THE SIMPLE WILD

ALSO BY K.A. TUCKER

Ten Tiny Breaths

One Tiny Lie

Four Seconds to Lose

Five Ways to Fall

In Her Wake

Burying Water

Becoming Rain

Chasing River

Surviving Ice

He Will Be My Ruin

Until It Fades

Keep Her Safe

THE SIMPLE WILD

a novel

K.A. TUCKER

ATRIA PAPERBACK

NEW YORK LONDON TORONTO SYDNEY NEW DELHI

An Imprint of Simon & Schuster, Inc.
1230 Avenue of the Americas
New York, NY 10020

This book is a work of fiction. Any references to historical events, real people, or real places are used fictitiously. Other names, characters, places, and events are products of the author's imagination, and any resemblance to actual events or places or persons, living or dead, is entirely coincidental.

First Atria Paperback edition August 2018

ATRIA PAPERBACK and colophon are trademarks of Simon & Schuster, Inc.

For information about special discounts for bulk purchases, please contact Simon & Schuster Special Sales at 1-866-506-1949 or business@simonandschuster.com.

The Simon & Schuster Speakers Bureau can bring authors to your live event. For more information or to book an event, contact the Simon & Schuster Speakers Bureau at 1-866-248-3049 or visit our website at www.simonspeakers.com.

Manufactured in the United States of America

20 19 18 17 16

Library of Congress Cataloging-in-Publication Data

Names: Tucker, K.A. (Kathleen A.)
Title: The simple wild : a novel / K.A. Tucker.
Description: First Atria paperback edition. | New York : Atria Paperback, 2018.
Identifiers: LCCN 2018016363 (print) | LCCN 2018019930 (ebook) | ISBN 9781501133459 (eBook) | ISBN 9781501133435 (pbk.)
Subjects: | GSAFD: Love stories.
Classification: LCC PR9199.4.T834 (ebook) | LCC PR9199.4.T834 S56 2018 (print) | DDC 813/.6—dc23
LC record available at https://lccn.loc.gov/2018016363

ISBN 978-1-5011-3343-5
ISBN 978-1-5011-3345-9 (ebook)

To Lia and Sadie,
The best things in your lives will never come simply.
They'll always be worth it.
But, ideally (for my sake), they'll have nothing to do with small planes.

Prologue

■ ■ ■

November 15, 1993
Anchorage, Alaska

Wren sets the two navy suitcases next to the stroller and then reaches for the cigarette precariously perched between his lips, taking a long, slow drag. He releases smoke into the frigid air. "Just these?"

"And the diaper bag." I inhale the musky odor. I've always hated the smell of tobacco. I still do, except on Wren.

"Right. I'll go and get that," he says, dropping the cigarette to the snowy ground and crushing it with his boot. He clasps his callused hands together and blows into them as he rushes back out to the tarmac, shoulders curled inward, to where the Cessna that delivered us here awaits its hour-long flight home.

I quietly watch, huddled in my plush, down-filled coat against the icy wind, fiercely holding onto the resentment I've been carrying for months. If I don't, I'll quickly be overwhelmed by the pain of disappointment and impending loss, and I won't be able to go through with this.

Wren returns and settles the hefty red bag on the asphalt, just as a grounds worker swings by to collect my belongings. They exchange pleasantries, as if this is just any other passenger delivery, before the man shuttles my things away.

Leaving us in tense silence.

"So, what time do you get in?" Wren finally asks, giving the perpetual brown scruff on his chin a scratch.

"Noon, tomorrow. Toronto time." I pray Calla can handle ten

hours of traveling without a meltdown. Though, that might distract me from having my own meltdown. At least the next plane is substantial, unlike the tiny things Wren insists on flying. God, how on earth did I *ever* think marrying a born-and-bred bush pilot was a good idea?

Wren nods to himself, and then pulls our sleepy daughter out of the stroller and into his arms. "And you? Are you ready for your first big plane ride?" His wide grin for his daughter makes my heart twist.

For the hundredth time, I wonder if *I*'m being the selfish one. If I should grit my teeth and bear the misery, the isolation of Alaska. After all, *I* made the bed I'm running from now. My father was quick to remind me of that when I admitted to my parents that life with Wren isn't as romantic as I'd convinced myself it would be. When I admitted that I've cried at least once a day for the past year, especially during the painfully long, cold, dark winter, when daylight is sparse. That I hate living in the last great American frontier; that I crave being close to my family and friends, and the urban bustle of my childhood. In my own country.

A deep frown line forms in Wren's forehead as he plants a kiss on our happy, oblivious seventeen-month-old's nose and sets her onto the ground. She struggles to toddle around, her stocky body bundled in a thick bubblegum-pink snowsuit to keep the icy wind at bay. "You know you don't *have* to leave, Susan."

As quickly as I'd been softening, I harden again. "And what? Stay here, and be miserable? Sit at home with Calla under a happy lamp while you're out, risking your life for a bunch of strangers? I can't do it anymore, Wren. Every day is harder than the last." At first I thought it was postpartum depression, but after months of flying back and forth to Anchorage just to talk to a therapist and refill a prescription for antidepressants that did little more than make me sluggish, I've accepted that it has nothing to do with hormones. And here I was, naïve enough to think Alaskan winters would be manageable, having grown up in Toronto. That being married to the love of my life would outweigh the challenges of living here, of having a husband whose chances of dying at work on any given day are alarmingly high. That my adoration for this man—and the attraction between us—would be enough to overcome *anything* Alaska threw at me.

Wren slides his hands into the pockets of his navy checkered down vest, focusing his attention on the giant green pom-pom atop Calla's knit hat.

"Have you at least *looked* into flights over Christmas?" I dare ask, my last-ditch attempt.

"I can't take that much time off; you know that."

"Wren, you own the company!" I throw an arm toward the plane he brought us to Anchorage in, to the ALASKA WILD logo across the body. There are plenty more with the same emblem that make up the Fletcher family business, a charter company left to him after his dad passed away five years ago. "You can do whatever the hell you want!"

"People are counting on me to be here."

"I'm your wife! *I*'m counting on you! *We* are counting on you!" My voice cracks with emotion.

He heaves a sigh and rubs the wrinkles from his brow. "We can't keep going 'round in circles like this. You knew when you married me that Alaska is my home. You can't just change your mind now and expect me to up and abandon my entire life."

Hot tears burn against my cheeks. I furiously smear them away. "And what about *my* life? Am I the only one who's ever going to sacrifice in this relationship?" I never planned on falling head over heels for an American charter pilot while I was in Vancouver for a bachelorette party, but I did, and since then, it's been all on me to keep us together, and I've done it with the reckless fervor of a woman madly in love. I moved across the country to British Columbia and enrolled in a horticultural program, just so I could be closer to Alaska. And then, when I found out I was pregnant, I dropped out of school and moved to Wren's hometown, so we could marry and raise our child together. Only, most days I feel like I'm a single parent, because Wren's always at the damn airport, or in the air, or making plans to be.

And what am I left with? Dinner plates that grow cold from waiting, a toddler who asks for "Dada" incessantly, and this inhospitable subarctic soil that I'm lucky to grow weeds in. I've just kept on giving this man parts of me, not realizing that I was losing myself in the process.

Wren looks past me, watching a commercial plane as it takes off from the nearby international airport. He looks desperate to be back in the air, away from this never-ending fight. "I want you to be happy. If going back to Toronto is what you need to do, then I'm not going to stop you."

He's right; we can't keep doing this, especially if he's not willing to sacrifice *anything* to keep me around. But how can he just let us go like this? When I announced that my ticket was one-way, he did little more than grunt. Then again, I shouldn't be surprised. Expressing feelings has never been one of Wren's strengths. But for him to simply fly us here and set our belongings on the cold, hard ground next to us . . .

Maybe he doesn't love us *enough*.

I hope that my mother is right, and a few months without a wife to cook his meals and warm his bed will jog a change in perspective. He'll realize that he can fly planes *anywhere,* including Toronto.

He'll realize that he doesn't want to live without us.

I take a deep breath. "I should go."

He settles those sharp gray eyes on me, the ones that ensnared me four years ago. If I'd had any idea how much heartache the ruggedly handsome man who sat down next to me at a bar and ordered a bottle of Budweiser would cause . . . "So, I guess I'll see you when you're ready to come home." There's a rare touch of hoarseness to his voice, and it nearly breaks my resolve.

But I hang onto that one word to give me strength: "home."

That's just it: Alaska will never feel like my home. Either he truly doesn't see that or he simply doesn't want to.

I swallow against the painful ball in my throat. "Calla, say goodbye to your daddy."

"Bye-bye, Da-da." She scrunches her mitten-clad hand and gives him a toothy grin.

Obliviously happy as her mother's heart breaks.

Chapter 1

■ ■ ■

July 26, 2018

That calculator's not mine.

I smile bitterly as I peruse the contents of the cardboard box—toothbrush, toothpaste, gym clothes, a tissue box, super-size bottle of Advil, cosmetics bag plus four loose lipsticks, hairspray, brush, and the six pairs of shoes that I kept under my desk—and note the pricey desktop calculator included. I convinced my manager that I needed it just last month. The security officer who was tasked with clearing out personal effects from my work space while I was busy getting fired from my job obviously mistook it for my own. Likely because "Calla Fletcher" is scrawled across the top in permanent black marker, an attempted ward against theft by my sly coworkers.

The bank paid for it, but screw them, I'm keeping it.

I hold onto the tiny shred of satisfaction that decision affords me as the subway sails through the Yonge line tunnel and I stare past my reflection in the glass, out into darkness. Desperately trying to ignore the prickle lodged in my throat.

It's so quiet and roomy on the TTC at this time of day, I had my pick of seats. I can't remember the last time that happened. For almost four years, I've been squeezing into jammed cars and holding my breath against the melding of body odors and constant jostling as I rode to and from work in rush-hour commuter hell.

But today's trip home is different.

Today, I had just finished shaking out and savoring the last drops of my Starbucks latte—venti-sized—and clicked Save on my morning Excel files when a meeting request with my boss appeared in my in-box, asking me to come down to the Algonquin Room. I didn't think much of it, grabbing my banana and my notebook and trudging off to the small conference room on the second floor.

Where I found not only my boss, but my boss's boss and Sonja Fuentes from HR, who held a thick manila envelope between her swollen hands with my name scrawled over it.

I sat across from them, listening dumbly while they took their turn giving a prepared speech—the bank recently introduced a new system that automated many tasks in my role as a risk analyst and therefore my position has been eliminated; I'm an exemplary employee and this is in no way a reflection of my performance; the company will provide me with ample support during the "transition."

I might be the only person in the history of mankind to eat an entire banana while losing her job.

The "transition" would begin immediately. As in, I wasn't allowed to go back to my desk, to collect my things, or to say goodbye to my coworkers. I was to be walked down to the security desk like a criminal and handed my belongings in a box, then shown the curb. Standard protocol when letting go of bank employees, apparently.

Four years of fussing over spreadsheets until my eyes hurt and kissing egotistical traders' asses in hopes that I could count on a good word come promotion time, staying late to cover for other risk analysts, planning team-building activities that didn't involve used bowling shoes and all-you-can-eat MSG-laden buffets, and *just like that,* none of it matters. With one impromptu fifteen-minute meeting, I'm officially unemployed.

I knew the automated system was coming. I knew they would be reducing the number of risk analysts and redistributing work.

But I stupidly convinced myself that I was too valuable to be one that they'd let go.

How many other heads rolled today, anyway?

Was it just mine?

Oh my God. What if I'm the *only* one who lost their job?

I blink away the sudden swell of threatening tears, but a few manage to escape. With quick fingers, I fish out tissues and a compact mirror from the box and set to gently dabbing at my eyes so as not to disturb my makeup.

The subway comes to a jolting stop and several passengers climb on, scattering like alley cats to grab a spot farthest away from anyone else. All except for a heavyset man in a sapphire blue uniform. He chooses the cherry-red seat kitty-corner to mine, dropping into it.

I angle my knees away to avoid them rubbing against his thigh.

He picks up the crinkled copy of *NOW Magazine* that someone cast aside on the seat next to him and begins fanning himself with it, releasing a heavy pastrami-scented sigh. "Maybe I should just hang out down here, where it's cool. Gonna be a real stinker out there, with this humidity," he murmurs to no one in particular, wiping at the beads of sweat running down his forehead with his palm, seemingly oblivious to the annoyance radiating off me.

I pretend I don't hear him, because no sane person makes idle conversation on the subway, and pull out my phone to reread the text exchange with Corey from earlier, as I stood in a daze on Front Street, trying to process what had just transpired.

I just got fired.

Shit. I'm sorry.

Can we meet up for a coffee?

Can't. Swamped. With clients all day.

Tonight?

We'll see. Call you later?

The question mark on the end makes it sound like even a quick phone call to comfort his girlfriend is not guaranteed at this point. Granted, I know he's been drowning in pressure lately. The ad agency he's working for has had him slaving around the clock to try and appease their biggest—and most unruly—corporate client, and he needs to nail this campaign if he ever has a hope in hell of getting the promotion he's been chasing for almost two years. I've only seen him twice in the past three weeks. I shouldn't be surprised that he can't just drop everything and meet me.

Still, my disappointment swells.

"You know, on days like this, I wish I were a woman. You ladies can get away with wearing a lot less."

This time, the sweaty man *is* talking to me. And looking right at me, at the bare legs my black pencil skirt has afforded his view.

I offer him a flat gaze before squeezing my thighs together and shifting my body farther away, letting my long cinnamon-brown hair serve as a partial curtain for my face.

Finally, he seems to sense my mood. "Oh, you've had one of *those* days." He points to the box of belongings on my lap. "Don't worry, you're not alone. I've seen more than a few people get walked out of office buildings over the years."

I'd peg him for his early fifties, his wiry hair more salt than pepper and almost nonexistent on top. A quick glance at his shirt shows me a label that reads WILLIAMSONS CUSTODIAN CO. He must work for one of those cleaning businesses that companies like mine contract out. I'd see them when I worked late, leisurely pushing their carts along the cubicle aisles, trying not to disturb employees as they empty waste bins.

"I quit," I lie as I slide the lid back on the box, covering it from his prying eyes. The wound to my pride is still far too fresh to be casually talking about it with complete strangers.

He smiles in a way that says he doesn't believe me. "So, what'd you do, anyway?"

"Risk analyst for a bank." Why am I still humoring this man's need for conversation?

He nods, as if he knows exactly what that means. If you asked *me* what that meant four years ago when I was collecting my degree from the University of Toronto, I couldn't have told you. But I was excited all the same when the job offer came through. It was my first step as a young professional female, the bottom rung of a corporate ladder in downtown Toronto. Half-decent pay with benefits and a pension, at a big bank. Plenty of boxes to check in the "good career" department, especially for a twenty-two-year-old woman, fresh out of school and good at math.

It wasn't long before I came to realize that all being a risk analyst entails is throwing numbers into spreadsheet cells and making sure the answers that the formulas spit out are the ones you want. It's little more than monkey work. Frankly, I'm bored out of my skull most days.

"So why'd you quit then?"

"I didn't," I finally admit through a shaky sigh. "You know, restructuring."

"Oh, yeah. I know it well." He pauses, studying me intently. "Did you love it, though?"

"Does *anyone* actually love their job?"

"You're too young to be that cynical." He chuckles. "Did you at least like the people you worked with?"

I think about my group. Mark, my micromanaging boss with chronic coffee breath who books meetings simply to validate his purpose and makes note of the minute you leave for lunch and the minute you return to your desk; and Tara, the obsessive Type A with no life outside of her job, who spends her weekends sending long-winded emails about process improvement suggestions with "Urgent! Action Required" subject lines to hijack everyone's in-box first thing Monday morning. Raj and Adnan are nice enough, although they've never gone out for drinks after work and can't accept a simple "Good morning, how are you?" from me without their faces turning beet red. And then there's May, who sits one cubicle over, who *never* sends her dailies on time and who eats fermented cabbage at her desk, even though there's an HR policy against bringing strongly scented food into the office. I have to leave my desk or spend ten minutes gagging.

Every.

Single.

Damn.

Day.

"Not really," I admit. To be honest, I can't remember the last time I didn't have to drag myself out of bed, or didn't watch the hours pass. I loved the feeling that came as I switched off my computer and grabbed my coat each night.

"Maybe being forced out is a good thing, then." He grins at me.

"Yeah. Maybe." Davisville station is approaching. With a sigh of relief that I can end this conversation without being overtly rude, I slip out of my seat. Balancing the cumbersome box in one arm, I hold onto the bar with a tight grip and wait for the subway to stop.

"I wouldn't worry too much about it. You're young." The guy hefts his body out of his seat as the car comes to a jarring halt. "Those jobs are a dime a dozen. You could be swiping your access card at another bank in a couple weeks."

He's just trying to make me feel better. I offer him a tight but polite smile.

The doors open, and I step out onto the platform.

The man lumbers close behind. "You know, I was you, fifteen years ago, carrying my own box of things out of my downtown Toronto office. Sure was a big hit to my ego, but it was also a kick in the ass. I decided to take the severance and start a cleaning business with my brothers. Never thought that'd be my calling, but turns out it's the best thing that ever happened to me. And I wouldn't want to be doing anything else, even on the worst days." He winks and waves the rolled-up newspaper in the air. "This is fate. You've got bigger and better things ahead of you, pretty lady. I can feel it."

I stand on the platform, hugging my cardboard box, watching the enthusiastic custodian stroll toward the exit. He's whistling as he tucks the paper into the recycling bin on his way, as if he's *actually* happy with a life of cleaning toilets and mopping floors.

Maybe he's right, though. Maybe losing my job today will end up being the best thing that could ever happen to me.

Giving my head a shake, I begin heading for the exit. I make it three steps before the bottom of my box gives way, scattering my belongings over the dirty concrete.

■ ■ ■

My skin is coated in a thin sheen of sweat by the time I trudge up the stone walkway of our house, a ten-minute walk from the station. Mom and I have lived here for the past fifteen years with my stepfather, Simon, who bought it at below-market from his aging parents, years before. A smart investment on his part, as the value of houses in Toronto continues to skyrocket. We routinely get real estate agents cold-calling us, looking for a chance to sell the substantial three-story Victorian, clad in brown brick and well situated on a sizeable corner lot. It's been fully renovated over the years. The last appraisal put the place at over two million.

It's almost noon. All I want to do is take a long, hot shower while I cry, and then crawl into my bed and avoid people—well-meaning or otherwise—until tomorrow.

I'm almost at our front steps when the side entrance that leads to Simon's psychiatry practice opens and a mousy, middle-aged woman in an ill-fitting black pantsuit darts out, sobbing. Our eyes cross paths for a split second before she ducks her head and runs past me toward a green Neon.

She must be a patient. I guess her appointment didn't go well. Or maybe it did. Simon always says that real breakthroughs don't come easily. Either way, it's comforting to know that I'm not the only one having a shitty day.

Once inside the house, I kick off my heels and let the faulty box fall to the floor, glad to finally be rid of it. Two of my forty-dollar lipsticks smashed on the concrete platform, and my left running shoe—from a brand-new pricey pair, no less—is still lying next to the subway tracks. I briefly considered climbing down to retrieve it, but then I imagined the ensuing headline: "Dejected Risk Analyst Leaps to Her Death," and I decided that that's not how I want to make the news.

"Hello?" my mom calls out from the kitchen.

I stifle my groan as my head falls back. *Crap.* That's right, it's Thursday. She doesn't go into the flower shop until two on Thursdays. "It's just me."

The hardwood floor creaks as she approaches, her rose-colored wrap skirt flowing breezily around her ankles with each step.

Simon follows close behind, in his usual plaid sweater vest, button-down, and pleated khaki pant combo. It doesn't matter how hot it is outside, he keeps the air frosty in here.

I stifle a second groan. I expected him to be home—he's almost *always* home—but I hoped he'd be tied up with his next patient and not hear me come in.

"What are you doing here?" Mom's frown grows as she looks from my face to the box on the floor. "What's that?"

Behind her, Simon looks equally concerned.

I'm forced to replay the dreadful morning for them, handing over the envelope with my severance package details, the lump in my throat swelling as I talk. I've done well, up until now, but I'm struggling to keep the tears at bay.

"Oh, honey! I'm so sorry!" My mom spears Simon with a glare and I know exactly why. Simon's best friend, Mike, is a VP at the bank. I got this job because of him. I wonder if Mike had any idea that I was on the chopping block. Did he warn Simon? Did Simon know how my day would turn out when I dropped my breakfast dishes into the dishwasher and waved goodbye to him this morning?

Simon has already put his reading glasses on to scan the severance paperwork.

Meanwhile, Mom wraps her arms around me and begins smoothing her hand over my hair, like she did when I was a small child in need of consoling. It's almost comical, given that I'm three inches taller than her. "Don't worry. This happens to all of us."

"No it doesn't! It hasn't happened to either of you!" Simon keeps complaining that he has more patients than he has hours in the day to treat them, and Mom has owned a successful flower shop on Yonge Street for the past eleven years.

"Well, no, but . . . it happened to your grandfather, and Simon's brother, Norman. And both sets of neighbors, don't forget about them!" She scrambles to find examples.

"Yeah, but they were all in, like, their *forties*! I'm only twenty-six!"

Mom gives me an exasperated look, but then the fine lines across her forehead deepen with her frown. "Who else lost their job?"

"I don't know. I didn't see anyone else at security." Is the rest of my team sitting around their desks, whispering about me at this very moment? Did *they* see it coming?

Her slender hands rub my shoulders affectionately. "Well, the place is *obviously* run by a bunch of idiots if they would let go of their best and brightest employee." Another eye-spear cast Simon's way, meant for Mike.

Of course she's going to say that. She's my mom. Still . . . it makes me feel marginally better.

I rest my head against her shoulder, finding comfort in the delicate scent of her floral perfume and the softness of her sleek, chin-length golden-brown bob, as we quietly watch Simon peruse the paperwork, awaiting his verdict.

"Four months' pay with benefits . . . retraining with an employment agency . . . looks fairly standard," Simon says in that charming Hugh Grant–esque British accent that still lingers, even after thirty-odd years of living in Canada. "You're in a good situation. You don't have rent or a mortgage to worry about. Your bills are minimal." He slides his glasses to the top of his thinning gray-haired head and settles his shrewd blue eyes on me. "But how does this make you feel?"

Simon is big on asking me how things make me feel, especially when he knows I don't want to talk about it. He's a psychiatrist and can't help but psychoanalyze everything and everyone. Mom says it's because he's teaching me to always be comfortable with expressing my emotions. He's been doing it since the first day I met him, when I was eight and he asked me how the thought of my mom having a boyfriend made me feel.

"I feel like I need to be alone."

He nods once, in understanding. "Quite right."

I collect my severance package and head for the stairs.

"Susan? Isn't there something else you ought to mention?" I hear him whisper.

"Not now!" she hisses in response.

When I glance back, the two of them are communicating through a series of glares, waggling eyebrows, and pointed stares. They're notorious for doing this. It's amusing . . . when it has nothing to do with me. "What's going on?"

Mom offers a tight smile and says in a light voice, "It's nothing. We can talk about it later, when things have settled down for you."

I sigh. "Just tell me."

Finally, Mom relents. "There was a call today." She hesitates. "From Alaska."

Unease settles into my spine. I only know one person in Alaska, and I haven't talked to him in twelve years. "What does he want?"

"I don't know. I missed getting to the phone, and he didn't leave a message."

"So then it's nothing."

Her tight brow tells me she doesn't think it's nothing. Even when we were on speaking terms, my dad was never the one to make the effort, to work out the time difference and pick up the phone to say hello. "Maybe you should give him a call."

"Tomorrow." I continue up the stairs. "I can only handle so much disappointment for one day."

And my father has already delivered enough to last me a lifetime.

Chapter 2

"Going out?" Simon checks his watch. He can't fathom the idea of leaving the house at eleven P.M. to see friends, but he's fifty-six years old and doesn't leave the house much, period, unless my mother forces him. His idea of entertainment is pouring himself a glass of sherry and catching up on the latest BBC documentary.

"I figured I may as well."

Simon peers over his glasses at me, doing a quick, fatherly scan of my outfit before shifting his gaze back to his book. I decided on my shortest, tightest black dress and my highest heels for tonight. In any other situation, the combination would be considered escort-worthy, but on a sweltering Thursday night on Richmond Street in July, it's practically standard uniform.

Simon rarely comments on my clothing choices, though, and I'm thankful for that. Lord knows what meaning he could find in tonight's ensemble. An ego boost after my pride's been trounced? An outcry for love and attention maybe? Deeply seeded daddy issues?

"With the usual suspects?"

"No. They're all away. Just Diana tonight." And Aaron, I'm sure. One can't be at a club for too long without the other. My best friend will demand a girls' night out and then act like it's a complete coincidence that her boyfriend shows up, even though I watched her text him our exact location a half hour before.

"No Corey?"

"He's working late," I mutter, unable to hide my annoyance. He wants to hook up on Saturday, though. So we can "de-stress," his latest text said. That's code for "get laid." Normally, a message like that wouldn't bother me. But today is different. Today, it bothers me. The fact that he can't even spare ten minutes to call and make sure I'm okay after getting the axe is a growing thorn in my thoughts. When did he become so focused on his career, in his bid for promotion, that I became a clear runner-up?

And how hadn't I noticed it sooner?

Simon's mouth curves into a frown. "I saw that photograph in the rubbish. The one of you two from last summer."

"It got mangled when the box broke."

"It's a nice picture."

"Yeah." It was taken last June at my friend Talia's cottage on Lake Joe, the same cottage where Corey and I had met a month before when he was visiting a friend's place three doors down for the long May weekend. We crossed paths on kayaks early that Saturday morning, in a quiet part of an otherwise bustling lake, slowing to float beside each other and exchange "gonna be a great day!" pleasantries. It was his silky blond curls that caught my attention; it was his mesmerizing smile and easygoing laugh that held it. I was even more thrilled when I found out he lived in High Park and worked only eight minutes away from my office.

By the time we paddled back to our respective shores side by side, we'd made plans to meet up for lunch. By the time the bonfire in Talia's pit was burning that night, we were playfully smearing melted marshmallow across each other's lips.

In the picture, we're sitting on a pile of craggy gray rocks that creep out into the lake. Hundred-year-old pine trees tower in the background. Corey's long, lanky arms are wrapped around my shoulders and we're both smiling wide, completely enamored with each other. That was back when we saw each other at least four times a week, when we'd make all our plans based around each other's schedules, when he responded to my texts with cheesy quips within thirty seconds of me hitting Send, and he'd order flowers from my mom's florist shop every week and have her put them by my bedside table—which solidified her adoration for him almost instantly. Back when I had to push him away—giggling, of course—as he stole another last kiss, no matter who was watching.

But somewhere along the line, things have changed. The flowers don't come every week anymore; the text responses sometimes take hours. And the kisses only come as a prelude to more.

Maybe we've just grown comfortable in our relationship.

Maybe *too* comfortable.

Maybe Corey and I need to sit down and have a talk.

I push that thought aside for another day. "I can always print another one."

Simon looks at me again, his narrow face hinting at mild concern. He adores Corey, too, possibly more than my mother does. Then again, they've always welcomed my boyfriends and there have been more than a few coming through our front door over the years.

Corey is the easiest to like, though. He's intelligent, soft-spoken, and easygoing. The corners of his soft hazel-green eyes crinkle with his laugh, and he is a master at giving you his undivided attention. He cares what other people think of him, but in a good way, a way that holds his tongue even when he's angry, to avoid saying things he'll later regret. He has always treated me well—never uttering a word of complaint when I hand him my purse to free my hands, holding the door for me to pass through, offering to stand at crowded bars to get my drink. A true gentleman. *And* he's hot.

What parents wouldn't want their daughter to be with a guy like Corey?

And why, as I stand here mentally going through Corey's best attributes, do I feel like I'm convincing myself of them?

"Well . . . Guard your drinks and stay together," Simon murmurs.

"I will. Kiss Mom good night for me." With the wedding season in high gear, she's already fast asleep, needing her rest before an early-morning rise to finish this weekend's bridal bouquets.

I make it all the way to the front door before Simon calls out, "Don't forget to take the rubbish to the curb."

My head falls back with my groan. "I'll do it when I get home."

"At three o'clock in the morning?" he asks lightly. Knowing full well that the last thing I'll be doing when I stumble up the steps at three A.M. is hauling the medley of garbage, recycling, and composting bins to the curb.

I open my mouth, about to plead for my stepdad to do it for me, just this once . . .

"Putting out the rubbish once a week as your *only* contribution to this household seems like a good substitute for paying rent and utilities, wouldn't you agree?"

"Yes," I mutter. Because it's true. We have a housekeeper come twice a week to clean and run laundry. Mom has our weekly groceries dropped at our door and ready-made dinners delivered from an organic, grain-fed, hormone-free, gluten-free, dairy-free kitchen, so I rarely have to shop or cook. And I always slide my blouses and dresses into the pile when Simon takes his sweater vests and pleated pants in for dry cleaning.

I'm a twenty-six-year-old woman with no debt, who has been living on her parents' dime despite earning a decent salary for the past four years, without a complaint from either of them because they love having me here and I love the lifestyle I can afford by living at home. So, yes, the least I can do is put out our "rubbish" once a week.

That doesn't stop me from adding, "You're just making me do it because *you* hate doing it."

"Why else do you think we've kept you around this long?" he calls out as I'm pulling the front door shut behind me.

■ ■ ■

"I'll meet you down there." The wheels on the compost bin rumble against the pavement as I drag it to the curb by one hand, past Mom's

Audi and Simon's Mercedes, my phone pressed to my ear. We're one of the few houses on the street that has a driveway, and one large enough to fit three cars. Most everyone is stuck battling it out for street parking, which is an especially prickly situation come winter, when there aren't just other cars but four-foot snowbanks to contend with.

"We're not going to get in anywhere if you don't hurry up!" Diana yells over the crowd of noisy people around her, panic in her voice.

"Relax. We'll get in somewhere, like we do *every* time we go out." Somewhere where we can flirt with the doormen and, worst case, slip them a few bills to let us bypass the line they've manufactured to make their club look like it's packed. Meanwhile inside it's a ghost town.

But being two attractive, young women has its benefits and I plan on taking full advantage of them tonight. For as crappy as I feel on the inside, I've compensated by making an extra effort on the outside.

"My Uber's on the way. Just pick a place and text me. I'll see you in fifteen." More like twenty-five, but Diana will abandon me if I tell her that. Setting down my phone on the hood of Simon's car next to my purse, I lug the recycling bin to the curb, careful not to chip a nail. Then I make my way back to tackle the gray garbage container.

Movement catches the corner of my eye a split second before something soft brushes against my leg. I leap back with a startled yelp, only to lose my balance and, stumbling over the curb, land flat on my ass next to an especially thorny rosebush. An enormous raccoon scurries past me. A second one follows quickly behind, chattering angrily at me.

"Dammit!" The touchdown was hard and I'll likely be bruised, but right now what hurts most is the four-inch heel lying next to my foot, snapped off the base. I peel the ruined Louboutin stiletto off my foot and aim for the raccoons, throwing it with all my strength. But they've already safely settled under the car, and now they watch me, the stream of light from the porch glinting off their beady eyes.

The front door opens and Simon appears. "Calla, are you still here?" He spots me sprawled out in the garden and frowns.

"Tim and Sid are back," I mutter. The pair stopped coming around last month, after frequenting our property every Thursday night for the better part of a year. I assumed they'd either found another family to terrorize or had been hit by a car.

"I had a feeling they'd return." He holds out the receiver. "From Alaska."

I shake my head, mouthing, "I'm not home," though it's already too late.

Simon's bushy brows arch as he waits, his arm outstretched. He'd never cover for me anyway. The psychiatrist in him believes in facing problems, not avoiding them.

And my biggest problem, according to Simon, is my relationship with Wren Fletcher. Or lack thereof, because I hardly know the man. I *thought* I knew him, back when I'd dial his number and listen to the ring, imagining the room and the house and the man on the other side. Of course, I knew what my real father looked like. My mom had shown me pictures of him, of his shaggy peanut-butter-brown hair and his soft gray eyes, wearing a navy-blue-and-black plaid jacket and jeans in mid-August, standing proudly next to a row of planes. She called him ruggedly handsome, and I somehow knew what she meant without understanding it at my young age.

Sometimes he wouldn't answer, and I'd be bereft for the entire day. But other times, when I was lucky, I'd catch him coming or going. We'd talk for fifteen or so minutes, about school and my friends, or the hobbies I was into at the time. It was mostly me speaking but I hardly noticed, happy to prattle on. Mom says Dad never was a big talker.

She also said that we would never live together as a family. That my dad's life was in Alaska and ours was in Toronto, and there was no way around that reality. I learned to accept it early on. I didn't know any different. Still, I'd always ask him to fly out to visit me. I mean, he had all these planes to choose from, so why couldn't he just hop in one of them and come?

He always had an excuse, and Mom never tried to coax him. She knew better.

Me, though? I only ever saw him through the enchanted eyes of a little girl who desperately wanted to meet the quiet man on the other side of the phone.

I pull myself up and dust the dirt off my behind. And then I hobble to the front steps in my one shoe, glaring at my ever-understanding and patient stepdad.

Finally, I take the phone from his hand.

"Hello."

"Hello. Calla?" a woman asks.

I frown at Simon. "Yeah. Who's this?"

"My name is Agnes. I'm a friend of your father's. I found your number among Wren's things."

"Okay . . ." An unexpected spark of fear ignites inside me. What was she doing in his things? "Did something happen to him?"

"I guess you could say that." She pauses, and I find myself holding my breath, dreading the answer. "Your father has lung cancer."

"Oh." I take a seat on the top of the steps, suddenly feeling wobbly-legged. Simon eases down onto the step beside me.

"I know things have been difficult between the two of you for some time, but I thought you'd like to know."

Difficult? More like nonexistent.

There's a long pause. "I only know because I found a copy of the test results in his pocket when I went to do his laundry. He doesn't know that I'm calling you."

I hear what she doesn't say: He wasn't going to tell me that he has cancer. "So . . . how bad is it?"

"I'm not sure, but the doctors have recommended a treatment plan." She has a reedy voice and a slight accent that reminds me of my father's, from what I remember of it.

I don't know what else to say except, "Okay. Well . . . I'm sure the doctors know what they're doing. Thanks for calling and letting me know—"

"Why don't you come here for a visit?"

My mouth drops open. "Here? What, you mean . . . to *Alaska*?"

"Yes. Soon. Before treatment starts. We'll pay for your ticket, if that's what it would take. It's high season right now, but I found an available seat to Anchorage for this Sunday."

"*This* Sunday?" As in three days from now?

"Jonah could bring you the rest of the way."

"I'm sorry, who's *Jonah*?" My head is spinning.

"Oh." Her laughter is soft and melodic in my ear. "Sorry. He's our best pilot. He'd make sure you got here safe and sound."

Our best pilot, I note. *We*'ll pay for your ticket. She said she was a friend, but I'm gathering that Agnes is more than that.

"And Wren would love to see you."

I hesitate. "He told you that?"

"He doesn't have to." She sighs. "Your father . . . he's a complicated man, but he does love you. And he has many regrets."

Maybe this Agnes woman is okay with all the things Wren Fletcher *doesn't* say and do, but I'm not. "I'm sorry. I can't just hop on a plane and come to Alaska . . ." My words drift. Actually, as of this moment, I have no job or other major commitments. And as far as Corey is concerned, I could probably fly to Alaska and come back without him ever being the wiser.

I *could* just leave, but that's beside the point.

"I know this is a lot to take in. Please, think about it. You'd get the chance to know Wren. I think you'd really like him." Her voice has grown husky. She clears it. "Do you have something to write with?"

"Uh . . . yeah." I pluck the pen from the breast pocket of Simon's button-down shirt—I can always count on him to have one at the ready—and jot down her phone number on the back of his hand, though it's likely already on the call display. She also gives me her email address.

I'm in a daze when I hang up with her. "He has cancer."

"I gathered it was something along those lines." Simon puts an arm around my shoulders and pulls me into him. "And this woman who called wants you to visit him."

"Agnes. Yeah. *She* wants me to visit him. *He* doesn't want me there. He wasn't even going to tell me. He was just going to go and die, without giving me *any* warning." My voice cracks. This man who I don't even know still wounds me so deeply.

"And how does that make you feel?"

"How do you *think* that makes me feel!" I snap, tears threatening.

Simon remains calm and collected. He's used to being yelled at for his prodding questions—by my mom and me, and by his patients. "Do you want to fly to Alaska to meet your father?"

"No."

He raises an eyebrow.

I sigh with exasperation. "I don't know!"

What am I *supposed* to do with this information? How am I *supposed* to feel about possibly losing a person who has only ever hurt me?

We sit quietly and watch as Tim and Sid venture out from beneath the car, their humps bobbing with their steps as they head for the bins at the end of our driveway, standing on their hind legs to paw at the blue one, attempting to knock it over with their weight. They chatter back and forth to each other, only bothering with an occasional glance at their audience.

I sigh. "He's never made an effort to get to know me. Why should I bother making the effort now?"

"Would there be a better time?"

That's Simon. Always answering a question with another question.

"Let me ask you this: Do you think you could gain something from going to Alaska?"

"Besides a picture with my mom's sperm donor?"

Simon grimaces his disapproval at my poor attempt at humor.

"Sorry," I mumble. "I guess I just have low expectations for a man who hasn't cared enough to meet his daughter once in twenty-four years." He was supposed to come to Toronto. He called me four months before my eighth-grade graduation, to say that he was coming for it. I started crying the moment I hung up. All the anger and resentment that'd been building up over the years, for all the birthdays and holidays he'd missed, disintegrated instantly. And I truly believed that he'd be there, that he'd be sitting in the audience with a proud grin on his face. I believed it, right up until he called, two days before the ceremony, to say that "something" came up. An emergency at work. He wouldn't elaborate.

My mother called him back. I heard her seething voice through the walls. I heard the ultimatum she delivered through tears—that either he sort his priorities out and finally show up for his daughter or get out of our lives for good, monthly child support checks and all.

He never showed up.

And when I stood on the stage, accepting my academic award, it was with puffy eyes and a forced smile, and a silent promise to myself that I would never trust him again.

Simon hesitates, his wise gaze peering out into the darkness. "Did you know that your mother was still in love with Wren when we got married?"

"What? No, she wasn't."

"She was. *Very* much so."

I frown. "But she was *married* to you."

"That doesn't mean she didn't still love him." A pensive look fills his face. "Do you remember when your mother went through that phase, when she changed her hair and started working out almost every day? She was *highly* irritable with me."

"It's fuzzy, but yeah." She dyed her hair platinum blonde, and started going to yoga obsessively, reversing the softening effects of middle age and turning her body hard again. She was throwing petty jabs at Simon between sips of morning coffee, picking at his personal faults over lunch, sparking colossal fights over everything he *wasn't* by dinner.

I remember thinking it was odd, that I'd never seen them fight at all, let alone that frequently.

"That all began after Wren called to say he was coming."

"No, it didn't," I begin to argue, before stopping myself. Simon would have a much better grasp of that timeline than I would.

"When your mother left Wren, she did it hoping that he would change his mind about staying in Alaska. He never did, but she never stopped loving him, despite it. Eventually she knew she had to move on. She met me, and we married. And then all of a sudden he was coming here, back into her life. She didn't know how to deal with seeing him again, after so many years. She was . . . conflicted about her feelings for the both of us." If Simon is bitter about admitting this, he doesn't show it.

"That must have been hard for you." My heart pangs for the man I've come to know and love as a more than suitable replacement for my birth father.

Simon smiles sadly. "It was. But I noticed a change in her after your graduation. She was less anxious. And she stopped crying."

"She was crying?"

"At night, when she thought I'd gone to sleep. Not often, but often enough. I'm guessing it was guilt over harboring feelings for him. And fear for what might happen when she saw him again, especially so soon after marrying me."

What exactly is Simon suggesting?

He presses his thin lips together as he wipes the lenses of his reading glasses on the cuff of his sleeve. "I think she finally accepted that neither of you would ever have the relationship you longed for with him. That wanting someone to be something they're not won't make it happen." Simon hesitates. "I'll selfishly admit that I wasn't entirely unhappy that he never came. It was clear to me that if Wren were willing to give up his home, my marriage to your mother would have dissolved." He toys with the gold wedding band around his ring finger. "I will always play second fiddle to that man. I knew that the day I asked her to be my wife."

"But why would you marry her, then?" As glad as I am that he did, for her sake as well as mine, it seems like an odd proclamation.

"Because while Susan may have been madly in love with Wren, *I* was madly in love with *her.* Still am."

That, I know. I've seen it, with every lengthy look, with every passing kiss. Simon loves my mother deeply. At their wedding, my grandfather gave a mildly inappropriate speech, commenting on the two of them being an unlikely pair—that my mother is this vibrant and impulsive woman, while Simon is a calm and practical old soul. "An unexpected match, but he'll sure as hell make her much happier than *that last one*" were my grandfather's exact words over the microphone to a room of a hundred guests.

The old man was probably right, though, because Simon dotes on my mother, granting her every self-satisfying whim and wish. They vacation at expensive, all-inclusive tropical resorts when he'd rather be visiting dusty churches and ancient libraries; he's her pack mule when she decides she needs a fresh wardrobe, schlepping countless bags through the streets of Yorkville; he humors her love of Sunday road trips to country markets and then comes home sneezing from the dozen allergens that plague him; he's given up gluten and red meat because Mom has decided she doesn't want to eat them. When we redecorated the house, my mother chose a palette of soft grays and pale mauves. Simon later confided in me that he despises few things and, oddly enough, the color mauve is one of them.

In the past, I've found myself silently mocking the gangly Englishman for never putting his foot down with my mother, for never showing a spine. But now, as I gaze at his narrow, kind face—his feather-thin hair long since receded from his forehead—I can't help but admire him for all that he's put up with while loving her.

"Did she ever admit her feelings to you?" I dare ask.

"*No,*" Simon scoffs, his brow furrowing deeply. "She'll *never* admit any of this to me and don't bother confronting her about it. It'll only stir up guilt that does none of us any good."

"Right." I sigh. "So, should I go to Alaska?"

"I don't know. Should you?"

I roll my eyes at him. "Why can't you be a normal parent and *tell* me what to do for once?"

Simon grins, in that way that tells me he's secretly delighted that I referred to him as a parent. Even though he's always said that he sees me as his daughter, I think he would have been happy to have children of his own, had my mother been willing. "Let me ask you this: What was your first thought when Agnes told you your father has cancer?"

"That he's going to die."

"And how did that thought make you feel?"

"Afraid." I see where Simon's going with this. "Afraid that I'll miss my chance to meet him." Because no matter how many times I've lain in bed, wondering why my father didn't love me enough, the little girl inside me still desperately wants him to.

"Then I think you should go to Alaska. Ask the questions you need to ask, and get to know Wren. Not for him, but for you. So you don't find yourself ruled by deep regrets in the future. Besides . . ." He bumps shoulders with me. "I don't see any other pressing matters in your life at the moment."

"Funny how that worked out, eh?" I murmur, thinking of the chatty custodian on the subway earlier today. "It must be fate."

Simon gives me a flat look, and I laugh. He doesn't believe in fate. He doesn't even believe in astrology. He thinks people who follow their horoscopes have deeply repressed issues.

I sigh. "It's not like he lives in the *nice* part of Alaska." Not that I remember *any* part of Alaska from my brief time there—nice or otherwise. But Mom has used the words "barren wasteland" enough to turn me off the place. Though she tends to be dramatic. Plus, she's a city lover. She can't handle the Muskokas for more than a night, and not without dousing herself in mosquito repellent every fifteen minutes while reminding everyone incessantly about the risk of West Nile.

"I'll think about it." I mentally start reorganizing my schedule. And groan. If I leave on Sunday, I'll miss next week's hair appointment. Maybe I can beg Fausto to squeeze me in Saturday morning. Highly unlikely. He's normally booked four weeks in advance. Thankfully I have a standing nail appointment on Saturday afternoons and I had my eyelashes done last weekend. "I *just* paid for ten more hot yoga sessions. And what about squash? Mom would need to find a replacement partner."

"All things you managed to work around when you went to Cancún last year."

"Yeah . . . I guess," I admit reluctantly. "But Alaska is a million hours away."

"Only half a million," Simon quips.

"Will you at least give me a script for Ambi—"

"No."

I sigh with exaggeration. "What fun is having a stepdad with a prescription pad, then?" My phone starts ringing from its resting spot on the hood of Simon's car. "Crap, that's Diana. She's in a line somewhere, mentally stabbing me." As if on cue, a black Nissan Maxima coasts up to the curb in front of the house. "And that's my

Uber." I look down at my missing heel and my soiled dress. "And I need to change."

Simon eases himself off the step and heads toward the waiting garbage can. "I suppose I can manage this last one for you. Just this once. After all, you *have* had quite the day."

He charges forward in a funny shuffle that sends Tim and Sid scurrying into the hedge before struggling to wheel the can into place. For all that makes Simon endearing, he is neither coordinated nor strong. Mom has tried and failed to get him to a gym to add some muscle to his spindly arms.

A thought strikes me. "What are you going to do about garbage day if I go to Alaska?"

"Well, of course your mother will take care of it." He waits a beat before turning to meet my doubtful smirk, and mutters in that dry British way he has, "That would be a bloody cold day in hell, now wouldn't it?"

Chapter 3

■ ■ ■

"You *have* to go!" Diana yells over the throbbing bass, pausing long enough to flash a pearly white grin at the bartender as he sets our drink order on the bar. "It's beautiful up there."

"You've never been to Alaska!"

"Well *yeah,* but I've seen *Into the Wild.* All that wilderness and the mountains . . . Just don't eat the berries." She makes a dramatic show of placing a ten-dollar tip down so that the bartender notices. A trick for priority service the next round.

Meanwhile, the bartender's eyes are busy dragging over the plunging neckline of my cobalt-blue dress, the first thing I yanked out of my closet in my rush to change and get out the door. He's cute but short and brawny, with a shaved head and a full sleeve of ink—not my tall and lean, clean-cut, inkless type—and, besides, I'm not in the mood to flirt in exchange for free shots.

I humor him with a tight smile and then turn my attention back to Diana. "It's not like that on the western side of Alaska."

"Cheers." We down our shots in unison. "What's it like?"

The sickly sweet concoction makes me grimace slightly. "Flat."

"What do you mean? Flat, like the Prairies?"

"No. I mean, yeah, it's probably flat like there, but it's *really* cold. Like, *arctic* cold." Whereas our midwest provinces are home to the vast majority of our country's farmland, nothing thrives where my dad is from, the growing season's too short. That's according to my mom, anyway, and the woman has a bachelor's degree in Plant Science from the University of Guelph. If anyone would know, I'd think it would be her.

"Arctic?" Diana's cornflower-blue eyes widen with excitement.

"Seriously, think how amazing that could be for Calla & Dee. You're the one who said we needed to find an original angle. *You* said we need to get out of the city."

"I was thinking more a trip to Sandbanks or Lake of Bays." New pretty and picturesque places that we can get to within a few hours by car.

"What's more original and out of the city than a lifestyle blogger in the *arctic*?" Diana's matte mauve-colored lips curl into a hopeful smile as no doubt a spiderweb of ideas is spinning in her head.

Last year, we started a small website aptly named Calla & Dee, an avenue to share our passion for the latest lipstick shades and shoe styles, just for fun. I should have known when Diana asked me to split the cost of a website designer that she already had lofty goals and that this hobby was going to grow legs of its own.

Now we exchange texts about the site *all day long*—ideas for future posts and who's doing what that seems to be working. Instead of a simple blog, we have entire sections—fashion, food, beauty, entertainment—and a strict weekly schedule to adhere to. I spend my commutes and lunch hours scrolling through newsletters and blog posts in order to educate myself on the latest—retailers announcing sales, fashion industry leaders announcing the latest trends, other lifestyle bloggers who we befriend online in the name of networking. My evenings are for updating links, loading content, tweaking aesthetics—tasks that Diana abhors but I don't mind and am actually good at.

Diana and I meet up in a new restaurant every Thursday night to bounce around ideas and taste-test appetizer menus for our "Grazing in the City" section. One Saturday a month is for scouring discount racks for trendy clothes to style ourselves with, and every Sunday afternoon we hunt for the perfect settings in downtown Toronto—colorful graffiti in alleyways, the spring cherry blossoms of High Park, the Distillery District's picturesque Christmas Market. We take Simon's pricey Canon with us, swapping out cute outfits in the backseat of Diana's Tahoe and taking turns pretending that we're not posing for the camera. I've learned far more about sight lines and shutter speed and the rule of three than I ever expected to, and it's all in the name of grabbing that perfect lifestyle snapshot—nice outfits on park benches and in city streets, with blurred backgrounds and feel-good captions about love and happiness and spirituality.

We get caught up in "what if" conversations *all the time*. What if we hit a hundred thousand followers? What if companies started sending us clothes and makeup samples to promote so we don't have to spend half our paychecks anymore? What if we become Instagram famous?

It's a daydream for me.

A goal for Diana.

But we have a *long* way to go before we're being featured on any "best of" lists, and more and more lately, I fear that all our efforts have been a waste. After a year of hard work, we have a frustratingly modest following of almost four hundred returning visitors to our website. Our separate Instagram profiles—the two halves of Calla & Dee—have more. Diana's is triple mine, which isn't surprising given she is *obsessed* with learning the latest expert tips and tricks about building an audience and curating photos and tagging appropriately; about how to word captions to be upbeat and inspirational. She responds to *every last comment* on her posts and spends her lunch hour interacting with strangers, hoping to attract their attention and their following.

Still, even with all Diana's die-hard efforts and determination, we can't seem to gain any traction. At this point, it's nothing more than a forty-hour-a-week hobby, grappling with finding ideas for "how to's" and "top tens" that haven't been done before, that people might want to read.

My gut says we're missing a key ingredient—originality. Right now, we're just two more attractive city girls who love to pose and talk about makeup and clothes. There's a sea of us.

"It's not *really* the arctic. Not where he lives, anyway. It's . . . somewhere *in between* the arctic and normal civilization. It's like . . . the last frontier?" I echo something I read about Alaska once, silently admitting that I don't know much about where I was born.

"Even better! And you'll have a bunch of planes at your disposal!"

"I doubt they'll be 'at my disposal.' *And* I'll be alone. How am I going to get any good shots?" We cringe in unison at the thought of a selfie stick.

Diana's not to be swayed, though. "Someone there will be willing to take pictures of a beautiful Canadian girl. Maybe a hot American pilot."

I sigh. "Have you *forgotten* why I'd be going in the first place?"

"No. I'm just"—her face turns serious, her perfectly shaped blonde brows ruffling—"trying to make it not so depressing."

We collect our martinis and ease our way out from the bar. Our spots are instantly swallowed up by the crowd. Diana wasn't exaggerating. This club must be testing fire code violations; I can't stand anywhere without being nudged from at least two sides at any given time.

I suck back a mouthful of my drink as we weave through the throbbing crowd, shrugging off the male hands that graze my arm and pinch my sides in brazen attempts to gain my attention, hoping I don't spill anything with all the bumping and jostling.

Finally, we squeeze into a small vacant space near a pillar.

"So, where's Corey tonight?" Diana asks.

"Working."

"Hmm . . ." Her nose crinkles subtly, as if a mild but unpleasant odor lingers and she's trying her best to pretend she doesn't smell it.

I think Diana might be the only person on earth who doesn't like Corey. It took five months and six margaritas apiece in the back of a Mexican restaurant for my best friend to finally admit that to me. He tries too hard to be liked, she said. And he's handsy. And the way he stares at her when she's talking feels flirtatious; it makes her uncomfortable. She simply doesn't trust him not to break my heart.

To say I didn't like hearing that is an understatement. I told her she was jealous that I had someone and she didn't. We parted ways under a dark cloud that night, and I woke up the next day with a throbbing head from the alcohol and an aching heart from fear that our friendship had been irreparably damaged.

Simon swiftly talked me down from that ledge, though, as only he can do, by pointing out all the times Diana had been there for me over the years, through all the boyfriends, even when she didn't have one, and that *if* she was jealous, it was more than likely because she felt her importance in my life was being threatened, a normal affliction for best friends at our age.

Diana and I made up that same afternoon, over plenty of tears and apologies, and she promised she'd give Corey another shot. Thankfully, Aaron came into the picture a few months later and I've firmly fallen to second rung. I'm not complaining, though—I've never seen her this happy, or serious about a guy. Just two weeks ago, she mentioned buying a condo with Aaron next year, which means she'll finally stop pestering me to move in with her. I love my best friend, but she drains hot water tanks with her long showers, she cleans *everything* with a skin-melting dose of bleach, and she likes to clip her toenails while watching TV. And if she can't sleep? No one is sleeping.

Have fun living with that, Aaron.

"So, when would you go?" Diana asks, her gaze flitting this way and that, searching the crowd even as she talks to me.

The sooner the better, if my dad is going to start chemo or radiation, or whatever the doctors are recommending. The only other person I've ever known with lung cancer was Mrs. Hagler, the old lady who lived in the house behind us. She was a longtime friend of

Simon's parents and didn't have any family of her own left, so Simon sometimes took her to the hospital for her chemo. That went on for *years* before she succumbed. Near the end, she spent a lot of time sitting in her backyard wearing a knit hat that covered her sparse fuzz, puffing away on a cigarette while her oxygen tank sat two feet away. She'd made peace with what was coming by that point.

"My dad's friend said there was a flight available for Sunday, so . . . I guess maybe then? If it's not taken by tomorrow. She said she'd buy the ticket, but I don't want to fly there on her dime. I mean, what if this ends up being a horrible idea and I want to leave as soon as I get there?"

"You'd feel like you owe it to her to stick around," Diana agrees. She takes a sip of her drink and makes a face. The bartender mixed this round extra strong. "Get Daddy Warbucks to buy your ticket from his secret stash, then. We all know the shrink is good for it." Diana is convinced that Simon has a secret vault beneath our century-old house and spends his nights inventorying his mountain of gold coins.

While he does make a lot of money on fragile psyches, it's highly unlikely that he could ever amass such riches, given my mother's taste for the finer things. She's even worse than me in that regard.

"But seriously, Calla, Simon's right. If you don't go and your dad doesn't pull through, you will regret it. I *know* you."

And she does, better than anyone else. Diana and I have been best friends since I started at the private school a few blocks away from our house. I was eleven and didn't know another soul. She painted my fingernails robin's-egg blue during recess. It's still my favorite color. She knows all about my father and the heartache that he's caused me over the years. She also knows all the unasked questions that I still long for answers to.

Mainly, why is Alaska Wild more important to Wren Fletcher than his own flesh and blood?

Still, this feels like a huge risk. One I'm not sure I have the guts to take. "What if he's nothing more than a deadbeat dad?"

"Then you'll know once and for all that he's a deadbeat dad." She pauses. "Or maybe he's actually a decent guy and there's this whole other side of him that you'll get to know and love."

"Yeah, I guess," I say doubtfully. Another, darker worry strikes me. "But then what if he doesn't get better?" It would be like losing him all over again, only this time it wouldn't be just the idea of him.

"Then you'll have something real to hold on to. Look, we can play this 'what if' game all summer long, or you can get answers. Oh hey!" Diana waves to someone behind me. A moment later, surprise, surprise, Aaron swoops in.

I avert my gaze as they share a long, movie-screen-worthy kiss, my annoyance flaring. Normally I wouldn't care, but tonight, after the day I've had, I needed my best friend's undivided attention, just this once.

"Heard about the job, Callie. That sucks."

At six foot four, even in my heels Aaron towers over me. I have to tip my head back to meet his inky blue eyes. "It does. But it's just a job, right?" Funny how that line comes out a little more easily, now that I have the distraction of my father to focus on.

"I wish *I'd* get canned with four months' pay," Diana laments. She works as a paralegal at a midsized law firm and hates every second of it, which I'm guessing is part of the reason she puts so much energy into our side project.

"My buddy's a headhunter for the banks. He'll hook you up with a new job right away," Aaron offers.

"Thanks." I sigh, pushing aside my dour mood. "Nice beard, by the way."

He smooths a palm over the well-trimmed licorice-black hair that coats his jaw. "It's holding up pretty good, eh?"

"It is," I agree, admiring the sharp lines. "Where on earth did you *ever* find such a talented barber?"

"It was a barberette, actually." He grins. "A smoking-hot barberette—"

"Stop hitting on my best friend. *And* making up words." Diana shoots him a stern look, but she follows it up with a wink.

Two months ago, Diana decided that we needed to do a post called "Turn Your Bushman Boyfriend into an Urban Gentleman." For the good of all womankind, she insisted. Or, at least, for the girlfriend of the attractive but hairy and unkempt server who plied us with copious amounts of wine and spanakopita at the Greek restaurant on the Danforth.

So she roped in Aaron to be our guinea pig for a live demo. Being the supportive boyfriend that he is, the baby-faced Aaron went without shaving, complaining only a hundred times. But he surprised us—and himself—by growing a respectably thick layer of hair.

Neither Diana nor I had ever shaved a man's face before, but I have more experience with clippers, given that I'd volunteered at an animal shelter for credit during high school and spent a semester beautifying bedraggled dogs to up their chances of adoption. So we decided I was up for the task. I devoured dozens of tutorials on YouTube, in preparation. And last weekend, under the watchful lens of Diana's iPhone camera, I transformed Aaron's shabby scruff into magazine-model-worthy beard status.

Aaron finally looks like a twenty-eight-year-old man instead of an eighteen-year-old boy.

Diana reaches up to draw dainty fingers along his jaw. "That was the most popular post we've done yet. All those thirsty females . . ."

Those thirsty females, *and* the fact that the company whose tools Diana bought featured our video in their social media, after we tagged them. My ears were ringing for a good half hour after Diana called me, squealing with hysteria.

Aaron grins, earning another eye roll from Diana. He's read

every last comment on that post, his ego basking in the glory. "I was hoping Calla could freshen it up this—"

"*No.*" Diana gives him a pointed look.

"But she's already done it once—"

"For Calla & Dee. But that's it. It's too *intimate*. Right, Calla?"

"I guess?" Aaron and I share a frown. "I mean, it didn't feel that way to me, but—"

"Besides, she's going to Alaska on Sunday."

"I haven't decided yet," I start to say, but Diana has already leaned in to Aaron's ear to reiterate the phone call from Agnes.

I watch his face fall. "I'm sorry, Calla. *Man,* you've had a shitty day."

"Cheers to that!" I lift my martini in the air.

"Well . . . my friend went to Alaska a few years ago and he still raves about it. I'm sure it'll be an experience, even if the reason behind it sucks."

"Did you know Calla was born in Alaska? Yeah, her dad owns a freaking *airline*!"

"It's more like a charter plane company." *I think?*

"Like, a hundred planes!"

"A couple dozen small planes, maybe," I guess, because I have no idea and the last time I tried trolling my dad on the internet, I found little more than a directory listing and an Alaska Wild landing page that said "check back soon."

"She's going to make her dad's pilots fly her *all* over the place so she can take cool shots for the site."

"Awesome." Aaron points to my half-finished martini. "I'll get you ladies another round." Though he has never said a word about it, I'm sure he'd be happy to *not* hear Diana talk about Calla & Dee for one night.

Stealing a quick kiss from her lips—because he *always* kisses Diana whenever he's stepping away from her, just like Corey used to—Aaron weaves through the crowd toward the bar.

"I fucking *love* this club!" Diana hollers, shimmying her shoulders to the music. The number of "fucks" she voices is in direct proportion to how many drinks she's had. She must be starting to feel the alcohol. I know I am.

"*Really?* I was just thinking it's getting a bit stale." I sip at my drink and let my gaze wander over the crowd again, wondering how many people they've packed in here. Five hundred? A thousand? It's hard to tell. I used to feel a rush as I stepped through these doors. I'd get giddy as the music vibrated through my limbs and all around me, a sea of revelers dancing, drinking, laughing, kissing.

I'm not feeling that rush. It's probably the day I've had, but the DJ is lackluster. His set is similar to last week's. In fact, I'll bet it *is* last week's set. And the week before's. And the week before that's. I doubt I can even muster the urge to dance.

"Hey." Diana nudges me with her elbow, her eyebrows waggling suggestively. "Arabian admirer at three o'clock."

I turn to my right, to see a tall, ebony-haired guy standing about six feet away with a group of friends, his near-black gaze locked on me, his smirk flirtatious.

A "whoa" slips through my lips, as a rash of butterflies churns in my belly. He's attractive and built. Not my usual type, but he's the kind of attractive that would make him *any* girl's type. God knows how long he's been sizing me up over there, waiting to catch my eye, hoping for a returning smile, the bat of my lashes, a wink . . . anything to give him the green light. I'll bet his voice is deep. I'll bet his skin smells of citrus and peppery cologne, and he has to shave twice a day to keep that chiseled jaw smooth. I'll bet he likes to stand inside a girl's personal space as he talks to her—not close enough to crowd her, but just enough to make her feel a hint of intimacy, a craving for a touch. I'll also bet he never leaves the club alone, but he always—gladly—wakes up by himself.

And that telling him I have a boyfriend won't scare him away.

But I *do* have a boyfriend, I remind myself. *Jesus, Calla.* This is the third time in the past few weeks that I've found myself drooling over an attractive guy—twice at a club and once while seated at a park bench over lunch, when a blond in a tailored pinstripe suit strolled past me, leaving me slack-jawed.

I make a point of hardening my expression and turning my back to him, hoping he won't mistake it for coyness and will simply move on. Picking up girls at clubs is like baseball for those kinds of guys, only with way more chances to swing before they strike out.

"Hey!" Diana frowns, her narrowed gaze now locked on the bar. "Isn't that Corey?"

I spot the familiar-looking mane of lush blond curls. "Maybe?" The tall, lanky guy certainly looks like Corey from behind. And his shoulders hunch over slightly, like Corey's do. And he's dressed like Corey would be—in a fitted and stylish black collared shirt and tailored dress pants.

The guy turns to show his youthful, clean-shaven profile, confirming our guess.

I try to ignore the feeling in the pit of my stomach as I dig my phone out of my purse, thinking that perhaps he called to check in after all.

Nothing. Not even a text.

Diana scowls. "Who's he with?"

I zero in on the faces around him. I've met three of them before. "Coworkers. I guess this is what he meant by having to work late," I mutter.

"Well, I guess we should go over there and . . ." Her words drift as there's a part in the crowd and the diminutive female tucked in beside him appears. The one whose back Corey has his hand settled on, midway down in a semi-affectionate way. The way that says they're not together but he desperately wants them to be.

We watch as he leans down, says something in her ear, and then pulls away. No doubt something witty. I've always loved his sense of humor.

Her long, chestnut-brown hair sways as she tips her head back and laughs, earning his grin. I can almost see the twinkle in his eyes, the same one that charmed me so long ago, when *we* would come out to the club with our friends and stand at the bar, his hand settled on *my* back like that.

A sinking feeling settles into my chest as pieces click together. Stephanie Dupont started working at the advertising agency about three months ago. I met her once, at a party. She had a boyfriend then. But does she still? Because Corey looks like he's putting in his application.

"So you're going to go over there and throw your drink in his face, right?" Diana says through gritted teeth. "No, wait. Don't waste your drink. Use this one." She grabs a random glass from the ledge where someone left it, half-full of melting ice and mangled lemon slices.

I contemplate it for a split second. "Why bother?"

Diane's eyebrows crawl halfway up her forehead. "Because he lied to you about working tonight? Because he's right over *there,* one drink away from cheating on you. And with a major downgrade, by the way. I mean, come on, look at *you* and then look at *her*."

I can't see her face, but I remember her being cute and wholesome, with deep dimples and a friendly smile.

I don't answer and Diana's voice turns shrill. "How are you not more upset right now!"

"I don't know." Sure, it stings, but if I'm being honest with myself, that bite probably has more to do with my ego than anything else.

My heart *should* be aching with loss.

My stomach *should* be twisting with betrayal.

My eyes *should* be burning with emotion.

But if anything, what I'm feeling right now could be described more like a mixture of disappointment and . . . relief?

Diana huffs. "Well, what are you going to do?"

I shake my head as I try to make sense of it. My yearlong relationship with the seemingly perfect guy is unraveling in front of me and I'm not feeling any urge to storm over there and fight for it?

"Wait, I know!" Diana spins around. "Where is he?"

"Who?"

"That guy. That beautiful guy over there who was drooling over you—"

"No!" I grab hold of her with my free hand to stop her, because when Diana gets an idea in her head . . . "I am *not* going to hook up with some stranger to get back at Corey."

"Well . . . But . . ." she sputters, "you have to do *something*!"

"You're right, I do." I clink my glass against hers before downing the rest of my drink, my legs itching to whisk me away before Corey notices me here. "I'm going home."

And then I guess I'm going to Alaska.

Chapter 4

■ ■ ■

"These are nice." My mother holds up the new pair of military-red Hunter rain boots.

"Right? Except they take up a lot of room. I'm not sure if I should bring them."

"Trust me. Bring them." She lays them into the suitcase I've reserved for footwear and toiletries—that's already brimming—and then takes a seat on my bed, her finger toiling with the small pile of price tags heaped by my pillow. Evidence of the "Alaska" wardrobe flash shopping spree I went on yesterday. "You sure you're only going for a week?"

"You're the one who taught me that 'overpacking is key.'"

"Yes, of course, you're right. *Especially* where you're going. You won't be able to just run out and grab something that you've forgotten. They won't even have a mall." She cringes at the very idea of mall shopping. "There is literally nothing there. It's a—"

"Barren wasteland. Yes, I remember." I cram a pair of wool socks resurrected from my winter clothing bins into the corner of a second suitcase. "You haven't been there in twenty-four years, though. Maybe it's changed. They have a movie theater now." I know because I Googled "Things to Do in Bangor, Alaska" and that popped up. It was the *only* indoor activity to pop up, besides weekly knitting classes and a community book club, two things I have no interest in. "Bangor could have doubled in size. Tripled, even."

She smiles, but it's the condescending kind of smile. "Towns in Alaska don't grow that quickly. Or at all, in most cases." Reaching for one of my favorite fall sweaters—a two-hundred-dollar soft pink cashmere wrap that Simon and Mom gave me for Christmas—she folds it tidily. “If I know your dad at all, that house is the same as when we left.”

“Maybe seeing it will jog an early childhood memory.”

“Or give you nightmares.” She chuckles, shaking her head. “That god-awful tacky wallpaper that Roseanne put up was the worst.”

Roseanne. My father’s mother. My grandmother, who I was too young to remember ever meeting. I talked to her occasionally over the phone, and she sent birthday and Christmas cards every year, right up until she died, when I was eight.

“Agnes probably took down the tacky wallpaper.”

“Maybe.” Mom sniffs, averting her gaze.

Do you still love my dad, even now? I bite my tongue against the urge to ask her about what Simon told me. He’s right; she’ll never admit to it, and I don’t want to make Simon’s life hell for the entire time that I’m gone. Things have already been tense around the house as it is. Mom went to sleep on Thursday thinking about blush rose table arrangements and orchid bridal bouquets, and woke up to news of a woman named Agnes, my dad’s cancer diagnosis, and my impending trip to Alaska.

I can’t tell what upsets her most—the fact that there’s another woman or that my father is seriously sick. All of it has left her unsettled. I’ve caught her standing in front of the bay window in the kitchen, clutching her mug and staring off into nothingness, at least a half dozen times. For a woman who’s always on the go, that’s a jarring sight.

Still, I can’t skirt the question entirely. “You would never leave Simon for Dad, would you, Mom?”

“What? No.” A deep frown pulls her brow tight, as if she’s reconsidering her answer after she’s given it. “Why would you ask that?”

“No reason.” I hesitate. “Have you talked to him at all?”

“No.” She shakes her head, then pauses. “I did send him an email a few years ago, though, with a copy of your U of T grad picture. So he'd know what his daughter looked like." Her voice trails, her eyes transfixed on a chip in her coral nail polish.

"And? Did he ever answer?" Did he care enough to?

"He did. He said he couldn't believe how much you'd grown. How much you looked like me." She smiles sadly. "I didn't keep the conversation going, though. I figured it was for the best. You're not going to need that," she says, eying the striped tank top that I've laid on top of my other clothes. Swiftly changing the topic.

"Didn't you *just* say to pack for every situation?"

"They're calling for highs of only fourteen degrees Celsius all week. Four, at night."

"Then I'll put a sweater overtop."

She smooths a hand over the bedspread. "So, Wren is picking you up in Anchorage?"

I shake my head through a mouthful of water. This intense heat wave that shifted into Southern Ontario has refused to vacate, making the third floor of this house stuffy, despite the air-conditioning that pumps through the vents. "Some guy named Jonah is picking me up."

"Why not your dad?"

"I don't know. Maybe he's not feeling well enough to fly." What shape will he be in when I get there? My email exchanges with Agnes have been focused on travel arrangements, not his current state of health.

"But he knows you're coming, right?"

"Of course he does." Agnes said *they'd* have my room ready and *they* were so happy I was coming.

Her mouth twists with worry. "What kind of plane?"

"One that stays in the air, hopefully."

She spears me with a sharp look. "This is not funny, Calla. Some of your father's planes are *tiny*. And you're flying through the mountains and—"

"It'll be fine. *You're* the one who's afraid of flying, remember?"

"You should have waited for a commercial flight. They fly those Dash 8s to Bangor daily now," she mutters.

"There weren't any seats available on *whatever* you said until Tuesday." I'm heading to Alaska and suddenly Mom's a plane-model expert. "Relax, you're being dramatic."

"You'll see . . ." She gives me a smug look, but it fades quickly. "When's he starting treatment?"

"I don't know. I'll find out when I get there."

Mom huffs. "And you're connecting through where again?"

"Minnesota, Seattle, Anchorage." It's going to be a grueling day of travel, and not even to anywhere exotic like Hawaii or Fiji, places I'd eagerly spend a day flying to. But the flip side is that, twenty-four hours from now, I'll be standing face-to-face with Wren Fletcher, after twenty-four *years*.

My stomach squeezes.

Mom drums her fingertips over her knee. "Are you sure you don't want me to drive you to the airport? I can get someone to start doing the arrangements for me."

I'm struggling to maintain my patience. "I have to be there at four a.m. I'll grab a cab. I'll be *fine*, Mom. Stop fretting."

"I just . . ." She tucks strands of her hair behind her ear. We used to have matching hair color but now that she dyes it to cover the invading gray, she's opted for a darker shade of brown with hints of copper.

I know what this all boils down to. It's not the long distance or the tiny plane or the fact that I'll be away for a week that's got her so unsettled.

"He can't hurt me any more than he already has," I say more softly.

The silence in the room is deafening.

"He's not a bad man, Calla."

"Maybe not. But he's a shitty father." I struggle to tug the suitcase zipper closed.

"Yes, he is. Still, I'm glad you're going. It's important that you meet him, at least once." She studies a small wound on her thumb, likely a prick from a rose thorn. "All those years of smoking. I begged him to quit. You'd think he would, after watching your grandfather wither away from damn cigarettes." Mom shakes her head, her brow—smoother than it should be at her age, thanks to rounds of laser skin care and fillers—furrowing ever so slightly.

"Maybe he did quit, and it was too late. But if he hasn't, I'm sure the doctor will make him quit now." I haul a suitcase to its wheels, dusting my hands for impact. "One down."

Mom's hazel-green gaze rolls over me. "Your highlights look nice."

"Thanks. I had to grovel to get Fausto to squeeze me in last night." I glance in a nearby mirror as I brush a strand of blonde hair off my face. "He went lighter than I wanted, but I don't have time to fix it before I go." I can't help but notice the dark circles lingering under my eyes, which even a thick smear of concealer can't hide. The last two days have been a whirlwind—of shopping, primping, packing, and planning.

Breaking up with my boyfriend.

"So, you and Corey are *officially* over?" Mom asks, as if she can read my mind.

"I cut the shiny red ribbon and everything."

"Are you okay?"

I sigh. "I don't know what I am. It feels like my life has been turned upside down. I'm still waiting for the dust to settle." After I left the club on Thursday, Diana made a point of bumping into Corey "accidentally"—because she would have exploded from indignation otherwise—to let him know that he'd *just* missed his *girlfriend*. I'd bet money that she delivered her perfect poison-laced smile as she walked away, satisfied to make Corey squirm.

I woke up the next morning to a voice message from him. His tone was lighthearted as he gave some lame-ass excuse about how he ended up at the club. He didn't say a word about Stephanie Dupont, or why he was practically draped over her at the bar.

I didn't respond right away, giving him a dose of the medicine he's been dishing out recently.

Childish?

Maybe.

But I needed more time to sort out my thoughts and feelings, something I still wasn't entirely clear on after spending the night staring at the slanted ceiling above my bed as the hours reached for dawn.

I needed more time to face the truth.

Corey did love me at one time. Or at least, he thought he did. And I was so sure I loved him, too, back at the height of our relationship, after the newness wore off but before the comfort began to fray at the seams. We had a good thing going on. We never argued; we were never jealous or rude to each other. If I had to choose one word to describe our relationship, it'd be "smooth." As in, our relationship has operated without a hitch.

There is no reason for us not to work.

We are textbook perfect together.

And we have grown bored.

Whatever magic there was in the beginning has been fizzling away, like a slow leak in a tire after it has taken a nail. You could go on for months without knowing something's wrong, until one day you end up stranded on the side of the road with a flat.

At least, that's what I've heard about slow leaks in tires. I've never actually experienced one. I don't even have my license. But I do have to face facts—the enamored "Calla and Corey" who posed for the camera on that pile of rocks last year took a long, sharp nail somewhere along the way, likely before Stephanie Dupont ever came into the picture.

It's the only reason I can come up with for why seeing Corey flirting with another girl didn't gut me, and why I wasn't more than mildly irritated that he couldn't make time for me after the day I'd had. And why I didn't bother trying to phone him after learning of my father's illness, in the small hope that he might answer and give me comfort in the sound of his voice.

I think, buried deep down somewhere, I already sensed that our relationship was evaporating. I just hadn't admitted it to myself yet. Maybe because I was hoping it wasn't true. Or, more likely, because once I did acknowledge reality, I'd feel like I would have to do something about it. And what if Corey didn't feel the same way I felt? What if he thought everything was perfect between us, and begged me not to end things?

What if I hurt him?

All unconscious worries simmering beneath the surface. All reasons to avoid confronting him. At least, reasons for me, a girl who is acutely allergic to confrontation. It's my one defining "Wren quality," my mom has said. My dad is ninja-level at avoiding conflict and, well . . . apple and tree, apparently, even if I landed fifty-five hundred kilometers away.

Sure, I can throw a verbal jab like the best of them when you push me far enough, but when it comes to truly facing someone or something that pains me, I run from my own shadow. But I'd run out of places to hide, the truth now glaringly obvious. I couldn't imagine flying off to Alaska to meet my dad with this on my mind. So I sent a text to Corey on Friday night, mentioning the trip and how I thought *maybe* it would be better for us if we took a break, with all he had going on at work "and stuff."

His response? *Yeah, I was thinking the same. Take care of yourself. Safe flight.* It's like he was waiting for an out. I shouldn't be surprised, though. He dances around sticky situations with the best of them. The best being me.

And thus, the official end to my fourteen-month relationship.

Via text, minimal confrontation achieved.

Mom eases off my bed. "It's late, Calla. You need to get some sleep."

"I know. I'm just gonna grab a shower first."

She reaches for me and gives me a tight hug that lasts several beats too long.

"Oh my God, I'll be back next Sunday!" I laugh, squeezing her slender frame back just as hard. "What are you going to be like when I move out?"

She peels away to stroke the long strands of my hair off my face, blinking against her glossy eyes. "Simon and I have discussed it and you're never moving out. We've begun building a dungeon for you downstairs."

"Next to his secret money vault, I hope."

"Across from it. I'll remove your collar when it's time for our shows."

"Or you could just put a TV *in* my dungeon."

She mock-gasps. "Why didn't I think of that! We wouldn't have to listen to Simon's whining in the background." Simon detests our mutual love of cheesy reality TV and violent Viking shows, and he can't help but pass through the living room while we're watching, sometimes dropping witty but mostly annoying commentary.

Finally releasing me, she moves languidly to the doorway. She lingers, though, studying me as I kneel on top of the second stuffed suitcase and tug at the zipper. "You should probably bring a book or two."

"You meant MacBook, right?" I can't get past a chapter in a book without falling asleep and she knows it.

"I figured as much." A pause. "I hope they have internet there."

"Oh my God, you're kidding, right?" Panic hits me as my mind begins to spin with the possibility that they don't. I spent a long weekend at a cottage near Algonquin Park once and had to drive fifteen minutes up the road to get enough bars on my phone to retrieve my texts. It was hell. But no . . . "Agnes answered her emails right away. They totally have internet," I say with certainty.

Mom shrugs. "Just . . . prepare yourself. Life out there is different. Harder. And yet simpler, if that makes any sense." A nostalgic smile touches her lips. "You know, your dad used to try and get me to play checkers. *Every single night* he'd ask, even though he knew I hate board games. Used to annoy the hell out of me." She frowns. "I wonder if he still plays."

"Kind of hoping he doesn't."

"You're going to be bored out of your mind within a day and looking for things to do," she warns.

"I'm sure I'll be hanging out at the airport a bit." I heave the second suitcase to its wheels. "You know . . . watching planes crash."

"Calla!"

"I'm *kidding*."

She sighs heavily. "Just don't make the same mistake I did and fall in love with one of those pilots."

I chuckle. "I'll try my best not to."

"I'm being serious."

"It's not a firehouse, *Mom*."

She holds her hands in the air in surrender. "Fine. I know. But there's *something* about those guys that work up there. I can't explain it. I mean, they're *crazy,* landing on glaciers and mountain ridges, flying through whiteouts. They're like . . ." Her eyes search for words within my walls. "Sky cowboys."

"Oh my God!" I burst out laughing. "Do I seem like the kind of girl who'd fall for some Alaskan *sky cowboy*?" I can barely get the words out.

She levels me with a flat look. "Do *I*?"

Fair point. My mom has always been glamorous. Her earlobes are never without diamonds and she could make a pair of leggings and a worn concert T-shirt look sophisticated. She'd set herself on fire before sliding on a pair of "mom" jeans.

I carefully navigate around my furniture, wheeling the two enormous suitcases to the landing outside my door.

"Those look back-breakingly heavy," Mom murmurs.

"They *are* back-breakingly heavy."

We eye the steep flights of oak stairs that wind all the way to the ground floor, recently stained a dark walnut, the spindles and risers painted a warm white.

And then holler in unison, "Simon!"

Chapter 5

■ ■ ■

"Yeah . . . there's only a couple carriers that work well enough up here." The middle-aged cab driver flashes a crooked-toothed grin over his shoulder as I scowl at the lack of bars on my screen.

"I guess mine isn't one of them," I mutter, tucking my phone away. So much for the US international plan I purchased this morning, while waiting for the first of my flights to board. I'm praying that my dad has Wi-Fi at his house or this week will test my sanity like never before.

The driver smoothly navigates the van along the road toward the small regional airport where my fourth—and last—plane awaits me. I found him standing at the baggage carousel, holding a sign with "CALLA FLETCHER" scrawled across it. After fifteen hours of traveling, thanks to a delay in Seattle, I'm grateful for the prearranged ride.

I shift my focus to a small ski plane as it climbs into the sky over us, its red paint vibrant against the bright blue canvas. How does it compare to the one I'm about to fly in?

"First time in Anchorage?"

"Yeah."

"What brings ya here?"

"I'm visiting someone." The man is just making conversation, but right now my stomach is rolling. I try to calm myself by taking deep breaths and concentrating on the scenery—on the tranquil cobalt water ahead, the lush evergreens in every direction, and the snow-capped mountain range in the far distance. This is the landscape that Diana assumed when I said Alaska. On the last flight, I had a window seat for the descent and I spent all of it pressed against the glass, mesmerized by the vast mosaic of treetops and lakes.

How different will my end destination look?

"Is Bangor far by plane?" It's early evening and the sun is still high, with no hint of it going down anytime soon. Will we get there before dark?

"About four hundred miles. An hour's ride. Somewhere in and around that, anyway."

I release a shaky breath against this odd mix of eagerness, dread, and fear. An hour and a bit until I meet my father.

"I take it that's where you're going, then? Bangor, I mean."

"Yeah. Have you been?"

"Not in years. But they've got them Dash 8s flying out that way a couple times a day. So who're you flying with?"

"Alaska Wild."

He nods. "Fletcher's planes. They're good. They've been around a long time."

There's something familiar in the way he says my last name, a way that pricks at my senses. "Do you know him? Wren Fletcher, I mean."

"Yes, ma'am." The driver nods for emphasis. "I've been doin' this job for twenty years now. You recognize faces after a while, and Wren's come out to Anchorage enough times for me to get to know him. In fact I gave him a ride to the hospital not that long ago. He had a nasty cough he needed looked at. Some sort of bug."

My stomach tightens. Yeah, a bug. One that will slowly kill him.

"Hey, wait a minute." He frowns as he lifts the clipboard with the sign he was holding at pickup. "You related?"

I hesitate. "He's my dad." Why does it sound deceptive to say that? It sounds like I *know* him, like I've seen him since leaving this very city twenty-four years ago. But the truth is, this shuttle driver knows him better than I do.

"You're Wren Fletcher's girl?" His murky green eyes catch mine in the rearview mirror and I see the incredulous look in them before he refocuses on the road ahead. "Didn't know he had one," he mumbles under his breath, but I hear it all the same.

I stifle my sigh. *I'm not sure he remembers he does.*

■ ■ ■

"Will we be taking off over the water?" I pause to give my foot a shake. The loose stone caught between my toes tumbles out.

"Nah. We've got a gravel runway, too." Billy, the short, twenty-something grounds crewman who met me at the main door of Lake Hood Seaplane airport, drags his work boots along the ground, my suitcases wheeling clumsily behind him. "Jonah flew in with his Cub."

"Is that a smaller plane?" I ask warily. And is it normal that *everyone* talks about planes in terms of models around here?

He looks over his shoulder at me, doing a quick head-to-toe—his seventh since I met him—and grins. "Why? You scared?"

"No. Just curious." I scan the row of planes to our left, and the people milling about them.

"Don't worry, you'll be fine. Jonah's one of the best pilots around. He should be done refueling by now. He'll have you on your way soon."

"Great." I inhale deeply, enjoying the crisp, fresh air after hours of breathing in who knows how many germs circulating in the cabins. It's an even more welcome change from the smog from back home.

Another sharp stone catches under my toe, one that doesn't easily shake out. I have to bend over and pick it out by hand, my other hand pressed against my Brixton to hold it in place. Wearing a wide-brimmed hat probably wasn't the smartest move for this many plane rides, but it's not like I could pack it. Maybe I should switch to my Chucks. But these three-inch strappy wedges are surprisingly comfortable and, more importantly, they look amazing with my ripped jeans.

"This way!" Billy hollers.

I look up in time to see him slow next to a blue-nosed plane with several portal windows. I quietly count the rows. It must seat *at least* six people. My mother had nothing to worry about. I pause to take a picture of the plane with my phone, and then one of the airport behind me, capturing the glassy lake and the mountainous backdrop beyond.

It's not until I've rounded the corner that I realize Billy hasn't stopped at the blue-nosed plane. He's past it, heading for one parked farther down the line.

"Oh my God. Is this for real?" I blurt out, gaping at the tiny yellow-and-orange thing. A toy plane, more wings than body.

Billy looks back to smile at me. "What do you mean?"

"I mean, there isn't even a seat for me!"

"Yeah there is. It's behind the pilot. Hey, Jonah!" Billy hollers in between his laughter, at the man whose broad back is to us while he fusses with something on the propeller. "I think you've got a nervous flyer!"

"Fantastic," the man grumbles in a deep baritone voice, tossing a tool into a bag on the ground beside his feet before he turns with obvious reluctance to face us.

Diana would have a field day with this one, I note, taking in the thick, shaggy, ash-blond beard that covers the bottom half of his face, jutting out at all angles. Between that, the reflective aviators, and the black USAF baseball cap that's pulled low over his forehead, I can't see his face. I can't even guess at his age.

And he's *big*. Even in my three-inch heels, he towers over me. It's hard to tell exactly how bulky he is beneath that checkered emerald-green and black jacket, but his wide shoulders make him look hulkish.

"Jonah . . . *this* is Calla Fletcher." I can't see Billy's face from this angle, but I don't miss the hidden meaning in the way he says that. An answer to a previous conversation. One I'd probably blush at if I overheard.

But I'm suitably distracted from wondering too much about any crude guy jokes, more focused on the plane that's supposed to carry me through a mountain range and on the yeti who's going to fly me there.

How the hell did he even fit into that plane?

I take a deep breath as I close the distance, trying to calm myself. To remind myself that it doesn't matter, that this giant got here in that plane and he'll get me back in that plane.

"Hey. Thanks for coming to get me."

"Aggie didn't give me much choice."

"I . . . uh . . ." I stumble over my tongue, searching for a suitable reaction to that response. And *Aggie?*

Jonah studies me from behind those impenetrable lenses for a long moment, and I get the distinct impression that he's doing a head-to-toe once-over. "What are you? One-oh-five? One-ten?"

I feel my brows pop. "Excuse me?"

"How much do you weigh?" he says slowly, enunciating each word with irritation.

"Who asks that as soon as they meet someone?"

"Someone who wants to get his plane off the ground. I can't take off if there's too much weight, so I need to do the math."

"Oh." My cheeks heat with embarrassment, suddenly feeling stupid. Of course that's why he's asking.

"So?"

"A hundred and thirty-five," I mutter. I may be thin, but I'm muscular.

Jonah reaches into the plane and pulls out an empty black nylon track bag. He tosses it to me and I instinctively reach to catch it, dropping my purse in the process. "You can use that for your things."

"What do you mean?" I frown at it and then at him. "My things are in these suitcases."

"Those suitcases aren't gonna fit in here. Billy, didn't you tell her that already?"

Billy merely shrugs in answer, earning an annoyed head shake from Jonah.

"But . . . I can't leave my things behind! There's *thousands* of dollars' worth here!" Clothes, shoes . . . I had to pay two hundred bucks in overweight fees to get them here!

"If you want to fly with me, you'll have to," Jonah counters, his arms folding over his wide chest as if getting ready to stand his ground.

I stare at my luggage with growing panic.

"I'm sure we'll have a cargo plane flying to Bangor tomorrow. I'll get the bags on the first one that can carry the extra weight," Billy offers in a placating tone.

My shocked gaze drifts between the two of them. What choice do I have here? If I don't go with Jonah now, I'll have to find a hotel room and stay in Anchorage until I can get a regular flight. Agnes said it's high season. Who knows how long that will take? "Why didn't Agnes send you here in a bigger plane?" I grumble, not really looking for an answer.

"Because the bigger planes are out making money. Plus, no one knew you were planning on *moving* here." His voice drips with sarcasm.

I'm quickly getting the impression that Jonah doesn't want to be flying me anywhere.

And that he's a giant asshole.

I make a point of turning my back on him to face Billy. "Will my things be safe here?"

"I'll guard them myself," he promises, crossing a finger over his chest for added impact.

"Fine," I grumble, tossing the track bag to the gravel, wishing that Billy were my pilot. Whether he can even fly a plane is of little concern to me at this point.

"And make it fast," Jonah adds. "There's heavy fog rolling in tonight, and I'm not getting stuck somewhere." With that, he disappears around to the tail of the plane.

"By all means, feel free to leave without me," I mutter quietly, because finding my own way to Bangor is sounding better with each passing second.

Billy scratches the back of his shaved head in wonder as he eyes the surly pilot. "He's not usually this grumpy," he murmurs.

"I guess I'm lucky, then." Or maybe *I'm* the reason Jonah's in such a foul mood. But what did I do to earn this hostile attitude? Besides pack too much, that is. I drop to the ground to begin rifling through my suitcases. Acutely aware of Billy standing over my shoulder, watching me as I consider my must-needs. This nylon bag is a weekender—just big enough to fit two or three days' worth of clothing. Less, when I include my cosmetics and toiletries bags, along with all my jewelry. There's no way I'm leaving any of that behind.

I glance up in time to find Billy's eyes perusing my collection of lace panties.

He quickly averts his gaze. "Ah, don't worry about Jonah. Something must have crawled up his ass." Billy pauses. "Something big."

"I hope he made sure to get its weight for takeoff," I mutter, reaching for my running shoes.

Billy's barking laughter carries through the cool breeze.

Chapter 6

▪ ▪ ▪

"It's gonna get bumpy on the way in," Jonah announces from his seat in front of me, his deep voice through the headset competing with the roar of the plane's engine.

"Worse than what we've been going through up until now?" Because my brain is rattling inside my head from the turbulence over the past hour.

"You thought that was bad?" He chuckles darkly as we cut through a low-hanging cloud. We may have taken off in blue skies, but on this side of the state a thick layer of gray drapes the horizon.

I tug my cable-knit sweater tighter around my body for comfort as much as to ward off the chill. Every jolt sounds clunky and hazardous, as if metal panels might pry right off the body of the plane at any moment.

Jonah probably wouldn't be so amused if he knew that I fished out a plastic bag from my purse and have been holding it open in front of me for the past fifteen minutes. How I've kept down the chicken tacos that I devoured in Seattle this long is no small miracle, but they're churning in my stomach now.

The plane's nose suddenly tips downward. I brace myself and yank on my seat belt to make sure it's snug. Then I concentrate on taking deep breaths, hoping that will soothe my frazzled nerves as well as my guts. What the hell was Agnes thinking, sending Jonah to get me in this death trap? I can't wait to phone my mother and tell her that she was right, that I'm *so not* fine with weaving around mountains while packed into a tin can like a sardine. That no sane person would be fine with this, *ever*.

These Alaskan pilots are *crazy* to *choose* to do this.

"How much longer?" I ask, trying to keep my voice steady as the plane tilts this way and that.

"Ten minutes less than the last time you asked," Jonah mutters. He radios the dispatcher and begins rhyming off codes and talking about visibility and knots.

And I glare at the back of his bulky frame, wedged into the pilot's seat. If he's uncomfortable in this tiny fuselage, he hasn't uttered a word of complaint. In fact, he's said barely anything to me this entire trip. Mostly "yups" and "nopes" and closed-off answers that stalled all attempts at small talk that I made. I finally gave up and instead focused on the frayed ash-blond wisps of hair that curl around the brim of his baseball cap and over the collar of his jacket, and *not* on the fact that just outside the thin metal walls and glass panels are thousands of feet through which we could plummet to our death.

A reality that seems more certain with each sudden and violent jerk.

The plane careens to the right, earning my panicked gasp. I squeeze my eyes shut and keep taking calm, steady breaths, hoping that will quell this bubbling nausea. *I can do this . . . I can do this . . . This is just like flying in any plane. We're not going to die. Jonah knows what he's doing.*

"That's Bangor, up ahead."

I dare peek out the window and below, hoping the promise of my toes touching the ground soon will help with my nerves. Lush, green, flat ground stretches out as far as the overcast skies allow me to see, a vast expanse of land mostly untouched by the human hand. It's peppered with streams and lakes of all shapes and sizes, and one wide river that snakes through it.

"*That*'s Bangor?" I can't hide the surprise from my voice as I study the crops of low, rectangular buildings huddled along the river's edge.

"Yup." A pause. "What were you expecting?"

"Nothing. Just . . . I thought it'd be bigger."

"It's the biggest community in Western Alaska."

"Yes, I *know that*. That's why I thought the buildings would be, I don't know, *bigger*. Taller." With all the scrambling of the last two days, I had little time to educate myself on where it is I'd be going. All I know is what I read on my phone while waiting for my plane this morning—that this part of Alaska is considered "tundra" for its flat land; that the sun barely sets during summer months and barely rises during the long, arctic winters; and that most of the towns and villages around here have Native Alaskan names that I can't pronounce.

Jonah snorts, and I immediately regret admitting my thoughts out loud. "Doesn't sound like you know much at all. Weren't you born here?"

"*Yeah*, but it's not like I'd remember anything. I wasn't even two when we left."

"Well, maybe if you'd bothered coming back before now, you'd know what to expect." His tone is thick with accusation.

What the hell is his problem?

We hit a pocket of turbulence and the plane begins jolting violently. I brace myself with a palm against the icy window as that queasy feeling begins to stir again, and the solid form deep inside me begins to rise. My stomach's preparing to empty its contents. "Oh God . . . this is *bad*," I moan.

"Relax. It's nothing."

"No, I mean . . ." My body has broken out in a sweat. "I think I'm going to be sick."

His quiet curse carries into my ear. "Keep it down. We'll be on the ground in five minutes."

"I'm trying, but—"

"You *can't* puke in here."

"Do you think I *want* to?" I snap, fumbling with my plastic bag. Of all the things I dreaded, vomiting is up there with the worst.

And now I get to do it sitting behind this asshole.

"Hell. Six other pilots available and *I* had to be the one to get you," Jonah mutters to himself.

I close my eyes and lean my face against the window. The ice-cold glass helps a bit, even with the jarring bumps. "'Don't worry, Calla.' 'It's no big deal, Calla.' That's what a decent person would say," I mumble feebly.

"I'm here to get your high-maintenance little ass to Bangor, not soothe your ego."

High-maintenance? My ego? I crack one lid to shoot daggers at the back of his head. All pretenses of politeness have dissolved. "Does my dad know you're such a giant dick?"

Jonah doesn't answer, and I'm glad for it, because talking makes my nausea worse. I push off my headset and go back to drawing long breaths through my nose and exhaling slowly through my mouth, fighting my body's urge to evacuate its contents at any given moment as I'm bumped and jostled in our descent toward the runway ahead.

The tiny two-seater plane teeters side to side like a seesaw before the wheels touch the ground, bouncing several times and then finally sticking.

Miraculously, I somehow succeed in keeping my tacos down through it all.

I breathe a sigh of relief as we coast down the runway. To the right, I spy several large rectangular buildings in various colors—forest green, fire-engine red, navy-blue—with two commercial planes like the ones I flew earlier today. We head left, though, toward a crop of smaller steel-gray buildings, the largest of them wearing a white and aqua-blue sign that reads ALASKA WILD.

My heart begins pounding in my chest.

I was here twenty-four years ago. Too young to remember, but I was here, and I've imagined this moment countless times since.

A short, stocky guy wearing a fluorescent vest casually waves his orange sticks, guiding Jonah to a spot at the end of a line of six planes. In front of us is a row of four more. Behind them, another two.

All of them are larger than the one we're in, I note.

I want to ask questions—Are these *all* my dad's planes? What part of the airport are we in? Is the collection of colorful warehouse-like structures *actually* the city airport? How many people work here?—but it's become apparent that Jonah has no interest in enlightening me about *anything*, so I bite my tongue. I can ask Agnes. I'm assuming she'll be more pleasant to talk to.

Or I can ask my father, who I'm about to meet.

The sudden urge to pee hits me.

No sooner has Jonah shut off the engine than he's yanking off his headset, popping open the door, and hopping out with surprising grace.

I remain a while, though, enjoying the crisp, cool breeze that skates across my face, working like a salve for my churning stomach.

"Come on, let's go!" Jonah barks.

I'm *almost* done having to deal with him, I remind myself as I slip out of my seat.

I stall at the plane's doorway to size up the distance to the ground, struggling to figure out how I'm going to hop out in my wedge heels—while keeping my purse on my shoulder and my hat on my head—without falling flat on my face or twisting an ankle. I should have changed my shoes when I was pilfering through my suitcase to get the essentials.

Without a word of warning, Jonah seizes me by the waist with his giant hands and hoists me down as if I weigh nothing at all, earning my squeal of surprise. Setting me onto the ground, he then dives back into the plane to retrieve the nylon bag tucked in behind my seat. He unceremoniously drops it to my feet like he's tossing trash to the curb. It lands in a puddle.

"Here. Puke all you want now." He thrusts the plastic bag into my empty grasp.

I peer up at his face—still masked by all the mangy hair and sunglasses and baseball cap, pulled low despite the lack of sun. How long has he been growing that bush for, anyway? *Years?* There are long, wiry hairs sticking out in every direction. I guarantee it's never seen a pair of scissors or a comb. *Ever.*

My disgusted expression stares back at me from the reflection of his lenses and my mother's words about falling in love with a pilot suddenly hit me.

I burst out laughing. Is Jonah what she would call a "sky cowboy"?

As if I'd ever fall for this guy.

The skin between the bottom of Jonah's aviators and the top of his unkempt beard flushes. "What's so funny?" he asks warily.

"Nothing." The cool wind picks up in a gust, sending strands of my long hair fluttering around my chin and threatening to lift my hat from my head. I brush away the strays and clear my throat. "Thanks for flying me here," I say politely, keeping my expression flat.

He hesitates. I can feel his heavy gaze on my face and it makes me uncomfortable. "Don't thank me. It wasn't my idea," he says, then flashes a tight, insincere smile, revealing straight, beautiful white teeth.

And here, I had assumed he'd written off *all* basic grooming and hygiene habits.

"Hello, there!" a female voice calls out, distracting me from thoughts of punching Jonah right in that perfect grill of his.

I gladly turn away from him, to see a petite woman marching toward us.

That has to be Agnes.

For the past three days, I've been imagining what the woman behind the calm, soft-spoken voice on the phone looks like. The "friend" who must be more than that. I guess I assumed—stupidly—that she'd look something like my mother.

Agnes is about as opposite to my mother as you can get.

For one thing, she's so small she's almost childlike, especially in an orange safety vest that's at least three sizes too big, baggy men's jeans, and clunky work boots. An outfit my mother wouldn't be caught dead in on her worst day. And, unlike my mother's sleek and impeccably colored bob, Agnes's raven-black hair—lightly peppered with gray—has been chopped to an unimaginative pixie length, almost as if she was annoyed with it one day and took a pair of scissors to herself without using a mirror for guidance.

For another, Agnes is an Alaska Native.

"You made it," Agnes says, stopping in front of me, giving me a chance to take in her features. She has a pretty, round face, aged with fine lines across her brow and conspicuous crow's-feet at the corners of deeply set, hooded eyes. I'd put her in her mid-forties, if I had to guess.

"I did."

She smiles wide, showing off pronounced cheeks and slightly crooked front teeth the color of bone china.

Finally. Someone around here seems genuinely happy to see me.

"So, is he . . ." My words drift as my gaze wanders from the door Agnes exited moments ago to the other buildings around us, where half a dozen workers in reflective vests load cargo into planes. I search their faces while I hold my breath, an odd mixture of nervous butterflies and nausea competing for attention inside me.

"Wren had to go up to a site near Russian Mission to drop off supplies," she explains, as if I know where that is. "He'll be back soon."

"Oh," I stammer. He's not here for my arrival? "He knew I was coming, though, right?"

"Yes, of course. He's excited." That wide smile wavers a touch, enough to make me suspicious.

He knew that his daughter, who he hasn't seen in twenty-four years, hasn't talked to in twelve years, was arriving tonight. Couldn't he have found someone else to drop off supplies, so he could be here to greet her? Couldn't he have sent Jonah instead? Or one of the six other available pilots, according to Jonah's grumblings not long ago?

Better yet, seeing as he's not too sick to fly, why couldn't he have come to Anchorage to get me?

Is my dad intentionally avoiding me?

Will I be dealing with another Jonah, who is less than thrilled that I'm here?

I struggle to keep my expression calm as my emotions war inside me. Disappointment swells after a day of counting down the hours and minutes until I'd meet the real-life version of the picture, until I'd hear the soft, easygoing timbre of his voice again. But with that disappointment comes a wave of the same pain-numbing resentment that absorbed me so many years ago, my way of coping with the raw realization that I would never be a priority for him.

And then tucked somewhere in the recesses of these volatile emotions is relief that I have a bit more time with my feet on Alaskan soil to gather my strength before I have to face him.

"How were your flights?" Agnes asks, as if sensing my suddenly heavy mood and wanting to keep it light.

"Fine. For the most part, anyway." I steal a withering glance over my shoulder. Jonah's tinkering with something on the plane, seemingly ignoring us.

Agnes's eyes trail mine and when they reach the burly pilot, her brow tightens a touch. But she's quick to shift her attention back, to wander over my face, stalling on each feature. "You've grown up so much." She must see my confusion because she adds quickly, "Your mother used to send your school picture to Wren every year. He kept them in a frame on his desk and swapped them out when a new one'd come."

Aside from my university graduation picture, the last school photo my mother would have sent was from eighth grade, which means Agnes and my father have known each other for a long time.

It feels awkward to ask within minutes of meeting this woman, and yet I can't hold back anymore. "So, are you and my dad married?" There's no ring on her finger, but she also doesn't look the type to wear jewelry.

"Me and Wren? *No*. We're just us. It's complicated." Her gaze shifts downward, skittering over my wedge heels before landing on the worn track bag. "Yours?" she asked doubtfully.

It doesn't sound like I'm going to get more out of her about their relationship yet. "No. My luggage is back in Anchorage. It wouldn't fit. I can't believe *I* fit, to be honest." I explain what Billy said about sending my bags over tomorrow.

She shakes her head. "I'm sorry. I told him to take one of the Cessnas."

Wait a minute . . . "Jonah told me that *that* one was the only plane available."

"Don't know what she's talking about," he calls out, though his focus seems glued to a clipboard as his giant hand passes over it with a pen, casually checking things off.

My mouth drops open as I stare at the lying bastard.

A soft sigh escapes Agnes. "Come on, Calla." She reaches down to grab the strap of the nylon bag and then hoists it over her shoulder as if it weighs nothing at all, even though it's probably half her size. "Let's get you settled before your dad arrives. I'm sure your mother would like you to check in."

"There's Wi-Fi at the house, right?" I wave my phone in the air. "Because I haven't been able to get a signal since Seattle."

"You must be dying," Jonah mutters under his breath, but loud enough for me to hear.

I roll my eyes.

"No, you won't get a signal. Only GCI works around here. But yes, you'll be able to connect from home," Agnes says. "Jonah, take care of things here for me, will ya?"

He grunts an answer, which I assume is an agreement.

Agnes seems to take it for that. She beckons me to follow her with a nod of her head, toward a small crop of vehicles parked on the far side of the office building.

"Wait! Do you mind taking a picture?"

"Oh . . . sure," Agnes says, her eyes widening with surprise.

I hand her my phone and then pick my path gingerly through the puddles to lean against the plane, angling my body in a pose that I know is especially flattering, my left hand pressed gently on the top of my hat.

"Smile!" Agnes calls.

"Oh, no, it's okay!" I call out as I look into the distance, at another plane that's descending from the clouds. Keenly aware of Jonah's eyes on me, my ears pricked to catch whatever snide comment he might have to make.

Thankfully, whatever thoughts he has, he keeps them to himself for once.

"I took three. Is that good?"

"Perfect. Thanks." I avoid Jonah's gaze as I collect my phone and follow Agnes. "So, you work here?"

She smiles at me warmly. "Going on sixteen years now."

"Wow." My dad and Agnes have known each other since I was ten. That's four years where we were talking and he didn't mention her. Has it been "complicated" for all that time or just part of it? "And what do you do here?"

"What *don't* I do is more like it. Fly planes . . . I don't do that. But I keep busy with a lot of other stuff—dispatch and payroll, bookings and shipment contracts; all that boring stuff. And I take care of the guys. We have . . . thirty-five pilots now."

My eyes widen. *"Seriously?"*

"'Course, they're not all full-time and they're scattered all over the place. We've got one guy in Unalakleet, two in Kotzebue . . . Barrow, of course, for the summer season. A few in Fairbanks . . . all over the place. It's like having dozens of sons. They can be a handful and I don't see some of them for months on end, especially the ones up north, but I love 'em like they were my own."

"I'll bet." Though how anyone but legitimate flesh and blood could love Jonah is beyond me.

I'm so distracted with my thoughts that I'm not paying attention to where I'm walking. My left foot lands in a deep puddle. I cringe from both the shock of the cold, muddy water against my toes and the damage it's going to do to the suede insole. "I guess it just rained?"

"It always 'just rained' around here." Agnes tosses the duffel bag into the back of an old black GMC pickup truck that's seen better days—the side of it is dented and scratched, and rust is eating away at the wheel well. "I hope you brought good rain boots with you."

"I did. Beautiful, expensive red Hunter boots." I pause for effect. "They're in Anchorage with the rest of my clothes."

"I'll make sure we get your things here soon." Agnes's eyes flicker back toward the rows of planes. She opens her mouth as if to say something more, but then decides against it. "Let's get you home."

I hazard a glance. Jonah is strolling across the lot toward the hangar, his gait casual and assured. He turns my way once, before dismissing me entirely without so much as a wave.

Good riddance. If I don't have to deal with him for the rest of the week, I'll be more than happy.

■ ■ ■

The drive to my father's house is not far—not even five minutes—and along lonely roads, the paved one riddled with yawning cracks, the dirt ones peppered with countless potholes. The few houses we see as we pass are basic, functional structures, mostly modular homes clad with colorful siding, all of them sitting above the ground on wooden legs. Because of the permafrost, Agnes explains.

I've made a mental note to look up "permafrost" in the dictionary when I have internet again.

Agnes has her seat pulled forward as far as it can go and sits straight-backed so she can see over the dash, her diminutive stature a challenge behind the wheel in a pickup truck. If I were in a more relaxed mood, I'd probably find it amusing.

But it helps to be with Agnes. She's as calm in person as she was on the phone, her voice a lull as she points out the basic landmarks: the "city" of Bangor about five miles to the east, and the Kuskokwim River beside it. That's the thick, snaking river I saw from above. She says it's a main artery off the Bering Sea and it stretches far to the north, allowing for travel between villages by barge and boat during the warmer months and by vehicle once it has frozen over in winter. It's the *only* way to drive a car to the villages, apparently, because there aren't any roads to connect Bangor to the rest of the state.

On a clear day, Agnes promises I'll be able to see Three Step Mountain in the far distance. Right now, though, all I see are miles upon miles of flat land freckled by low bushes, and capped by foggy skies.

And a sleepy moss-green modular home at the end of a long, narrow driveway, banked by a garage and two small utility sheds.

"Well . . . here we are," Agnes murmurs, cutting the engine.

My father's home. The place where I spent the first two years of my life.

Even though I don't remember any of it, everything about this moment feels surreal.

I take a deep breath as I climb out of the truck and trail Agnes up a set of creaky wooden steps, and through a single door, only vaguely aware that she didn't bother to use her key. The door was already unlocked.

I stop dead in my tracks and my eyes widen with shock as I take in the army of green mallard ducks. The atrocious wallpaper covers every square inch of kitchen wall. It's not a large kitchen, by any means, which makes it feel all the more enclosed.

As horrendous as it is, I stifle the sudden urge to giggle. This *must* be what my mother was talking about. I can't wait to tell her that she was right, that she *does* still know my father.

Agnes tosses the truck keys onto the counter. "Wren always forgets to open these before he leaves in the morning." She stretches onto her tiptoes to yank the cord attached to the blinds on the window over the sink, allowing the murky daylight in to illuminate the golden oak cabinets, the cream-colored laminate countertop, and the matching shade of vinyl flooring—a pattern of squares with small burgundy triangles accenting each corner. It reminds me of the flooring my grandparents had in their basement.

With only the small window above the sink, the one in the door, and a single-bulb light fixture above, it's dim in here. I can only imagine how oppressive it would feel during the long winters.

"When does it get dark, anyway?" I ask, curling my arms around my chest more for comfort than heat.

"At this time of year? The sun sets just before midnight, and then rises around a quarter past four, but it doesn't get *really* dark at night right now. Not like it does in the winter."

My eyes widen. I knew the days were long, but a midnight sunset?

"I replaced the blackout shades in your room. The old ones were tattered. You'll definitely want to draw those. Unless you're like your father, who doesn't mind sleeping in daylight." Agnes wanders to the fridge. "You must be hungry. Help yourself to whatever's in the . . ." Her brow crinkles as she holds the door open to show shelves bare of food, save for some condiments and a few beverages. "He promised he'd go grocery shopping," she mutters under her breath, quiet enough that I don't think she meant me to hear it. She lifts the carton of milk, to open it and give it a sniff. Her nose crinkles. "I wouldn't drink this, if I were you."

"It's okay. I can't drink milk anyway. I have a dairy allergy." I was diagnosed with it when I was five. Something I'm sure my father doesn't remember.

She pushes the fridge closed. "I'm sure he was waiting until he could see what you like." She gives me a tight smile. "Meyer's opens at eight thirty. He'll take you there first thing."

It's a good thing I'm not hungry, then.

Yet again, I can't help but wonder if my dad actually wants me here. Surely he could have grabbed a few basic food items to have in the house to feed his daughter when she arrived. *If* he cared enough to.

"When exactly did you tell him that I was coming?"

Agnes hesitates, reaching for the stack of mail that sits on the counter, slowly rifling through it, her eyes stuck on the labels. "Last night."

I think back to our email exchange from Friday, when I wrote to tell her that I had booked the plane ticket—thank you, Simon, for footing the bill. She wrote back saying that my dad was so happy that I was coming.

That was obviously a lie.

Why didn't she tell him on Friday, right after receiving my email? Why did she wait another day? Was she expecting him to be something other than "so happy"? What did he say when she told him? What words were exchanged within these walls about my arrival, and with what tone?

Abandoning the unopened mail, Agnes sets to picking dried leaves off a basil plant that sits on the top shelf of a tiered stand by the door, her face pulled into a frown of concentration. "Make yourself comfortable, Calla. Your dad should be back soon."

"Sure." My gaze flutters about. I feel anything *but* comfortable right now. The kitchen certainly has all the necessities—the basic white stove and fridge, a simple round wooden dining table set that wears plenty of dents and scratches from years of use, a worn stainless steel sink with a window above it that overlooks the sprawling, flat landscape. And yet, nothing about the space is particularly welcoming. It's not like our spacious and bright kitchen in Toronto, with the dreamy bay window and the cushioned window seat that runs alongside it, an inviting corner to curl up in with a book and a hot chocolate on a cold winter's day.

But maybe my discomfort has nothing to do with the décor and everything to do with the fact that whatever excitement I was feeling over seeing my father has quickly been squashed by the mounting dread that I am unwelcome here.

I inhale. The air is ever so faintly tinged with the acrid smell of burnt wood and ash, like that from a woodstove. Not cigarettes, I note. "He quit smoking, right?"

"He's working on it. Come on. I'll show you to your room." Agnes leads me out of the kitchen and into a long, narrow living room. At least this side of the house is free of mallard ducks, but it's also void of any personality. Equally dim, even with a light shining from overhead. The walls are white, with a few pieces of unremarkable snowy landscape artwork; the carpet is a shabby oatmeal color, a worn path from the threshold to the simple black woodstove atop beige tile in the far corner visible.

"When your dad's not working, this is where you'll find him. Here, or out there." She casts a hand toward a screened-in porch on the other side of a window that's larger than the one in the kitchen but still much too small for this size of room.

Aside from a few folded newspapers sitting in a heap on a wooden coffee table, it doesn't look like the room is used much. As ever, Alaska Wild is clearly his priority.

But there, sitting on a side table on the far end of the gold-black-and-green woven couch, is the infamous checkers board. I wonder if it's the same one from oh so long ago.

I feel Agnes's eyes on me. "It's . . . cozy," I offer.

"You're as bad a liar as Wren." She smiles. "I keep tellin' him the place needs freshening up. I've even left a few of those home renovation shows playin' on the television for him," she waves a hand at the small flat-screen that sits in the corner, opposite the woodstove and across from a tan-colored La-Z-Boy, "but he keeps saying he's not around enough to bother." Her voice drifts, her gaze settled on that chair, her seemingly permanent smile slipping.

Why doesn't she do it herself, then? Won't he allow her?

"He'll be home more in the coming weeks, though, right?"

"Yes, I suppose so."

There's no point dancing around the topic of my dad's cancer diagnosis anymore. "How bad is it, Agnes?"

She shakes her head. "That slip of paper was full of medical babble that I couldn't understand."

"But he told you what the doctors said, right?"

"Who, Wren?" She snorts softly. "He was sick for weeks with a terrible chest cold before I finally convinced him to go see someone. The doctor decided to run an X-ray and that's how they found the tumor. He didn't tell anyone, though. He just took his antibiotics, and I assumed he was getting better. Then the bugger flew to Anchorage for a secret biopsy and more testing." I can hear the frustration in her voice. "All I've been able to get out of him is that he has lung cancer and the doctors have suggested chemo and radiation."

"It sounds like they have a plan, then." I'd spent a bit of time on the Canadian Cancer Society website while waiting for my connecting flights today, reading up on types and stages and treatment options for lung cancer. It was a lot to sift through, and difficult to understand. All I managed to take away is that treatment is crucial and survival rates are among the lowest of all cancers.

"If I could see that paperwork, maybe I could Google—"

"I don't know where it is. He took it when I confronted him. Made me promise not to tell anyone."

A promise she obviously broke by calling me.

My own frustration begins to build. "When do the doctors want to start it all?"

"Next week. He has to go to the cancer clinic in Anchorage for it; that's the closest one. Jonah said he'd fly him back and forth, so he can be comfortable at home on the off days."

It's a good thing Jonah's much more willing to fly to Anchorage for my father than for me, at least.

My gaze drifts over the inhospitable living room. "Why don't you go ahead and redecorate, then, while he's gone?" Some paint color, new artwork, a few lamps. Anything would be an improvement at this point.

Amusement flashes in her eyes now. "Just come over to Wren's house and tear down that hideous wallpaper in the kitchen?"

Her words catch me off guard. "You mean you don't live here?"

"Me? No. I live in the little white house across the road. We passed it on the way in."

"Oh . . ." The puzzle pieces that I'd begun putting together—an understanding of my father's life—suddenly don't fit. "So you're *neighbors*?"

"For thirteen years now. Your dad owns the house. I rent it from him."

Neighbors. Coworkers. Friends.

And "it's complicated."

I trail her down the narrow hall, digesting this new information. "I still think you should do it. My mom painted Simon's bookcases one weekend while he was out of town for a convention." Simon had paid a small fortune for the golden oak custom units before he met my mother. She *despises* golden oak.

I remember watching the blood drain from his face when he walked through the door to see the new and improved soft white ones.

He got over it . . . eventually.

"Yeah, well . . . I'm not Susan." Agnes sighs, in a heavy way that carries deeper meaning with it. She leads me into a small corner bedroom with chalky walls and a pink crystal chandelier dangling in the center of the room. "You should have seen all the boxes he had stuffed in here. Took me all day yesterday to move them out."

It took Agnes all day, I note. Not Agnes and my dad.

The room is now empty of everything save for a metal-framed twin bed tucked into the corner by a small window, a wooden kitchen chair next to it, and a simple white chest of three drawers on the opposite side. There's a narrow closet with a louvered door on the wall directly beside me. The kind of old-fashioned folding door that our house in Toronto used to have, too, before we remodeled.

Not until I move farther into the room do I realize that the walls aren't plain white, but adorned by faint pink calla lilies of various sizes.

It finally dawns on me. "This was my room." My mother once told me that she spent the long, dark months waiting for me to be born painting my namesake flower on the walls of my nursery. An entirely new hobby for her, inspired by boredom and the fact that she couldn't grow the real thing. Or anything, for that matter. In the end, it kept her sane until the trip to Anchorage to wait out my due date at a family friend's house, as was necessary back then if you wanted to guarantee that a doctor would deliver your baby.

Her skill has improved greatly over the years. She still paints sometimes, usually in the winter, when the gardens around our house are asleep and she's looking for a quiet escape from the daily grind of the florist business. Her "studio" is directly across from my bedroom, taking up the front half of the third floor. The room is bright and spacious, and decorated in canvases of ruby-red tulips and vivid peonies, bursting with pink-tipped petals, all done by her hand. Some of her pieces now grace the walls of local restaurants and stores, a small sign beneath them naming her price to sell. But she's not in her studio often anymore, claiming that she doesn't need to paint flowers when she's elbow-deep in real ones all day long.

But twenty-six years ago, in a land that is unforgiving for so many things, this was her garden.

And my dad has preserved it all these years.

Agnes looks thoughtfully at me. "I figured you might like it."

"I do. It's perfect. Thank you." I toss my purse to the floor.

"It gets chilly at night, so I put plenty of blankets down to help keep you warm." Agnes gestures at the colorful and eclectic stack of folded quilts at the foot of my bed, and then looks around the space, as if searching for something. "I think that's everything. Unless there's something else?"

I hold my phone up. "The Wi-Fi password?"

"Yes. Let me find that. The bathroom is out here to the left, if you want to freshen up. Your dad has his own in his room, so this one is all yours."

With a weary sigh—if I weren't running on the adrenaline of anticipating meeting my father, I'd probably nose-dive right into that bed—I unzip the nylon track bag and begin emptying it, noting with frustration how little clothing I was able to fit.

And how most of it is damp.

"Dammit!" My black jeans are cold and wet against my fingertips, as is my sweater, my running gear, and the two other shirts I hastily stuffed into the right side of the bag. The side that Jonah so casually tossed into the puddle of muddy water. Gritting my teeth to keep my anger at bay, I fish out a small woven hamper from the closet and toss everything in.

"Found it." Agnes holds out a slip of paper between stubby fingers. Her nails are naked of any polish and chewed to the quick.

"Great. Thanks. Where can I do laundry? My clothes are wet, thanks to Jonah." I don't bother hiding the bitterness in my voice.

She huffs softly and then reaches for the basket. "Jonah lost his father to cancer a few years back and he's having a hard time dealing with Wren's news. I think maybe you got the brunt of it today."

"So, he *does* know."

She nods. "Wren didn't want to tell him yet, but Jonah's too aware. He weaseled it out of me earlier today. Anyway, I'm sorry if he was a bit difficult."

Is *that* what crawled up Jonah's butt and put him in such a foul mood? If it is, it's still far from acceptable, but I don't have to dig too deep to find sympathy for him.

But shouldn't he also feel at least a shred of sympathy for me, then?

"The machines are off the kitchen. Come on, I'll show you." She slows, her dark eyes widening as she takes in the myriad of hair product, brushes, and pretty cosmetics cases that ate up half the track bag and now cover the top of the chest of drawers. "Do you use *all* of that every day?"

"Pretty much . . . yeah." There's double that sitting in my room at home; I only brought the staples with me.

She shakes her head, murmuring, "I wouldn't even know where to begin."

A car door slams somewhere outside. Agnes turns toward it, pausing to listen. A few moments later, heavy footfalls land on the wooden steps leading up to the front door.

She takes a deep, sharp breath and for the first time since hearing her voice in the receiver, I sense nervousness radiating from her. Still, she smiles. "Your dad's home."

Chapter 7

■ ■ ■

I hang back, watching Agnes's slight form as she walks calmly and casually down the hall, laundry basket balanced on her right hip.

Nothing about this is calm or casual.

Flutters thrash in my stomach, an odd combustion of anticipation and dread. Will Wren Fletcher be the version I imagined as a small child growing up, his picture firmly grasped between my small hands? A quiet but kind man who would pick me up and toss me in the air after a long day of flying planes?

Or will I be facing the version he became later, after he broke my heart? The real version. The one who has never made an effort to know me.

"So? How did it go?" Agnes leans against the wall that leads into the kitchen, her back to me. As if this is another typical day.

"They've got their supplies," comes the deep male response, with a hint of rasp.

An odd sense of déjà vu rises deep inside me. I've heard that voice say those words before. Many years ago, through a receiver, carried along thousands of kilometers of wire, occasionally tinged by static and the hint of an echo. Probably when I asked him what he'd done that day.

"And the elk?"

He responds with a faint chuckle and it sends shivers down my spine, because that sound is familiar, too. "They finally chased them off the sandbar and to the east. Took 'em long enough, though. I almost had to turn around."

Silence lingers for one . . . two . . . three beats.

And then . . . "So?"

One word with such heavy meaning.

"She's in her room, getting settled. Jonah was a pain in the ass."

Another chuckle. "When isn't he?"

If my dad is angry with Agnes for bringing me to Alaska, he's hiding it well.

"Well . . . I'll let you go and say hello." Agnes disappears into the kitchen.

I hold my breath as my heart races, listening to the floor creak and the footfalls of approaching boots.

And then suddenly I find myself face-to-face with my father.

He's so much older now than he was in that tattered picture still tucked beneath my sweaters at home, and yet it's like he stepped out of the frame and into real life. His wavy hair still hangs a touch too long, like something from the 1970s, but the brown has been mostly replaced by gray. Where his skin used to be taut and smooth, age has carved deep lines and crevices. He's wearing the same outfit—jeans, hiking boots, and a layer of checkered flannel.

And he looks . . . healthy. Only now do I realize that I'd been preparing myself for a male version of Mrs. Hagler—brittle and hunched over, with an ashen complexion and a chest-rattling cough. But to look at him, you'd never know he has lung cancer.

Ten feet lingers between us and neither of us seems to be ready to make a move to close it.

"Hi . . ." I falter. I haven't called him "Dad"—to him—since I was fourteen years old. Suddenly it feels awkward. I swallow my discomfort. "Hi."

"Hello, Calla." His chest rises and falls with a deep breath. "Gosh, you're all grown up now, aren't you?"

Since the last time you saw me, twenty-four years ago? Yeah, I should hope so.

But I don't feel like a twenty-six-year-old woman right now. Right now, I feel like an angry and hurt fourteen-year-old girl, brimming with insecurity and doubt, acknowledging that *this* man—the one not moving a muscle to close this last bit of distance—made a conscious decision to *not* be in my life.

I don't know what to do with my hands, but I feel the urge to do *something* with them. I tuck them into my jeans pockets, and then pull them half out, only to remove them completely to ball them into fists. From there it's a fold and tuck into my armpits, as I hug my arms around my chest.

He clears his throat. "How were your flights?"

"Fine."

"Good."

The bang of a metal door and the crank of a dial in the background reminds me that Agnes is still here.

"Are you hungry? I didn't have a chance to go shopping—"

"No. I'm fine. I ate in Seattle."

He nods slowly, his gaze studying the worn carpet beneath our feet. "How's your mother?"

"Great." No doubt on her third glass of wine and driving Simon insane as she paces circles around him in his chair, waiting to hear from me. I hesitate. "She's shocked by the news." I don't think there's any need to elaborate further.

"Yeah, well . . . it is what it is." He reaches into his coat pocket to pull out a pack of cigarettes. "I'll let you get settled, then. See you in the morning." He turns and, just like that, he's gone, the kitchen door letting out a loud groan to signal his exit.

I stare at the empty space where he stood.

See you in the morning?

Four planes, 5,500 kilometers, and *twenty-four years* later, and all I get from my father is two minutes of polite conversation and "see you in the morning"?

Disappointment threatens to bowl me over.

I sense eyes on me and look up from my daze to find Agnes there, her dark, worried gaze studying me. "Are you okay?"

I swallow away my emotion. "I'm fine." My shaky voice betrays me.

"Wren isn't the best at expressing himself. This is a lot for him to take in."

I let out a breathy laugh, but all I feel is the urge to cry. "For *him*?" What about for *me*?

At least the smile she gives me is sympathetic. "I'll move your clothes to the dryer for you. Go on and get some sleep. Tomorrow will be better."

I'm glad for the dismissal. I duck into my bedroom, pushing the door shut behind me, fighting against this prickly feeling that's growing, the one that says I've made a terrible mistake, coming here.

I know the moment my phone has connected to the Wi-Fi because a rapid-fire succession of chirps sound, all text messages from my mother.

Have you made it to Anchorage yet?

Let me know when you get to your dad's.

Are you there yet?

Okay, I checked your flights and saw there was a delay from Seattle into Anchorage. Call me as soon as you can.

I called Alaska Wild and they said you landed about fifteen minutes ago. Have you made it to your father's?

My thumbs pause over the screen, deciding what to say. If I give her an honest rundown, she'll insist on calling, and I don't have the energy to dissect this disastrous reunion with her and Simon yet.

I made it. You were right about the small planes. I'm exhausted. I'll call you tomorrow.

First thing, okay? We love you!

And remember to take lots of pics!

I quickly swap my clothes for my pajamas—one of a few clothes items that didn't get wet, thankfully—and dart into the bathroom to wash up. My father and Agnes are nowhere to be found, which makes me think they're outside, talking.

Shutting myself into my bedroom once again, I draw the curtain and crawl under the blankets with my phone, hoping to distract my dark thoughts.

I pull up the picture that Agnes took earlier. As horrifying as the flight in that thing was, we pose well together, the plane's cheerful colors especially striking against the gloomy backdrop.

The only flaw is the asshole standing inside the frame.

Jonah's back is to the camera, his clipboard is gripped in his hand, but his head is turned to showcase the fur around his face and the fact that there's no mistaking it—he's watching me. If it were any other guy, this picture might tell a different story, a romantic tale of a man drawn to a woman.

So not the case here.

I play around with the various photo editing tools, cropping, tweaking, and filtering, until I have a stunning snapshot for Instagram, sans angry bush pilot.

But my thumbs stall over the keyboard, unable to come up with a suitable caption. Diana's voice preaches in my head. *Be upbeat and inspirational! Bonus points for funny!*

I feel the opposite of those things right now.

I always struggle with writing captions. Not Diana. Then again, most of her posts don't sound like her, at least not my best friend Diana, the girl who shoves sweet potato fries into her mouth five at a time while she gripes about the lawyers at her firm.

How can I make anything about today upbeat or inspirational?

How should I lie?

By keeping it superficial, that's how. Simple and light and happy.

I quickly type in the first thing that comes to mind: "City girl in the Alaskan wild. Love my life!" I throw in a bunch of hashtags—another golden rule à la Diana—and hit "post."

All the while I'm biting my lip against the worry that comes with my growing reality—that *everyone* would be happier had Agnes never made that phone call.

■ ■ ■

I wake to soft ocean waves lapping rhythmically at the shore, a peaceful sound courtesy of the white-noise app I use every night.

For a split second, I forget that I'm unemployed and single.

And in Alaska to meet a father who may be gravely ill but *still* doesn't want me here.

Pushing the sleep mask off my face, I let my eyes adjust, focusing on the faint glow of daylight that creeps around the edge of the curtains. My muscles ache with weariness after yesterday's long, grueling day of travel. Or maybe it's this bed. My bed at home is a king—big enough that I can sprawl sideways and never have a limb dangling over the edge—and dressed in memory foam to mold to my body. This one has all the qualities of a Salvation Army cot by comparison.

The pillow's not much better, hard and lumpy against my face. I must have punched it a dozen times last night, trying to soften it, before giving up.

I paw at the small wooden chair next to me until my fingers grasp my phone.

I groan. It's not even six a.m. and I'm awake. Then again, I shouldn't be surprised—my internal clock thinks it's ten.

I *also* shouldn't be surprised that my mother has sent three more texts.

Are you awake yet?

How is your father doing? Does he look well enough?

Let me know when you're awake!

She's also tried calling.

I'm not ready to handle the Susan Barlow inquisition just yet. I mean, what would I even tell her? He looks healthy, meeting him was brief and awkward at best, and I don't know why the hell I came?

There are also two messages from Simon.

Be patient with your mother.

Remember, you are a stranger to him, as he is a stranger to you.

"No shit, Simon," I mutter. I'm sure there's a deeper meaning behind his words. There always is. Simon is who I need to speak with right now. I'm desperately in need of one of his shrink pep talks. But I'm sure he'll be prescription-pad-deep with real patients all morning, so my issues will have to wait.

If there's one good thing about waking up this early, though, it's that I've bought myself a few hours before I *have* to call home.

I sigh with satisfaction as I open up my Instagram to find more "likes" on my bush plane post than usual, and a dozen new followers. I can always count on Diana to leave a comment riddled with emojis and exclamation points, along with the usual comments from my friends and a few regular followers, the "Love your outfit!", "Beautiful shot!", "You're so pretty!", "I have that hat, too!" But there are a few other ones, too. People claiming how lucky I am to be in Alaska, how adventurous I am, and how they've always wanted to go.

These people—strangers—see a pretty, well-dressed girl embracing life. None of them know the *real* story—of why I'm here, of why I'm already thinking about going home. They can't sense my loneliness, or the knot in my stomach. That's the magic of social media, I guess. But there's also an odd comfort to hiding behind the illusion. If I stare at myself beside the orange-and-yellow toy plane long enough, and reread the effervescent caption enough times, maybe I'll start to buy what I'm selling, too.

I spend a few minutes answering people, until basic human needs win out.

Throwing off the heavy layers of blanket, I pull myself out of bed and quickly change into the outfit from yesterday, my skin prickling with gooseflesh from the crisp, cool air. It's refreshing in comparison to the stifling summer heat and the stale air circulating through the vents back home.

The smell of fresh-brewed coffee teases my senses as soon as I crack my bedroom door. To my delight, I find the basket of my clean clothes—folded—sitting by my feet. I push it aside for the moment and pad softly down the hall, that same conflicting mix of anxiety and excitement churning in the pit of my stomach that I had last night.

The living room is empty.

So is the kitchen.

"Hello?" I call out and wait.

Nothing. Not a rustle or a floorboard creak, or a tap running from his en-suite. It's eerily quiet, the tick-tick-tick of the kitchen wall clock the only sound.

But my dad's been here, I can see, by the not-quite-full pot of coffee and the used mug sitting next to it, spoon resting inside. I poke my head out the door to see if he's having a cigarette. An old black Ford truck that's in only slightly better condition than Agnes's sits outside, but there's no sign of him, or so much as the lingering scent of nicotine.

It's not until I've stepped back inside that I notice the sheet of lined paper sitting on the counter, next to the fridge. My name is scrawled across the top in tidy all-cap print. Next to it is a stack of American twenty-dollar bills.

> *Didn't know what you'd want to eat. Keys are in the truck. Meyer's is five miles away. Go east to the end of the road, turn right, then make your 2nd left in town. The rain should hold off for the morning, if you want to go for a walk.*

At the bottom of the page, there's a scribbled-out "W," as if he started writing his name and then decided against it. But he didn't replace it with "Dad."

I'm guessing he's gone to work. Does he always leave for work *this* early?

Or was he avoiding me?

On impulse, my fingers graze the ceramic of his used mug. It's still warm. Evidence that he *was* here, and not that long ago. He probably bolted the second he heard movement coming from my room, I realize with dismay.

How he got to work without his truck, I can't guess. Maybe he got a ride from Agnes?

Regardless, it clearly didn't cross his mind that I might not have my driver's license.

"No, no, *you* go ahead to work, *Dad*. What? But we haven't seen each other in twenty-four years? No biggie. I would *never* expect you to take an hour or two off. Seriously, I'll take care of myself," I mutter, trying to squash the sting in my chest.

I spend a few minutes rifling through the bare fridge and disorganized cupboards to learn that my father lives off coffee, cheap sugar-loaded peanut butter, and frozen macaroni-and-cheese dinners.

It's a good thing I'm not hungry. What I am, though, is desperate for one of Simon's frothy soy milk lattes. I don't have a lot of vices, but my regular dose of caffeine in the morning is number one on a short list. On the rarest of occasions that I miss my fix—I could count those days on one hand—my head is throbbing by midday.

Five years ago, Simon surprised us at Christmas with a fancy barista machine that can rival Starbucks. I swear he sits at the breakfast bar every morning with his cup of Earl Grey and his *Globe and Mail* and listens for the first creak of steps from the third floor, just so he can hit Brew. By the time I'm staggering down to the kitchen half-asleep, he's sliding a hot mug into my hands. To keep the Kraken at bay, he claims, though I'm pretty sure it has more to do with his secret fascination with the frother.

A pang of homesickness stirs inside me, but I push it aside, focusing on the matter at hand. This Meyer's place doesn't open for another two and a half hours. That means I have time to kill while I figure out how I'm going to get there so I can survive this day.

■ ■ ■

BEADS OF SWEAT trickle down my face as I pause for a gulp of water and to catch my breath, my gaze landing on my father's mossy green home in the distance. I lasted twenty minutes in that eerily quiet, uncomfortable house with nothing but my tense thoughts and my laptop before my disquiet forced me out. Throwing on my running gear and investigating my surroundings seemed like as good an excuse for escape as any.

I can see Agnes's house in the distance, too. It's like a mirror image of my father's house—same size, same distance from the road, same wooden porch leading up to the door—except it's white, and there's no truck in the driveway. It was already gone when I ventured out. I assume she's at work, too.

The mileage tracker on my phone claims I've run ten kilometers and I haven't lost sight of either house this entire time. There's been little to obstruct the view—fields of low bushes and a few scattered houses—and not another living soul to distract my focus.

Not a single person driving by, or riding a tractor, or walking their dog. Not even an echoing bark to carry through the stillness. It's unsettling. I'm so used to the constant flow of people, the blasts of horns and roars of engines, and the clatter of construction. It's white noise for me, and I've come to need it as I need the rhythmic waves of an app to sleep. Add the fact that I don't have a working phone and I feel *completely* cut off from the world out here.

How can *anyone* find this peaceful?

"Ow!" I slap my thigh, leaving a squashed tiny corpse clinging to my skin where my palm made contact. The mosquitoes have been relentless all morning, swarming my damp, bare flesh.

A second and third pinch on my arms and calves gets me running once again. That seems to be the only way for some respite.

I keep a steady, solid pace along the road, the rhythmic pounding of my running shoes against dirt the only sound, until a low, familiar buzz catches my ear. A yellow charter plane climbs the sky above me, leveling off just below the thick layer of tufted clouds the color of sheep's wool, the kind that promise rain at any moment. I can't discern the logo on the side of the plane, but it could very well be an Alaska Wild charter.

It could very well be my dad.

Trying to get as far away from his daughter as possible.

Can he see me down here in my hot-pink running outfit and matching running shoes?

At least they *used* to be pink. Now they're covered in mud splatter, thanks to the dirty roads. A week of this place and I might as well toss them onto the Davisville subway station tracks to join the others.

The plane fades into the distance and once again I'm completely alone. Just me and a million blood-sucking mosquitoes.

Up ahead is a cluster of shed-like buildings surrounded by a low, spindly hedge. They're all shapes and sizes, all with ruby-red roofs. A few look like houses, but others look like barns. But for what? My mom insisted that nothing can grow in this climate. As I get closer, I see the clear structures set up behind the buildings. They're definitely greenhouses. There are pickup trucks and tractors, and garden patches scattered throughout, with rows of vegetation. Some are covered with white plastic, others with white semicircular hoops lining them.

And beyond are fields of vegetables. Rows upon rows of heads of lettuce and tall stocks of green onions, and chartreuse carrot fronds, and things I can't discern from here. Two people toil around a lemon-yellow barrel, hoses in hand.

There *is* life out here after all.

And things to grow. Either the soil has changed drastically in twenty-four years or my mother was wrong about the barren wasteland. Or maybe she gave up on growing things in Alaska before ever trying.

A sharp pinch pricks me and, quick as a swatter, my hand flies up to slap against my neck. I cringe as three squashed mosquitoes cling to my hand and then take off at a clipped pace, desperate for sanctuary from the bugs and a long, hot shower.

And then I guess I'll have to wait until *someone* gives a damn that I'm here and checks in on me.

■ ■ ■

What are the chances that a cop would pull me over around here, anyway?

I consider this as I peer out the kitchen window at my dad's pickup, the dull ache behind my eyes from lack of caffeine quickly growing to a gnawing throb. I felt it coming a half hour ago and attempted to choke down a mug of black coffee out of desperation. I gave up after three sips and then spent ten minutes scrubbing the bitter taste out of my mouth with my toothbrush, unable to swallow any more.

To make matters worse, my stomach is now growling in protest and my heart is being tested by the raw reality that I am one right turn, one left turn—or five miles, per the note—from civilization and I've been all but abandoned by my father.

Agnes was wrong. Today is not better.

I check my Uber app. No cars available in my area.

With gritted teeth, I Google the number to Wild Alaska's main line. Because, of course, my dad didn't think to leave me his contact number.

Agnes answers on the third ring.

"It's Calla."

"Oh, good morning. How was your sleep?"

"Fine. Is my dad there?"

"Uh . . . no. He took off a little while ago, on his way up to Barrow to check on things. Won't be back until this afternoon." There's a pause. "He said he left you the truck, though, so you could go into town."

"I don't have my license."

"Oh." I can almost see the deep frown lines in her forehead. "So you're stuck there."

"Pretty much. With nothing to eat." I don't bother hiding the irritation from my voice.

"Okay. Well, let's see . . ." I hear papers shuffling in the background. "Sharon can cover for me while I drive you in."

"Perfect."

"She'll be in at noon."

"Noon?" I don't know who Sharon is, but I can do math, and noon means four o'clock Toronto time.

I'll be dead by then.

"Oh, wait, you know what? Jonah has a late start today. He'll drive you into town."

"Jonah?" I feel my face twist in disgust. She's got to be kidding me.

"Is his truck still in the driveway?"

My disgust morphs to suspicion. "What do you mean 'in the driveway'?"

"Next door."

I dart to the window to spy the neighboring house maybe fifty feet away. It's another simple and quiet modular home, clad in butter-yellow siding that could use a power wash. My eyebrows pop. "*Jonah* lives *next door*?"

"Is he still there?"

"There's a forest-green SUV parked out front." But no signs of life, otherwise.

"Okay, good. Run on over and ask him to take you to Meyer's."

This keeps getting better by the minute.

"He doesn't want to drive me anywhere," I grumble. And the absolute last thing I want to do is ask him for a favor.

"He'll drive you." She sounds confident. I note, though, that she doesn't argue about his lack of desire.

"And then what? Abandon me there? You know he took that tiny plane yesterday on purpose, don't you?"

There's a long pause. "Jonah likes to play little games, sometimes. Keeps himself from getting bored." Agnes's soft chuckle fills my ear. "But he's a teddy bear. And don't worry, I've already talked to Billy. He's putting your suitcases on the Caravan flying in this afternoon."

I heave a sigh of relief. Finally, some good news.

"Ask Jonah for a ride into town. It'd be good for you two to get along. He and your dad, they're close. And don't be afraid to put him in his place. He can get as well as he gives."

I gaze warily across the lawn again.

"Or wait until I can come get you at noon. Up to you."

Ask the angry yeti for help or starve to death. The latter may be less painful.

"Oh, and you and Wren are coming for dinner tonight. I hope that's okay."

"Sure." If I survive that long.

Before I can think too much about it, I stuff the cash my dad left into my purse, slip on my wedge heels, grab my sunglasses, and march out the door. I'm dressed smartly in jeans and a fitted lightweight navy sweater, yet the mosquitoes swarm me all the same, forcing me into a mad rush past the truck and through the wet grass. My feet sink into the marshy ground with each step and by the time I've made it to the small wooden porch off the front of the house, my toes are soaked and uncomfortable, the soles of my shoes squishy and most certainly ruined. Just another reminder that I don't have my rain boots thanks to the jackass I'm about to ask for help from.

I struggle to remove the sour look from my face as I rap my knuckles against the solid white door.

After a good ten seconds, I knock harder.

"Hold on a second!" that gruff voice calls out. Heavy footfalls sound and then a moment later the door is yanked open, and Jonah fills the doorway, halfway through sliding his shirt down over his stomach.

I flounder for a moment.

Jonah isn't much older than I am, I realize, now that he's not disguised behind a ball cap and sunglasses. Early thirties, maybe, with only the faintest of lines creasing his brow. His hair hangs long, damp, and scraggly to his jawline, the ends tattered as if not touched by a pair of scissors in years.

He's not as bulky as his jacket made him look yesterday, either. Or rather, he's big but he's surprisingly fit, as just made evident by the glimpse I caught of a ribbed torso before his black shirt hid the pleasant sight away.

But it's his eyes that are the most jarring to me. They are piercing in their hard gaze, but his irises are the lightest, prettiest shade of ice blue I've ever seen on a man.

Beneath all that unkempt hair, Jonah is actually attractive.

"Calla!"

I startle.

"Did you need something?" he asks slowly, in an irritated way; a way that tells me I missed his words the first time, too busy gawking at him.

Too bad those pretty eyes come with that callous tongue.

I clear my voice. "I need you to take me into town."

His gaze flickers toward my dad's house. "What's wrong with Wren's truck?"

"Nothing. But I don't have my license."

His bushy brows pop. "You're kidding me. You're *how* old and you don't have your license?"

"I've never needed it," I say defensively.

A slow, knowing smirk touches his lips. "You get everyone else to drive you around, don't you?"

"No! I live in a *city* with *public transit*. Do you know what that is?" I snap, my temper flaring instantly. Something that doesn't normally happen with strangers. Sure, when I do leave Toronto, it's at the mercy of someone else—my mom or Simon, Diana, or a slew of other friends who have cars—but there's nothing wrong with that. And it's beside the point, anyway.

I knew coming to Jonah was a mistake. "You know what? Never mind. I'll drive myself. Thanks *so much.*" Spinning on my heels, I march down the steps and across the lawn, heading straight for my dad's truck. I yank the door shut behind me and spend a few moments in a murderous rage, my hands flailing about wildly, smacking the glass, the dashboard, and myself, killing the small horde of mosquitoes that followed me inside.

Not until I'm sure every last one is squashed do I let myself settle back into the driver's seat with a huff of grim satisfaction, fingers curling around the bottom of the steering wheel.

It smells like tobacco in here. There's no evidence—no butts in a cup, no empty cardboard cast aside, not even that thin plastic strip that seals a fresh pack—but I can smell the cigarettes all the same, the smoke permeated into the worn fabric of the seats.

The keys are right where my dad said they'd be, sitting in the ignition, waiting for me or anyone else to hop in and drive away. The threat of "anyone else" is clearly low.

I could drive into town. It's two turns, his note said. An empty dirt road that probably leads into a paved one. A few stop signs. Some lights. Green means go, red means stop. It's not rocket science, and I've been a passenger enough that I can figure this out.

"Crap." I eye the gear stick jutting out of the floor with dismay. It's a standard transmission. That is something I can't figure out, no matter how many times I've ridden shotgun.

I let my head fall back as a loud groan escapes my lips. All this open space around me and I'm trapped.

The passenger-side door opens. Jonah slings his arm over the top. "Why do you *need* me to drive you into town?" His tone is still gruff, but less confrontational.

"Because there's *nothing* to eat in that house."

"*Nothing* at all." He smirks.

"Nothing," I snap, more from frustration than anything else. "Spoiled milk and ketchup. My dad left money and a note, and took off before I was even awake. And Agnes can't come until noon. My head is throbbing because I haven't had a coffee yet and I'm *starving*." And in an increasingly foul mood.

"That's not at all dramatic," Jonah mumbles, glancing at his watch, and then to the east, where a plane descends. He heaves a sigh. "Learn how to ask next time."

"I *did* ask."

"No, that was closer to a demand, and I don't respond well to those."

I glare at him, as I mentally replay my exact words. I asked, didn't I? Maybe not.

"Well?" Those icy blue eyes widen. "I don't have a lot of time. And you better make it quick because I've got a full day of flying if the weather cooperates." He slams the door and begins trudging back across the road.

With equal amounts of relief and trepidation, I hop out and follow him all the way to his SUV—a boxy, older-model forest-green Ford Escape that's missing the tailgate tire but is in otherwise decent condition.

With the same surprisingly lithe, sleek movements that I noticed yesterday, he retrieves that black baseball cap from the backseat, the one from yesterday with the letters USAF scrawled across the front in white. With one hand holding his long, scraggly hair back, he slides it onto his head. And then he gets behind the steering wheel.

I climb into the passenger seat, inhaling the faint scent of spearmint gum as he adjusts the vents and turns a dial for the heat on the console, bringing a small gust of warmth into the chilly, dated interior. How old is Jonah's car, anyway? I can't remember the last time I was in a car that had a handle on the door to crank the window.

A mosquito floats in front of my face. "Are they *always* this bad?" I clap my hands together to squash it in my palm.

"They don't bother me."

"They ate me alive this morning."

"Maybe try putting on clothes next time you go running."

My mouth drops open. "There's *nothing* wrong with what I run in." Granted, my shorts *are* short and snug, for comfort. So is the tank top. And the outfit works better along city streets that aren't infested with bugs, so I guess I can see his point. Not that I'll ever admit that to him. And wait a minute . . . "Were you *spying* on me?"

He snorts. "I happened to look out the window to see you running up the driveway in clothes that leave *nothing* to the imagination, flailing your hands like a madwoman." He throws his SUV into drive and we coast along the bumpy driveway in loaded silence, my cheeks burning.

"Thanks for driving me," I finally offer. He might not be thrilled about it, but at least he *is* helping me.

I get only a small grunt in response. And then, "Why haven't you had a coffee yet? Wren always makes a full pot and leaves it on. You couldn't just pour yourself a cup?"

Why does everything out of his mouth sound like a direct assault? "I need soy milk."

"Of course you do," he mutters.

I don't know what that's supposed to mean, but I'm guessing it's not flattering.

We ride the rest of the way into town in silence.

■ ■ ■

Bangor, town of sixty-five hundred and the largest community in Western Alaska, is a shithole.

At least, that's my first impression.

I bite my tongue against the urge to say as much, as we drive along a snaking main road, passing intersections with street signs for more rural roads—some gravel, others with asphalt that's so badly cracked, they'd have been better off leaving it unpaved.

Single- and double-story buildings are scattered along either side. They remind me of the ones from the airport, rectangular and clad in siding, topped with metal sheets. Some are drab creams and browns; others are weathered peacock blues and emerald greens. Where there are windows, they're disproportionately small. Meanwhile some have no windows at all. And *all* of them are connected by silver pipes that run along the grassy ground, from one property to the next.

"Is this an industrial area?"

"Nope."

I stifle the urge to roll my eyes. Jonah's second favorite word, behind "yup."

We pass by one property that has a playground set erected in the yard. Two young children dangle from monkey bars as a husky sits on its haunches, looking on, no parents in sight. Many of these buildings are family homes, I realize, now noticing the bicycles lying on lawns and baseball bats propped against walls, and a lopsided trampoline. Homes with not a shred of curb appeal. No leading walkways or pleasing gardens, no welcoming front entrance. Only scraggly shrubs and dust-covered ATVs, and unsightly cylindrical tanks.

It's because we're on the outskirts, I convince myself. As Jonah takes me farther into this town in the middle of nowhere—with no roads connecting it to the rest of Alaska—we'll come across a visage that I'm more familiar with. Actual neighborhoods with brick houses and driveways lined with daylilies and rosebushes. A main street with some degree of city planning, with proper storefronts and decorative streetlamps and people dressed in something other than value-brand jeans and plain cotton shirts.

Areas where there aren't spray-painted Dumpsters on every corner like the one we just passed, decorated with rainbows and suns and "Bangor is the Best" messages. Meanwhile, the streets are littered with debris that's been dragged through the weedy grass by animals.

The farther in we drive, though, the less confident I become.

Thank you, Mother, for getting us the hell out of here when you did.

There aren't even sidewalks along the streets. Everywhere I look, I see people walking along the ditch at an unhurried pace. Some carry brown paper grocery bags. Most don rubber boots or hiking-type shoes, and seem unconcerned about stepping in muddy puddles or the spots of dirt spattering their pants.

They're of all ages, some as young as ten or eleven, one an elderly Alaska Native man whose limp is so pronounced, he should be walking with a cane. "He's going to fall and hurt himself," I murmur, more to myself, not expecting a response from Jonah, beyond maybe a grunt.

"Yupik people are tough. That man probably walks three miles every day."

I frown. "What people?"

"Yupik. Some are Athabascan, or Aleut." Jonah makes a left turn. "The villages that we fly into are mostly Yupik communities."

"Is that what Agnes is?"

"Yup. She grew up in a village up the river. Her mom and brothers are still there, living a subsistence lifestyle." He adds quickly, perhaps after seeing my frown, "They live off the land."

"Oh! So, sort of like farm-to-table?" Unlike all the other exchanges I've had with Jonah, I feel like I'm getting useful information about Western Alaska.

"Sure. If you want to compare an entire culture's way of life to the latest culinary trend . . ." he murmurs dryly.

I study the faces of people as we pass them. About half of them are Alaska Natives, while the other half are Caucasian, except for the one East Indian who's standing next to a battered Tahoma with its hood propped up and steam swirling from its engine.

"What are *those* people doing?" I point to three men in their twenties trudging along the road, two supporting either end of a mattress, the third carrying an awkward-looking box. A woman walks about ten feet ahead with a lamp in one hand and a toddler perched on her hip.

"My guess would be moving."

"By *foot*?"

"They're probably just shifting a block or two. People don't want to burn gas for that, not at almost seven bucks a gallon."

"I take it that's a lot?" I hazard, quickly adding, "We pay in liters." Not that I could gauge the value in any measurement, but I'm tired of feeling like an idiot in front of Jonah.

Jonah lifts a hand in casual greeting at a passing man on an ATV. "Double the gas price in Anchorage. Almost three times as much as the Lower Forty-eight."

The Lower Forty-eight? Do I dare ask? Or will that earn me another dry, thinly veiled "you're so ignorant" response.

I reach for my phone to Google the term, but then my hand freezes as I remember my phone doesn't work here.

"That's what we call the rest of America," Jonah murmurs, as if able to read my mind. "Up here, all our fuel comes in on a barge, and then gets dumped into a fuel farm for storage or carried up the river to the villages in smaller boats. That's a lot of added cost in transportation and storage. And that's just to keeping a car going. Every one of these vehicles cost thousands to get here, on top of what they cost to buy. A lot of people around here don't own one. Those who do take good care of them so they last."

I guess that explains why my dad is driving a truck that's at least fifteen years old when it sounds like by normal standards he could afford better.

I quietly take stock of the vehicles we pass as if to prove Jonah's words. They're all older, worn models, with plenty of bumps and bruises. Fords, GMCs, Hondas. A lot of pickup trucks. Not a shiny BMW in sight.

A worn white sedan with orange writing on its side that reads TAXI CAB and a phone number drives by, surprising me. "You have cabs here?"

Jonah snorts. "Plenty of those. More per capita than any other US city. Five bucks flat will get you anywhere you want to go in town. Seven to the airport."

I wish I had known. I would have gladly called one instead of dealing with Jonah. Though, he's being civil now. *More* than civil, actually. He's using full sentences.

Maybe that's why I dare ask, "Have you lived in Alaska your whole life?"

There's a long pause, and I wonder if maybe I misread his civility, if maybe I should have shut up while I was ahead.

"I was born in Anchorage. We moved to Vegas when I was twelve. I moved back about ten years ago."

"*Vegas*. Really . . ."

Sharp blue eyes glance over at me quickly. "Why do you say it like that?"

"No reason. I've never met anyone who actually *lived* in Vegas." My only weekend there was a drunken, costly three-day blur with Diana and two other friends for our twenty-first birthdays. By the time I curled up in my seat to fly home, I was more than ready to leave.

"Yeah, well, there's more to it than the Strip. Most locals won't be caught dead down there."

"Do you miss it?"

"Hell, no. Couldn't wait to get out of there."

"Why?"

He sighs, as if he doesn't have the energy to answer a question like that. "Too fast, too loud, too materialistic—take your pick."

The exact opposite of Bangor, I'm quickly gathering. "But why this part of Alaska? I mean, why didn't you go back to Anchorage, if that's where you grew up? It looks nice. Peaceful. From what I saw, anyway." And from what I read, it's a *real* city.

"I like it better here."

I'm sensing he could say a lot more but has no interest to. Still, I'm too curious to stop asking questions. "How'd you end up working for my dad, anyway?"

"One of the pilots was an old friend of my father's. He hooked me up."

Mention of Jonah's father reminds me of what Agnes revealed yesterday. I hesitate. It's a sensitive topic, but it's also a connection between us. "I heard your dad had cancer, too."

I hold my breath, waiting for him to say something—when his father died, from what type of cancer, how long he suffered, how long he fought. I want to ask if Jonah was close to his father, if it still hurts. Maybe that bit of information will make him seem more human; maybe he'll soften when he realizes that we have at least one thing in common.

"Yup."

His hand tightens around the steering wheel and I instantly regret bringing it up. Though, I think I got the answer as to whether it still hurts.

I quickly search for a new, safe topic to switch to.

I find it in the form of a golden-yellow sign. "Hey! You guys have a Subway!" I don't even like subs and yet I'm excited, for no other reason than it's something familiar.

He relaxes his grip. "It's the only chain you'll find around here."

"So . . . I guess that means no Starbucks?" I hazard, topping it off with a playful grin.

Icy blue eyes flicker to me a moment before adjusting to the road. "Nope."

"Is there somewhere I can grab a coffee?"

We come to a stoplight, the first one so far. With his hand still curled around the steering wheel, he points a long index finger—the nail bitten off, cuticle cracking—at a forest-green building. "Right there."

A white bristol-board sign hangs over the darkened entryway. "Berta's Coffee *and Bait Shop*?" I read out loud.

"Yeah. You know . . . fish eggs, leeches, herring, shad, chunks of dead—"

"I get it," I cut him off with a cringe. "But in a *coffee* shop? That's got to be a health code violation."

"People need to diversify to keep their businesses afloat around here."

"I guess." I'm still cringing when I notice the ramshackle building next to it, a medley of ill-sized plywood boards and metal sheets and worn paint, and a wooden board slapped to the front that has SZECHUAN's scrawled across it with, I'm guessing, a wide paintbrush. "Oh my God. Is that . . . a *Chinese food restaurant*?" Because it looks like a backyard clubhouse built out of scrap material by a bunch of ten-year-old boys.

"It's been there forever."

That place would be shut down for a slew of health and building code violations in a day, anywhere else in North America.

"Where the hell am I?" I mumble, aiming my phone. Wait until Diana sees this.

I feel his steady gaze on me. "Do you want me to pull over, so you can run in and see if they have a fresh pot of—"

"No thanks. I'll wait." I'd rather deal with this pounding headache than accept a coffee from someone who most certainly didn't wash their hands enough after sticking them into a vat of writhing earthworms.

I think there's a small smile lurking behind that beard, but it's hard to see. Still, I feel an odd sense of accomplishment at the possibility that this "teddy bear"—by Agnes's description—might not despise me as much as he seemed to initially.

He makes another turn—either my dad's directions on that note were wrong or Jonah took me the long way—and we're now on Main Street, a wider road lined with more of the same simple siding-clad buildings, only with business signs. Bangor seems to have all the service staples—law office, dentist, chamber of commerce, bank, even a real estate broker—as well as a string of sandwich, pizza, and family restaurants that are basic but *don't* look like they're serving up listeria.

My stomach grumbles as we roll past Gigi's Pizza & Pasta, a cute upbeat yellow place with more windows than anyone else on the street. But the neon OPEN sign by the door isn't illuminated. If it were, I'd ask Jonah to drop me off there and I'd catch a cab home.

Jonah swerves into a parking lot and pulls in next to an ATV. A giant warehouse is ahead, finished off with an earthy brown siding and a gently sloped black tin roof. The sign above the door reads MEYER'S GROCERY, CLOTHING, AND HOUSEHOLD GOODS.

"Look, if you want to wait—"

He pops his door open and with sleek moves, exits his truck and rounds the front of it, before I have a chance to finish my sentence. And then he simply stands there, arms folded across his broad chest, waiting for me.

"I guess I'm going grocery shopping with Jonah," I mutter to myself. At least this way he can't abandon me here.

I hope.

I slide out of the passenger seat, adjusting my fitted sweater over my hips and waist.

Jonah's eyes catch the subtle move and then he turns away, looking wholly disinterested. That's fine, because I'm not trying to attract him. What *would* be his type anyway, I wonder. I couldn't even hazard a guess, other than to say "hardy."

He marches for a set of stairs that lead to the main door.

And despite the fact that he's a jerk, I can't help but admire the curves of his shoulders and arms as I follow him in. He has an impressive upper body. The upper body of someone who lifts weights regularly. His lower body, I can't discern. His jeans are too loose to show any real definition, plus he should tighten his belt a few notches because they're sagging on his ass.

I look up in time to meet his eyes. Jonah has caught me and it probably looks like I'm ogling him.

"I thought you were in a rush." I nod my chin to urge him forward, feeling my cheeks burn.

He tugs on a shopping cart handle, pulling it free from the rack. "Where to, first?"

Good question. One of the luxuries of still living at home is that I don't have to think about meal planning. Sure, when my friends and I head off for a weekend, we'll stop at the grocery store and load up a cart with burgers and the like, but Mom takes care of planning food for the week. When was the last time *I* had to do it?

Have I ever?

The interior of Meyer's is pure chaos, I realize, as I take in the sea of products that seem to occupy every available square inch of real estate. This is not what I'm used to. On the rare occasion that I have to grab something we've run out of, it's at the local Loblaws, a sleek, stylish store with spacious aisles, polished floors, and tempting produce displays.

As far as aesthetics go, this place sorely pales by comparison, with everything from its flickering low-voltage lights above to the scuffed gray floors and narrow aisles, the shelves crammed with product and topped with brown cases for excess stock. Islands of soft drinks and toilet paper sit on pallets, creating obstacles for carts to navigate around. Everywhere I look, there are oversized SALE signs, but the prices marked can't possibly be right because ten dollars for a box of Cheerios? *Thirteen* bucks for a twelve-pack of bottled water? *Thirty-two dollars for toilet paper?*

The one thing Meyer's *does* have, I note with delight, is a small coffee bar next to a glass case of cream pies and icing-laden cupcakes to my right. A whiteboard hangs on the wall above the metal chest-level counter, with a handwritten menu of hot drink options.

I make a beeline to where a young girl hides behind the stacks of paper take-out cups. "I'm *desperate* for caffeine." A painful throb flares in my head as if to emphasize my need.

Her near-black eyes do a once-over of me. "What size?"

"The largest you have. A latte, with soy, please."

"We don't make those."

I glance up at the sign, to double-check that I'm not hallucinating. "It says you do."

"Well yeah. We make lattes. *Normal* ones."

Six fifty—American dollars—for a *grocery store* latte is not normal, I want to say, but I bite my tongue. "It's the same thing, just made with soy milk."

"I don't have soy milk," she says slowly, as if to help me understand.

I take a deep, calming breath. "Okay, do you have almond milk or cashew or . . ." My words drift with her shaking head.

"So . . . I guess you don't want the latte, then." She sounds put out.

"No, I guess I don't." I can't recall the last time I stood in front of a barista—if that's what I can even call her—and was told that there was no alternative option. I don't think it's ever happened.

"She giving you problems, Kayley?" Jonah asks, coming up from behind me.

"Hey, Jonah." The girl—Kayley—grins at him, dismissing me entirely.

She isn't so much girl as woman, I now realize as I study her more closely. Early twenties, maybe mid, with large, almond-shaped eyes and high cheekbones. Not a smudge of blush or a swipe of a mascara brush has touched her face today. She's naturally pretty, and the fact that her brunette ponytail is masked by a hairnet doesn't detract from that.

I wore a hairnet once, when I was sixteen and rebellious, and decided that I couldn't handle working weekends for my mother at her florist shop. So I got a job at the cupcake shop three doors down. I lasted one Saturday before I went back to my mother, because as difficult as she seemed, she didn't make me wear an unflattering headpiece.

"Why aren't you flying today?" the girl asks, her idle hands lazily stacking and restacking paper cups, her hawkish gaze never leaving Jonah's face.

"I'll be in the sky within the hour, as soon as I'm off day-care duty." He tips his head toward me. "This is Wren's daughter. She hasn't figured out where she is, yet."

"In hell, at the moment," I snap, my irritation flaring unexpectedly. I'm hungry, my head is pounding, and he's making jokes at my expense.

He gives me a flat look before leaning in to rest his sinewy forearms on the counter. "Hey, any chance you can grab a carton of whatever it is she needs off the shelf and make her that coffee so she'll be a bit more pleasant?" His voice has turned soft, gravelly.

Kayley's lips twist with reluctance. "Yvette doesn't like us doing that. It always ends up going to waste."

"Don't worry. We'll take the carton with us and pay for it up front. Won't cost you a thing. Come on, Kayley, you'd be doing *me* a huge favor." I can only see his profile, but by the way his eyes are crinkling, I can guess the look he's giving her.

Is he . . . *flirting* with her?

Does the yeti actually know how to *flirt*?

Kayley rolls her eyes but then tilts her head to the side, her lips twisting playfully. "Sure, Jonah. Give me a sec."

I can't help the momentary glare, but then cover it up with a wide, fake smile. "Thanks *so* much, Kayley. I'm *so* sorry for any inconvenience."

She ignores me, disappearing around the corner, her hips swaying slightly. She has a thing for Jonah. She's hoping for something romantic between them. That or something romantic has *already* happened between them.

Both scenarios mean she's clearly masochistic. Also, possibly a psychopath.

I feel Jonah's gaze on me. "What?"

He shakes his head. "Couldn't wait to get home, could you?"

"You know what? Thanks for the ride. You can head on over to fly your little planes now. I'll be fine."

I'm expecting him to jump at the chance to ditch me, but instead he leans against the shopping cart handle, amusement in his eyes. "And how are you gonna get everything the five miles home?"

"I'll borrow a duffel bag for the essentials and fly the rest later," I mock, staring pointedly at him. Though a cab would be easy enough to grab.

He holds a hand up in a silent greeting to an older gentleman who passes by. "Relax. Your clothes will be here today or tomorrow."

"Today, thanks to Agnes and Billy." *And* not *you*.

"Billy?" Jonah's brows pop and then his head tips back. An unexpectedly loud, boisterous laugh sails from his mouth, turning numerous heads in the vicinity. "Billy spent last night with his hands in your things."

"He did not!" I scoff.

"Brought your suitcases home, emptied them onto his bed. Got naked and rubbed his—"

"Oh my God! Stop it! Gross!" I don't know whether to cry or laugh. He's joking, right? He *must* be joking.

His expression makes me think he might not be joking.

"You might want to wash your panties before you wear them again."

My face is twisted with disgust when an older Alaska Native woman wearing an oversized New York Knicks sweatshirt and a floral pink headscarf over short, gray hair sidles her cart up to Jonah. She settles a hand on his forearm. "I could hear Tulukaruq's laugh from a mile away."

What did she just call him?

Her face reminds me of Agnes's, though age and weight has made her cheeks heavy and her wrinkles much more prominent. She's also short like Agnes. I'd put her at five foot one, which makes the height difference between her and Jonah almost comical.

Jonah peers down at her, and even that beard can't hide his genuine smile. "What are you doing down the river, Ethel?"

"Gathering supplies." She waves a weathered hand at her sparsely filled cart of rice, pancake mix, and a can of Coke.

"How's Josephine and the baby?"

Mention of a baby cracks the old lady's face into a wide grin. "He's getting nice and fat, finally. And Josephine's strong."

"All you villagers are strong."

Ethel grunts, shrugging off what I sense is a high compliment from Jonah, her dark eyes shifting to me. "Who's she?"

"Wren's daughter. She's visiting."

She nods as she studies me intently, her wise gaze impossible to read.

I squirm under the scrutiny, offering a soft "hi."

"She's pretty," Ethel finally states with a nod, as if passing her approval of me. As if I'm not standing right here.

"Albert bring you down?" Jonah asks, quickly changing topics.

"Yeah. He's at the hospital, getting his hand looked at."

"What's wrong with his hand?"

"Cut himself at the fish camp back in June."

Jonah frowns. "Must be bad, for him to come all the way down to see a doctor."

"It's festering," she admits solemnly. "The healer said it will get worse without medicine." Then she lets out a bark of laughter. "I told him I would cut his hand off at the wrist while he was sleeping before the infection spread. I guess he believed me."

"That's because he *knows* you," Jonah says, shaking his head. He's smiling, but I get the sense that he believes the old woman might carry out her threat.

"When are you going to come to the village again?"

"We'll see." He shrugs noncommittally.

"Make it soon. We'll have meat for you." She turns her eyes on me again. "Jonah saved my Josephine and her baby's lives. She went into labor too early and he flew in to get them when it was dangerous. When no one else would. The baby was blue when he came out and Josephine lost a lot of blood—"

"Just doing my job," Jonah mutters, cutting her off suddenly, as if uncomfortable. "Tell Albert I said hi and to learn how to gut a fish."

Ethel chuckles, patting his arm affectionately. "See you up the river."

I watch her shuffle away. "Is that true? That you went and got them when no one else would?"

"It was a bit of snow. She's exaggerating," he mumbles, turning away from me to search the aisles, for Kayley perhaps, or just to close off a conversation he clearly doesn't want to have.

Is it that he's modest? Because something tells me that old woman doesn't exaggerate much, and that when *she* labels conditions as "dangerous," they're apocalyptic by other people's standards.

Kayley appears at the counter again, distracting my thoughts. She holds up a carton of soy milk that I've had once before. "You said 'large,' right?"

"Yeah, but . . ." I hesitate. "You wouldn't happen to carry the Silk brand?" It's the only one I've had that doesn't taste like liquid chalk.

Her face sours with irritation. "This is the only one we have. Do you still want it?"

I sigh. "Sure. Extra foam, please."

Kayley's brow furrows.

"Our little princess will have it however you can make it, and thank you for going out of your way for her," Jonah interrupts in an overly patient tone. "Right, Calla?"

"Of course." My cheeks burn. How does he make me feel absurd over ordering a simple thing like a coffee, the way I like it?

He nods toward the produce section, letting go of the shopping cart with a little push. "Why don't you go ahead and I'll bring it to you as soon as it's ready."

Is he offering because he wants a few moments alone with Kayley? Or a few moments away from me? A few minutes to mock "our little princess"? I decide I don't care either way. "Sounds great!" I stroll away with a wide, satisfied smile.

Because Jonah will have to fork over the $6.50 for my shitty cup of coffee.

■ ■ ■

"So, we're done here, right?" Jonah pushes the cart toward the cashier lines, stealing a quick glance at his watch. No sooner had he handed me my steaming paper cup—without a sleeve to keep my fingertips from being scorched—than he seized control of the cart. I'd say he was being helpful, but given that I had to speed-walk the aisles to keep up with him, it likely had more to do with getting out of here fast than any kindness. To his credit, though, he hasn't ditched me yet.

"I . . . think so?" I choke down the last of what might be the worst coffee ever known to man and toss it into a nearby bin. At least my headache is beginning to fade. But I don't know how I'm going to survive the week, drinking this crap. I wonder if Amazon delivers here . . .

"Last chance," he warns me.

I scan the cart—fruit smoothies for breakfast, green salads with chicken breast for lunch and dinner, along with a bag of almonds, a dozen eggs, ingredients for sandwiches, and bananas for snacks. Basically what I eat at home. I also remembered the twenty-dollar can of bug spray that will likely cause DEET poisoning, thanks to Jonah. He strolled down the household goods aisle—past an ATV and boat motor, because apparently in Alaska you can buy ATVs and boat motors at the grocery store—and tossed it in without asking, announcing loud enough for everyone two aisles over to hear that if I insist on jogging naked, it's the only mosquito repellent that will work.

And yet I can't ignore this nagging feeling that I've forgotten something.

"Come on. Let's go. Get Wren to bring you back if you forgot something."

"As if." I let out a derisive snort. "He's too busy making a buck to make time for his own daughter. He doesn't even want me here."

Jonah scowls. "Who told you that?"

"No one has to. It's pretty damn clear." If it weren't for Agnes, I wouldn't even know he was sick.

Agnes.

Dinner tonight.

That's what I was forgetting. "Red or white?"

"What?" Jonah frowns in confusion, caught off guard by my question.

"Agnes invited me and my dad to dinner tonight. I need to bring something for her." Plus, I think I hear a bottle of vodka calling my name, to get me through this week. "Red or white wine?"

He waves it away. "Don't bother. She doesn't expect it."

"I'm not going to show up to someone's house empty-handed," I mutter, my eyes roving the store signage, searching for the liquor aisle that we obviously missed. "Who does that?"

"*I* do it all the time," he retorts, as if proud of that fact.

"Yeah . . . well . . ." It was a rhetorical question, but I shouldn't be at all surprised that the yeti doesn't understand basic etiquette. Meanwhile, my mother had me bringing cookies and cupcakes to my friends' houses as a thank-you for arranged playdates when I was as young as eight. "It's considered good manners to bring something for the hostess. Like wine," I say calmly, with as little judgment as I can muster in my voice.

He levels me with that icy gaze for three long beats. "Aggie doesn't drink. Your dad will have the occasional beer."

"Great." Maybe if I show up with a six-pack, he'll feel obligated to talk to me for more than a minute. "Where can I get—"

"You can't. It's a dry community. They don't sell alcohol in Bangor."

"What?" I feel my face twist with shock. "You're lying."

His eyebrows arch. "You're arguing with me about this?"

"What the hell is this, the 1920s prohibition?"

"*No.* It's Western Alaska, where alcoholism is a serious problem," he says, his voice carrying with it a condescending edge. "People will drink so much, they pass out in snowbanks and freeze to death in winter."

"So *no one* can buy any alcohol, then?" That seems a bit drastic.

"Nope. Not even you." He's enjoying this way too much.

"Well, how does my dad get beer, then?" I counter. "*You* said he drinks beer."

"He brings it home with him when he goes to Anchorage or Seward. And no . . . I'm not flying there to grab you a damn six-pack." His perfectly straight, white teeth glint with a wide, spiteful smile. "I guess you'll have to forgo proper dinner etiquette for tonight."

"That's fine. I'll buy her flowers." I eye the green pail next to the cash register, where three sad-looking bouquets of lemon-yellow daisies sit, the bright dye in the petals unable to hide the browning edges. My florist mother would *die* witnessing this, I think, as I grab one and trail Jonah to the last cashier, all while glaring at his back.

A *dry* community? What do people order at the bar on a Friday night? Cocoa and cream sodas? Come to think of it, I didn't notice any flashing neon lights or the word "bar" anywhere.

So what the hell do people do around here for fun?

"Shouldn't you be working?" the cashier—a white woman in her fifties, with blonde hair, soft blue eyes, and a slight Southern accent, the kind that's faded with time—smiles up at Jonah, while stealing frequent, curious glances at me. I'll take that over being blatantly stared at by every other person in this place. Elderly women hunched over bins of discounted canned vegetables, *staring* at me through cataract-clouded gazes. Stock boys, pausing with their hands in midair, gripping produce, *staring* at me—my face, my chest, my shoes—as I edge past. Middle-aged ladies in unflattering jeans and clunky shoes, their hair pulled into messy ponytails, quieting in mid-conversation, *staring* at me like I'm some sort of circus sideshow. Or, more likely, like they know I'm an outsider and they're trying to figure out what on earth brought me to Bangor, Alaska.

I'm quickly sensing that everyone knows everyone around here, and if they don't directly know them, then it's through one or two degrees of separation at most, and they'll strike up a conversation to find out exactly how. Coming to Meyer's seems to be a social activity as much as a life necessity. Shoppers meander up and down the aisles, blocking paths as they slow to comment on the sale on ground beef and lettuce, or the forecasted break in the rain, or who's coming in from Anchorage. No one is in much of a hurry.

No one except Jonah.

"Hey, Bobbie." Jonah starts chucking produce onto the belt. "Yeah. I'm supposed to be. I was ambushed on my way in."

I roll my eyes. Jonah's gone from babysitter to hostage. "Thanks. I've got this." I yank the green pepper out of his hand before he can toss—and bruise—it, too. "Do you mind bagging things? Over *there*." Away from me. I punctuate my words with a little push against his bicep, rock hard beneath my palm.

The cashier—Bobbie—continues ringing things up, her fingers flying over the keyboard with memorized vegetable codes. "George said they're calling for a few clear days this week. I'm tired of getting my hopes up. Still, it'd be a nice change from all the rain."

"You should be used to the rain by now," Jonah says gruffly, stuffing my groceries into brown paper bags.

"Is anyone ever used to it?" There's a pause and then, "So, is this your sister? Or a cousin?" She's asking Jonah, but she's looking at me.

"This is Wren's daughter, Calla."

Her quick fingers stall. "Oh . . . right! George said something about you going to Anchorage to pick her up. George is my husband," she explains, now addressing me directly. "Him and Jonah's dad used to fly together in the air force. Now he flies for Wren."

I'm guessing this George guy was the connection to Alaska Wild that Jonah mentioned earlier. And this Bobbie lady has also given me another piece of information—Jonah's father was a pilot in the US Air Force, and it sounds like Jonah followed in his footsteps, as far as flying goes, anyway. That must be his father's hat.

Bobbie shakes her head. "I forgot Wren had a daughter all those years ago. Gosh, it's been forever. You and your mom ended up in . . ." She lets that hang, waiting for me to fill in the blank.

"Toronto."

She gives a small nod, like that answers an unspoken question. "And this is your first time here?"

"Since we left, yeah."

"So . . . you figured it was time for a visit?"

"As good a time for a vacation as any, right?" Jonah answers for me, his piercing eyes on mine, the warning in them clear.

From what Agnes said, my dad doesn't want people knowing about his cancer diagnosis yet. I guess that includes his employees.

"Yeah. Had some time to burn and I've always wanted to see Alaska," I add, solidifying our lie.

Bobbie gives me a polite smile—one that says she was hoping for a juicier answer than that—and then finishes ringing up the rest of my groceries.

My eyes bulge at the final tally as I count out the bills. How do two bags of groceries cost *that* much?

Bobbie laughs. "That's some sticker shock, huh? Well, you enjoy your time in Alaska, Calla. And be careful," she warns, nodding Jonah's way, "or that one will charm you so much, you won't want to leave."

"Yes, I'm already struggling to control myself." My voice drips with sarcasm.

Her head crooks, confusion filling her face.

And my mouth drops. "Oh my God, you're not kidding."

An awkward chuckle sails from her thin lips. "Make sure you send that husband of mine home right after work, Jonah. He gets to talking and next thing he knows, the sun has gone down."

Jonah throws a flat-faced wink her way as he scoops up the grocery bags in one arm, his biceps straining beneath his cotton sleeve. "Will do."

I trail him out, cradling the bouquet of near-spent flowers, feeling countless eyes on my back.

I can't help myself. "So, if *you're* charming, what would Bobbie consider an asshole?"

"There's one right now."

I follow his nod and find a reflection of myself in a window.

He's quick with the comebacks, I'll give him that much.

Jonah peers up to the sky, squinting, and I can tell he's searching for a looming rain cloud.

"People really obsess about the weather around here."

"Why wouldn't they? Strong winds, thick fog, too much rain or snow . . . any of it will ground us for hours, a day. Even longer, sometimes." His boots scrape along the dusty ground. "People rely on planes for food, medicine, doctors, mail. Everything."

I try to ignore the heavy gazes of two teenaged boys of maybe sixteen, with cans of Coke in their hands, gawking openly at me. "And they stare even more than they obsess about the weather," I mutter, more to myself.

"They're not used to seeing a real, live Barbie doll is all."

I frown. Did he just call me . . . "I am *not* a *Barbie* doll!"

"No?" He gives me a sideways glance, amusement in his eyes. "Fake hair, fake face, fake nails . . ." His eyes dip to my chest before flashing away. "Is anything on you real?"

My jaw drops. "*These* are not fake!" And I've never had anyone insinuate otherwise. They're not even particularly impressive.

"I don't care one way or the other. You wondered why they're staring at you. That's why," he says in a bored tone. He pops the hatch of his SUV, and then sets the grocery bags in.

And I simply gape at him, astonished. At least twenty-five people said hello to him in Meyer's. All those little waves and friendly greetings, as if people are *actually* happy to see him. Bobbie called him charming. Agnes claims he's a teddy bear. Ethel talks about him like he walks on water.

Am I in some sort of alternate universe?

One where everyone else sees Jonah in one way and I see the truth?

"Have I done something to make you not like me?" I finally blurt out.

He chuckles darkly. "No. I just know your kind and I've never had much patience for it."

"My kind?"

"Yup." He slams shut the gate of his SUV and turns to settle a stony gaze on me, his muscular arms folded over his chest. "The shallow, self-absorbed, entitled kind."

My mouth hangs open for three beats. "You don't know *anything* about me."

"Really . . ." He bites his bottom lip in thought. "Let's see . . .

you show up in Anchorage with an entire closet's worth of clothes for a one-week visit, expecting, what, a private jet to bring you the rest of the way? *And* looking like you mistook the airstrip for a fucking runway in Milan."

I push aside the shock that he knows a thing about the fashion industry to defend myself. "I had to pack for this moody weather—"

"Were you going for a jog or to a nightclub this morning, with all that makeup on? I'd bet my left nut that no one's seen your real face in years. You spend all your money on looking pretty and all your time posting pictures to prove to complete strangers how pretty you are."

My spine begins to tingle. Is he talking about my Instagram profile? How could *he* know about that? And, oh my God, did he just make a reference to his *balls*? "So, *some* people take pride in their appearance." I give him a pointed look, even as my cheeks burn from being picked apart.

He goes on as if I hadn't spoken. "You're dramatic, entitled, and judgmental. You like attention and you're used to getting it. You don't know much about the world outside your little bubble. You didn't even bother educating yourself a little about where your dad's from. Where *you* were born."

"It's not like I had much time—"

"You're twenty-six years old and you've *never* had time?" His eyebrow arches in that doubtful way. "You decided you weren't gonna like Alaska before your toes ever touched the soil, and you've had your nose turned up to everyone and everything ever since."

"I have not!"

"Agnes figured you might have a hard time up here, but you could at least try for a damn week. You haven't seen your father in basically your entire life, and when you finally show up here, you're pissed that the fridge isn't full for you? You probably haven't even considered how tough things have been on Wren, or how he might not know *how* to talk to you after this long"—he drops his voice—

"or what he's going through right now. But no, you're more focused on getting your fucking *soy latte* and what hostess gift you should bring to dinner tonight." He smiles smugly. "How am I doing so far? Do I have you all wrong?"

"Completely," I counter with a wavering voice, unable to manage more in my current state of shock. I'm used to Simon—to his gently probing questions, his thoughtful pauses as he quietly evaluates the real meaning behind my words, the way he tries to help me see myself for who I am. It's his nature, given his profession. There have been times that it's annoyed me, when I've screamed at him to stop psychoanalyzing me. But he's never done it in a vindictive, disparaging way.

And then here comes *this* guy, who I met twelve hours ago, making all kinds of unfounded assumptions and picking me apart as if there's no real substance to me at all.

The cold amusement fades from his eyes, leaving something that looks almost sad. "I *wish* I was wrong. Because then maybe you'd get over yourself, cut Wren some slack, and use the time you have to get to know him."

"You don't even know what happened between us," I mutter. "I can't just forgive and forget, and give him a big hug."

"No one expects you to. But if you're smart, you'll be willing to try and salvage even a shred of what you used to have, for your own sake." Jonah glances at his wrist to check the time again—I have yet to see him slide a phone out of his pocket—and then rounds the truck and climbs into the driver's side. Leaving me standing there, feeling rebuked and I'm not even entirely sure for what. Several shoppers linger nearby, having witnessed my humiliating and raw dissection.

The SUV's engine roars to life and a moment later, there's a holler of "Come on! We're not all on vacation around here."

Yeah, Bobbie . . . He's charming the panties off me, alright.

I'd rather walk five miles wearing nothing but a million mosquitoes than sit next to Jonah right now.

There's a cab parked a few spots over. The driver, a man with shaggy black hair and a bored expression, lounges in the driver's seat with his window rolled down, casually puffing on a cigarette. Watching the spectacle.

I wave my hand, still gripping the bouquet of overripe daisies, at him. "Are you available?"

He dips his head once—*yes*—and then takes a long drag.

Are cabbies allowed to smoke in their cars around here?

Holding my head high—I won't give Jonah the satisfaction of knowing his words cut me—I stroll over to the taxi and climb in the backseat, trying my best to ignore the waft of tobacco smoke that lingers.

An engine revs and I glance over to meet Jonah's cold gaze, glaring at me through his windshield. We stay locked like that for three . . . four . . . five seconds before he peels off, his wheels kicking up dust clouds and stones as he leaves the parking lot. *Good riddance.*

"Where to?" the cab driver asks, his dark eyes peering at me through the rearview mirror.

Crap. How do I get back to my dad's again? Where did Jonah turn? Was it before or after that sketchy coffee shop? "Do you know where Wren Fletcher lives?"

He shakes his head, and for a moment I panic. I'm about to tell him to take me to the airport, but then I remember that I have my dad's address in an email from Agnes. I quickly find it and read it out loud for the man. And then sink into the cracked, tobacco-scented leather with a sigh of relief. I don't need Jonah at all. "How much for the scenic way there?"

Chapter 8

■ ■ ■

"I *still* can't believe you have six kids," I murmur.

"Seven, come December." Michael chuckles as he turns into my dad's driveway. "I told you, I was eighteen when my oldest was born."

"Still."

He grins mischievously, flashing nicotine-tinged teeth and a slight overbite. "What can I say? I'm lucky my wife likes babies."

I can't recall the last time I offered more than a polite hello and nod when seated in a cab or Uber, intent on getting to my destination, my attention glued to my phone. And, truth be told, if I had a phone to use, and if I wasn't trying to avoid Jonah, I probably wouldn't even know this guy's name.

But, forty-five minutes after climbing into this taxi, I'm more familiar with Michael than with anyone else in the entire state of Alaska.

Michael is only three years older than me, which is mind-boggling. He mostly lives with his brother, and the two of them run a thriving cab company in Bangor together. Meanwhile his wife and kids live up the river in a village of about three hundred, with his parents and her sister. His wife wants nothing to do with Bangor and this way of life. She claims it's too loud and busy. Ironically, she must not think that having seven children is too loud and busy, because she's been popping them out like a Pez dispenser.

Michael gave me a tour around Bangor, stopping by a lively riverfront, teeming with villager boats, and a landmark church—the first structure ever to be built in the town. He even agreed to play cameraman and took a few posed pictures of me while we were there, and the results aren't half-bad.

"You must miss your kids a lot."

He shrugs. "I see them when I go back."

"And how often is that?"

"Depends on the season. It gets harder when we're waiting for the river to freeze over, or thaw. Can't take the boat through, and it's not safe to drive. Sometimes I have to wait weeks." His voice has an easy, unhurried way about it. Much like Agnes's does.

"Must be hard." But what's it like compared with not seeing your child for twenty-four years, I wonder.

"I can provide for my family better this way. Here." He passes a business card over the seat to me. "Call me anytime you need a ride. I'm always working. Even when I'm sleeping."

"Cool. Thanks." I frown at the name. "Wait, I thought your name was Michael."

"Michael is my kass'aq name."

"Your *what* name?"

He chuckles. "My kass'aq name. 'Kass'aq' is what we call white people."

"Oh. But *this* is your real name? This . . ." I frown at the spelling, sounding out cautiously, "Yakulpak?"

"Ya-gush-buck," he corrects, emphasizing each syllable.

"Ya-gush-buck," I repeat slowly. Coming from a city as diverse as Toronto, it's not the first time I've struggled with—and butchered—a name. "So . . . not at all how it's spelled, then?"

"Not for a kass'aq." He grins. "Stick with 'Michael.'"

"Sounds good." Scooping up the bouquet of flowers, I hand him the thirty bucks we agreed on, plus a tip he more than earned. "Thanks for being my tour guide." I slide out of the back of the car, noting with relief that Jonah's Escape is nowhere to be seen.

"No problem," Michael says with a wave, his brakes squeaking as his car begins to roll away. He didn't ask about that scene with Jonah in the Meyer's parking lot, for which I'm glad.

The moment I step through the door and into my dad's eerily quiet, dark house, my phone picks up the Wi-Fi connection and begins chirping with a string of text messages and voice mails from my mom and Diana. I sigh, knowing I can't avoid calling home much longer.

Right after I eat.

Two paper bags lie on the counter, empty and folded. When I open the fridge, I find to my surprise that my groceries have been tucked away, lined up much too neatly for a man who was chucking vegetables on the checkout belt only an hour ago. And here I was, expecting my salad supplies to be strewn across the front lawn.

Maybe this is Jonah's way of apologizing for being a complete asshole. "Well, that's something. I guess," I murmur. But it's going to take a hell of a lot more than this for me to forgive him.

■ ■ ■

"You're virtually strangers, Calla." Simon pauses to take a sip of his afternoon tea—in his favorite Wedgwood china cup, no doubt; the guy is so predictable—before I hear him set it down on his metal office desk. "It's going to take time for both of you to get comfortable and figure each other out."

The kitchen chair creaks as I lean forward to sop up the last of the egg yolk with a piece of toast and shove it into my mouth. "I'm only here for a week." Can I even begin to understand my father in that time?

"That's a self-imposed deadline. You can push your return flight and stay longer. That's why we paid more for this ticket. So you have options."

"I thought it was so I had the option of flying back *earlier*, if this trip was a disaster." Of course Simon would see it another way. "With how things are going right now, a week already feels like a death sentence."

"You knew this wasn't going to be easy."

"Yeah, well, it's going to be impossible if he runs every time I come into the room."

"Is he running? Or are you chasing him away?"

I frown. "What do you mean?"

"You're holding onto a lot of resentment, Calla. Years of it, that you've used to shield your pain. You don't hide it well and Wren isn't the type to confront it. If you two are going to reconnect, and in such a short amount of time, you need to find a way to communicate, even if it's around the proverbial elephant. At least for the time being."

"I'm trying, but . . . it's hard." How do you form a relationship with someone without forgiving them first?

"Just remember . . . you can't control him, but you *can* control how you act toward him."

I groan inwardly. Why do Simon's soft words seem to carry the same message as the blunt-force-trauma version that Jonah delivered earlier?

"Has Wren mentioned anything about the prognosis or treatment options? Anything at all?" Mom interrupts, her voice sounding distant over the speakerphone. She's pacing around his office. I swear, it's one of her favorite pastimes. Simon complains that she's worn a circular track in his grandmother's Persian rug.

"We talked for, like, two minutes last night, Mom," I remind her. "But Agnes said he's going to Anchorage next week to start chemo and radiation. And he doesn't look sick at all."

"That's good. They must have caught it early." There's no mistaking the relief in my mom's voice. Simon must notice it, too. How does that make him feel? Oh my God, I'm starting to sound like my British shrink stepfather.

A bell dings, signaling that the door to Simon's practice was just opened. "That's my next patient. Call me tonight if you'd like to discuss this further."

"Thanks, Simon."

"But not between ten and eleven p.m. my time, if you can help it. There's a BBC documentary on . . ."

I tune him out, my mind straying to thoughts of how I'm going to fill the rest of my day, waiting for dinner at Agnes's. I could head over to Alaska Wild, to get a better look at the planes and people who my father prioritized over his own daughter. But then I'd be risking another uncomfortable two-minute conversation with him. And, worse, a run-in with Jonah.

Thank God I brought my computer.

"Don't hang up, Calla," my mom calls out. There's a flurry of muffled sounds and clicks, and then her soft and melodic voice is in my ear as she leaves Simon's office with a receiver. "Hey."

"Did you get the pictures I sent? They should have come through by now."

"Let me see . . . Yes! Here they are. Oh my God! Is *that* what you flew to Bangor in?"

"I almost puked."

"But you can't even fit luggage in there!"

"Which is why all my things are on a cargo flight from Anchorage today."

"*Why on earth* would they come to get you in *that*?"

"Because Jonah is a jackass and he pretty much hates that I'm breathing his precious Alaskan air." I fill her in on the day's events, Jonah related, earning numerous gasps and groans.

"But you have a dairy allergy! That's not being high maintenance. That's a legitimate medical condition," she snaps.

"Right?" I sink into a creaky kitchen chair, feeling vindicated. *Finally,* someone else is reasonably annoyed with Jonah's antics. I can always count on my mother for that. "He is the biggest asshole I've ever met."

"Why does Wren keep him around?"

"Because I'm in the Upside Down, where everyone likes him." I roll my eyes, even though she can't see it.

"Just avoid him. I don't want him making your time there harder than it already is."

"I'm trying to, but it feels like every time I round a corner, that bushy face is there. *And* he lives next door! I can't get away from him."

"I'm sorry, honey."

"Whatever." I release a heavy sigh. "I don't want to talk about Jonah anymore."

"I don't blame you. What else did you send me . . ." There's a pause as she scrolls through the pictures. "Is this lettuce?" I can almost hear her frown.

"Yeah. Literally hundreds of heads of lettuce. Maybe more. There are farm fields down the road."

"Huh. I guess some things *have* changed in twenty-four years."

"Not *everything*." I grin, waiting for her to scroll to the next picture.

She gasps. "The ducks are still there!"

"In all their tacky glory."

Her mortified laugh sings out. "They're as ugly as I remember them being."

My gaze wanders over the busy wallpaper.

She gasps again, more softly, and I know she's scrolled on to the next picture, the one of the calla lilies in my bedroom. "How did I forget about those? You know, I stayed up every night for weeks painting every last petal, all fat and swollen, trying to get them done before you were born."

"Yeah, I remember you telling me."

"Gosh, that was a lifetime ago, wasn't it?" She murmurs wistfully. There's a long pause, as she no doubt drifts back to her time here. "So? What are your plans for the rest of the day?"

"Besides scratching all my mosquito bites?" I mutter, my nails raking at the back of my calf, where a red bump is beginning to flare and itch. "I may as well set up a bunch of posts for the site. Diana woke up with new ideas." I've had at least ten texts from her today.

"Diana *always* wakes up with new ideas. I wish I had that girl's energy . . . Oh! The time escaped me. I've got to get to the shop to finish up a few things. You wouldn't believe this woman that came in this morning. She was insisting on having baby's breath in her bouquet, even after I told her that I don't work with it because it cheapens the look of the arrangement. She had the nerve to . . ."

I lose track of my mom's little tirade as something odd on the wallpaper catches my eye. I feel my face twist up. "Do ducks have nipples?"

There's a pause. "Sorry. *What?*"

I lean forward to take note of the six distinctive dots perfectly spaced out on the underbelly of the duck. There are slight variations in dot size and spacing, though, which tells me that someone's done this by hand with a black marker. To every last duck on this wall. "Did *you* do this?"

"Calla, what on earth are you talking about?"

By the time I'm done explaining, we're both howling with laughter.

"It would have taken *hours*. There are, like, *hundreds* of ducks on this wall alone."

"Well, it wasn't me, but I wish it had been."

I settle back into my chair, in awe. "Maybe Agnes did it. I don't think she likes the ducks much, either."

Mom's laughter dies down. "So . . . what's going on there?"

"No idea, but whatever it is, it's 'complicated.' We're going over to her house for dinner tonight. She lives across the road."

"Good. You'll get more than two minutes with him there. Wren was always a slow eater."

"To be honest, I'm dreading it right now." How awkward will it be, to sit across the table from him? Will he at least attempt polite conversation? Or will he completely ignore me?

At least Agnes will be there, too, to serve as a soft-spoken buffer.

"It'll be fine. Just be yourself. And listen, don't worry about what that jerk pilot said. He doesn't know you at all."

He doesn't, and yet I haven't been able to shake Jonah's words from my mind.

"Thanks, Mom. Love you." I set my phone down on the table with a heavy sigh, and then crack open my MacBook.

Chapter 9

■ ■ ■

Agnes's driveway is as long as my father's, giving me plenty of time to study the rectangular house ahead of me as I approach, my sweater pulled over my head to protect my hair from the gloomy drizzle that's been falling all afternoon.

It's a mirror image of my father's house, save for the white siding and the front door, painted a deep crimson that delivers a much-needed punch of color. She doesn't have the additional garage, but there is a small shed on the left, with a large green garbage can propped against the side. Agnes's truck is parked in front of it.

Gripping the sad bouquet of daisies in one hand, I knock on the door. A moment later, I hear Agnes's reedy voice holler, "Just come in!"

Warmth and the delicious scent of roasted chicken and herbs envelop me as soon as I step inside, and I steal a moment to marvel at how different this house feels from the cold, dark one across the road. For one thing, the kitchen, dining room, and living room are all open-concept, filling the length of the house. A short hallway divides two sides of the back, leading to the bedrooms, I presume.

For another, it feels like a family home. It's simply furnished in beiges and grays, the furniture bland in style but clean and well maintained. But, where my dad's place is void of character, Agnes has infused small touches of personality everywhere. Rich hues of red and burnt orange color the walls. The couch is adorned with cushions with birds hand-stitched into their fronts. Wooden masks and swirling artwork that must be tied to her Native roots hang on the wall, and the entire wall beside the hallway is filled with framed photographs of people, many wearing colorful beaded headdresses and animal-pelt coats. Her family members, I presume.

"So? You survived your first day in Alaska well enough?" Agnes asks, her back to me as she inspects a golden chicken sitting in a pan atop the stove, looking fresh from the oven.

"It was touch-and-go for a while there, but yes," I joke. I spent most of the day updating links on the website and setting up draft posts for Diana so they're ready for her to add her words. I floated from the duck-infested kitchen, to the painfully bland living room, to the screened-in porch—which could be comfortable enough if not for the piles of clutter and decrepit vintage-style aluminum lawn chairs—and then finally my bedroom, where I ended up drifting off for an hour.

All in all, it was a peaceful yet uneventful afternoon, after a difficult morning.

"I hope you brought your appetite. We'll eat as soon as the guys get here."

The guys? "Which guys?" I ask warily.

"Just Wren and Jonah. They should be here soon. Jonah got stuck up near Nome with the fog, but it was beginning to clear when I left. He figured he'd make it back in time."

"*Jonah*'s coming, too?" I struggle to hide my displeasure.

Agnes smiles. "It'll be fine. I promise."

I sigh heavily. Yeah, I'm guessing everything "will be fine" in Agnes's eyes.

Fucking hell. I can't get away from this guy.

"Jonah has worked for your dad for over ten years now. He's like his right-hand man. Does all the risky off-airport landings for the hunters and fishermen, sorts out most of the plane issues. And the customer issues, not that we have that many. Helps Wren make the tough decisions. He's a good guy, once you see past that hard shell." She glances over her shoulder at me, her eyebrows arching when she sees the daisies.

"Just something to say thanks. For dinner . . . and everything else you've done."

She smiles wistfully. "I can't remember the last time anyone brought me flowers. It's been a while."

I damn well know Jonah hasn't. But has my father, ever? Is he the kind of man who would? Have they ever had the kind of relationship where he *should*?

"Do you have a vase that I can put them?"

"I think I have a tall jar. I'll have to dig it up. Just leave them on the counter for now."

Setting the bouquet down, I yank my sleeves up and head for the sink to wash my hands. "What can I help with?" I note that the table has already been set.

Agnes peers at the tall pot that sits on a trivet, and then at me, as if considering. "The potatoes need mashing, if you don't mind?"

"No problem." I can't remember the last time I mashed potatoes. Mom has all but eliminated them from our house, the carbohydrates "devastating" to her waistline. But every once in a while, I come into the kitchen late at night after she's gone to bed, to find Simon at the table with a bowl of instant mashed and a sheepish look on his face. Where he's ferretted those packets away, I haven't figured out yet.

"The masher is over there." She juts her chin toward a drawer. "And there's milk and butter in the fridge. Wait, can you have that? Because we can make it without."

I smile, appreciating her concern and the fact that she remembered. "It's fine. I'll skip the potatoes." I push up my sleeves and set to work. "So, did my dad say anything about bringing my luggage home today?"

"No, but I expect him to. The plane should have arrived an hour ago."

"Thank God. All my shoes are getting ruined." I found an old scrub brush under the sink today and spent an hour gently brushing the mud from my wedge heels. I'm afraid it was in vain, though.

Footfalls stomp up the six wooden steps outside then, and a moment later the door flies open.

My stomach tightens automatically as I turn, preparing myself to greet one of two men, both of whom seem to cause me anxiety, for entirely different reasons.

Instead I find a teenaged girl facing me, long, glossy hair the color of espresso pulled into a messy, off-kilter ponytail, her inky black eyes sparkling with curiosity. "Calla! You're here!" She kicks off her muddy boots.

"I am," I say warily. She seems to know who I am, and yet I have no idea who she is.

"I was gonna come over last night but my mom said you were tired, and then I stopped by on my way to the farm and Jonah said you were still in town."

Her mom . . . My gaze flickers to Agnes and then to the dining table, where the four chairs tricked me into not noticing five settings, and then past, to the wall of pictures, to the child's face that graces more of them than I first realized, and it suddenly dawns on me. "This is your daughter?" Agnes has a child? Did she mention her last night and I missed it, too wrapped up in my own worries?

Agnes smiles. "This is Mabel. She's a fireball of energy, just to warn you now."

Mabel's face splits into a wide grin that rivals her mother's. Her face is not as round as Agnes's, I note. But she certainly has the same deeply set, hooded eyes, only larger.

"So, you're from Toronto, right? That's so cool! I want to visit Toronto *so bad* one day. George has been there and he said it's amazing! I've creeped, like, your *whole* Instagram account. You should be a model. You're *so* pretty!"

"Toronto's great," I agree, taking a moment to process all that just flew from Mabel's mouth. She's definitely not shy, and she talks a mile a minute, in an oddly husky voice for a girl, and with an inflection that's slightly different from her mother's.

But most importantly, *how* does this girl from Western Alaska know my Instagram handle?

"There was a link at the bottom of your email," Agnes explains, likely able to read the confusion on my face. "I was curious, so I clicked on it and found your website. I swear, Mabel's scoured every last corner of it."

"Ah. Right." My automated signature. I completely forgot about that. Now it makes sense.

"So, you took a cab to the river today?" Mabel asks.

"Uh . . . yeah." It takes a moment to connect the dots. I posted a few pictures from earlier, and decided to ignore Diana's captioning advice and talk about my day in Bangor, about the friendly cabbie whose name isn't really Michael, with the six kids and one on the way, and how he uses the river to see them. It just seemed more interesting and way more honest.

I posted those *maybe* an hour ago, but I guess even all the way up here in the middle of nowhere, teenagers are linked to their phones.

"Mabel, why don't you go wash up for dinner and then pull out that chair from my room." Agnes begins carving the chicken with expert strokes of her knife, setting the freshly cut meat onto a small white platter.

Mabel wanders over and leans in to inspect the chicken as her mother just did. She's taller than Agnes by at least three inches, and dressed in the same type of department-store-brand budget jeans. "So did I pick a good one?"

Agnes tugs at the left leg. The meat begins to separate, and clear juices dribble over the golden skin. "You did. Though I would have liked a bit more fat on its thighs."

"He was the slowest one of them! I barely had to run to catch him!"

"You *caught* our dinner?" I blurt out.

Mabel grins at me. "Barry let me bring one home this week, for helping out on the farm."

"Is that the farm down the road? I think I saw it when I went for a run today."

"The Whittamores," Agnes confirms. "It's pretty famous. No one's been as successful at farming around here as Barry and Dora. They grew over *fifty thousand pounds* of vegetables last year. And who knows how many eggs in that underground chicken coop of theirs. We fly their produce to a lot of the villages."

"I was surprised to see it," I admit. "My mom's big into growing things and she wasn't ever able to do it."

"The season's longer and warmer now than it was twenty-four years ago. But, still, it's *a lot* of work to grow anything around here. Like the Whittamores do, anyway," Agnes murmurs. "Barry's out there thawing and tilling and prepping the soil for two years before he can plant anything in the ground."

"Yeah, he puts up these *huge* tunnels so we can start seeding things in February. There's no wind or snow, and it's way warmer in there."

Agnes chuckles. "That's where I find her most days after school, in the winter. That or in their root cellar."

"Oh. That's right!" Mabel exclaims, as if she's just remembered something important. "Barry said he saw you this morning. You were in bright pink, tearing down the road."

At least he didn't say I was naked. "That was me. Getting eaten alive by mosquitoes," I add, giving my arm a scratch where an itch suddenly springs.

Mabel's sweet face scrunches up. "The mosquitoes and no-see-ums will get you good."

"The *no-see-ums*?"

"Yeah. They're bad this year. Make sure you wear jeans and a hoodie when you go out, and you'll be fine."

"I'll be sure to do that." When my hoodie gets here from Anchorage, that is.

"How was it at the farm today, anyway?" Agnes asks.

"Same ol'. Kinda boring."

"Remember how lucky you are. There are plenty of people around here who'd collect eggs and vegetables in exchange for fresh produce and the occasional chicken."

"I'll bet they'd rather do it for cash," Mabel mutters.

"When you're older, I'm sure he'll pay you with real money. Unless you keep showing up whenever you feel like it. In that case, he might not hire you at all," Agnes scolds, in that gentle way of hers.

How old is Mabel exactly, that this farmer doesn't feel comfortable paying her in cash?

Mabel waves her mother's worries off with an annoyed frown. "Barry doesn't care what time I come in. And besides, the hens lay twice as many eggs when I'm around. I'm his chicken whisperer." She gives me a toothy grin and then stretches to her tiptoes to pull out a bag of chips from the cupboard.

Agnes promptly plucks the bag from her grasp and tosses it back into the cupboard. "We're eating dinner soon, Chicken Whisperer. Go on and get washed up."

With a groan, Mabel retreats down the hall, leaving me staring after her.

"She *does* have a lot of energy."

"It's something, trying to keep her busy enough to burn it all off, especially during the summer break. I'm so thankful to Barry for giving her something to do." Agnes pauses and then says more quietly, "She doesn't know about Wren yet. I'm going to tell her soon. I just . . . He asked me to wait."

He also asked her not to tell me or Jonah, but she didn't stick to that request, I note.

Two more sets of boots clomp up the six wooden steps of the porch then, these ones heavier, and moving more slowly.

I peer over and find unreadable glacier-blue eyes watching me intently from the other side of the window. I can't help but glare back at him, even as my chest tightens with anxiety.

A single knock sounds, followed immediately by the creak of the door opening.

"Doesn't smell like muktuk," my dad says, bending over to unlace his boots. His voice instantly stirs something familiar inside me.

"Thought we'd ease Calla into Alaska before I start feeding her whale blubber."

I struggle to keep the disgust off my face, earning Agnes's chuckle.

"Did she catch a fat one this time?"

"Fat and slow, apparently. Not as slow as you two, though. I was beginning to think you weren't coming." Agnes smiles, even as she softly reprimands him for being late.

"You know how it is." He saunters in farther to study the platter of chicken, my eyes on him the whole time as my hand moves mechanically, crushing the white potato flesh as I'm absorbed in a surreal fog.

I'm actually here, in Alaska. With my father. I'm a spectator, watching his daily life as it happens, surrounded by *his* people, inhaling the faint waft of cigarette smoke that trails him.

"Mabel home yet?" he asks.

"Washing up. She'll be out in a minute." A bit lower, but loud enough for me to catch, "As soon as she hears Jonah's voice."

My dad groans. "I'll be happy when that crush wears off."

Mabel has a crush on Jonah? My eyebrows pop in surprise as I peer over my shoulder, just as the supposed object of her affection comes into view, having removed his outer clothes and hat.

I'll admit, he's far from bad-looking, even with all the hair. If only I could take a pair of scissors to him . . . My fingers twitch just thinking about it.

And then Jonah's words from earlier ring in my ear—his claim that I've been picking everyone apart since I got here—and guilt has me turning away from mentally grooming him.

I find my dad's gentle gray eyes watching me keenly.

"So? How was your day, Calla?"

Simon's words echo inside my head.

Is he running? Or are you chasing him away?

You can't control him, but you can control how you act toward him.

"It was . . . good." Aside from the tongue-lashing from his right-hand man over there. I press into the potatoes. "Quiet."

He nods slowly. "I suppose it's a lot different from what you're used to."

"Yeah. A little bit." I smile my agreement. How many days will I be able to survive out here, before I long to be back in my city? Or any city, for that matter.

"Did the truck give you any problems? Getting into second gear has been a bit sticky lately."

"Uh . . ." I glance at Agnes questioningly, to see the subtle head shake. I guess she didn't tell him that I can't drive. And, obviously, neither has Jonah. Should I?

Things are already uncomfortable between us; I don't need to make them more so by pointing out all the things he *doesn't* know about me right out of the gate.

"Nope. No problems."

"Good . . . good . . ." His head bobs slowly. An awkward moment stretches.

"Did Calla's suitcases come in?" Agnes asks.

"Right. About that . . ." Dad scratches his graying hair, hesitating. "They couldn't make room for them on today's flight."

"You're kidding me!" My disappointment swells. "But I *need* my clothes! My rain boots!"

"We can do another load of laundry tonight," Agnes offers.

"Yeah, I guess," I mutter, though that's not the point. "How could they all of a sudden not have room?"

"There were some last-minute supplies that needed to get to one of the villages today. It's just the way things go around here." My dad gives me a sympathetic look.

"Food. Medicine. You know, *real* necessities," Jonah adds, his tone laced with amusement.

"We'll get your things in tomorrow." Agnes smiles with assurance, even as she adds, "Probably."

"Don't worry, I'm sure Billy's taking *really good* care of it all."

I grit my teeth and return my focus to the potatoes while I take a calming breath and work my frustration out, because there's nothing I can do about the luggage and bludgeoning Jonah to death with this potato masher would put a damper on dinner.

"Hey, Aggie. I grabbed these for tonight."

"Wow! First flowers from Calla. Now this?"

A familiar clanking sound against the counter has me turning in time to see Jonah set a six-pack of Budweiser cans down.

My jaw drops. I abandon the potatoes—which are basically pulverized—to face him. "You said I couldn't buy beer in Bangor!" My voice is thick with accusation. "You said it was a *dry* community."

"*You* can't," he says simply, pulling two cans off the rings and tossing one to my dad, who smoothly catches it.

I glare at his smug face. Another one of his fucking games. He probably hatched it from the grocery store aisle as he was lying right to my face.

"Bangor's technically a damp community now, because they passed a law that allows the sale of it," my dad says. A snap and sizzle sounds as he pulls the tab on his can to crack the seal. "But the town hasn't been willing to issue any licenses yet because they're so worried about the villages. So you either have to fly or go to one of the bootleggers, which I don't recommend you doing, Calla. Some of the stuff they have will make you go blind." He shifts his gaze between Jonah and me, his brow furrowing a touch. "Let me know what you want and we'll get it in for you next time someone's in the city."

"Thank you." I breathe through my irritation. "And I promise *I*'ll bring something better to dinner than cat piss." I nod toward the red-and-white cans with distain, aiming that slight at Jonah.

Jonah snorts. "Your dad happens to *love* cat piss. But I guess you wouldn't know that, would you?"

We square off against each other, my jaw clenched tight as I search for a retort. Yes, Jonah knows my dad better than I do, and he uses that as a weapon, jabbing whenever he sees an opportunity.

Our tense showdown is broken up by laughter.

My dad and Agnes, doubled over, tears streaming down Agnes's plump cheeks.

I steal a wary glance at Jonah. He looks as confused as I am.

"I think you need to expand your palate, Wren," Agnes says, transferring a large hunk of succulent white breast meat onto the platter.

My dad takes a sip and then makes a point of smacking his lips. "I don't even like cats."

Jonah hangs his head for a long moment, and then his shoulders begin to shake and a genuine, deep-in-the-gut sound that reverberates in my chest fills the room.

"What do you know? Satan *is* capable of laughter," I mutter, though my own smile is emerging, the tension in the kitchen dwindling quickly.

My dad shakes his head, still chuckling. "Exactly how hard a time have you been giving my daughter, Jonah?"

My daughter. Such foreign words, and yet the simple acknowledgment makes me blush.

It quickly evaporates as Jonah's heavy arm lands on my shoulder and he pulls me into his side. He's a brick wall compared to Corey's lanky frame. "Me? Give this *patient*, *delightful, down-to-earth* girl a hard time?"

I try to wriggle free but Jonah only tightens his vice-like grip, pulling me in closer, until I'm practically molded to his torso and hip, my cheek pressed against his chest. The faint woodsy-scented soap on his skin is gone after a day of work, but he still smells indescribably pleasant.

The last thing I want to be doing is *smelling* Jonah.

"We couldn't be getting along better if we tried. Peas and carrots, Wren. Fucking *peas* and *carrots.*"

I use my hands for leverage, digging fingers into his ribs, hunting for a sensitive divide. I find nothing but a thick layer of muscle and hard ridges. So I do the only thing I can think of: search the hard plane of his chest with my fingers until I find what I think is a nipple.

And squeeze, then twist.

He releases me with a grunt of pain.

"More like vinegar and milk, I'd say," Agnes says, still thoroughly amused.

Soft footfalls pad down the hallway. "What's going on out here? What's so funny?" Mabel saunters into the kitchen, changed into black leggings and a plain but fitted white T-shirt that shows off narrow hips and the small buds of breasts. Long, poker-straight hair hangs halfway down her back, recently brushed. Her innocent eyes flitter quickly at our faces before settling on Jonah's to linger.

And I instantly see the truth behind Agnes's claim.

Mabel has a serious crush on Jonah.

Oh, God. *Why?*

"Hey, kiddo." My dad ropes an arm around Mabel's shoulders and pulls her to him. "How was the farm today?"

My stomach clenches. That's *my* nickname. He used to call *me* that.

"Fine. Kinda boring. Why can't I hang out at Wild?" Mabel fakes a pout.

He chuckles. "Because that's got to be even *more* boring. What twelve-year-old wants to spend their entire summer sitting in an airport?"

She's only twelve? She acts so much older. Granted, I haven't hung around with any twelve-year-olds since *I* was twelve.

Mabel rolls her eyes. "Twelve years plus almost one month. And I wouldn't be sitting if you'd teach me how to fly."

"Oh, here we go . . ." Agnes murmurs.

"What? He said he would!"

"When you're fourteen," Agnes reminds her.

"Yeah. And that's only one year and eleven months away. Don't forget." Mabel pokes her finger into my dad's stomach and his body buckles slightly.

"How could I forget?" He ruffles her hair. "You've only been reminding me every week since you were six."

A distinct wave of jealousy bowls into me. My dad and *I* used to talk about how he'd teach me to fly a plane one day, so many years ago, back before I realized that I prefer my feet on the ground. And here he is now, his arm around Mabel, promising her the very same things he used to promise me. Acting every bit the father I imagined he could be for me.

An uncomfortable suspicion begins to bloom in the back of my conscience.

Agnes and my dad have what she calls a "complicated" relationship. She says they've known each other for almost sixteen years. And, just by the look of Mabel, I'd bet money that her father is not Yupik, or any other type of Alaska Native.

Blood rushes to my ears.

Twelve years plus almost a month. That would mean her birthday is at the end of June. My dad was supposed to fly to Toronto for my eighth-grade graduation twelve years ago, this past June.

Is that merely a coincidence? Or . . .

Is Mabel a defining part of Agnes's cryptic "it's complicated" comment?

Do I have a half sister that *no one* has told me about?

Back when Simon and my mom married, I desperately wanted a sibling. And when I hit high school, I remember wishing my mom would get pregnant accidentally, so she'd be occupied with someone else and stop breathing down my neck.

But to have had a little sister all these years and not even know about her existence?

That's not something I was prepared to find out when I boarded the plane here.

Is Mabel the reason my dad canceled on me?

Did it not have anything to do with Alaska Wild after all? Is *she* the reason he ditched me?

Did he choose *her* over *me*?

"Calla?" My dad peers at me. "Are you okay? You're looking a little bit pale."

"Yeah." I clear my wobbly throat. "I mean, no, actually. I'm not feeling well." The last thing I can do now is smile and pretend everything is fine. I need to gather my thoughts.

Agnes and my dad share a worried look.

"Why don't you lie down?" Agnes says. "My room is to the left—"

"No, I think I should go home." Across the road.

And then, if I'm right about this . . . get on a plane, back to Toronto.

I sense Jonah's gaze boring into me as I sweep past him, shoving my feet into my muddy sneakers, stumbling as I hurry out the door.

"Calla!"

I turn back to see Jonah charging down the driveway toward me, his boots unlaced and splayed open. He is the *last* person I want to deal with right now. I rush on, tripping through a pothole, my eyes stinging from threatening tears as a foggy truth swirls around me.

Jonah's faster than I expected him to be, and he catches my arm as I'm climbing the steps to get inside my dad's house. His tight grip keeps me from escaping.

"What was that all about, back there?"

"I'm not feeling well—"

"Bullshit, you were feeling fine and then Wren put his arm around Mabel, and you freaked out. Don't tell me you're jealous of a twelve-year-old kid?"

Agnes was right. Jonah *is* too aware. And I guess that's what it would look like, to anyone on the outside.

I take a deep breath and then turn around. The second porch step puts me at eye level with him, and I find myself peering into an unreadable cold blue sea. "She's my half sister, isn't she?" My voice is shaky.

Did they not think I'd figure it out?

Did they honestly think it was okay to hide that from me?

Mixed in with my shock and hurt is a growing anger.

Jonah opens his mouth to speak, but pauses, frowning in thought. "What have they told you about Mabel?"

"You mean that girl in there that I'd never even heard of until ten minutes ago?" His question feels like the confirmation I needed. A single tear trickles down my cheek and I quickly brush it away with my free hand. I *hate* that I cry so easily when I'm upset.

"Wren never told you about her?"

How much does Jonah know about our estranged relationship?

"Not a word. Not since he bailed on being *my* father." But not hers, apparently. Another tear slips out. I don't bother brushing it away this time. "I've had twelve years to come to terms with the idea that he cared more about his planes and Alaska than about me," I let out a derisive snort, "and now I find out it's actually because he had another kid."

Jonah releases his grip of my arm. "God dammit, Wren," he mutters, along with something else I don't catch, but there's definitely a string of curse words mixed in.

I move to climb the rest of the steps, to duck inside so I can be alone with my thoughts.

"Mabel's father worked for Wren. He was a pilot for Wild," Jonah calls out, stalling my feet.

"Wait. So . . . my dad's *not* her father?"

"No, he's not," Jonah says slowly and clearly.

My shoulders sink with an odd sense of relief. "So where is Mabel's father now, then?"

"He died in a plane crash, a few months before Mabel was born."

"Oh. That's . . . shitty."

Jonah pauses a beat, seemingly in thought. "Why'd you come to Alaska, Calla?"

I frown. "What do you mean? So I could get to know my father before, you know . . . *Just in case.*" I shouldn't have to spell it out further.

"Maybe you should get to know Wren, *just because.* And stop looking for reasons to keep hating him."

"I don't *hate* him. And I'm not *looking* for anything. It's . . . You don't understand."

He sighs heavily. "It's none of my business what happened between you two. You've gotta sort your own drama out. But I do know what it's like to decide you want to try to forgive someone, only to realize that you waited too long." His gaze flickers to the ground before settling back on my face. "Trust me, you don't want that hanging over your head." Even through that scruffy beard, I can somehow sense the tension in his jaw.

Is he talking about his father? What happened between them? I hold that steely stare of his for one . . . two . . . three long seconds.

He's the first to break away, his eyes drifting to Agnes's house, to where my dad leans against the rail, his hand lifting to his mouth for a moment before pulling away. He's smoking.

Stomach-churning embarrassment washes over me. I got jealous for no good reason and stormed out, basically ruining dinner and making things exponentially more awkward than they already were.

So much for not letting my resentment get the better of me. So much for controlling my own actions.

"You know, you're definitely Wren's daughter," Jonah mutters.

"Why do you say that?" I ask warily. Do I want to hear this answer?

"Because neither of you have the guts to speak your mind when it matters most."

I watch him stroll away, gravel crunching under his boots.

Chapter 10

■ ■ ■

I'm scratching feverishly against a mosquito bite on the back of my calf when the patio door from the living room slides open.

My dad pokes his head out. "There you are." His gaze drifts over the patchwork quilt I dragged from my bedroom and cocooned myself in, a ward against the evening chill as I sit curled up in the wobbly aluminum chair. "Hungry?"

"A little," I admit sheepishly, feeling my cheeks flush all over again from my embarrassment at the scene I caused.

He appears with two dinner plates balanced in one hand. "Agnes fixed this for you. Said you don't eat mashed potatoes, so she gave you extra of everything else." He sets a plate down on the worn coffee table in front of me. It's loaded with a heap of white and dark meat—more than I can possibly eat—and, funny enough, peas and carrots.

He nods to the chair beside me, the orange-and-red woven strips torn in several places, looking ready to give way with the slightest weight on it. "You mind if I join you?"

"No. Of course not. Go ahead."

He sinks into it with a groan, setting his own plate on the stack of plastic bins piled next to him. "Agnes makes a mean roasted chicken. I've never met anyone who doesn't go back for seconds."

I reach for my plate. "I'll bring these back to her when we're done so I can apologize for earlier."

He opens his mouth to say something, but then seems to change his mind and instead slides a can of beer from his vest pocket. "Thirsty?"

Normally I'd decline, but something inside urges me to accept it.

He pulls a second out of his other pocket. The sound of the can cracking open cuts into the silence of the calm evening.

I watch him for a moment as he sips his beer, his thoughts lost in the acres of fields beyond us.

Do I bring up that fiasco from earlier?

Do I wait for him to bring it up? What if he doesn't bring it up?

Maybe I should avoid the entire topic of Mabel and keep the mood light, not make things more awkward?

"I'm sorry," I blurt out before I can think too much more about it.

"It's okay, Calla," he murmurs, holding a hand up. "Jonah explained where your head went." He chuckles softly. "Right after he told me what he thought about me, and how I've handled myself with you. Man, that guy doesn't hold back any punches. He can make you feel *this* small." He holds up two fingers, an inch of air in between, to emphasize his point.

"Yeah, I've noticed," I mutter, frowning. Jonah said he wasn't getting involved with our *drama*.

"He's right, though. I owe you an explanation. Even if it can't fix anything. Even if it's twelve years too late." Dad's eyes settle on a pile of old worn shoes, cast haphazardly into a corner, and sits there for so long that I wonder if I'm going to get one.

"The January before I was supposed to come to Toronto to see you, one of my pilots, Derek, was flying through the Alaska Range when the cloud level came down fast. We think he got confused and took a wrong turn. Flew right into the mountainside."

"Was that Mabel's father?"

He nods. "It was supposed to be *my* run. But I was buried in problems here—a fuel shortage, two grounded planes, a bunch of paperwork that I couldn't ignore. You know, taxes . . . that sort of stuff. So I asked Derek to come in on his day off and do the run for me."

Understanding hits me. "You would have crashed that day."

My father would have died that day.

"I don't know if I would have. Derek had only been flying maybe five years by that point, and not a lot of time in those mountains. Me? I couldn't even guess how many times I've done that route. I know my way through there. I would never have made that mistake." He takes a long sip of his beer. "I should never have sent him."

I search for words, but I don't know what to say. "That must have been hard to deal with."

"It was. For everyone at Wild. But especially Agnes. Mabel was due that coming August, but there were complications and she ended up born in June, a few days before I was flying to Toronto to see you. She had a heart defect that needed surgery right away. They rushed them both to Anchorage by medevac and I flew myself over." He sighs heavily. "After what happened to Derek, I couldn't leave Agnes to deal with that on her own. Not if Mabel didn't survive. That's why I canceled my trip to see you."

I replay the bits and pieces of that devastating phone conversation from twelve years ago in my head. The call that severed any relationship with my father. All these years, I thought he bailed on me for something as seemingly trivial as his job. "Why didn't you tell me that? I would have understood."

"You were fourteen, Calla. You'd been begging me to visit for years. I'd been disappointing you for just as many. I figured the reason didn't matter. Especially not when it involved someone else's little girl. I didn't know how to explain that to you. It was easier to blame it on Wild. At least you were used to that excuse."

His words give me pause. I *was* fourteen and I *was* desperate to see him, to know that I mattered to him. No matter how solid his reasoning, would I have understood back then?

Do I even truly understand now?

"Did you tell my mother all this?" God, if she knew about this and didn't tell me . . .

My dad shakes his head. "Your mother was . . . Things were complicated between us. They've *always* been complicated between us."

Complicated. That seems to be the buzz word when it comes to my dad.

"Because she was still in love with you?" I ask quietly.

An awkward laugh escapes his lips. He gives the back of his shaggy-haired head a scratch, his gray eyes drifting to mine to linger for a moment, searching for something—what, I don't know—before returning to the pile of shoes. "What do you know about that?"

"Just what Simon told me. That he thought she was still in love with you and would leave him if there was hope of you guys getting back together." I hesitate. "Was he right?"

He rubs at his furrowed brow. "Look, I don't wanna be the cause of any rifts between you and your mom."

"How would you cause a rift between us?" I ask warily.

He seems to struggle to gather his thoughts. "Your mother and I were never gonna fit. I knew that the moment I met her and yet she somehow convinced me otherwise. Hell, I wasn't gonna argue with her. I knew she'd wake up one day and realize she was too good for me. Until then, I'd take what I could get. A woman like that . . ." He shakes his head more to himself, a small, secretive smile touching his lips.

"I wasn't surprised when she packed you up and left. I was surprised she'd stayed that long to begin with. And I couldn't beg her to stay, even though I wanted to. It wouldn't have been fair to put her through that. I knew she'd never be happy here."

"It wasn't *you* she left, though." If he'd been willing to start a life where they'd both be content, I wouldn't be sitting across from a complete stranger right now.

"Alaska may be where I live, but it's as much a part of me as anything. I can't really explain it. This place, this life . . . it's in my blood." A frown touches my dad's forehead. "Your mom called me after I told you I was coming to see you."

"Oh, yeah?" I don't remember her ever telling me that, but maybe she did and I've forgotten.

"It was quick, that first call. You know, to find out where I was thinking of staying, and for how long."

Unease settles along my spine. He said *that first call.* "How many more times did she call you?"

He hesitates. "A few times," he admits, in a way that tells me "a few" is far more than three in this case. "God, it was good to hear her voice again after so many years." He studies his hands intently. "Problem was, it also stirred up a lot of feelings. It got confusing for a bit there. On both sides."

"What do you mean?" I sink into my chair as my stomach clenches. What exactly is my dad telling me? "Were you and my mom having an over-the-phone affair?" Is that part of the reason why everything went to shit?

"Hold up, Calla. Just . . . wait a minute. Don't read too much into it." He holds his hands in the air in a sign of surrender, and then takes a moment to continue. "You both seemed to have a good thing going for you there, in Toronto. I didn't want to mess it up for you or Susan, not when in the end, nothing had changed. I wasn't going to be able to give either of you what you really wanted. I knew that, and she knew that." He heaves a sigh. "So, after I canceled on the trip because of Mabel, I decided it was probably also time to finally bow out and let you both move on. And maybe it was the wrong decision. Lord knows I've made enough of those in my life. Can't change any of them, though." After a moment, he turns to give me a sad smile. "But maybe not. You seem to have grown up well."

Thanks to Mom and Simon, I want to say.

Despite the fact that I can't count the number of nights that I cried myself to sleep wondering why he didn't care.

I'm still having trouble processing this. Why would *anyone* get involved with a person in the first place when they're so sure it's doomed to fail? Why get married and bring a human being into the world with them?

And, if you're going to do it, why not at least *try* to make it work? I mean, I know that getting pregnant with me was an accident, but still.

My dad swaps the can for his plate and, setting it on his lap, begins cutting into his chicken. "So, how are things at home?"

"Uh . . . Fine. Good." I stumble over my words, startled by how quickly my father has steered the conversation out of the trenches of the past to safe, smooth territory.

"Your mom? Your stepdad? What's his name again?"

"Simon."

He nods to himself. "What is he again? A doctor?"

"Psychiatrist." I push around a piece of chicken with my fork, not hungry anymore. Finally I force myself to take a bite, and silently marvel at how tender and juicy it is.

"I knew it was something like that. Smart guy."

"Super smart. And patient. It's annoying sometimes, how patient he is."

Dad's face cracks a smile. One that fades quickly. "But he's been good to you and your mom?"

"He's been the best." *He's been a real father to me.*

And he would remind me to quiet that voice that fuels this lingering bitterness right about now, and remember why I came to Alaska.

But does he know about these phone calls that happened so long ago? He pays the bills. I've seen him combing through statements. Would he have figured out that it wasn't me calling Alaska, but my mother?

My anger with her flares suddenly. Does she realize how good Simon is to her? That she might not deserve him?

My dad chews unhurriedly. Mom said he's a slow eater. I wonder if that's the case now, or if he's using it as an excuse to avoid further conversation.

Eventually, he swallows. "So, tell me what you've been up to since we last talked."

"You want to know about the last *twelve years* of my life?" I don't mean it to come out sounding snarky.

He shrugs. "Unless you've got big plans tonight."

"No, I can't say I do." Smoothing on a face mask and killing hours on social media until I fall asleep.

"Well then, I guess we've got time . . ." He lifts his can in the air and winks. "And Jonah's beer."

■ ■ ■

"Why are you smiling like that?"

My dad shakes his head, his smile growing wider. He's long since finished his dinner and is leaning against a porch post about ten feet away from me, a cigarette burning between his fingers. "Nothing. It's just, listening to you talk, it reminds me of all those phone calls over the years."

I grin sheepishly. "You mean when I wouldn't shut up?"

He chuckles. "Sometimes you'd be on such a roll that I'd have to put the phone down and walk away if I needed a restroom break. I'd come back a minute later and you'd still be talking away, none the wiser."

"Are you saying you need to use the bathroom now?"

He eases open the porch screen door and empties the last dribs of his beer on the grass. We've shared two cans apiece, the remnants of Jonah's six-pack that my dad brought back with him. "Actually, I think I'm going to hit the hay. I'm wiped."

Tension eases back into my spine. I'd lost it for a time there—busy filling my dad in on my degree, my job, my recent layoff, Diana and the website, even Corey, who I'd given no thought to since leaving Toronto. Somewhere along the line, I forgot about reality. Now it comes back with a vengeance.

Is he tired because he's had a long day?

Or because of the cancer inside his body, slowly leaching away his energy? Because, despite any bitterness that may linger beneath the surface, I don't want my father to die.

I hesitate. "Agnes said you were starting treatment next week?"

His head bobs, the previous humor from his face fading.

"So . . . how bad is it?"

"It's lung cancer, Calla. It's never gonna be good," he says quietly. "But I've waited twenty-four years to see you. I don't want to think about that until next week. You're here now. That's all I want to be thinking about. Okay?"

I feel the smile curve my lips, unbidden. "Okay." It's the first time he's made any indication that he's happy I came.

A car door slams, pulling our attention toward the direction of Jonah's house, just as an engine comes to life. Tires spit gravel as they spin away a moment later. "I think he might have another flight."

"Now?" I check my phone. It's nine p.m.

"Gotta take advantage of the daylight while we've got it. These guys work long days in the summer. They're taking off at six in the morning and still in the air at midnight some nights."

I grimace. "Where's he going?"

"You know? I can't remember him sayin' anything about going anywhere tonight. But Jonah runs his own schedule most of the time." He snorts. "Who knows. Maybe he's on the hunt for another six-pack."

I force thoughts of my dad's health from my mind for the moment. "Good. Maybe we can drink that one, too."

Dad chuckles. It sounds as smooth as it did over the phone for all those years. Warmth spreads through my chest, appreciating that I'm now *finally* hearing it in person.

"How do you deal with him every day? He's . . . *insufferable*." That's Simon's favorite word. Wait until I tell him I used it in a sentence.

"Who, Jonah?" Dad wanders over to the far side of the porch, to peer at the butter-yellow house, out of my view. "I still remember the day he showed up at Wild ten years ago. He was this skinny twenty-one-year-old kid from Vegas, full of piss and vinegar and desperate to fly planes. Damn good at it, too."

That would make Jonah thirty-one, and only five years older than me. "He said he grew up in Anchorage."

"He did. He resented his dad for taking them away. Came back as soon as he had the chance. I doubt he'll ever leave again."

Just like my dad won't ever leave, I guess. But why? What hold does Alaska have on them? What makes this place worth giving everything else up?

"He may be a pain in the ass sometimes, but he's the best bush pilot out there. Possibly one of the craziest, too, but we're all wired that way to some degree. Some more than others."

"He's definitely embraced the whole crazy bush *man* look. Don't know if I agree with you about the best bush *pilot* part yet."

"The Cub was a bit too small for you." My dad nods, as if he's already heard the story.

"He flew that tiny plane intentionally, to scare me. I thought I was going to die."

"Not with Jonah flying," he says with such certainty. "He might take risks that even *I* don't have the guts to take, but he's always smart about it."

Like flying in to save Ethel's family, I'm guessing. "I almost puked. Had a bag ready and everything."

My dad smirks. "Well, that would have served him right if you had. You know, this one time, he was flying a group of school kids home from a wrestling meet and two of them got sick on the way. He was the color of pea soup when he climbed out of that plane. He can't handle the sound of it happening."

"I wish I *did* puke now," I admit, through a sip of beer. Though that may have made landing the plane difficult for him.

Dad's soft chuckle tickles my ear as he butts his cigarette out in the empty beer can. "I'll talk to him. Make sure he eases up on you. But he's not so bad, once you get to know him. You might even find you like him."

"Let's not get carried away."

Dad wanders toward the door, collecting the empty dinner plates on his way. "There's a bunch of movies in the cabinet beside the TV, in case you're looking for something to watch."

"I'll probably just hang out here for a while and then go to bed, too. I'm still jet-lagged. But thanks."

His gaze drifts over the porch. "Susan used to sit out here every night during the summer. 'Course, it was a lot nicer back then. She had a bunch of potted flowers and this big wicker thing." He smiles as he reminisces. "She'd curl up with a blanket, like you are. Like a caterpillar in a cocoon."

"She does that at home, too. We have a little sun porch off the back of the house. It's a quarter of this size, but . . . it's nice. Cozy."

"Is she still growing her flowers and all that stuff?"

I chuckle. "Our house is a jungle of thorns and petals. She owns a flower shop now, too. It's doing well."

"That sounds right up her alley." He purses his lips together and then nods with satisfaction. "Good. I'm glad to hear that. Well . . . 'Night, Calla."

"'Night." I feel the urge to tack on "Dad" at the end, but something holds me back.

"Oh, and don't mind Jonah. He likes to get under people's skin." He slides the door softly behind him, leaving me to myself.

"Like a damn parasite," I murmur.

And yet, if I'm not mistaken, that parasite helped force a lot of truth to the surface tonight.

Truth that was needed if I have any hope of reconnecting with my father.

Chapter 11

■ ■ ■

I cringe at the acrid taste of sweat and bug spray on my lips as I amble up my dad's driveway, my heart pounding from a rigorous run. So far today feels much like a repeat of yesterday—another unintentional early rise, another overcast sky, another quiet, lifeless house, save for the aroma of a freshly brewed pot of coffee, evidence that my dad was there, but gone by the time I poked my head out.

Except today, things don't feel as hopeless between Wren Fletcher and me as they did yesterday.

On the flip side, I haven't begun to wrap my mind around how I feel about these phone calls between him and my mother. Angry, on Simon's behalf, that's for certain. Though something tells me Simon knows more than even he let on that night on the porch steps.

What if those calls hadn't started? What if the feelings between my parents hadn't resurfaced? Would my father still have decided that it was best for everyone if he distanced himself?

My gaze drifts to the green Ford Escape next door as I climb the porch steps, panting. I didn't hear it roll in last night. Jonah must have come home after I went to bed.

I push through the door into the kitchen.

And yelp at the hulkish figure inside, pouring a cup of coffee into a travel mug.

"What are you doing in here?"

"What does it look like I'm doing?" Jonah slides the half-full pot back on the burner. He's dressed much the same as yesterday, swapping the black shirt for charcoal gray, the cotton material clinging nicely to his shoulders. His jeans are still too loose. The same ratty USAF baseball cap keeps his straggly blond hair off his face.

"You don't have a coffeemaker at your place?"

"Wren brews a full pot every morning for the both of us. That's our routine. I always come over to fill up my mug."

I frown. "Did you come in here yesterday, too?"

"Yup." He turns and leans against the counter, settling his pretty blue eyes on me. "You were in the shower." Did he trim his beard? It's still long and full, but it seems less mangy than yesterday. Or . . . I don't know. Something's different about him. He looks a bit less wild and unappealing.

Bringing the mug to his lips, he takes a long sip, his gaze flickering over my sweat-coated body—clad in the pink shorts and tank top that he claimed leaves *nothing* to the imagination—before settling on my face. "Did your bug spray work?"

I can't read him, not even a little bit, and that's unsettling. "Seemed to," I murmur, suddenly feeling self-conscious. Which is probably his goal. Setting my jaw stubbornly, I stroll over to the kitchen sink.

"Agnes warned you about the water, right?"

My hand freezes mid-swipe over my lips. "What do you mean? Is it contaminated?" I haven't intentionally drunk any, but I've been brushing my teeth with it.

"No, it's clean. But we're on a hauled water system out here. A truck comes out once a week to fill that big tank outside. If you use it up before the next truck comes, you're shit outta luck."

"Does that happen a lot? Running out of water?"

"Not to people who don't leave the tap on while they wash up," he says pointedly, as water gushes freely from the faucet.

I slap a hand down to shut it off. "Thanks for letting me know."

"No problem." A pause. "Those bites look nasty."

I can feel his gaze on the backs of my thighs, on the angry, itchy red welts that cropped up overnight.

My cheeks begin to flush. "I'll be fine."

The floor creaks with his heavy footfalls as he heads for the door. "Have fun playing dress-up, or whatever it is you do all day."

And . . . I guess he's back to being an ass. Too bad, because for a while there, I thought I might be able to like this guy.

"Have fun annoying people, or whatever it is *you* do all day."

His deep chuckle vibrates in my chest as he disappears out the door. I watch through the window as he strolls confidently across the lawn toward his SUV, as if without a care in the world.

"Bastard," I mutter. At least the animosity that I felt for him yesterday has dulled considerably. Now I'm just mildly aggravated. I pour half a mug of coffee for myself and then, with great reluctance, reach into the fridge for the liquid chalk to top up the other half.

I frown at the fresh carton of Silk sitting front and center on the shelf.

That wasn't there earlier this morning.

Did Jonah leave that in there?

I poke my head out the door, in time to see his Escape pulling out of his driveway and onto the main road, speeding off toward Alaska Wild.

What did he do, go out last night and buy it for me?

A quick Google search on my phone shows one other grocery store in town. I guess they must carry it. But still, for Jonah to even consider doing that for me . . .

I fill the rest of my mug, diluting the otherwise bitter taste, and then take a long, savoring sip.

It's not Simon's latte, but I can live with this, I decide with a small, satisfied smile.

■ ■ ■

"Thanks for the ride." I push the taxicab door shut, my gaze wandering over the small assembly of grounds crew workers ahead, their orange vests fluttering in the cool breeze as they wheel skids loaded with packages toward the planes.

"Anytime. But you know it's not that far to walk from your place," Michael says as he lights up a cigarette.

"It's closer than I thought," I admit. Still, it would take me more than a half hour. I watch a curl of smoke sail upward. "You shouldn't smoke." At least he doesn't do it while I'm in the car, or I'd have to find myself another cab driver.

"Yeah, yeah. I know. I've tried quitting." He dismisses it in an apathetic tone.

"Keep trying until it sticks. For your kids' sake." He talks about them enough that I know he cares, despite their living situation.

The car begins rolling away, Michael's arm dangling out the window, the cigarette burning as he casts a lazy salute my way.

With a heavy sigh, I push through the front doors of Alaska Wild, an unexpected rash of butterflies suddenly stirring in my stomach. When I was young, I used to picture my dad's company inside one of those cavernous architectural-masterpiece airport terminals like the ones I saw in TV movies, with hordes of people rushing like little black ants in all directions, frantic to catch their next flight, suitcases dragging behind them. I asked my mom once if that's what Alaska Wild looked like. She laughed. "No, Calla. It's not like that at all. It's rather simple."

So I tried to reset my imagination to picture a "simple" airport with planes and pilots and my father at the helm. I couldn't.

Now, though, standing inside the spacious lobby, taking in the faux wood-panel walls, the dark gray linoleum floor layered with aged forest-green runners that wear scores of dusty boot prints; the panels of lights above, checkered amongst a tile ceiling; and the only window, a large one that overlooks the runway, I finally understand what she meant.

It looks like a mechanic's shop my mother and I ended up at once, after a strange whistling sound coming from her engine interrupted our weekend wine-touring trip to Niagara. Even the water cooler in the corner, with its sad little paper cone cups jammed into a dispenser beside it, is eerily similar.

At least it doesn't smell like motor oil in here, though. I can't describe the scent. A faint waft of brewed coffee and damp air, perhaps.

Rows of navy-blue chairs—the typical uncomfortable airport seats—fill the open space. There's enough to accommodate thirty people, by my eyeball calculation. All of them are empty at the moment.

A thin brunette with rosy cheeks sits at the far end, behind one of two computers at the customer desk. Her round hawkish gaze is doing a once-over of me. When she sees that I've noticed her, she grins. "You *must* be Calla." Her voice—a distinctive American accent that I can't place except to say she's not from Alaska—seems to echo through the open space.

I'm not sure how to take that.

I force a smile. "Hi. I'm looking for Agnes."

"She's in the back." She gestures to a doorway behind her. "I'm Sharon, by the way."

"Right. Agnes mentioned you the other day. I'm Wren's daughter, Calla." I shake my head at myself as I approach. "Which we just covered."

She laughs and nods to the doorway. "Go on through."

It's not until I round the desk that I notice the basketball under Sharon's shirt. My eyes widen involuntarily.

"All baby, right?" She pats her swollen belly. "And *a lot* of it."

"When are you due?" Because she looks ready to burst.

"Eight more weeks, and I am *so* ready to be done."

"I'll bet." She can't be older than me. She might be even younger. I struggle not to grimace at the thought of being in her shoes. Maybe a baby will sound more appealing to me in a few years.

Like, ten years.

"Well . . . good luck." I wander through the doorway and into a much smaller room decorated in the same outdated fashion, half of the space filled with filing cabinets of varying sizes and shades of metal gray, the other half by three large desks. Maps plaster the walls all around, and off to the far left is a small office with a door that wears a gold plaque with the name "Wren Fletcher." It's empty.

A portly white-haired man sits at a desk in the corner, stabbing at the keys of a clunky calculator with the eraser end of his pencil. The printer churns and a strip of white paper spits out at a steady stream. It's a scene right out of one of those cheesy old movies that Simon insisted I watch, sans the thick haze of cigarette smoke and rotary phone.

Agnes looks up from her monitor, a pair of glasses that are much too narrow for her round face perched on the end of her nose. "Hey, Calla. Looking for your dad?" She's not at all fazed that I've shown up here, but she never seems fazed by anything.

"No, actually I wanted to talk to you for a minute. Can you take a quick break?"

"I was just thinking I needed a coffee refresh." Agnes stands and collects a green mug from beside her desk, and then the red one beside Calculator Man. "Another one, James?"

"Uh-huh." He doesn't even look up.

She hesitates. "Calla's here."

His hand pauses mid-poke, his bushy eyebrow lifting as he regards me. "Good God, you're Susan's spitting image," he mutters, before glaring at the sheet in front of him. "Dammit, where was I?"

"James is 'in the zone,' as Mabel would say." Agnes nods toward the door. "We try not to interrupt him. He gets grouchy." She pokes her head around the corner. "Sharon? Keep an ear out for dispatch, will ya? Wren should be calling in soon."

"Can do!" says the chirpy receptionist.

"Wren went up to St. Mary's to check on some repairs to the station building." Agnes leads me through a different door and into what I'm guessing is the staff room—a long corridor with a small kitchenette on one side, a rectangular table in the middle, and an eclectic collection of three worn couches in a U-shape on the far end, the pillows misshapen from years of being burdened by weight. A coffee table in front of them is stacked with tattered magazines and poorly folded newspapers.

It feels like it's several degrees colder in here. I hug myself, trying to warm up. "So, that guy back there remembers my mother?" James, I think she said.

"*And* you." Agnes retrieves the half-full pot of coffee from the maker and fills both mugs. "James has been coming in here every week to update Wild's books for *forty-eight years* now. Can you believe that?"

Wow. "And he doesn't use a computer?"

"Nope. Just that big calculator and his ledger books."

"You're kidding, right?"

Agnes shakes her head, amusement in her eyes.

"Is that the way things are in Alaska?"

"That's the way things are in Alaska Wild." She turns the tap on and begins washing a dirty mug left by the sink. The paper taped to the wall above that reads, "You use it, you wash it" was clearly ignored. "It's the same reason your dad still books flights on scrap pieces of paper that I have to fish out of his pockets, and why we only take reservations in person and over the phone." She chuckles. "In case you haven't noticed, Wild is behind a few decades."

"I couldn't even find a website," I admit. "Not one that had anything on it, anyway."

"That *is* our website." Agnes chuckles and then rolls her eyes. "You wouldn't believe how long it took me to convince Wren we should have one. He argued that we didn't need to pay someone thousands of dollars because everyone in Alaska already knows us. Anyway, I finally got him to agree and we hired this designer guy from Toledo. He took our money, set up the website address, and then never did anything else. I chased him for a few months, until my emails started bouncing back." She shrugs. "We haven't gotten around to finding someone new yet."

"You don't need to pay someone. You could do it yourself."

She snorts. "I finally figured out how to build a simple staff schedule on Excel. I know what my limits are."

"What about that girl out front. Sharon?"

"Sharon's good with dealing with customers. That's her strength. Same with Maxine. She's not here today, but you'll meet her another day."

"Well . . . what about Jonah, then?"

"Jonah?" She chuckles. "That guy refuses to answer his phone half the time. No . . . Jonah's good at flying planes and telling everyone what to do, and fixing our problems. He wants nothing to do with computers."

"Don't planes use computers?" I mutter wryly. That explains the wristwatch, though. "Well, maybe *I* could do it for you guys while I'm here," I offer, without thinking. "I mean, I don't know anything about planes or charter companies, but I'm sure I could figure it out." Most of what I do for the Calla & Dee site has been self-taught.

"Ah, it's not that important. We'll get to it, eventually. You're only here for a week. You should spend it getting to know your dad."

I guess.

If he's around long enough.

Agnes rings out the dish sponge and sets it out to dry. "Did Mabel come by this morning?"

"No. Why?"

"Oh, just wondering. I told her to give you space, but she doesn't listen too well sometimes. There's not a lot new and exciting around Bangor." She smiles. "*You* are something new and exciting. And she can be overwhelming sometimes."

Mention of Mabel reminds me why I came to Alaska Wild this

morning in the first place. I hesitate to bring it up and risk making our conversation awkward. "I'm sorry about last night."

She waves it away, much like my father did. "We can see how that confusion might have happened and how it would have been shocking for you."

I watch Agnes's profile for a moment as she quietly wipes spilled sugar and coffee from the countertop. Is she *truly* this understanding? "My dad told me about Mabel's father. Derek, right?"

"Right." A wistful smile lifts her cheeks. "I still remember the first day he showed up here from Oregon. He was the loud, goofy new pilot and I fell for him right away. We got married a year later." She wanders over to sit opposite me at the table, her coffee cup gripped in her small hands. "When we got the call that he hadn't shown up, I just knew. It took them two days to find his plane because of the fog. I was sitting on that couch over there when they told us that they'd found it." She nods toward the baby-blue one and a ball of emotion swells in my throat.

"That's . . . horrible."

Pain flashes through her eyes and then, just as quickly, it's gone again. "It was. But I always knew it was a possibility. It is with *any* of these guys, the conditions they fly in. We've lost a good few friends over the years. I can't tell you how many times Jonah has stressed me out. Anyway . . . I was thankful that I had Mabel on the way. She's a piece of him that I got to keep."

"Does she ask about him a lot?" As much as I used to ask my mom about my father when I was young?

"Not a lot. Sometimes." Agnes leans back in her chair, her eyes roving the tile ceiling. "She reminds me of Derek so much. She's a ball of energy just like he was. She even has that raspy voice of his."

"It's funny how that can happen, isn't it?"

I feel Agnes's dark gaze land on me as I draw a finger over the wood-grain swirls in the tabletop, with hands that my mother swears are identical to my father's.

"It was Derek's death that made Wren decide to come visit you in Toronto. Derek had been pushing him to go and then, after he died, Wren felt he owed it to him."

Didn't he feel that he owed it to *me*?

I push that bitter thought aside. "Because he blamed himself for Derek dying. He told me."

Agnes makes a disapproving sound. "No matter what way you slice it, Wren has a way of twisting the accident to take the blame. Either Derek wasn't experienced enough to find his way through those mountains, which means Wren made a bad judgment call, or there was no avoiding it, and it should have been Wren flying into that ridge. It happens enough through those passes when the weather's dicey. Pilots mistake one river for the next and they don't turn when they're supposed to, or turn too early. Either way, Derek should still be here. According to Wren, anyway. No one else ever saw it that way but him." She hesitates, studying me. "He never told me that he canceled his trip to go see you until it was too late. If I'd known what he was planning, I would have insisted that he go. I feel partially responsible for what happened between you two. I'm sorry for that."

"No . . . You had nothing to do with it. That was his choice." And perhaps his mistake, but perhaps not. What would have happened to our family? Would Simon have been cast aside?

Would my mother have done something that she couldn't take back?

What would my life look like right now, had my dad come to Toronto?

I sigh heavily. "I wish he'd told me. Even if I didn't understand it at the time, I'd like to think I would have eventually."

"If it makes you feel any better, Wren won't say it but I know he has a lot of regrets. You and your mother are at the center of most of them." Agnes stands and wanders over to a block of cupboards by the utility sink. "He can be an infuriating man, I'll admit. He says little and is slow to act on feelings. It's not that he doesn't care, though. Far from it. You just sometimes have to watch extra close to see how he shows it." She stretches onto her tiptoes to reach the cupboard above the sink and begins shuffling things around, searching and rearranging boxes and tins that are already in order, doors smacking against their frames to fill the quiet.

She needs to keep busy, like my mom.

At least they have one thing in common.

Over the past two days, I've been able to slowly cobble together a sense of Agnes's relationship with my father, and yet one thing remains uncertain. "So . . . have you and my dad ever . . . I mean, was there a time when you two were *more* than friends?"

She occupies herself with a clipboard and pencil that hangs on the wall, marking something off—inventory, maybe? "There was a time when I *hoped* we could be more than what we are."

"But not anymore?"

She doesn't answer immediately, as if giving her words careful thought. In the end, all she says is, "Not anymore."

A knock on the door sounds then and we both turn to see Sharon filling the doorway, her pregnant belly all the more pronounced now that I can see her long, thin legs.

Agnes's eyes twinkle as they take her in. "How're you hangin' in there?"

Sharon's hand settles on the underside of her bump as she waddles toward the fridge. "I'm peeing every twenty minutes, I'm forgetting *everything*, and this heartburn . . . ugh. And Max is irritating the hell out of me."

"Max is the father. He does our regular run up to Nome," Agnes explains to me, watching Sharon as she stands in front of the open fridge, a confused look on her face as she searches the shelves. "He's just excited."

"And *I'm* excited for this little guy to get out," Sharon says with certainty. "Agnes, have you found anyone to replace me and Max yet?"

"Jonah's interviewing a new pilot next week. Nothing yet for front desk. It'll be me, Maxine, and Mabel for the next little while, I guess. Unless I can convince Calla here to stay longer." She chuckles. "What do you think? Take over for Sharon when they move back to the Lower Forty-eight? You'd get to spend more time with your dad . . ." She dangles that out there as if it's bait.

Did my dad tell her about the bank's restructuring? That I'm unemployed and technically *could* stay longer?

I wonder why Sharon and Max are leaving, anyway. Do they not like Alaska?

"*That's* why I came in here. God, this baby brain!" Sharon groans. "Wren radioed in. He'll be landing in ten."

"Good. Finally." Agnes beckons me with a wave of her hand. "Come on, Calla. Let's watch your dad fly in."

■ ■ ■

I hug my body against the chill that's moved in over the past hour, the damp air and murky clouds hinting of the approaching rain. At least the mosquitoes have taken to ground with the cool breeze.

"Look! There he is!" Agnes points up at the sky, to the small speck quickly taking shape as it nears. She smiles. "I never get bored of watching these guys fly home."

I'll admit, I do feel a small thrill, being at an airfield, surrounded by all these planes, and this surreal reality that they're the only means for rejoining civilization. It's definitely a different way of life from stepping onto a subway or car to get to your destination.

"Does my dad go out every day?"

"No, he usually spends his days stuck on the phone, checking in with all the pilots and watching the weather reports. But he's been going up more over the last week. I think he's trying to get in as much flying time as he can before he has to give it up."

I frown. "What do you mean, give it up?"

She glances around us. "He'll have to declare his medical condition soon, and when he does, they'll ground him. He can't fly when he's going through treatment. As it is, he should have already reported it. I think that's why he's only doing solo trips. He doesn't feel as guilty about breaking the rules that way, if it's only his life up there." Agnes pauses. "I think that's the worst thing for him out of all this. Not being able to take off whenever he wants."

I quietly watch the speck grow larger. "He *really* loves flying."

"More than anyone I've ever met, and Alaska has *a lot* of pilots," she agrees. "James said your grandmother was convinced that Wren screamed when he came out of the womb because he didn't want his feet touching the ground. But if ever there was a man born to live in the sky, it's your dad." She smiles in thought. "You know, we could always tell when he had gotten a phone call from you. He'd fly off without telling anyone where he was going or when he'd be back. Wouldn't answer dispatch or the other pilots." She chuckles. "Drove us all nuts. Of course he'd always be back within the hour, but it was still reckless. Eventually, we learned that it was his way of dealing."

"By going kamikaze?"

"By being in his favorite place, high up in the sky, getting away from everything he'd lost down on the ground."

I can't tell if she's defending my father's choice to let his family go or trying to explain it. Either way, there's a glaring distortion to reality. He was never a victim. "He didn't have to lose us. Alaska skies aren't the only skies. There are plenty of bush pilot jobs all over the place. The Pacific Northwest, British Columbia, Alberta, Ontario. He lost us because he didn't even try."

She's silent for a moment, her eyes narrowed on the approaching plane, as if weighing her words. "Did you know that your dad lived in Colorado for a while?"

"Uh . . . no." But there's a lot I don't know about my father, so I guess I shouldn't be surprised. "When was that?"

"He was twenty-one. He went to stay with his uncle—your

grandmother's brother. That's where your grandparents were originally from. They moved up to Alaska a year before Wren was born. Anyway, Wren had never been outside of the state. He wanted to see what it was like in the Lower Forty-eight before he took over Alaska Wild for good. So he went down and got a job with a search-and-rescue team. He'd been flying up here since he was fourteen and he had more than enough experience. He had three offers within the day.

"He traveled a bit while he was there, too. California . . . Arizona . . . Oregon. Can't remember where else. Oh, New York, for one weekend." She chuckles. "He hated that city. Said he couldn't get out of there fast enough. And even after a year of living down there, he felt like a visitor in a foreign country. It was so different. The people were different. The lifestyle was different. Priorities were different. And things moved too fast. He was terribly homesick."

"So he moved back to Alaska."

"He didn't have much choice. Your grandfather got sick and had to go to the hospital in Anchorage. So Wren came back and took over Wild. He always knew he would, but it was a lot sooner than he expected. You know, he was only twenty-three when his dad died."

"I didn't realize he was that young."

"It had to be overwhelming, though Wren's never been the type to complain. This place was a lot for him to take on, for a lot of years. Your grandmother helped as much as she could. But still, it was a lot of responsibility. In some cases, people's lives." Agnes watches the approaching plane with keen eyes. "Life up here may be simple but it's not easy, and it's not for everyone. Water runs out; pipes freeze; engines won't start; it's dark for eighteen, nineteen hours a day, for months. Even longer in the far north. Up here it's about having enough food to eat, and enough heat to stay alive through the winter. It's about survival, and enjoying the company of the people that surround us. It's not about whose house is the biggest, or who has the nicest clothes, or the most money. We support each other because we're all in this together.

"And people either like that way of life or they don't; there's no real in-between. People like Wren and Jonah, they find they can't stay away from it for too long. And people like Susan, well . . . they never warm up to it. They fight the challenges instead of embracing them, or at least learning to adapt to them." Agnes pauses, her mouth open as if weighing whether she should continue. "I don't agree with the choices Wren made where you're concerned, but I know it was never a matter of him not caring about you. And if you want to blame people for not trying, there's plenty of it to go around." Agnes turns to smile at me then. "Or you could focus on the here-and-now, and not on what you can't change."

I get what she's saying. That maybe the demise of my parents' marriage doesn't fall just on my dad's shoulders, that maybe my mother never really tried, either, despite what she claims.

The small white-and-black-striped plane grows closer, descending in the sky, lining up with the short runway below, its wings teeter-tottering from side to side. "Do they always look so unstable coming in?" I ask, warily.

"Depends on the crosswinds. Don't worry, though. Wren could land that thing in his sleep."

I distract myself from my growing anxiety with a gaze around the lot. Several of the planes that were being loaded when I arrived are now closed up and appear ready to go. "What are those planes carrying? I saw the guys loading up boxes."

"Cargo. Lots and lots of packages and other mail to the villages."

"Wild delivers mail?"

"Oh, yeah. We've had a contract with USPS for years. We fly out thousands of pounds of cargo every day. Letters, online orders, food, fuel. Water treatment chemicals. Two weeks ago we flew two ATVs up to Barrow on the Sherpa."

"Wow. I didn't realize the scope of the business," I admit sheepishly.

She nods knowingly. "It's quite an operation. There are a lot of people working here, between all the locations. Used to be even *more*, but our competition has been poaching our hunt camps and tour guide companies away from us. Even the private one-off bookings coming in from the Lower Forty-eight are less and less." She snorts. "There was one day when Wren made me call all our lines to make sure they were working, the phones had been so quiet. But . . . we'll manage." She says it almost airily, but the tightness I see in her profile tells me it's nothing to take lightly. She smiles with assurance when she sees the worry in my face. "It's nothing for you to think about, Calla."

We watch quietly as the wheels of my dad's plane touch down on the gravel runway, bouncing twice before sticking. I traipse after Agnes as she strolls forward to where my dad coasts in, guided by the same short, stocky guy with the glow sticks from the night I arrived.

My dad slides out of the plane with surprising ease for a fifty-three-year-old man. We reach him as his boots hit the ground.

"How'd it go up there?" Agnes calls out.

"Rain's still leaking in the back corner and the guys seem more interested in taking their lunch break than figuring it out. I'll need to send Jonah up there to bark at them in a few days." His soft gray eyes flicker to me. "You been up a while?"

"Since sunrise," I admit. Though there's no sun.

"It'll take a few more days to adjust."

"Just in time for me to head back home."

"That's how it usually goes," he murmurs, frowning up at the sky as rain begins to spit. "Hopefully we'll have some good weather for you before then."

"She came to check out Alaska Wild and see her dad fly a plane," Agnes says, winking at me. "Maybe we should get her up in the air, so she can see more than Bangor."

"Today?" My stomach instantly tightens with nerves. It's one thing to watch a plane land. It's another to hop in and fly off with no mental preparation, after my last horrendous experience.

My dad seems to sense my panic. He chuckles. "I think Jonah may have scarred the poor girl."

"She'll be fine. You and Jonah can take her out in Betty," she urges.

I frown. *Betty?*

"Can't," the grounds worker pipes up from behind us, unloading my dad's plane. "Betty's in the hangar."

His gaze wanders to the big warehouse, where a banana-yellow plane sits. Two men stand next to it, talking. One is tall, with gray hair and a potbelly; the other a small man in denim-blue coveralls, holding a tool. A mechanic, I'm guessing.

"Sonny!" a deep voice booms, pulling my attention to the left, to the looming figure that marches toward us. "Did you remember the supplies from the fridge?"

"Shit," the grounds guy—Sonny, I assume—whispers. He steals a glance at me and then scurries off, the panicked look on his face saying that he indeed forgot whatever Jonah is referring to.

"There's a strong downwind and rain north of us. Better get going," my dad warns by way of greeting.

"I'll be in the air in five." Jonah comes to a halt beside me. "I called River Co. and shook their tree. They said they'll pay the bill by the end of the week."

My dad nods. "Good. That'll help. I know they're busy as hell, but that's no reason not to pay."

"Yeah, busy pushing all their clients to use Jerry," Jonah grumbles. "If they're not gonna pay on time, we need to cut ties."

"Can't afford to lose them," Agnes adds in gentle warning.

"We already pretty much have," Jonah throws back.

Dad sighs wearily, as if they've had this conversation too many times already. His gaze heads back toward the hangar. "What's going on with her?"

"George said she felt funny up there today."

"Funny? Like *how,* funny?"

"Couldn't say exactly. Just didn't like it."

"Twenty-seven years flying planes and all he has is 'it felt funny'?"

"You know how George gets with his 'feelings.'" Jonah gives my dad a look. "Who knows. Maybe he didn't rub his lucky rabbit foot three times before takeoff. Anyway, she was due for her maintenance check soon, so I've got Bart doing a full look-over."

Something familiar finally jogs in my mind. "You name all your planes," I say slowly. He used to talk about them like they were actual people—family members.

They turn to look at me and a wistful smile slowly stretches across my dad's face.

"Wasn't there a . . . Beckett?" I struggle to recall the exact name as memories flood back to me now. *I flew so-and-so up to the North Pole today.* He even made me ask my mom to show me where the North Pole was on the map. Apparently, it's in Alaska.

"Becker. After George Becker, the geologist. That's one of the Beavers." My dad is full-out beaming now. "Your grandfather named the planes after Alaskan explorers. We have an Otter called Moser. And a Stockton, and Turner. Those are Pipers. We had to retire Cook a few years ago after one of our pilots hit a moose in a white-out landing. He was fine." My dad waves off my cringe. He's suddenly alive with names and facts. "Bering, after Vitus Bering, is getting an engine overhaul. Huh . . ." My dad scratches the thin layer of stubble on his chin. "I can't believe you remember that."

"Neither can I." I'd also forgotten how easy it is to talk to my dad when it has anything to do with planes. "So *Betty* was an explorer, too?"

All three of them chuckle.

"I may have strayed a little off course," my dad admits with a sheepish grin. "We now have Betty, who's in the hangar. And this is Veronica. She's a Cessna. She's my special girl." He raps his knuckles against the plane he just flew in, then points to the larger orange-and-white plane not far away. "That one's Archie." He pauses, looking expectantly at me.

"Don't get your hopes up, Wren. I doubt she's ever read a comic book," Jonah butts in, and I can sense that condescending smirk from beneath his bushy face without being able to see it.

This is one time he won't get the better of me. I stroll past the smug bastard and stop in front of a white plane with a navy-blue nose and a row of portal windows on either side. "So this is Jughead, then?" I steal a glance at Jonah to see the surprise in his icy blue eyes. A wave of triumph rushes over me, and I let my own smug smile blossom over my face.

There's no way in hell I'm admitting that not only is Jonah right and I've never so much as held *any* comic book—because they're pointless and I'm not a seven-year-old boy—but I wouldn't be able to name a single Archie comic character including the namesake, had it not been for Netflix.

The point is, I've proven Jonah wrong and I'm feeling way too much satisfaction over something so petty.

My dad wanders over to smooth his hand over Jughead's blue nose. "He's our school sports team workhorse. He does a lot of back-and-forth between the villages through the year, shuttling the kids to their games."

"Students *fly* to all their games?"

"You should see the school travel budgets." A knowing smile crinkles his eyes. "It's a very different way of life up here."

"Speaking of budgets . . . James ran the numbers for how much we lost when we were grounded last week," Agnes says in a low, serious tone. "You've got a few things to figure out."

The lightness fades from my dad's face as he nods solemnly.

And unease grows inside me.

First, Agnes's offhand comment about the competition, and now this. Is Alaska Wild having money issues? It's bad enough that my dad has his health to worry about, but does he have his family's business to stress over, too?

Sonny's back, running awkwardly across the pavement toward a nearby waiting plane, his short arms hugging a sizeable white Styrofoam cooler. "Just the one, right, Jonah?"

"Yup. Alright. I'm off," Jonah announces, dragging his feet with the first steps toward his plane, as if reluctant.

"Why don't you take Calla with you?" Agnes says suddenly.

I can't help the glare I shoot at her. "No, thanks." Is she insane? As if I'm going to get into a plane with Jonah alone ever again.

Jonah chuckles, slipping on his sunglasses, hiding his heavy gaze from my view. "That's okay. Maybe Wren can teach you how to drive while I'm gone." He turns and saunters toward his plane.

"Have a *great* flight!" I holler, my blood simmering with annoyance. *Shithead.*

"Make sure you call in when you land," Agnes adds.

"Always do."

"Sooner." She sounds like a doting mother asking her children to check in.

"Yup."

She sighs softly, the only sign that she could be frustrated with him, and then turns back to us. "Why don't you go talk to James and I'll take Calla into town to get some Benadryl for those bites. It looks like she's having a reaction."

"That'd be great." I punctuate it with a scratch against my arm.

"Yeah." My dad frowns in thought. "What did he mean about the driving thing, anyway?" His gaze searches the parking lot, no doubt for his truck.

I sigh.

Thanks a lot, Jonah.

Chapter 12

■ ■ ■

"What about 'Leisure Looks for the *Wild*.' That has a nice ring to it, doesn't it?"

"Yeah, not bad," I murmur as I scroll through Alaska Aviator's website. They claim to be the best charter plane company in Alaska. I don't know if that's true, but I'm guessing any tourist planning a trip here would take them for their word.

Everything I could possibly want to know is listed—their history, their types of planes, their excursions, their pilots. Safety records, rates, recommendations for lodging and camps—the list goes on. And they have proof in pictures, too! A gallery of picturesque Alaskan landscape and wildlife, taken in every season, meant to lure people in.

If I were a tourist looking to book an excursion, this Alaska Aviator company would likely be at the top of my list. And if not them, then one of the ten other companies I've spent the past several hours perusing from my rickety chair on the porch.

It would certainly *not* be Alaska Wild, which was *far* down the screen on the search results and didn't offer me any information besides a directory listing.

"You're not paying attention to me, are you?" Diana snaps.

"I am! I swear," I lie. "I think it's great. Except it'll be 'How to Stretch One Leisure Look for an Entire Trip in the *Wild*' if I don't get the rest of my clothes. I guess that'd be good for backpackers," I add, half-heartedly.

"You *still* haven't gotten your suitcases? That's madness."

"Should be today." Hopefully.

"Okay, so you'll still have four days to put something together."

"I guess."

"Calla! What is your problem? It's like you don't care."

"I don't know. I'm tired, I guess. I took Benadryl for these bites and it's making me sleepy." I wince as I inspect the giant, red welts on my calf. "I don't think it's working, either. My skin is all hot, too."

"Oh . . . that's not good. I hope that doesn't turn into cellulitis."

"Cellulite *what*?" I squawk, panicked.

"Not *cellulite*. Cellulitis. It's an infection. Get a pen and draw a circle around the outside edge. If the redness spreads outside it, you probably need antibiotics."

"How do you know this?"

"Hi, have we met? Because my mom's a nurse."

"Right," I murmur.

"But I'm sure you'll be fine. It'll take another dose or two probably, and then you'll be good to go. Oh! I was also thinking we could do a post on . . ."

My attention wavers as Diana prattles on, something about Viking braids and hot springs. The truth is, I don't think my lack of enthusiasm has anything to do with my missing clothes or antihistamines. It's more that Calla & Dee seems so . . . trivial right now.

"What about the yeti?" she asks suddenly, instantly pulling me in.

"What about him?" Diana has heard the gory details of my first and second encounters with Jonah, the text conversation littered with four-letter words and hopes for an unfortunate sexual encounter with a feral animal.

"I don't know. Maybe we can do a second round of 'Bushman to Gentleman.' Alaska edition."

I snort. "Believe me, it would take a whole lot more than a pair of shears to uncover anything gentlemanly about him. Plus, I think he likes that look." He must. Why else would he allow it to go so long?

"Crap. I've gotta go. Beef Stick's waving me over," Diana mutters. "It's like I'm his personal secretary or something."

"He *does* own the firm," I remind her. The fact that Diana's boss lives off those long, skinny meat sticks you find at convenience store counters doesn't change that.

"Man, I've gotta find a new job. Talk to you later," she says in a rushed whisper, and then hangs up.

I stick my earbuds back in, turn on my music, and return to my research, picking at the ham sandwich I made for lunch while I read up on Alaska Wild's competitors, until I decide that a sandwich is not what I feel like after all. So I head into the house to fix myself a plate of hummus and carrots, and a glass of a ready-made green smoothie.

I step back out through the sliding door.

And yelp. There's a raccoon perched atop the table, its busy paws pulling apart the slices of bread.

"Shoo! Go on!" I yell, expecting it to hightail out the cracked porch door where it clearly snuck through.

But it merely glares at me with its beady eyes before turning back to my sandwich.

I give a nearby plastic bin a kick. "Get out of here!"

The raccoon chatters at me, that odd squeaking sound grating on my nerves.

And then it scampers forward.

I take several stumbling steps back, losing half my plate of food to the floor and spilling my smoothie all over my jeans as I try to get away from it.

It's temporarily distracted by a rolling carrot, picking it up in its nimble paws, flipping it this way and that.

Are Alaskan raccoons different from Toronto raccoons?

Will this one attack?

There's a straw broom perched in the corner. I dump the plate and glass on a nearby ledge and grab the handle, getting a good grip with two hands, ready to take a swing.

"Bandit!" a deep voice calls.

The raccoon stands on its hind legs and turns toward the voice, pausing to listen.

"Bandit! Get over here!"

It takes off, squeezing through the ajar porch door. I watch, with the broom handle still gripped within my fists, as the animal trots across the lawn toward Jonah, to stop a mere foot away. It stands on its hind legs and reaches up into the air.

"Hey, buddy. You getting into trouble?" Jonah gives the raccoon's head an affectionate scratch, to which it chatters back excitedly.

"You have got to be kidding me!" My face twists in horror as realization sinks in. "He's your *pet*?"

"No. You're not allowed to have raccoons as pets in the state of Alaska," Jonah says matter-of-factly.

"So, what is he, then? Because he sure looks like a pet."

"He's a raccoon that likes to hang out around my house." Jonah's gaze narrows at the broom in my hand. "What were you planning on doing with that?"

"Chase him out of here before he bit me."

"He won't bite you unless you give him reason to."

I think of Tim and Sid, their humps bobbing as they scurry down the driveway after rooting through bones and rotten, smelly meat packaging, and I cringe. "You know they carry diseases, right?"

Jonah gives the raccoon one last pat before standing tall again. The raccoon scampers away. "Bandit's fine."

"You *named* him."

"Yeah. You know, because of the black mask around—"

"I get it," I interrupt. "*Super* original." But also, fitting. "He stole my sandwich."

Jonah shrugs. "Don't leave your sandwich lying around where he can steal it, then."

"I didn't leave it lying around. It was on a plate, on a table, inside *here*. *He* came in *here*. *And* he made me spill my drink all over myself." I throw a hand at my jeans, covered in thick green liquid. My socks are soaked through.

Jonah's eyes crinkle with amusement. "Don't be so clumsy next time."

I shoot a glare at him—why is he even here? I thought he was working!—and then, picking up my mangled food and dishes, I head inside to change into the only clean pair of clothes I have left and grab a banana to eat.

When I return, Jonah's sitting in my seat. Thankfully, there's no raccoon in sight.

"What is this?" he asks, nodding toward my MacBook.

"A computer."

He throws me a flat look. "Why are you looking up charter company websites?"

"Because I wanted to know more about my dad's competition."

"For what? You suddenly interested in taking over the family business?" he mutters.

"No," I scoff through a bite of my banana. "But I noticed that Alaska Wild doesn't have a website and I think that's a huge mistake. *Everyone* has a website nowadays. The sixteen-year-old girl in our neighborhood who walks dogs has a website *and* an online payment option. It's the most basic way to market yourself."

Jonah leans back, his legs splayed in that guy way, his arms folded across his chest. He's made himself comfortable in my chair. "We don't need to market to the villagers; they all know us. Same with our shipping contracts and the schools."

"Yeah, but what about the tourists? Agnes said you're losing business with them."

"Yeah, we are," he admits. "But a website's not gonna help that."

I settle into the other seat. It teeters under my weight, the metal legs uneven. "If *I* were coming to Alaska and looking to go sightseeing or fly to another city, I wouldn't even know about Alaska Wild."

"Of course you would. We're listed on all the big Alaska tourism pages. And we're in the directory."

"Yeah, but there's no information. Nothing about what planes you have, or what your rules and refund policies are, your flying schedule, how much it would cost . . ."

"We tell them all that when they call," he says, as if it should be obvious.

Entirely missing my point.

"Jonah, maybe that's how people do it around here, but if you're trying to attract people from the Lower Forty-eight—or whatever you called it—or from other parts of the world, it's not enough. People don't phone companies, not until they've already narrowed down their choices. People *hate* talking over the phone. *I* don't even talk to my *friends* over the phone if I can help it. *Everyone* goes online, Googles what they're looking for, picks their top two or three choices, and *then* calls. A lot of people don't even call if they have questions, they email."

"So they can email us."

"And how are they going to find the address? You have nothing on your website. And they're not going to go hunting for it in some directory, believe me." I forge on, because it seems like Jonah is listening to me. "A lot of people book online, print out their receipt, and show up. And if there are other charter companies around here who have a website and all this information and pictures of planes and videos of flying to make it easy for them to decide, people are going to skip right over Alaska Wild. And honestly? If I'm paying to come to Alaska and then forking over even more money to go see mountains and wildlife, or to fly into a camp, it wouldn't be with the company that can't even get a basic website together."

It's not like I have specific data to prove anything I'm saying, but it's all common sense, isn't it? I mean, *everyone* knows this, right?

Jonah still looks doubtful.

"Look, say I'm John Smith from Arkansas and I want to come

to Alaska to hunt. I've never been before, so I look up Alaskan hunt camps and find this one." I stand just enough to drag my seat over closer, until I can reach my laptop. Jonah makes no effort to move, forcing me to lean over his thigh to reach my computer. I flip over to the tab with the camp that appeared at the top of the search earlier. "And when I click on 'how to get here,' it takes me to Alaska Aviator."

"Because they've got a deal with them. We've got the same thing with River & Co."

"The one that's *not* paying their bills on time?" I lean forward, navigating to their page, accidentally bumping my knee against his. "Sorry," I mumble. "They have Alaska Wild *and* Alaska Aviator listed as options for travel there." I tap the screen with my polished tip to prove it, bumping his knee again. He doesn't shift away. "So right away, when John Smith is planning his trip, Alaska Aviator is looking better to him because he has nothing to compare it against and he has to make a decision, all the way in Oklahoma."

"I thought you said Arkansas."

"Whatever. The point is, the only draw for him to Wild would be if it was a lot cheaper."

"They're pretty even."

"Well, then guess who John's going to be going with when he books his hunting trip." I lean back in my chair, feeling satisfied that I've proved my point. "Maybe River & Co. isn't the problem. Maybe they're not telling these tourists to fly with these other guys. Maybe these tourists are going to them because they made it easy to pick them."

Jonah's piercing gaze weighs heavily on me, his usually cold, indifferent expression replaced with curiosity. "You know how to do that? Build a website, I mean."

"Yeah. I pretty much built this." I lean forward to flip to the Calla & Dee tab.

"It's *pink*."

I roll my eyes. "That's all aesthetics. I could figure something out for Alaska Wild."

"In four days?"

"Yeah. I think so. A simple one, anyway." I shrug. "What else do I have to do here?"

He nods slowly, his brow furrowed in thought. "It won't cost much, will it?"

"No. I'll use the same web designer platform that I used for that site. It's next to nothing. And I have my camera, so I can take some pictures. I'm not a professional, but I'm decent enough. I took these." I click on a post that I know has a lot of scenery.

"'Sequins in the City,'" Jonah reads out loud.

"Forget the title and look at the pictures."

"Who's that?" He nods to Diana, who's posing in High Park, her short, blush-colored sequined skirt identical in shade to the cherry blossom trees in bloom behind her.

"That's my best friend."

"*Damn.*"

"Okay. Great. So you're into leggy blondes. Surprise, surprise," I mutter. "But *look* at the picture."

"That skirt barely covers her ass."

"Jonah!" I growl through a laugh, and then smack his chest, noting how hard and curved it is beneath my fingertips. "Forget Diana and her short skirt. My point is I'm pretty okay at taking pictures. And in any case, it's better than what's there now, which is nothing."

His eyes are crinkled with amusement as he watches me, and I feel my mouth curling into a stupid grin in response, even though I'm mildly annoyed. "You're not taking me seriously."

"I am. I swear." His hand lands on my knee, giving it a quick but tight squeeze, before leaning back in his chair again. "So go ahead and do it."

"Really?" I can't hide my surprise.

He shrugs. "You make a good argument. I still don't know if I buy what you're selling, but it can't hurt."

"Should I ask my dad first?"

"Nah. Just tell him you're doing it. He'll be happy."

"You think so?"

"You kidding? His kid showing interest in Wild?"

I wouldn't exactly call it an interest in Wild so much as an interest in feeling useful and having something to do. But I keep that to myself. "Well . . . okay, then."

"Okay, then." He nods resolutely. "You and me can bang this out together."

Whoa. Wait. *"Us?"* I feel my eyes pop.

"How else are you gonna add all that stuff about planes, and Wild's history, and all that? You think you can figure all that out? In *four days*? And I know everything there is to know about this place."

"Right. I guess." Me and Jonah, working together on a website for Alaska Wild. "This should be interesting," I mumble, under my breath.

His lips curl into a smirk. "Why do you say that?"

"Because you're . . . *you*."

"And you're *you*," he retorts, adding more softly, "except you're *actually* smart. I'm shocked."

"Shut up." A spark of satisfaction flickers inside me. Jonah thinks I'm smart.

He sighs, his gaze settling on his folded hands. "Alright, alright. Look. We got off on the wrong foot and that's on me. Yeah, I can admit when I've been an ass."

"So . . . is this, like, a truce or something?" Is Jonah capable of being civil?

"Or something." He glances at his watch and then eases out of my chair. His heavy boots thump against the floorboards as he heads for the door that leads off the porch.

"My dad told you to be nice to me, didn't he?"

"Nope."

I don't buy that, especially since my dad said he'd tell Jonah to ease off me. And something makes me think they're too close for Jonah to shrug my dad's requests off.

"Hey."

He pauses at the door. "Yup?"

"What do you know about my dad's diagnosis?" My dad made it clear that he doesn't want me to bring it up with him, and Agnes has already told me what she knows.

So the only person left to ask is Jonah.

His shoulders sag with a heavy exhale. "I know he has cancer, and he doesn't want to talk about it while you're here."

"What do you think that means?"

"That he has cancer and he doesn't want to talk about it while you're here," he says, matter-of-factly.

I roll my eyes at his back. "But he hasn't let on how bad it is?"

There's a long pause, and then he admits, almost reluctantly, "He asked me if I'd ever consider buying the company from him."

Surprise hits me. "He's thinking of *selling* Alaska Wild?"

"He's weighing his options. He said he might want to retire."

My dad, retiring. He's only fifty-three. Then again, he's been running the place since his early twenties. Maybe, after thirty years, he's finally had enough. But what would he do?

Would he stay in Alaska?

Or would he be ready to finally try something new?

"What'd you tell him?"

He chuckles. "I don't have that kind of money. Plus, I don't wanna be stuck behind a desk all day long for the next thirty years. I like the way things are right now. No matter what, though, I told him I'd take over running Wild for as long as he needs me to."

Much like my dad took over for my grandfather, when he started his treatment.

I swallow the growing lump in my throat. "That's nice of you, to be willing to do that."

"Yeah, well, Wren's family to me. There's nothing I wouldn't do for him." He clears the gruffness from his voice.

My chest tightens at the rare hint of emotion. "Do you think he'll get through this?"

"I think . . . that if there's any way you can stay longer, you should."

"I could," I blurt out, without thinking.

Jonah turns to regard me, his eyebrow arched in question.

I shrug. "I got restructured out, so I don't have a job to get home to right now."

His gaze roams my features. "Then you should stay another week or two. Or even longer, if you can grow a pair and deal with how things work around here."

I give him a flat look.

But there's no hint of humor on his face. "Trust me, Calla, you'll regret it for the rest of your life if you don't."

He sounds so definitive.

Does that have anything to do with regrets from his own past, with his father?

And what would that even mean? A full *month* in Bangor, Alaska?

Would my father be okay with a house guest for that long?

Jonah's gaze drifts over the soft pink cardigan I've wrapped around myself. "I called over to Anchorage to check on your stuff before I came home. Sounds like they've got a mechanical problem with the plane. Your suitcases won't be coming today."

I groan. *"Seriously?"*

"Roll with it." He leaves me stewing, strolling out the door and across the lawn toward his house, a little bounce in his step.

■ ■ ■

THE KITCHEN DOOR creaks open, and I look over my shoulder in time to see my dad step through.

"Long day, huh?" He's been at work for almost fourteen hours.

"They all are." With a tired-sounding sigh, he tosses some paperwork on the counter and then rubs his eyes. "Something smells good."

I dump a handful of pepper slices into the bowl. "I'm making us dinner. Chicken Greek salad with homemade dressing." That should be bottled and marketed as liquid gold for what it cost me in basic ingredients plus cab fare. "It'll be ready in five. I hope you like black olives."

"That's . . . Yup. Sure do." There's a long pause, and I can feel his gaze on me. "Thank you, Calla. This is nice."

"No big deal." It's just the first meal I've ever made for us, I think with a small smile. One of those seemingly small and inconsequential things in life that I'll probably remember for the rest of my life.

"How was your day?"

I'm itching to tell him about the plan to build a website for Wild.

I'm desperate to ask him if he's truly considering retiring.

Where exactly do I start?

Quick footfalls pound up the front porch stairs, and a moment later the door flies open. Mabel bursts through with a wide grin on her face, out of breath, as if she ran down the driveway. "Just in time!"

"Hey, kiddo." Dad's face instantly softens with a smile. "What d'you got there?"

"My specialty." She holds up the foil-covered glass dish in her oven-mitt-clad hands, announcing with dramatic flair and an energy that I don't think I could manage on my wildest day, "The cheesiest, sauciest, most delicious pasta you've *ever* had. Just came out of the oven." Setting the dish down on the table, she peels the foil back, letting the long strings of cheese dangle in the air. "I've finally perfected it!"

My digestive system would explode if I ate that.

"*Wow*. And there's enough here to keep me fed for a week," my dad chuckles. To me, he explains, "Mabel has discovered a passion for cooking. She's been experimenting in the kitchen a lot this past year, and using me as her guinea pig. I think this is the . . . eighth week you've made this?"

"Ninth," she corrects proudly. "But *this* is the one, I'm telling you."

"*Nine weeks in a row* of cheesy pasta." He gives me a pointed look, and I stifle my laugh, even through the distinct twinge of offense I feel inside. This clueless twelve-year-old girl has inserted herself into one of only a handful of nights I have with my father. *I* don't live across the road. *I* can't just trot down the driveway with dinner in my hands anytime I wish. *I'm* supposed to be making dinner for him.

She's only twelve and I doubt she's barged in on my night with my dad with malicious intentions, and yet I can't help feeling this resentment for her right now.

This does, however, explain the empty fridge. *And* how my dad survives on a regular basis.

"Calla, wait until you try this." Mabel pulls three plates from the cupboard.

"I wish I could, Mabel. But I have a dairy allergy," I explain with an apologetic cringe.

"Really? That sucks. So what are you gonna eat, then?" Mabel wanders over to look in my bowl. Her nose crinkles. "*Oh*. Well, it's a good thing I made dinner for us, then."

I frown. "Why?"

"Because Wren *hates* vegetables with a passion. Especially salad."

My dad cringes. "I think 'hate' is a strong word, Mabel—"

"No it's not! Mom calls him Baby Wren when he comes over for dinner because she has to cut them up into *tiny* little bites and hide them in sauce so he'll eat them." She grins at me as she digs out a serving spoon from a drawer.

So he was being polite, earlier. Now that I think back to it, there weren't any peas and carrots on his dinner plate last night.

He sighs, and then offers me a sheepish smile.

Scooping a generous portion of pasta onto two plates, Mabel collects them and heads for the living room, hollering back, "Are you black this time, or is it my turn?"

"I can't remember. You pick." He stalls at the doorway. "We usually play a game of checkers every night. Missed a couple there."

Because I came to Alaska, I gather.

He hesitates, biting his bottom lip. "So . . . a dairy allergy."

"Yeah."

"That's why there's all that *soya* milk in the fridge."

"Soy," I correct. "And yeah. It's for my coffee."

"Huh. Well . . . now I know."

"Right. Like now I know that you wouldn't have eaten *any* of this." I wave the knife in my hand over the salad bowl.

"I would have eaten every last bite, kiddo," he says with certainty, then disappears into the living room.

Leaving me smiling at a wall of ducks.

■ ■ ■

Mabel lets out a whoop, snatching the black checker piece from the board and adding it to her growing pile. "What's it like, losing fourteen games straight to a little *girl*?"

My dad's brow is pulled tight as he puzzles over the game board, as if replaying the last moves. "Seems I've taught you *too* well," he murmurs, leaning back in his La-Z-Boy. His gaze wanders over to the couch where I sit cross-legged, my MacBook nestled in my lap. "You sure you don't want to give it a try, Calla? 'Cuz I'm on the search for an opponent I can beat. My ego needs it."

"Maybe tomorrow," I say in a noncommittal way.

Dad chuckles. "Thank you for lying to spare my feelings. Your mom always flat-out refused."

Mabel's curious eyes drift from me to Wren, and back to me. I wonder how much she knows about our history. Can she sense the tension in the air when we're in a room together? A tension that, thankfully, seems to be ebbing away ever so slowly.

My dad begins placing pieces back on the board. "Same time, same place, kiddo?"

I try to ignore the way my gut tightens. He's called her that at least a half dozen times tonight and every time has been like a siren for me, a stark reminder that this kid has something with him that I never had, even all those years ago when I'd still call and he'd still answer.

Despite the fact that they're not blood-related.

Despite the fact that he and Agnes aren't even together.

They have a genuine father-daughter relationship.

Mabel glances at the clock on the wall and says with reluctance, "Fine." But then adds with a devilish spark in her eye, "I'll let you win tomorrow."

"That'd be a nice change."

"It's on. See ya." She leans forward and plants a quick kiss on my dad's forehead, with not a hint of hesitation, as if it's something she'd done a thousand times.

How will she react when she finds out he has cancer? The fact that everyone has sheltered her from that grim truth so far tells me it won't be well.

She grabs the sweater she draped over the back of my dad's chair. "Hey, Calla, you should come berry picking with me tomorrow. A bunch of us from in town are going in the morning."

I push aside my dark thoughts. "Yeah, maybe?" I can't remember the last time I did that.

"Okay." She shrugs, like it doesn't matter to her one way or another, but based on what Agnes said about me being the shiny new thing, I'm guessing that's an act.

Just as quickly and easily as Mabel strolled through the door, she now strolls out, leaving a palpable calm in her wake.

"I hope you liked the pasta," I murmur, biting into my apple. "There's enough left to feed twenty people."

"To be honest, I can't tell the difference between this week's and the last eight weeks' worth," my dad murmurs, eying my empty plate, which I filled twice with my own dinner. "Too bad you can't help me with it. Seems like you can put away a lot, for such a tiny person."

"I think the time difference is messing with my appetite," I admit. "Plus Jonah's trash panda ruined my lunch, so I didn't eat much today."

My dad frowns. *"Trash panda?"*

"Raccoon."

"Ah." My dad nods knowingly, smiling. "So you've met Bandit."

"He's keeping that thing as a pet. You know that, right?"

Dad chuckles. "Jonah found him living under his house last year. He was just a kit; guess he'd lost his family. So he started tossing him scraps of food to help him out until he moved on his way. But he never did."

"Of course he didn't. No one's going to leave an all-you-can-eat buffet to starve in the wild."

"Jonah built him a little den on the porch and he lives in there. Seems quite comfortable."

"He was *petting* it today." I cringe.

"Bandit's a friendly enough little guy. He likes the attention." Dad sounds like he approves of this.

"You guys *do* realize that raccoons carry disease, right?"

Dad waves my concern away. "Nah, he's fine. Jonah's friend is a vet. She gave Bandit his rabies shot. Boy, did they have a time of it. Jonah had to put a sleeping dart into him." He pauses. "'Course, I don't think Marie's supposed to be vaccinating them so, as far as anyone knows . . ." He gives me a look of warning.

"Who am I going to tell?" Besides my mother, and Diana of course.

Dad shifts checker pieces around absently. "What about you? I remember you being pretty set on getting a dog, way back when. Did that ever happen?"

"No. Simon's allergic to pretty much everything on four legs. That's fine, though. I have too much going on in my life anyway. I had a fish one time, though. For Christmas."

He frowns in thought. "You know, I think I remember that."

"His name was Guppy. He was . . . a guppy." I roll my eyes at my childish simplicity. "He lasted a week before he went for the golden flush."

"So . . . no pets."

"No pets." I snort. "Not unless you count Tim and Sid."

My dad's eyebrows arch in question.

"These two neighborhood raccoons that have been terrorizing me for*ever*."

"Terrorizing you," he echoes, amusement flickering in his gaze. "They sound like horrible creatures."

"They *are* horrible! And huge. Twice the size of Bandit. And vicious." Not that they've ever done more than annoy the hell out of me.

"Did you know that raccoons aren't native to Alaska?"

"I did not know that," I say slowly.

"Yes. They were introduced into the state in the 1930s for the fur trade."

"That's . . . fascinating." I can't keep the dryness from my tone, but it earns his soft laughter.

"Truth is, we're more worried about the foxes, as far as rabies goes. Those little buggers are always getting into villages and attacking the dogs. Marie flies in from Anchorage once a month for a few days to run a clinic in Bangor, and Jonah usually takes her out to the villages so she can give rabies shots to the strays. She's a bit of a crusader, that one."

"This Marie person and Jonah sound pretty close, if she's risking trouble to vaccinate Bandit for him," I say casually. "Are they, like, together or something?"

My dad's brow furrows. "No, no . . . they're just friends. As far as I know, anyway. Though Jonah doesn't talk about the girls he's . . . *dating*." He falters over that word, making me think that "dating" wouldn't be the best word he'd use to describe what Jonah does with girls he's interested in. "Of course, Agnes is convinced that Marie would like to be more, but she says that about most girls that come around him."

"I don't get it," I murmur, baffled. Kayley the coffee girl . . . Marie the vet . . . even twelve-year-old Mabel has a crush on the big brute. Though I'm guessing Jonah's a hell of a lot nicer to them than he has been with me, if that flirtatious interaction between him and Kayley is any indication.

But what I *really* don't get is that twinge of *something* I felt when Jonah was ogling Diana in her short skirt. It's been lingering in my stomach ever since. It feels like a shade of disappointment, but it can't possibly be, because I *don't like* Jonah that way. I'm barely tolerating him at this point.

My dad regards me peculiarly for a long moment. "You two still not getting along?"

"I think we might have turned a corner today. He's going to help me build a website for Alaska Wild." Maybe we'll come out on the other end of it as friends.

That, or one of us won't come out on the other end at all.

My dad's eyes widen. "A website?"

By the time I'm finished explaining the reasoning, just as I explained it to Jonah earlier today, my dad's gaze is thoughtful. "Did he ask you to do this?"

"No. I offered."

"And that's what you've been working on all evening?" He nods toward my computer.

"Yeah. I've already got a skeleton set up." I climb off the couch and walk over to set my laptop where the checkers board had been. "We can play with the colors and styles, to make it better, and then all we need to do is add content and pictures."

"I wish I had half your business sense. Would have made running Wild a lot easier." He smiles thoughtfully. "You turned out pretty smart, kiddo."

I feel a flutter of nostalgia in my stomach. I know that nickname isn't reserved solely for me anymore, but it still feels like a connection to oh so long ago.

"Jonah also told me you asked him if he wanted to buy Alaska Wild."

"He told you that, hey?" My dad presses his lips together, his gaze drifting to the matted carpet.

"Was he not supposed to?"

"I guess I didn't tell him not to," he says after a moment. "Of everyone I know, he's the one who'd do right by it. There's been some interest from Aro Airlines to buy me out, but Wild would get swallowed up." He smiles sadly. "Don't know if I'm ready to see that happen yet."

But Jonah says he doesn't have the money anyway, so what option does that leave my dad with?

"He said you were thinking of retiring."

He takes a long, deep breath. "Considering it. It's been a long thirty years. Wouldn't mind taking a bit of a rest." He pauses, and then asks, "You tired?"

"Not really. I had a nap this afternoon." That Benadryl knocked me out. Thankfully, the swelling has not expanded beyond the blue ink lines I drew.

"I've got some movies over there in the cupboard. They're old, but they're some of my favorites."

Is my dad asking me to watch a movie with him in a roundabout way? Is this Wren Fletcher, trying to get to know his daughter again?

"I could go and pick one for us to watch," I say, tentatively.

"Yeah? Well, okay then."

I shut down my laptop and cast it aside, and then head for the corner cabinet.

But not before catching the small smile of satisfaction touching my dad's lips.

Chapter 13

■ ■ ■

I stir to the distant sound of someone knocking.

A moment later, the knock sounds again, only it's more like pounding.

And it's on my bedroom door.

I push off my eye mask and squint against the glow of sunlight from around the edge of the curtains. "Yeah?" I call out, my voice hoarse with sleep.

There's no answer, only more knocking. It's an urgent sound, and it puts me on edge.

I wrestle with my covers to free myself and stumble for the door, throwing it open.

Jonah is filling the doorway.

"What's wrong? Is my dad okay?" I ask in a panic, searching the hall for any signs of him.

He stares hard at me for a long moment, his gaze skating over my features.

"Jonah?"

He blinks several times. "So *this* is what you look like, without all that shit on your face."

I sigh with exasperation. "I'm not in the mood for your crap this early. What do you want? Where's my dad?"

Jonah's eyes drop to my chest, reminding me that I'm in a cotton tank top, braless. And the air is crisp.

I fold my arms across myself reflexively, even as a strange shiver dances along my skin.

His gaze snaps up. "He had to fly to Anchorage. I thought you'd be up."

I study those glacier-blue irises for a moment. They look somehow darker. Heated. Is he . . . turned on? "We stayed up late to watch a movie and then I couldn't fall asleep. What time is it, anyway?"

"Seven. Get dressed. You're flying today."

That pulls me out of whatever fog I'm trapped in. "I'm *what*?"

"It's a clear day and your dad wants you to see more of Alaska. You've been here three days already. It's time you get in a plane."

"With *you*?" I say doubtfully.

He smirks. "Come on. You can get some pictures for Wild's website. You said you wanted to do that, right?"

Anxiety is quickly rising in my belly like a twirling windstorm at the thought of getting into a plane—with Jonah—again. But with it is a strange sense of excitement. Besides, I don't want to spend the day sitting around, looking for ways to kill time until my dad comes home. "Fine. Give me an hour."

He barks out a laugh. "You have five minutes."

"Yeah, right. I can't get ready in five minutes. I'm not *you*."

I get a flat look in return. "You're in Alaska. Throw on some clothes, brush your teeth, and let's go."

"Half an hour." If I skip showering and rush my makeup, I can do that.

"Five minutes."

"Twenty," I barter.

His normally icy gaze slides over my mouth, my throat, my chest, and farther, before coming back up to meet my eyes. His hard swallow fills the silence. "You don't need all that to look good, Calla. Seriously."

My words falter. Was that a compliment?

From *Jonah*?

And why is this heated gaze I'm seeing not making me uncomfortable?

Why does it seem to be doing the exact opposite, sending a

small thrill through me? Am I . . . ? No, even if the top half of his face is attractive and his body is impressive, I *can't* be attracted to him. I can't get past the yeti hair.

But something about the look in Jonah's eyes is arousing my curiosity.

"Fifteen minutes," I say, clearing the wobble from my voice.

"If you're not out in *five,* I will come in here, throw you over my shoulder, and carry you out."

"You will not."

He gives me a wicked smile in return, one that makes my blood start to flow. "Try me. And just know, I won't care if you're not dressed." He pushes a few buttons on his watch.

"Did you just start a *timer* for me?"

"Five minutes. I'll be waiting in the truck."

I glower at his retreating back.

"Tick tock!"

"Asshole." With a huff, I dive for my jeans.

■ ■ ■

"Are you *trying* to hit every last crack in the pavement?" I snap, glaring at my own reflection in the vanity mirror as I attempt to apply a second coat of mascara to my eyelashes.

"You're in the Alaskan bush. Stop with all that," he mutters, but slows a touch. Still, the ground is too bumpy for a steady hand.

I give up on a second coat, cap my mascara, and throw it into my purse. "Why does everyone keep calling it 'the bush' anyway? 'The bush' means dense forest where I'm from. There's no forest here. There're barely any trees. *No* bush." I add quietly, "Besides the one on your face."

"Aren't we a bit plucky this morning." He sounds amused.

I slide my sunglasses on to block the blinding sun, a welcome change from the drizzle but not when it's shining directly into my eyes. "If you don't like it, next time don't drag me out of my bed and chase me out the door." I'm never in good spirits when I'm forced to rush in the morning.

"I gave you an extra three minutes."

"You're too kind." I reach for the travel mug of coffee I managed to fill before Jonah plowed into the kitchen, his watch alarm dinging. "I don't know how you keep all the women around here from beating down your door."

His soft chuckle sends a warm shiver down my spine. I *hate* that he has an appealing laugh. "Glad to see that you have a little fire in you, after all."

"I guess you bring out the best in me," I mutter. I'm not normally like this. It's as if I'm itching for a fight.

He takes the next right turn too quickly and coffee splashes onto my white cotton T-shirt.

"Dammit!" I brush it away, but it's no use.

"Relax. It's *just* a T-shirt."

"It cost me a hundred bucks."

"You paid a *hundred bucks* for that?" Jonah's eyebrows tighten as he looks at me with a clear "you're an idiot" expression.

"What! It wears well and still looks new after fifty washes."

"For a hundred bucks, I sure as shit hope it washes itself."

"Are you saying that your *high-quality* clothing from the local grocery store doesn't?" I cast a cutting look at his shirt, which, despite being basic, looks nice on him.

He smirks. "Have you been enjoying your soy milk these last couple mornings?"

Crap. I completely forgot. And of course he'd bring that up after I delivered a low blow, just to make me feel extra small. He doesn't fight fair. "Thank you for that." I hesitate. "That was nice of you."

"I didn't do it for you. I did it for everyone who has to be around you."

I grit my teeth to stop from responding and turn my body away from him, focusing on the airport ahead.

So much for our truce.

■ ■ ■

Agnes's sharp eyes shift from me, to Jonah, to me, the curiosity shining in them. "Two go out, two come back, right?"

"She needs me to fly, so she can't do away with me." Jonah accepts a small ambulance-red case with a strap from Sonny and hoists it into the back of the orange-and-white plane. "At least, not until we get back."

Thank God this plane is bigger, I note, eying the two seats side by side in the front, and another row behind. The seat material is a deep burgundy that clashes terribly with the orange stripe on the exterior. Not that color coordination matters to me. I just want this thing to stay in the air.

"Here. You'll need that." Jonah tosses a thin-knit black hoodie to me.

Agnes studies my face as I tug it on. "You look different today, Calla."

"That's because Jonah barely gave me time to pee, let alone put makeup on." I feel naked and self-conscious. I can't remember the last time I went out in public bare-faced. I don't even go to the gym without my eyes done.

Agnes smiles warmly. "I like the barely-time-to-pee look. It suits you."

I yank the zipper closed and roll up the long sleeves that reach an inch past my fingertips. It's far too big for me, but I'm not drowning in it as badly as I'd expect, given it's Jonah's. And I can tell it's Jonah's because it smells like him, like woodsy soap and minty *something*. "Do you think I'll get my clothes today?"

"Yes, definitely. Your dad is bringing your suitcases back with him."

"Oh, thank God. I can't wait to have my rubber boots." I peer down at my dusty running shoes. Ruined.

"All set?" Jonah asks, looming beside me. There's an odd energy about him that I haven't felt before. Is he always like this when he's about to fly?

I didn't feel it yesterday.

"Where are we going, anyway?"

"Would it mean anything if I told you?"

"No," I admit. "But is it in the mountains?" Because after my first experience, plus that story about Mabel's father, I'm out if mountains are involved.

"Nope." Jonah lifts his baseball cap to smooth his scraggly mop of hair back, before sliding the cap back on. "Hey, Aggie, did George leave for Holy Cross already?"

"Still waiting on a package. He'll take off as soon as it shows up."

"And the supply run to St. Mary's?"

"Joe's probably landing right about now."

"Good. Finally. Those guys have been waiting weeks for that ammunition ahead of the coming hunt," he murmurs.

Despite my annoyance with him, I can't help but admire the guy, seeing firsthand how in-tune Jonah is to Wild's day-to-day operations. I can see why my dad relies on him so much. And why he'd think Jonah would be a suitable fit to keep the family business—that's been the Fletchers' lifeblood for decades—alive. And how critical Jonah's help is going to be in the coming months, and years.

"Okay, then. We're set."

Where my stomach was tight before, now it begins to twist and turn with an odd mix of dread and excitement as I watch Jonah climb into the plane and slide on his headset.

"Have fun, Calla!" Agnes begins backing away.

Sonny is waiting for me with one hand on the door, anxious to close it. Orange sticks dangle from his free fingers.

I climb into my seat. It's not nearly as crammed in here as it was in the Super Cub, but it's far from roomy, which means Jonah's arm is pressed against mine from shoulder to elbow and will be for as long as we're in here. There's no way around that with a pilot his size, I accept, and so I try to focus my thoughts on the front of the plane instead. It's nothing but a panel of dials and switches and levers, with carved-out space on either side for our legs. Jonah's fingers smoothly flick and press and pull over the panel with the expertise of someone who has done this a thousand times over.

A low rumble erupts from the engine of the plane and the propeller rotates once . . . twice . . . before the individual blades blur.

Jonah wordlessly holds a headset out for me. I accept it, acutely aware of how our fingers graze in the process.

Even if I am not attracted to him.

Even if I still want to punch him in the face.

"Can you hear me?" His deep voice rumbles in my ear.

"Yes. How *old* is this plane?" Because it looks like one of those cars from the movie *Grease,* with the quilted sides and the big metal handles to wind down the window in the door.

"Older than both of us."

"Oh, *great.*" Cars half my age fall apart on the road and I'm supposed to trust this hunk of metal in the air?

"Don't touch the yoke."

"The what?"

His muscular arm bumps me as he reaches out to tap the black thing in front of me that reminds me of an oversized arcade game controller. It's identical to the one in front of him. "Or the pedals on the floor. Those control the rudders."

I don't even know what rudders are. More importantly, "Where's the barf bag?"

"You won't need it."

"My one experience flying with you says otherwise."

"You're not gonna get sick."

"You can't just *will* me not to. *Where* is it?"

He shakes his head and sighs heavily. "Under your seat."

While Jonah signals in to the airport's air traffic controller, I reach below and search, until my fingertips catch the soft paper edge. I pull it out and tuck it into a narrow holder on the side of the door.

"Relax, there's no need to be scared," Jonah warns into my ear as the plane begins to roll forward.

I don't bother answering, instead focusing on Sonny as he strolls alongside us, waving those orange sticks. The plane bumps and jolts over the cracks in the pavement, bringing back an odd and dreaded sense of déjà vu.

I tug on my seat belt to tighten it, peering around at the small army of my father's planes, some being loaded by busy grounds crew workers, others awaiting small clusters of tourists. I can't tell if the runway ahead of us seems narrow and short against the wide expanse of flat land that surrounds us, or if it's because the runway is in fact narrow and short.

"I don't know how you can be Wren's daughter and freak out this much in a small plane."

"Because my first time in a small plane was a horrendous experience with a horrible, *mean* pilot," I throw back.

His chest heaves. "Look, it was a shitty thing for me to do and I'm sorry."

We've reached the end of Wild's runway. I turn to meet his icy blue eyes and find rare sincerity in them. "Why'd you do it, then?"

"I don't know. I guess I wanted to see what Wren Fletcher's daughter was made of."

"What I'm *made of*?" I snort. "Well, you came close to seeing what my stomach contents were made of."

"Yeah, that wasn't part of my plan." His brow furrows tightly. "I saw all those pictures of you and figured you were one of those uppity city chicks that I can't stand."

I frown. "What pictures?"

"I don't know. The ones Mabel showed me on her phone."

He must be talking about my Instagram account. "What's wrong with those pictures?"

"Nothing. Just, when girls look like you do . . ." He shakes his head. "I guess I wanted to knock you down a few pegs from the get-go."

Like I do. Like a Barbie doll, according to him. "So what? I'm not an uppity city chick that you can't stand anymore?"

"You're definitely uppity." His lips twist with a wry smile. "But you're alright." He radios in to the air control tower while that strange mix of fear and thrill swirls inside.

We wait in silence for the approval to take off.

"So, I was your first time?" Jonah murmurs mildly.

"What?"

"That's what you just said. I was your first time."

It clicks and I roll my eyes, even as my cheeks flush. "Yes, and you were subpar. You should be embarrassed."

His deep chuckle reverberates in my chest.

Air control calls in, giving him the all-clear message.

"If I die today, I'm going to kill you." I clench my thighs against the sudden urge to pee.

"That would take talent," he murmurs, his strong hands gripping the yoke.

"Seriously, though, where are you taking me?"

He flicks a few more switches. "I'm going to show you that Wild is about a hell of a lot more than making a buck," he says, echoing the bitter words I'd spoken only days ago, next to the Meyer's cashier.

I hold my breath as the plane begins to accelerate.

Chapter 14

I gape at the expanse of deep blue and rich green below. "I've never seen so many lakes before!" Countless oddly shape bodies of water are scattered as far as I can see. So many that I can't tell if the land is interspersed with water or if the water is interspersed with land.

And in the center of it all is a colony of rectangular buildings, their roofs a vibrant collection of reds, greens, and blues.

"This is all part of the Yukon-Kuskokwim Delta. Ahead of us is the Bering Sea," Jonah explains, his deep voice filling my ears.

I aim Simon's Canon and attempt to capture a few pictures of the breathtaking landscape. The glare from the sun bouncing off the glass makes it challenging.

"How are you feeling?"

"Fine. This is definitely a better plane. Am I yelling, though?"

He grins, flashing that perfect, white-toothed smile. "Nah, you're good." His hawkish eyes rove the skies around us. "It's a great day for flying. Not as much wind as normal."

"Plus you're so much better than that *last* asshole pilot I had." I struggle to keep a straight face as I snap pictures of the colorful town, feeling his gaze on my profile. Waiting for his clever response.

"That's Kwigillingok, where we're going," he says instead.

"It feels like we just took off."

"It's only a thirteen-minute flight. Most of the trips to the villages are that short. Even getting all the way up to Barrow takes less than two hours from us and that's Alaska's northernmost point." Jonah tips the plane to the right and I feel a surge of butterflies in my stomach.

Though, I'll admit, it's not nearly as terrifying as it once was.

■ ■ ■

While the view may be picturesque from above, the reality down below is another story.

I finally find my breath and my tongue again. "Are *all* the village airports like this?" If you can even call this place an airport. Because if they are, I have no interest in seeing more of Alaska.

"Nah. This is one of the most dangerous ones," Jonah says casually, seemingly unfazed by the jerks and bumps of the plane as he steers us along a narrow, uneven gravel road with water on both sides. We basically just landed on a patch of an island.

"And you thought it'd be a *great* idea to bring me with you?"

"Baptism by fire."

"I've already been baptized, thanks." Not that I've been to church in two decades. I take a calming breath. "I thought we were going to skid into the water."

Jonah smirks, pulling off his headset as we finally come to a stop not far from a windowless cerulean-blue shed where two people linger, an ATV beside them. He flicks a series of switches that brings the propeller to a slow halt and cuts the engine. "Maybe you would have with another pilot. But I'm *that good*."

And that cocky.

Unfastening his seat belt, he stretches his body to reach behind my seat, his solid chest pressing against my shoulder as he wrestles to unsecure something. I can smell the mint on his breath. It makes me press my lips together with worry that my breath isn't nearly as fresh.

The two people are walking toward our plane. They're clad much like everyone else I've seen in Alaska so far—layers of casual flannel and cotton on top, jeans, and boots.

"Why are we here, again?"

"To drop off a portable ventilator." Finally he heaves out the red case by one arm. I'm forced to shift away so as not to get knocked in the head by it. "Come on. Time to meet one of Wild's customers." Throwing open his door, he deftly slips out.

I'm not nearly as graceful in my descent, losing my footing and stumbling on my way down. By the time I round the plane, Jonah's already handing over the case.

". . . with all the sand kicking up in the wind, the past couple days," the woman says. "At least today's not so bad." She's a middle-aged Alaska Native woman with a kind face and sooty-black hair tied in a ponytail. She has a slight accent that is similar to my dad's, and Agnes's and Michael's, and pretty much every other person I've met who has lived in Alaska their whole life. It reminds me of a girl from university, who grew up almost eight hours away in Sault Ste. Marie. She had a distinctive way of saying things. Vowels sounded longer, certain consonants were left off. In general, she didn't rush her words. Even though the dialects aren't the same, there's a distinctively "northern" sound.

"This should help her out. I'm sorry it took so long to get here." Jonah does his hair-hat-smoothing thing. I wonder if his hat actually needs adjusting, or if it's an unconscious move.

"These new ones are so much smaller." The woman marvels at the case in her hand. "Evelyn said you harassed Anchorage until they gave it up?"

"They were telling her next week and that's bullshit. They had this one sitting in a storeroom, just in case."

"You're a lifesaver, Jonah." The woman's curious gaze shifts to me.

"Enid, this is Calla, Wren's daughter. She's visiting from Toronto. I'm showing her what we do."

The woman's face melts with a smile. "Everyone around here knows your dad. And Jonah." She nods at him. "They always help. It costs, but they help."

"Keeping planes in the air isn't cheap," Jonah says in a lecturing tone.

She waves it away with a gentle chuckle. "I know, I know. I'm teasing. You guys are the best, though. I can always count on you."

"We're gonna head out. You get that ventilator to the little girl right away and call the office if you need anything else," Jonah says, already taking steps backward.

"Tell Wren to visit soon. I'll have some red seaweed for him," Enid calls out.

I smile and, with a small wave, we begin our trek back to our plane.

"Red seaweed?"

"They eat a lot of it here."

"Does my dad—"

"*Hates* it, but you *never* turn down food from a villager. They hunt and gather *everything* they eat. It's a lot of work, and it's a big deal when they offer it to you."

"Is Enid the doctor?"

"Nah. She's kind of like a nurse. She's been trained to give basic care and she reports in to the doctors in Bangor regularly. Sometimes we'll fly a doctor out to run a clinic and see the villagers."

"So if someone needs to get to the hospital—"

"Medevac for emergencies, otherwise they call us. We've picked up people in some serious pain before." His tone turns somber. "Those flights always feel five times as long."

But I'll bet Jonah never balks at doing them. He may be an ass, but he seems to be an ass with a drive for helping others.

"What's wrong with the little girl?"

"Severe asthma, and her inhaler hasn't been helping much lately. She needs the ventilator and the one they had—a dinosaur, from the sounds of it—quit last week. Now, at least the poor kid will be able to breathe again." He sighs, and in that simple sound I sense great relief.

"Why would her family live all the way out here if she's got medical problems? If I were them, I'd move to Bangor."

He steals a glance my way, the frown on his forehead deep. "Because her family has lived here for hundreds of years. This is their home. This is what they know. This is how they want to live." He says it so matter-of-factly, as if there's no other explanation and there's no need to elaborate.

"I don't get it."

"You don't have to; you just have to respect it."

Now *I'm* the one getting lectured by Jonah. Another thought strikes me. "Is this why you rushed me out the door this morning?"

"Do you mean, was this little girl's ability to breathe more important than your vanity?"

I roll my eyes, taking that as confirmation. "You could have told me. Then I wouldn't have assumed you were just being your usual dick self."

"Where's the fun in that?" He opens my door and holds it for me.

"So you *do* have manners," I murmur, climbing into my seat.

"I usually reserve them for ladies, but I'll make an exception in this case," he throws back without missing a beat, slamming my door shut before I have a chance to retort.

"Bastard," I mutter, biting my bottom lip against the smile that threatens to form. His cutting quips don't come with the same sting they did in the beginning, though.

I actually think I'm beginning to enjoy this banter.

I wait for him as he does two slow circles around the plane, his callused fingers smoothing over the metal body, his brow furrowed in intense scrutiny. Finally, he climbs in.

"Is there something wrong with the plane?"

"No cracks, no leaks. We're good."

"So . . . Where to next?" I ask, as he starts flicking switches again.

"You mean you're not bailing on me yet?" He says it in a joking tone, but I sense a degree of doubt.

"Do you *want* me to bail?" Has he reached his limit of having me for a passenger?

There's a long pause. "No. I don't."

"Well, good then. Just don't go into the water, okay?"

He grins, sliding on his headset. "If you thought landing here was exciting, wait till we take off."

■ ■ ■

Jonah cuts the engine. After a day of listening to its near-constant roar, the ensuing silence is all the more serene.

Pushing off my headset, I sink back into my seat and gaze over the Alaska Wild buildings. The sun is still high in the sky, even though it's after eight at night. My head throbs from weariness and overstimulation, and lack of food. All I've had today is an apple, a banana, and a handful of crackers that Agnes offered me during one of our returns to base.

"So . . ." Jonah sighs. "Just making a buck, right?"

If he's on a mission to make me eat my words today, he's succeeding brilliantly. It was a long and tiring day of teeth-gritting landings on bumpy airstrips that are nothing more than short dirt roads, isolated by thousands of miles of mostly uninhabited land in every direction. Almost every trip today was to meet villagers to hand off essential supplies that had been ordered weeks before. Jonah knew all of them by name. He'd joke with them and apologize for the wait. They'd thank him for coming, even though most of them had been waiting by those airstrips for hours. One of them on and off for days, thanks to a heavy fog that kept pilots from being able to land there.

And all I kept thinking about as I smiled at that guy was how many times I've ordered makeup or clothes online, only to feel utterly disappointed when I arrive home from work and find it not delivered. And my mother, who dropped her phone in the sink that one time and ordered a new one for next-day delivery. She lingered at home, anxiously waiting. Her package finally arrived just as I was coming home from work, and so I had the pleasure of witnessing her dress-down of the deliveryman firsthand—how she's lost an entire day of her life, how a phone carrier should understand how vital a phone is to society, how the mail carrier company needs to upgrade their system to give smaller, more accurate delivery windows, how they don't value their customers' time and she deserves compensation for her hours of work lost—all while the man in uniform waited with forced patience and a glazed look for her to sign for it. As if he was so used to people yelling at him over seemingly important packages that it all just slid off his back. And I'll bet it happens all the time.

My mother, who would never be described as patient, berated a complete stranger about a cell phone—that arrived the day it was supposed to; meanwhile, this villager was cheerily catching up with Jonah, showing him pictures of the huskies he was training for some big dogsled race, the penicillin that he'd waited days in this field for, that the village clinic had waited *weeks* for, sitting by his feet.

I'm not surprised my mother didn't adapt well here.

And I'm beginning to see how Jonah would take one look at me—the twenty-six-year-old girl who showed up in wedge heels and a Brixton hat, her two giant suitcases in tow—and want to set me straight.

"Just making a buck *and* delivering pizza," I correct, jokingly.

"Right." He chuckles. "But did you see how that kid's face lit up?"

"The happiest little birthday boy I've ever seen."

He shakes his head. "And you almost ruined it."

I let out a groan. "That would have been *your* fault."

He shoots me a look of bewilderment and I can't help but start to laugh. "Why would I believe you?" When a cab pulled up and handed Jonah two pizza boxes from Gigi's earlier today, I assumed that lunch was being delivered. And then, when Jonah said we were taking it to a village for a little boy's sixth birthday along with some other cargo, I assumed he was messing with me.

I was reaching for the crust to rip off a piece and peel off the cheese—starved—when he hollered and snatched the box away.

Thank God, because the mother and the little boy were waiting for us by the airstrip when we arrived at the village of three hundred, the boy's eyes wide with glee and anticipation. His mom explained how, ever since the village teacher—a woman from Chicago—told the class about the popular food staple last year, all he's wanted for his birthday was a pizza party.

Speaking of pizza . . . "I'm hungry." And exhausted.

"Yeah, me, too. Good thing we're calling it a day." Jonah sighs and unbuckles his seat belt. But doesn't make to get out just yet. His mouth opens, and I sense him wanting to say something, and then changing his mind. We're left in awkward silence.

"Hey, thanks for taking me out. And not crashing," I offer, hoping to break up the sudden, odd tension. "I had fun." And, even more important, I'm starting to get a sense about how integral Alaska Wild is to so many people; how many villages rely on my dad and Jonah, and the other pilots, to bring them what they need to survive.

And to think my dad's had the weight of that on his shoulders since he was in his early twenties.

Meanwhile, I'm twenty-six and I don't even want the responsibility of keeping a pet alive.

Jonah's gaze flickers to me for a moment before it drifts out his side window. "Thank your dad. He made me take you."

"Sure he did," I murmur as Jonah slips out of the plane. Why can't he just admit that he enjoyed today, too?

My dad and Agnes are strolling toward the plane when I step out.

"So? Where'd you guys end up?" my dad asks, his curious gaze shifting between us.

"Calla?" Jonah prompts.

Suddenly I feel nine years old again, coming home to the painful "what'd you learn in school today" interrogation. Except back then my answers were reluctant and amounted to "stuff," and now I'm listing off village names I can't pronounce and passing on well-wishes from the people I met.

"I take it you got some pictures?" He nods toward Simon's Canon.

"Until the battery died on me halfway through."

"You'll have to go out with Jonah again tomorrow, then," Agnes says casually, a tiny, amused smirk touching her lips.

I'm just about to say "Sure!" when Jonah's hands go up in surrender.

"I've done my penance. We've got plenty of pilots around here."

I feel my face fall unexpectedly and my stomach sink.

"Seriously, Wren. She might be the worst passenger I've ever had. You should be embarrassed."

My jaw drops. "Hey! I was a *great* passenger!"

That hard expression finally cracks with his smile.

He's joking, I realize. Relief washes over me.

Followed by a wave of confusion. Why am I relieved? Why do I even care if Jonah wants to take me out again?

Because even though I spent a good portion of it gripping my seat and saying small prayers under my breath every time we took off or landed, it was a terrifying and exhilarating day like nothing I've ever experienced before, that's why.

A day I can't describe. A day I'll probably remember for the rest of my life.

And the fact that I was with Jonah probably played a part in that.

Sure, he's rough around the edges. He can be too brash and too blunt and too outspoken. In fact, he sorely needs to learn how *not* to speak his mind just because it suits him. But he can also be playfully witty and thoughtful. And no matter how hard he tries, he hasn't been able to hide the fact that he cares about these people.

"Hey, did Bart find anything wrong with Betsy?" Jonah asks, doing his hat-hand-hair move.

My dad shakes his head. "Said he's gone back and forth over her twice and can't find anything. Starting to think it's all in George's imagination, which is totally possible. The guy's still convinced that bird flew into his propeller because Bobbie didn't sew up the hole in his lucky socks."

"And that he hit that stump and snapped off his landing gear because of that black cat on his front step," Jonah adds.

"George is a bit superstitious," Agnes explains to me in an exaggerated whisper.

"I don't think I blame him." *Birds in propellers? Snapping off landing gear?* I'm glad we didn't start the day off with these stories.

"We can't afford to have her sitting in the hangar any longer than she needs to be, especially not with that big weather system coming in. We could be grounded all weekend," my dad says.

"All weekend?" I echo. "Will I be able to get to Anchorage for my flight on Sunday?"

"Might not," he admits and then adds slowly, "If you're worried about it, Jonah could fly you to Anchorage on Friday morning. The rain isn't supposed to start until that night. You could spend a couple days in the city." His eyebrows squeeze together. "That might be a bit more your style anyway."

"Friday *morning*." That means I'd have only one day left here. One day left with my father.

"Just to be sure you make that Sunday flight home." His gray eyes shift to the ground, as if searching for something in the potholes.

Is he feeling what I'm feeling?

That I just got here and I'm not ready to say goodbye yet?

I *could* stay, I remind myself. But why won't my dad just ask me to stay longer, then?

Other than the obvious answer—that he doesn't want me here.

I hush the insecure little girl's voice in my mind and search for another reason.

Maybe he thinks I *want* to leave. Maybe he doesn't want to say anything and make me feel obligated. Just like he never asked my mother to stay.

I feel Jonah's heavy gaze on me. As if able to read the swirl of conflicting thoughts in my mind, he gives me a wide-eyed "you know what you have to do" nod.

I hesitate. "*Or* I could just move my flight out to next weekend."

My dad's eyebrows arch as he studies me. "Is that something you'd want to do?"

"I mean, if you're okay with having me stay at your house longer. I know you're starting treatment on—"

"It's okay with me," he answers quickly, following it up with a smile and, if I'm not mistaken, a sigh of relief. "It's your home, too. Here, in Alaska."

"Okay. I'll stay a bit longer, then." Am I making the right decision?

Agnes is beaming and Jonah gives me a tight-lipped nod, and it makes me think that I am.

The wind has picked up since earlier and it sweeps past us then, rustling my hair and sending a shiver through me, reminding me that I don't have my warm clothes. "Did you get my bags, by the way?"

"Yeah. About that . . ." My dad's face pinches. "When Billy went into the storage room to grab your suitcases, he couldn't find them."

And just like that, the happy little bubble that had been growing around me bursts.

"What do you mean, 'couldn't find them.' They *lost* them?" My clothes . . . my shoes . . .

"With all the delays and shuffling back and forth, they probably just got shoved somewhere. I'm sure they'll turn up soon."

"And if not?" My voice has turned shrill.

My dad frowns in thought. "Insurance usually covers a couple hundred bucks. You got insurance, didn't you?"

"Yeah, it'll replace maybe a sweater and a pair of heels," I mutter. My exhilarating day has just taken a nosedive into the ground. "I've been wearing two pairs of jeans since I got here. How am I supposed to manage even longer?"

Jonah, who's been quiet this entire time, offers with faint amusement in his voice, "I'll be more than happy to take you to Meyer's to grab a few things."

I stab the air in front of him with my finger. "This is *your* fault. If you took the bigger plane in the first place, my luggage wouldn't be lost."

"If you'd packed for a week instead of a year, we wouldn't have had to leave your things behind," he retorts smoothly.

"Hey, you admitted to being a jackass about that whole thing earlier!" Why is he changing his tune again?

"Give it a day or two," Agnes says calmly, the ever-gentle referee stepping into a feud between opposing teams. "These things happen, but they have a way of working out."

I grit my teeth against the urge to call bullshit. I know she's only trying to help.

My dad sighs. "Come on, kiddo. Let's go home."

Chapter 15

■ ■ ■

When Jonah strolls through my dad's door the next morning, I've already gone for my run, showered, dressed, and am filling half a travel mug with coffee while scrolling through my Instagram feed. To my delight, I woke up to a slew of new followers and comments, thanks to the aerial shot above one of the villages that I posted last night, along with a quick story about the little boy with the pizza and a recap of the terrifying landing, which people seemed to find amusing. "So where are we going today?" I ask, pushing aside thoughts about our little spat last night over my luggage.

Jonah sidles in next to me, smoothly lifting the pot without hesitation, his callused hand—nearly twice the size of mine—momentarily grasping mine in the process.

My heart stutters.

"I'm taking a group of hikers and their guide into the interior." His voice sounds especially deep, cutting into the stillness of the house. "There aren't any extra seats."

"Oh." I frown, a wave of disappointment hitting me. I thought he was joking yesterday about doing his "penance" by taking me out for the day. But maybe there was some truth to it.

I focus on filling the other half of my mug with soy milk.

"Did you want some coffee with that?"

"I don't like the taste of coffee. That's why I always drink lattes at home." I tell him about Simon's Cadillac of barista machines.

He eases the pot back onto the burner and shuts the machine off. "Sounds like you've got a decent stepdad."

"Yeah. He's been pretty great to me and my mom." When I

texted home last night to tell them that I'd decided to stay, Simon sent me his credit card number in case the airline charged me. And then he told me that I was doing the right thing and he was proud of me.

"My stepdad's a dick," Jonah murmurs. "Then again, so was my dad."

I steal a glance as he takes a sip from his mug, squinting against the bright sun as his gaze drifts to the yawning fields beyond the window. He's opened a door for me, just a sliver. I prod through gently. "So your parents were divorced, too?"

"Yup. My dad was a selfish jerk who didn't treat my mom right. Look, I've got a supply drop for a camp this afternoon, if you want to come out with me then."

"Okay!" I say, a little too quickly, too eagerly. "Maybe I'll come in to the office this morning anyway. I can work on the website some more. Download the pictures I took yesterday." I didn't get much of anything done last night, the excitement from the day catching up with me as I listened to Mabel trash-talk my dad before beating him at checkers for the fifteenth day in a row. I can't figure out if he's letting her win or not.

Jonah doesn't seem to be in as much of a rush as usual, wandering aimlessly through the kitchen, his mug to his mouth. Eventually he pauses in front of the small kitchen table, his eyes roaming over the wallpaper.

"Do you know who drew the nipples on those ducks?" I keep forgetting to ask my dad.

"Drew *what*?"

"Nipples. On those ducks."

He frowns at the wall. "What are you talking about?"

"Those!" I close the distance and lean over the table, tapping the wall with the tip of my fingernail. "See? *Nipples*. There . . . There . . . Someone drew nipples on *every* last one of these ducks."

"Say it again for me?"

"What?" Frowning, I turn to find him struggling not to laugh. It finally dawns on me that he knew what I was talking about all along. "Oh, shut up. You are *so* immature."

He peers down at me, his gaze crawling over my eyes, my cheeks, my mouth. "You looked better yesterday, by the way. Without all that crap on your face."

I feel my cheeks flush with a mix of embarrassment and anger. "You look the same as yesterday, with all *that* crap on your face."

He reaches up to drag his fingers through his beard. "What's wrong with this?"

"Nothing, if you're planning on living alone in the mountains and foraging for food. And not walking quite upright."

"So you're saying you don't like it." There's no mistaking the amusement in his voice.

"Definitely not."

He shrugs. "A lot of women like it."

"No they don't."

"It's my style."

"No. Hipster is a style. Rockabilly is a style. *Yeti* is *not* a style." I search the mass of wiry hairs for what might be hidden beneath—a hard jaw, cutting cheekbones—but it's impossible to find. "I have *no* idea what you look like under all that."

He pauses in thought. "And that's important to you? Knowing what I look like?"

"No! It's just . . . why wouldn't you want . . ." I stumble over my words, my cheeks heating. Why am I so curious—and hopeful that there's a handsome face buried beneath that?

The corners of Jonah's eyes crinkle with his chuckle. "Come on, Calla. Time to get to work."

■ ■ ■

THE SLEEPY CUSTOMER lobby of Wild is gone, replaced instead by a crowd of backpack-clad bodies and a low buzz of excited voices, plus a wailing newborn baby.

"The bears haven't gotten you yet?" Jonah smiles and reaches toward the tall, slender guy in the army-green jacket holding a clipboard.

"Not yet. Good day for flying, hey?" They clasp hands and jump into easy conversation. I'm guessing this is the group Jonah is taking out and that he knows this guide well.

I make my way toward the back, where a plump, dark-haired receptionist behind the desk gives me a knowing wave while holding a phone receiver to her ear. I'm guessing that's Maxine.

I mouth a hello to Sharon, who has commandeered a young Alaska Native woman's mewling baby and is pacing and rocking and shushing the child cradled within her arms. A tall, handsome blond guy with a brush cut stands next to her, his arm casually settled around her shoulders as he watches Sharon with an adoring gaze. That *must* be Max. Meanwhile, the new mother looks on, a duffel bag by her feet, the heavy bags under her eyes evidence of her sleepless nights.

The noise cuts considerably the moment I push past the door and into the back office. ". . . move this delivery to the afternoon and send Jean up there to get her," my dad is saying, hovering over a giant paper map that's stretched out across a desk with Agnes, both with reading glasses perched on their noses. An older man with a handlebar mustache and a small potbelly stands with them. I recognize him as the one standing next to Betty in the hangar the other day.

Dad looks up and his frown of concentration fades instantly. "Morning, Calla."

Agnes flashes her typical wide smile. "George, this is Wren's daughter."

"Hey there." The man seizes my hand. His is large and sweaty. "It's good to finally meet you. My wife said you came through the other day, with Jonah. At first she thought he'd gone and gotten himself a beautiful girlfriend."

The pieces click. "Your wife works at Meyer's."

"Yeah. That's Bobbie." He chuckles. She was ready to throw a party!" He has a heavy Midwestern American accent. "So, how are you likin' Alaska so far?"

"It's great. Different, but great," I admit.

He belts out a laugh. "Sure is. There ain't nothin' like it out there."

"So? What have you got planned for today?" My dad eyes the laptop poking out of my purse.

"Not much, really. Jonah said he doesn't have room in the plane to take me out this morning, but he can take me out this afternoon."

"Why don't you go out with your old man! Hey? You can take a quick break, can't you?" George slaps my dad on the shoulder with another barking laugh. "Maybe convince her to take up the family tradition."

My dad chuckles, but even I can hear the strain in the sound. Agnes said he's only doing solo flights to ease the guilt that he shouldn't be flying at all. "Yeah, I'd like that, but I've gotta focus on this schedule right now and work in this surprise trip. And figure out what we're gonna do with all the weekend flights ahead of the storm, and . . ." The excuses tumble out of him like poorly cast die, the truth gripped tightly within his palm.

"And I want to get this website up and running for you guys, stat," I add.

"You're more than welcome to park yourself over there." Agnes points to the desk that James the bookkeeper was at the other day.

"Great. Thanks." I wander over to set myself up as they refocus their attention on the map.

A thought strikes me. "Hey, Dad . . ."

He falters. "Yeah, kiddo?"

And my breath catches, as it dawns on me that it's the first time I've called out to him like that in years. He must have realized it, too.

"Um . . ." It takes me a moment to regain my thought. "I was thinking, if there's room, you should come with me and Jonah later." That would solve any worries he has about piloting and I'd get to fly with him.

"Why'd I hear my name?" Jonah plows through the door then, interrupting an answer. "What's she saying about me now?"

"She was just marveling at how you're such a strapping young lad." George grins and then winks at me. It seems like Bobbie isn't the only one on a hunt for a girlfriend for Jonah.

"Funny, she told me I looked like a yeti earlier," he mutters, lifting a binder off the table, his penetrating gaze scanning it.

Agnes, mid-sip on coffee, snorts and breaks off in a coughing fit. My dad delivers a few whacks against her back to help it clear, himself chuckling.

"Jim's flying Betty to bring that girl and her baby home?" Jonah frowns. "I don't know, Wren."

Dad shrugs. "What do you want me to do? I've got a good mechanic with thirty-five years' experience saying she's good to go. We've gotta trust him, Jonah. Every other plane is in the air today and the poor girl just wants to get home to her husband and family. She's been stuck in Bangor for over a month."

Jonah turns to George, whose expression has gone sheepish.

"I forgot Jillian that day. I guess it threw me off."

"Who's Jillian?" I whisper to Agnes.

"This is Jillian." George pulls out a little hula-girl figurine from his pocket, the kind you affix to your car's dash that sways back and forth with the movement. "My first Wild passenger gave her to me and I've had her with me on every flight ever since. Except that one. It was the first time. Like I said, it threw me off."

"Yeah . . . maybe." But Jonah doesn't sound convinced. His frown is severe as he studies for another minute what I assume is the day's schedule, before tossing the binder back onto the desk. It lands haphazardly on the map. "I'm just gonna take her for a quick spin first. Give it my own gut check."

"You've got people out there, ready and waiting for you," my dad reminds him with a warning tone. "And a jam-packed schedule ahead of this storm."

"And I just got a call for an emergency pickup," Agnes adds. "A villager needs to get to the hospital today. We were just trying to figure that out . . ."

Jonah is already out the door.

"No point arguing with that one," George mutters.

My dad sighs heavily. "Stubborn ass."

■ ■ ■

"She checks out. I ran every test I could think of on her, and she checks out!" Bart the mechanic scratches his chin as he stands with my father and me, watching the bright yellow four-seater plane at the end of the runway. "That son of a gun never believes me."

The wind whips my long hair across my face, forcing me to scoop it back with a hand. I'm wishing I hadn't given Jonah his black hoodie back. It's more practical than the pink cashmere wrap I'm trying to hold in place.

"You know Jonah. Doesn't take anyone's word for it, even if he knows how ridiculous this whole thing is," my dad mutters. "He better hurry up, though. We're still a day out and we're already at"—he peers at the orange flag-like cone that flutters ahead—"thirty knots."

"That's what those are for? Measuring wind?" I've seen them lining runways at airports before. I always assumed they were just markers.

"They're called windsocks. They determine the wind speed and direction and let us know how risky taking off and landing is going to be. If it reaches forty-five, we won't be able to fly with any passengers."

"Huh . . . The more you know."

"What about you?" Bart leans forward to peer at me through squinty green eyes. He's a foot shorter than me, making him almost at eye level with my chest, and I've caught him taking advantage of that line of sight once or twice. "You gonna learn how to fly one of these while you're here? Maybe take over the family business one day, when your dad finally kicks the bucket?"

It's an innocent question, made in jest—Bart has no clue—and yet my stomach spasms all the same. My gaze can't help but flicker to my dad, whose eyes are locked on Betty. I can't read anything in that expression, but I don't miss the way his chest rises with a deep inhale.

"I think I'll settle for just riding passenger without wanting to puke, thanks."

"You sure? 'Cause you've got the best teacher standing right here," Bart pushes, oblivious to any tension.

"Actually, the best teacher is out there." My dad points to Betty as the engine roars with acceleration.

"You're kidding me, right?"

His gray eyes flutter to me, suddenly serious. "No. I'm not."

"I've met two-year-olds with more patience than him," I say doubtfully.

The air fills with the distinct hum of a small plane as it begins gaining speed. A few short seconds later, it's lifting off the ground. Betty's wings tip this way and that, battling with the breeze, as Jonah climbs.

"He puts on a good show, I'll give him that," my dad murmurs, winking at me. Something tells me he's not talking about Jonah's flying abilities.

"See? I told you! She's good as good," Bart proclaims, turning toward the hangar, wrench in hand. "I gotta get back to fixing things that have real problems, not pretend ones."

My dad sighs. "Well, that's good. Now we just have to figure out . . ." His words drift, his hard gaze on the sky. "Hey, Bart?"

"Yeah, boss?" Bart calls out, slowing in his retreat.

"Do you hear that?" There's an edge to his voice.

I frown, my own ears perking, searching for whatever's gotten my dad's hackles up.

It takes me moment to realize that the constant buzz, that telltale sound of a bush plane in flight, has cut off.

"What's going on?" I ask warily.

"I don't know. The engine's off, though. He might be trying to restart it." They both pause to listen.

Meanwhile all I can seem to hear is my own heartbeat, pounding in my ears.

The plane begins to descend.

A phone rings and my dad reaches into his pocket to retrieve it. I didn't even know he had a phone. "Yup? . . . Okay." He ends the call. "That was Agnes. Jonah just radioed in to say he's got an engine fire. He shut it off on purpose. He's gotta bring her down on the other side of Whittamores'. Come on."

My stomach is tight as I rush to keep up with my dad, who has taken up a pace much faster than I've seen from him thus far. "Is he going to be okay?" I note the edge of panic in my voice.

"Yeah, don't worry. He'll just glide in. He knows how to land in an emergency," he assures me, pulling his keys from his pocket and hopping into the driver's seat of his truck.

I don't think twice, climbing in to take the middle seat, between him and Bart.

Whatever few seconds of calm my dad's words gave me quickly evaporate as he guns the truck's engine and peels down the road.

■ ■ ■

I feel like a storm chaser, our truck speeding down the dirt road, the yellow plane gliding toward the ground alongside us.

"It's really flat around here. That's good, right?"

"Yup. That's good," my dad promises, reaching over to pat my knee. "Jonah's landed on everything from glaciers to a mountain ridge even I wouldn't land on. Don't worry."

"Of course there's the wind and the bushes and the power lines, and that lake, and a few houses that he's got to watch out for. And if that fire didn't die out—"

"Bart!" my dad barks, making me jump.

I've never heard my dad raise his voice before.

"What is it? . . . It's . . . nine in ten emergency landings that end without a scratch. Yeah, he knows what he's doing," Bart mutters, drumming his fingers impatiently on his door.

I want to believe him, but the way he said that makes me think he was just pulling those numbers out of his ass.

For as flat as the land around here is and as far as I can see on my morning runs, there's a ridge and bush line up ahead that masks Betty's descent as Jonah brings her to the ground.

A few seconds later, there's a loud bang.

"Is that normal?" I ask with panic in my voice.

My dad doesn't answer, veering onto a muddy path. A private road for tractors or other vehicles, I'm guessing. It's narrow, and full of deep divots that he doesn't bother navigating around, instead racing right through, sending us bumping around in our seats. Finally he brings the truck to a jarring stop. "This is as far as we can drive."

We pile out. I don't wait for them, charging forward, around the crop of bushes, my running shoes sinking into the wet ground.

If Bart's numbers are accurate, then Jonah is the one out of ten.

I don't know when exactly I start to run, but I'm moving fast now, my blood rushing in my ears as I race toward the wreckage, stumbling over the uneven ground and around the bits of yellow metal debris, doing my best not to focus on how one of Betty's wings is jutting into the air at an odd angle, and how the rest of her is riddled with dents and scratches. A stretch of torn land, grass, and muddy streaks lead me in.

Sitting on the ground some distance away, with his back pressed against a crop of rocks, is Jonah, rivulets of blood snaking down over the bridge of his nose, his left eye, and his beard, like some victim in a horror film.

"Oh my God." I dive down to kneel next to him, shifting strands of his long, straggly hair back to reveal the source of the blood, a gash across his forehead.

"Am I still pretty?" he murmurs dryly.

I let out a shaky laugh. Amid my struggle to catch my breath, I'm hit with an overwhelming wave of relief that not only is Jonah alive, but his sarcastic tongue seems to be flapping just fine.

"We need to get something on that." I look around, only to remember that we're in a field. "Here. Use this." I strip off my sweater and hold it against the wound.

"Thanks." He sighs, reaching up to press his bloodied hand over mine to clamp my sweater in place.

Bart is the first to reach us.

"Nothing wrong with her, hey, Bart?" Jonah mutters.

"But . . . I . . ." Bart sputters.

A bout of coughing announces my dad's approach. "Jesus Christ." He presses his hand against his mouth, trying to stifle it. "What happened?"

"There was a strange sound and then the engine warning light came on. And then I smelled oil burning, so I shut 'er down," Jonah explains. "Everything was fine coming in until I hit that patch of rock. I couldn't see it until the last minute. Tried to avoid it, but I couldn't. Fuck, I'm sorry—"

"Are *you* okay?" my dad interrupts abruptly, as if he doesn't want to hear Jonah's apologies.

Jonah shifts his body and winces. "Pretty sure my shoulder popped out for a second while I was trying to shimmy my way out, but yeah, I think I'm good."

"Did you hit your head?"

"No."

"Let me see."

I pull my hand away and stand to get out of the way. My dad crouches next to Jonah. He peels away my bloodstained sweater and I cringe at the sight.

"It's shallow and pretty clean. Probably got grazed by a piece of metal. I'd say you're in for at least ten stitches."

One eye—the one not covered in blood—looks up to regard me. "Was that exciting or what, Barbie?"

I shake my head in exasperation at him.

"That girl ran like I've never seen anyone run before," my dad murmurs.

"She wanted to make sure the ground finished me off."

I wanted to make sure you're okay. Because I was worried. Because I care.

"No. I figured you'd jump at the chance to ruin my favorite sweater," I say instead.

"Hmmm." Jonah's lips part in a bloody smile as he presses the soft, pink cloth against his forehead again. "At least one good thing came out of this, then."

Sirens sound in the far distance.

Jonah groans. "Who called them? The hell if I'm being carried out of here." He uses my dad as leverage to get to his feet, wincing in pain, his movements slow and graceless. Even injured, though, he's a looming presence. He stops to take in Betty's mangled frame. "Damn. So what is she? Number nine?"

"She would be number ten. But, hey, ten planes in fifty-four years ain't too shabby." My dad shakes his head and sighs. "Never gonna doubt George and his funny feelings ever again."

Bart snorts his agreement, a dumbstruck look on his face as he shifts a piece of metal with his boot.

Chapter 16

■ ■ ■

"Hey." My dad's arm dangles out the open window of his truck. "You sure you're alright?"

"I'm fine. I'm just gonna grab some lunch and then chill for a bit on the porch." I went back to Wild with my dad after the accident only to find myself unable to sit still in that office, partly because of the adrenaline still pumping through my veins, but also because my shirt has Jonah's blood smeared all over it.

Wild's planes are grounded until the FAA says otherwise. Dad said he was heading back to the crash site to meet with one of their investigators, so he offered to drop me off at home.

My gaze wanders over to the quiet little house next door. "When do you think Jonah will be home?"

"A bit, still. They're gonna want to check him over well before they let him go, in case he has a head injury."

I nod solemnly. That feeling in my gut—that dread that seized my insides when I saw the wreckage—still lingers, hours later.

"He's gonna be fine, Calla."

"Yeah, I know." I shrug it off.

"Okay. Well, call me if you feel like coming back later." My dad coughs a few times and then clears his throat. "You still got my number?"

I hold up the slip of paper he gave me before we left, five minutes ago, as proof.

The truck begins to roll forward but stops abruptly. His lips twist in thought. "You know, I think your mom's old chair may still be in the garage. The one she used to use on the porch. Anyway, there's a bunch of stuff tucked in the back that she wrapped up and put away for the winter."

"You mean, the winter twenty-four *years* ago?"

"Yeah . . ." He scratches his chin, a sheepish smile on his lips. "Anyway, you might find something useful in there." With that, he sets off, the truck bumping and jostling down the driveway. I watch him quietly, wondering if he's really so calm about today's crash or if he just hides it well.

I notice him slow on the main road to talk to a passing girl on a bike. It takes me a moment to realize it's Mabel.

She sails down my dad's driveway, her long hair fluttering wildly with the wind. By the time she reaches me, she's panting, and I know she's heard about Jonah. Her eyes widen at the sight of my shirt.

"It was just a cut. Ten stitches, probably," I assure her, quoting my dad.

She shrugs her backpack off. It falls to the ground with a thud. "I was in town, getting groceries, when I heard someone say that Jonah crashed his plane and had to go to the hospital. So I went there, but they wouldn't let me in to see him, and I couldn't get hold of my mom at first, but then I did and she told me he was fine and to just go home, but I was so worried," she rambles, her words quick and panicky, her breath ragged, as if she had pedaled as hard as she could all the way here.

"He'll be home in a few hours. But he's fine."

"Okay." She nods slowly, as if it's taking time for her to absorb that answer, to trust it. She brushes her hair off her forehead. "Can I hang out with you until then?" There's desperation in her voice. He might be fine, but he so easily might not have been. Something scary happened to someone she cares about and she doesn't want to be alone.

Neither do I, I realize.

"Of course you can." I smile. "I hope you feel like digging through old junk."

■ ■ ■

"Are you okay?"

"Of course I'm okay. I wasn't in the plane, Mom."

"But still, that must have been scary for you to witness."

"It was," I admit.

Her sigh fills my ear. "I remember those days, hearing some of the stories of things that'd go wrong. I'd do the math on how many times they went up in the air each day, and the odds of something bad happening being that much higher because of it. Especially in those little planes. They're not like the big jetliners that practically run on computers and have backups of backups. It got to the point where every day, your dad would walk out the door and I'd wonder if that was the last time I'd see him alive."

"That would have been hard to deal with."

"Hard? It drove me nuts. I was never meant to be a bush pilot's wife."

Simon's profession is certainly much safer than my dad's. Aside from that one patient who launched a silver-plated Sigmund Freud head statue at him—missing him completely but putting a hole through the wall—Simon's biggest occupational hazards have been paper cuts and chair ass.

"Thank God for this George guy. Imagine what *could* have happened?"

Yeah, thank God for George, and Jillian, his little hula girl.

But, more importantly, thank God for Jonah's stubborn need for a gut check. If he hadn't insisted on taking Betty for that quick flight, there would have been a young mother and newborn baby in that plane when the engine caught fire.

Who knows if that landing would have been any smoother.

Jonah very well may have saved their lives today.

"They still work!" Mabel exclaims behind me. I turn to find her with her arms held wide, a string of red, blue, and green Christmas bulbs stretched between them.

"I can't believe it!"

"I know, right?" Mabel giggles. "I'll check the rest."

"What can't you believe?" my mom asks.

"Hold on, Mom," I murmur, shifting my phone away from my mouth. "If we have enough, we can string them up all over the ceiling, like a canopy."

Mabel's eyes widen. "Oh, that would look *so* cool."

"Calla! Who are you talking to?"

"Agnes's daughter, Mabel. Did you know Dad kept all your stuff? Like *all* of it." Mabel and I spent almost two hours rooting through stacks of dusty plastic tubs from the deepest corner of the garage, to find everything from holiday decorations to garden gnomes and whimsical sundials.

"Agnes has a daughter? Why didn't you tell me?"

Why didn't you tell me about all those phone calls between you and my dad? I want to throw back, but I bite my tongue against the urge.

"I haven't had a chance." To be fair, we haven't spoken over the phone since Monday afternoon. There's plenty I have to fill her in on that I can't do over text. But now is not the time. "We found your wicker chair under a tarp. It's in decent shape," I say, trying to sway the conversation back to lighter things. The cushions have long since succumbed to time, moisture, and some animal—likely mice—but the chair's frame itself is sturdy enough to bear weight.

We dragged it all out, and then Mabel helped me clean off the porch, lugging the decrepit lawn chairs, fishing rods, and other miscellaneous things that have collected over the years into the garage. And she did it all without a single complaint.

It's my first time spending real time with Mabel without the buffer of my father and a game of checkers. She's quirky and plucky and talks nonstop about three different topics at once, often trailing off mid-sentence. I'm starting to think she may have issues with attention.

And I'm growing more fond of her with every minute.

"Listen, I've got to go. There's a customer here," my mom says. "You'll fill me in on *everything* later, right?"

"Sure." I know she means later *tonight,* but I'm not exactly rushing to dive into that conversation. Does she *really* need to know why my dad canceled his trip all those years ago? Would she care if Alaska Wild has run into financial challenges, and that I'm trying to help while I'm here? Maybe she would. But maybe I also selfishly want some time for just me and my dad, without her complicated relationship with him entering the picture.

I end the call just as a truck engine sounds.

Mabel drops the strand of lights in her grasp and bolts out the door. "It's Jonah!" she yells. Her feet pound across the grass as she runs for his driveway.

And I feel the inexplicable urge to run right behind her. But I resist, occupying myself with my bottle of water and an apple I washed hours ago to eat but couldn't find an appetite for.

Finally, I decide I've waited long enough and make my way over.

Jonah's leaning against his truck, an easy smile touching his lips as he listens to Mabel prattle on. I'm halfway across the lawn when he notices me coming, and begins stealing frequent glances my way.

"They let you drive yourself home?" I holler, struggling to keep my pace slow and casual. As if I haven't been silently counting down the hours, anxious for him to get home.

He eases off the truck to stand taller and takes steps toward me. "Who was gonna stop me?" He's not wearing any bandages. A thin, tidy line of black stitches runs across his forehead, about an inch below his hairline. The cut is smaller than I expected it to be, for as much blood as it produced. Still, it looks like it'd be painful. Most of the blood has been washed from his skin, but his beard is matted and sticking together in crimson clumps.

A bite my lip against a smile as a fresh wave of relief and happiness washes over me. I nod toward his forehead. "How many?"

"Just nine. Should heal up nicely." His lips part with a sly smile.

"Doc said it'll only add to my good looks. I think she was flirting with me."

"Right. Of course she was." I roll my eyes but laugh. "And everything else was fine?"

"Shoulder's a bit sore but doesn't look like anything's torn. I was lucky."

"I'll say." Again, I think of how today *could* have gone, and I shudder.

"Come and see Wren's porch!" Mabel insists, reaching for his hand.

"Later, kiddo," he says, dropping my dad's pet name for her. "I've gotta shower and change. Maybe take a nap." The dark navy of his cotton shirt hides the bloodstains well, but not completely. He nods to something in the distance, smirking. "Looks like *someone*'s interested in seeing it, though."

We turn to see Bandit scampering toward my dad's house.

"The chips!" Mabel exclaims and takes off running.

Jonah chuckles. "He's gonna eat well while you're around."

"Whatever. He can have it all. I'm not hungry after today." I wrap my arms around myself to ward off the chill in the wind.

He opens his mouth to say something, but then seems to change his mind. Reaching through his driver's-side window, he pulls out a red-and-black-checkered flannel jacket and tosses it to me. "Figured you didn't want your sweater back. It's the smallest they had. Should fit."

"Wow. It's . . . Thanks." I slide my arms into the sleeves and tug it on, reveling in the soft material against my fingertips. "Now I look like I belong here."

"I wouldn't go *that* far," he says, but he's smiling.

"Do you know when my dad's coming home?"

"Probably a while, still. FAA cleared us to take off again."

"Yeah, we've been seeing planes for the last hour." My dad has a perfect view of the skies around the airport from his porch. I can't help but wonder if that was intentional or just a lucky coincidence when he moved here.

"He's still dealing with the investigator, but him and that guy go way back, so hopefully that'll speed things up. Not that there should be any problems. We've got all the maintenance records. Should be a quick clear for me to be back in the air." His tone is casual. Not the tone of someone who's rattled because he could have died today, but also not the Jonah who's just waiting to poke at my temper.

I shake my head. He just got home from the hospital after crashing a plane and he's already itching to get back in the air. "Freaking sky cowboys," I mutter under my breath.

"Hmm?"

"Nothing." I nod toward his house, hugging the jacket to my body. "Thanks again for this. You should go and rest."

Jonah begins walking to his porch, his steps slow and seemingly reluctant.

"Hey . . . Did you get far with that website today?" he calls over his shoulder.

"Not really."

"You're not much for hard work, are you?"

There's the Jonah I know. "Maybe if you'd learn how to keep a plane in the air, I wouldn't be so distracted."

His responding chuckle is deep and warm, and it sends a small thrill through my body. "Bring your computer over after you have dinner and we can work on it."

I frown. "You sure?"

"Gotta get it done, right?" His pace picks up as he climbs his stairs and disappears into the house.

■ ■ ■

The skies are still bright with sunshine—deceptively so, for eight p.m.—when I leave my dad and Mabel in the living room and stroll across the marshy grass. I have a plate of leftovers in hand and my MacBook tucked under my arm. I hesitate for only a second before I rap on the door with my knuckles.

"Yeah!"

I wait another moment, listening for approaching steps.

"I'm not getting up!"

I ease the door open. The scent of lemons and mint catches my nose as I step into a tidy little kitchen that's a duplicate of my father's in layout and style—right down to the color of the cabinets and countertops. And yet it feels fresh and clean and new.

Probably because there isn't an army of ducks.

But also because I'd been preparing myself for the smell of stale beer and three-day-old pork chop bones, something that might suit the life of an Alaskan bush pilot and bachelor who puts little effort into his appearance.

"Hey," I call out, kicking off my mucky running shoes, my curious frown still firmly in place. "I brought you a plate of Mabel's cheesy casserole in case you haven't eaten. My dad said it's pretty good."

"Just leave it in the kitchen." Almost as an afterthought, he adds, "Please."

I set it down and then venture farther in, into the living room. Another room that's identical in basic layout to my father's—a sliding door that leads out to a screened-in porch, small black woodstove atop beige ceramic tile in the far corner, simple Ikea-style floor-to-ceiling bookcases tucked in the other corner—and yet feels distinctively different.

And, again, unexpectedly tidy.

The carpet has been updated to a fluffy-pile mocha that's still new enough not to show wear patterns. The walls have been painted a warm gray and decorated with framed photographs of vibrantly colored bush planes against backgrounds of snowy tundra. Table lamps cast a warm, cozy glow to a room in shadow, despite the burning sun outside.

To be frank, it looks Jonah's house has been decorated by a woman.

Jonah is sprawled out on one side of a charcoal-gray faux suede sectional. His stained clothes from earlier are gone, swapped out for a pair of black track pants and a soft gray T-shirt that lays loose across his abdomen and yet still manages to highlight his muscular ridges. He's cursing quietly as he fusses with a pill bottle.

"Here, let me."

"I'm good."

I yank it from his grasp, my nails scraping against his dry, rough palms. With one swift turn, I have the cap off. "You're right. You're perfectly fine." I make a point of letting him see me roll my eyes as I hand the bottle back. "What are they for?"

"Thanks," he mutters, fishing out a pill. "Muscle relaxers." Strands of his hair dangle down either side of his face, freshly washed. He obviously just showered, but there are still flecks of dried blood tangled within that mangy beard of his. Nothing short of a pair of scissors will get all that out.

His eyes are on me now, narrowing suspiciously. "What?"

"Let me get you some water for that." I hunt through his cabinets for a glass, temporarily mesmerized by the state of his kitchen. It's spotless. Everything is organized tidily, and there's no clutter or obvious dirt. Two plates with pink flowers etched around their rim sit drying in the dish rack, along with a handful of other dishes, the stainless steel in the sink gleaming.

But the most bizarre discovery for me is the canned goods cupboard. A guy like him, I'd expect to chuck cans in haphazardly. But every last can is grouped by type and size, their labels facing out, stacked in tidy rows. "Hey, have you ever seen *Sleeping with the Enemy*? You know, the one with Julia Roberts and the crazy ex-husband?" The one who likes his cans to be organized this same way. Ironically enough, the one I watched with my dad the other night.

"I don't watch TV." A pause. "Why?"

"No reason." I add more softly, "I'll bet good ol' psycho Martin didn't watch TV, either." *Dog food?* Why does Jonah have a dozen cans of chunky chicken and liver alongside peaches and creamed corn and black beans? He doesn't have a dog.

But he *does* have a raccoon, I remember.

"What are you doing in my kitchen?"

"Nothing." I fill a tall floral-etched glass with water and bring it to him, setting it on the coffee table.

"Thanks." Jonah promptly downs his pill and starts chugging.

"Did you sleep earlier?"

"No. My shoulder's throbbing too much. It'll be fine once these pills kick in."

"Have you taken them before?"

"Yeah. The first time I dislocated my shoulder, back in high school. When I was playing football."

"Huh. I wouldn't have taken you to be a team player." I wander over to the bookcase, noting what I didn't notice earlier—that there isn't a TV in here.

"I wasn't. I got kicked off the team halfway through the season."

I shake my head but smile as I examine the tatty spines, curious what interests Jonah besides flying planes and being generally abrasive.

"Those are called books," he murmurs, the timbre of his voice soft and smug.

The Great Gatsby . . . *Crime and Punishment* . . . "My, aren't we literary."

"And what were you expecting?"

"I don't know . . . *How to Skin a Squirrel in Four Steps*? *101 Ways to Cook Beaver*? *What Happens to You When Your Parents Are Related*?" I mock.

He chuckles darkly.

There must be over two hundred books crammed in here. "You've read all of these?"

"That's what you do with books, Barbie."

I ignore the nickname, because he's just trying to get under my skin, and turn my attention to the one shelf reserved for framed pictures. "Is this your mom?"

"Yup. *Way* back, when we still lived in Anchorage."

I study the stunning and svelte woman in the cherry-red bikini, perched on the edge of a dock, her long white-blonde locks looking windblown, her slender legs crossed at the ankles. "She looks a lot like this Norwegian fashion Instagrammer that I follow. Really pretty."

"She *is* Norwegian, so that would make sense."

A grinning boy of maybe six sits next to her, his scrawny, tanned legs dangling over the edge, equally light hair glowing under a bright summer sun. His piercing blue eyes, though so innocent there, are an easy match to the man lying on the couch behind me.

"Is she still in Vegas?"

"Oslo. She moved back when she remarried."

"Do you see her much?"

"It's been a couple years. I was supposed to go see her this Christmas, but I doubt I'll be going now."

"Why not?"

"Because of Wren." He says it so matter-of-factly, like "why else wouldn't I go see my mom for Christmas, other than for Wren?"

"Right. Of course." Jonah will be running Wild and flying my dad back and forth to Anchorage for treatment. Jonah, who's not even blood-related. "Are you still going to be able to fly him on Monday morning?"

"Me, or someone else."

A pang of guilt stirs in my chest. Am I wrong to be leaving a week into my father's treatment? I mean, I pushed my ticket back, but should I be staying longer? Should I be staying to help him while he's at home? I *am* his daughter after all, even though we're only just newly acquainted. Do I owe him that?

And if not for him, then for Jonah, and Agnes, and Mabel, to help share the burden?

And if not for them, then for myself?

I need to call Simon later. He's always my voice of reason.

The next picture is of a tall, gangly, teenaged version of Jonah standing stiff and somber-faced next to a man dressed in military fatigues. A fighter jet is parked behind them. This must be Jonah's father. It's not a surprise that he'd have such a beautiful wife, himself a handsome though stern-looking man, with a jawline that could crease paper. I hold the framed photo up. "How old are you in this?"

"I don't know. Maybe thirteen?"

Still at the beginnings of puberty, definitely, his face boyish and soft, his lips too full for the rest of his features—if that's ever truly a problem. Young, but already likely capturing fellow classmates' hearts.

"Did he teach you how to fly?"

"Yeah. He was a kick-ass pilot."

"And you didn't want to join the air force?"

"Nope." A pause. "I was supposed to, though. *He* wanted me to. *Expected* me to. I applied, went through all the testing, but when it came to sign on the dotted line, I changed my mind and walked away." There's a somberness in his voice.

"But he must have been okay with you doing what you're doing, right?"

"He was, eventually. Near the end. Not at first, though. He didn't understand why I'd want to waste my time on a bunch of Eskimos. Those were *his* words, obviously." There's another long pause. "We didn't talk for seven years."

"And then you reconnected when he got cancer?" I ask quietly.

Jonah sighs. "He'd already been fighting it for a year by the time I finally went to visit him in the hospital. He died a few days later."

I steal a glance over my shoulder to find Jonah staring at the ceiling above him. "And you regret not going sooner." He's already told me as much, in more subtle ways.

"He was too stubborn to apologize for all the shitty things he'd said and done over the years, and I was too stubborn and proud to forgive him for it." His gaze flickers to me, where it settles. "And there's nothing I can ever do to change that."

But I can, because I still have time. No wonder Jonah's been pushing me to make peace with my dad, to build a relationship where there isn't one. He doesn't want me to feel whatever weight still sits on his shoulders. His situation isn't unlike my own. And, had I not had someone like Simon sitting beside me that night, helping me past my resentment, would I have been so quick to come to Alaska?

Jonah needed a Simon in his life.

Everyone needs a Simon in their life.

I pick up another picture, one of my dad and Jonah, sitting side by side in the pilot and copilot seats, turned to smile at whoever was behind the camera in the backseat. My dad's hair is mostly brown still, the wrinkles across his forehead less pronounced.

But it's Jonah I can't peel my eyes from. I can actually see his face, free of that unsightly beard and the straggly long hair.

"When was this taken?"

"First or second summer I was here. Can't remember." There's a pause. "Why?"

"You have dimples," I blurt out. Two low, deeply set dimples that accentuate a perfect pouty-lipped smile and offset sharp cheekbones and a hard, angular jaw. Even the shape of his head is appealing—his blond hair cropped short to his skull. All beautiful features—many from his Scandinavian mother, I see proof of now—hidden by that unsightly mask of hair.

All features that, coupled with those sharp blue eyes, make Jonah almost . . . dare I say, pretty? And this was at around twenty-one, twenty-two, when he still had a slightly boyish look. Ten years later . . .

I turn to frown at Yeti-Jonah and find him smirking at me. As if he knows *exactly* how attractive he is and can read my mind right now.

"So . . . are we gonna do this or what?" he says casually.

"Excuse me?" My cheeks flush.

"Work on this website. You brought your computer, right?"

Oh. I exhale slowly. "Right."

"Good, 'cause once this pill kicks in, I'll be lights out for the night."

Setting the picture of my dad and Jonah back on the shelf, I retrieve my laptop from the kitchen and settle myself onto the other end of the couch.

Acutely aware of Jonah's gaze on me the entire time.

■ ■ ■

"You said 1964, right? Jonah?"

"Hmm . . ." His eyes are shut and his broad chest is rising and falling at a slow rhythm.

"Jonah?" I call out softly.

He doesn't stir again.

"Well, I guess that's that." Twenty minutes of help is better than nothing. Though, I couldn't actually work on the website because, along with the lack of TV, Jonah doesn't have internet.

What normal thirty-one-year-old male doesn't have a television and internet access in his house?

I shut my laptop and then simply stare at his relaxed face for a moment, chewing my lip in thought. I already knew he wasn't like any other guy I've ever met. And what would possess him to hide a face like that? Lord knows it's not a confidence issue. He seems pretty damn happy with himself.

But it's not like he's let himself go, either. He's not slouching on the couch with a bag of Doritos, wiping cheesy fingers over his boiler belly before he reaches for his tenth can of beer. Even lying there in baggy sweatpants and a T-shirt, it's obvious he's fit.

A chattering sound calls from outside. Bandit is perched on something in the screened-in porch, his front paws pressed against the glass, staring at me through beady black eyes.

"I am *not* letting you in." I shake my head at him.

He chatters back in answer and then hops down. An odd thumping noise sounds. Curious what he's up to, I wander over to the window, to find him standing next to an empty metal bowl, pawing at it like a dog. "You're hungry," I realize. "And I guess *I'm* supposed to feed you." With a reluctant sigh, I head to the kitchen to put Jonah's dinner in the fridge and, I guess, get a can of dog food for his not-pet raccoon.

"I can't believe I'm doing this," I mutter, pushing the sliding door open, an open can and spoon in hand. Jonah's porch doesn't have much on it. Basically just a few shelves and storage bins on one side and a giant plywood box on the other that I'm guessing is Bandit's haven. There isn't even anywhere to sit.

Bandit stands up on his hind legs and paws excitedly at the air. How much does this thing even eat? He's half the size of Tim and Sid. A runt really. And cute as far as raccoons go, I guess.

"Shoo! Back up!" I scold, wary of his sharp claws as I scoop out half the can's contents, my nose curling in disgust as the congealed mess flops into the bowl. "Ugh!" I cringe, feeling a slimy chunk land on my hand.

Bandit shoves his triangular face in and starts devouring it, not bothering to come up for air.

With an overwhelming urge to wash my hands, I turn to head back inside.

That's when I notice the small wheels peeking out from beneath a heavy wool blanket, tucked into the corner. Wheels that remind me of suitcase luggage wheels.

A sneaking suspicion creeps over me and when I pull back one corner of the blanket and see a silver hard-case suitcase—*my* silver hard-case suitcase—I'm left gaping.

How the hell did *my* suitcases end up on Jonah's porch, hiding under a blanket?

There's only one way, really.

Jonah must have put them there.

Which means he's been intentionally keeping my things from me.

How did he even get them? I feel my face screw up as I work through the possibilities. Did he fly to Anchorage and get them? If he did, he couldn't have done it today. Or yesterday—because we were together all day. That means he must have gone the day before. And, what, *stole* my luggage from Billy?

He's had my things for days.

But . . . *why?*

I glare at the sleeping giant through the window, feeling the overwhelming urge to march in there and slap him awake to explain himself. If he hadn't been in a plane crash today, I might.

Fucking Jonah.

Have we gone a whole day yet without him irritating the hell out of me?

I make a point of banging the door frame as I drag my suitcases into the house, the hard plastic thumping against the metal. He doesn't stir.

I wheel them past the couch, intentionally checking my hip against the side where his head rests, hard enough that I might have earned myself a bruise.

Nothing.

"You son of a bitch," I growl as my anger boils over, letting the cases roll into the kitchen cabinets with a thud while I go back to get my laptop. "I should open the door and let Bandit in. Wouldn't that be something to wake up to, asshole. You'd sure as hell deserve having your place ransacked." What is he even going to say when I confront him tomorrow? Will he just smile smugly at me and throw a clever line?

And what will Agnes and my dad say? Will they shrug it off? Will my dad say he'll have a talk with him? Will Agnes wave her hand and say, "Oh, he likes to play games," or something along those lines again?

Looking at him lying there, blissfully dead to the world, that mop of straggly hair scattered over the pillow, that wiry, tangled bush on his face, I should just . . .

I feel the vindictive smile slowly stretch over my face.

Chapter 17

■ ■ ■

You can't walk around downtown Toronto without passing the homeless. They hide in plain sight beneath layers of blankets as they sleep. They sit on street corners, with Tim Hortons paper coffee cups held in their grasps, their matted hair hanging over their grim faces, waiting for the loose change of a charitable stranger.

I've sometimes wondered what those people look like beneath all that grime and poverty. What a hot shower, a comb, and a razor might do for them. If people might not speed up when they pass them, might not disregard them so quickly. If they might look at them in a different light.

Kind of like the way I'm looking at Jonah now, more than a little awed at what kitchen shears and clippers, which I discovered tucked away in a bathroom cabinet, could achieve.

It was supposed to be one cut. One highly noticeable chunk taken from the right side of his beard with a pair of scissors, one of those practical jokes that guys play on their friends when their friends pass out drunk on the couch. Just enough maiming to force him to take action when he woke up.

But then I thought to myself, *What if he leaves it like that, just to drive me insane?* Because that's something Jonah would do.

So I started cutting.

He didn't stir once.

Not when I lopped off handfuls of blood-flecked hair. Not when the buzz of the clippers filled the silent living room. Not while I carefully—with the most delicate touch—trimmed and combed that formless bush covering half his face. It kept shrinking and shrinking, until I had uncovered the full, soft lips and the sharp cheekbones and the promise of the chiseled jaw I knew was beneath.

Jonah now has a thick but tidy beard, the kind that inspires envy from men, that causes girlfriends and wives to shove magazines into the faces of their bearded significant others, demanding, "Make yours look like this!"

I didn't stop there, though. I hacked off that straggly mop on his head, shaving the sides and back—as well as I could given his horizontal position. I left a strip of hair about two inches long on the top, which I've styled because, lo and behold, Jonah also had an old bottle of cheap gel tucked away in the vanity.

Now I sit back and admire the ruggedly handsome man I uncovered under all that wild, dark-ash-blond hair, in peaceful slumber, itching to smooth my hand over his face. He's even more attractive than the picture version I was drooling over earlier, his face filled out with age and weight, the delicate lines making him more masculine.

And I wonder, how the hell did this go from a simple act of vindication to me sitting here, fawning over the conniving bastard?

I groan. "You're an ass even when you're unconscious, aren't you?"

His head shifts to the right and I inhale sharply. I hold my breath as his eyelids begin to flicker.

And release it with a heavy sigh of relief only after he stills again.

I don't want to be here when he wakes up, I realize as mounting dread shoves aside whatever glory I've been basking in up until now.

Because how is Jonah going to react when he sees what I've done to him? Will he laugh it off in a "well-played" manner?

Or did I just go *way* too far?

I mean, I cut off a plane crash survivor's hair while he was sleeping off his injuries.

Anxious flutters fill my chest as I scoop up the obvious evidence and dart to the kitchen.

This isn't just about his taking my clothes, I remind myself, as I shove my weapons into a drawer and toss the bag of hair under the sink. He's been a dick to me over and over again. I finally snapped. That's what happens when you push someone too far—they snap and cut off all your hair while you're sleeping.

I grab the pad of paper and pen that sit on the counter and scrawl a quick note, and then leave it on the side table next to his pills and a full glass of fresh water for him when he wakes up. A pretty lame peace offering.

Where I was intent on using my luggage as a battering ram earlier, now I tiptoe, easing each suitcase out the door and down the steps with painstaking efforts to not make a sound. It's an absolute nightmare, lugging each weighty suitcase across the wet, marshy land, and my arms are burning by the time I finally reach the safety of my dad's house.

My dad is settled into his recliner in the living room. He turns away from the baseball highlights on the TV to peer over at me. "How's our guy doing?"

Such a simple question and I'm hit with a sudden wave of guilt. "He's asleep. He took some pills that knocked him out."

"I'll bet he needs the rest. That was quite a day." My dad covers his mouth against a bout of coughs.

"Are you feeling okay?" I noticed he was coughing through dinner, too.

He waves it off, clearing his throat several times. "Shouldn't have been running through fields, is all. So . . . did you two get a lot done tonight?"

"A little bit. He passed out pretty fast."

"You were there for a while." There's something odd in his tone, something I can't pinpoint.

I glance at the clock on the wall. It's almost eleven. "I also fed Bandit and then . . . spent some time checking out books." I stumble over my words, averting my gaze as my cheeks flush, hoping he can't read me well enough yet to know that I'm hiding something. But I can't bring myself to admit what I just did to Jonah.

What if my dad says I went too far?

What if he's disappointed with me?

"Find anything interesting?"

"What?"

"The books . . ." His gaze drops to my empty hands.

"Oh. No, I'm not a big reader. Anything good on TV?"

"Nah. I just threw it on for a bit. I was sitting outside on the porch for a while tonight. You and Mabel sure made it look good. Brought me back a few years."

"Wait until the sun goes down." We had enough strands of old Christmas lights to crisscross the ceiling twice over.

He sighs and, hitting the power button to cut the picture, tosses the remote to the side table. "Maybe tomorrow night. Today's excitement wiped me out."

"Yeah, I'm pretty tired, too."

His movements are slow as he pulls himself out of the chair, collecting his dirty mug. "You sure you're okay? You seem a bit . . . jittery."

"I'm fine. Hey, what time are you going in tomorrow morning?"

"Probably the usual. Before six, anyway."

"I should get a ride in with you since Jonah won't be going anywhere."

He chuckles. "A few stitches across his forehead won't keep him away from Wild, even if he can't fly yet."

"Right. Okay." *Great.* I press my lips together.

My dad gives me another curious look. "Well, okay then. I'll see you in the morning."

"Yup."

He spots the two suitcases sitting in the doorway by the kitchen. "Hey! Told you they'd turn up!"

"Yeah, they turned up alright," I mutter under my breath. Do I tell him what Jonah did? A part of me wants to tattle on his golden boy, but a bigger part wants to hear Jonah's bullshit reasoning myself first.

Besides, this is between him and me now.

My dad frowns. "How'd they get here, anyway?"

"A cab. Just as I was coming home."

"Hmm . . ." His frown deepens, as if he knows that's a flat-out lie. But then he shrugs. "Well, you've got all your clothes now. That's good. 'Night."

"'Night, Dad."

He pauses to give me a small, satisfied smile and then disappears into his room.

I let out a shaky sigh the second my bedroom door shuts behind me. Jonah got what he deserved. Besides, it's not like I *disfigured* him. And hair grows back. If he prefers looking like he belongs in a cave, carrying a club around, it won't take him *too* long to transform back.

I set to unpacking my things.

■ ■ ■

Two hundred and forty-four.

Someone drew nipples on two hundred and forty-four ducks.

That's one thousand, four hundred and sixty-four hand-drawn nipples in my father's kitchen.

"Calla?"

I turn to find my dad standing in the kitchen doorway. "Hey! I'm making coffee for us. It's just finishing up."

His surprised gaze shifts from me to his coffeemaker as it noisily dispenses the last drips of hot liquid from its spout, and then back to me. "You feeling okay?"

"Yeah. I couldn't sleep, so I figured I'd get ready and go in with you."

He studies my tired eyes that no amount of concealer and Visine seemed to be able to fix. "I didn't sleep well last night, either," he admits, the bags under his eyes telling. "I'll bet seeing Jonah like that unsettled you."

"Yeah, maybe." My sleepless night has everything to do with Jonah, but less to do with the crash and more to do with his potential wrath when he wakes up and finds he's been shorn like a farm animal. Will he laugh it off or will we be back to square one in our relationship—mutual loathing? "Anyway, I figured I might as well get an early start to the day. With you."

"Nothing wrong with that." He pours himself a cup from the pot and takes a sip.

And starts choking. "How many spoonfuls did you put in?"

"Whatever the package said. Is it bad?"

He presses his lips together and shakes his head, and then says in a tight voice, "It's great."

I give him a flat look. "You're lying."

"It might be a *tad* bit strong." He smiles as he takes another sip, turning away to hide his grimace.

"I'm sorry. I don't know how to make coffee. You don't have to finish it."

"You kidding?" Another forced sip, followed by a fake thirst-quenching sound. "My daughter made this here cup just for me. Damn straight I'm gonna drink it."

I'm lost in laughter as I mix my own cup—extra heavy on the soy milk—and watch him force down the rest of it, alternating between dramatic cringes and full body shudders. Setting his dish in the sink, he grabs his vest and keys. "Well, if I wasn't awake before . . ."

I trail him out the door and toward his truck.

"Those are nice." He admires my red Hunter boots with a smile and nods at the red flannel jacket from Jonah, folded over my arm. "And they match."

"Shockingly. At least I *finally* have something appropriate to wear." I'd dug out my favorite ripped blue jeans, coupling them with my silvery off-the-shoulder knit shirt and matching lace bra.

"You had every right to be frustrated. It takes some getting used to, the way things work around here."

My luggage problems weren't on account of Alaska, I want to say. They had *everything* to do with the sleeping giant next door.

Both our gazes fall on the quiet yellow house.

"Wonder how he's feeling this morning," my dad murmurs. He climbs into the driver's side, slamming the door shut behind him. The engine comes to life.

I round the hood of the truck, unable to steer my eyes away from Jonah's house. My breath catches as I think, maybe, the gauzy kitchen curtain shifted. Just a touch.

But it's six a.m. Jonah's not up yet, I assure myself.

Still, I scuttle into my seat and buckle my seat belt, my guilty conscience not abated.

My dad's hands are on the steering wheel, but he makes no move to drive. "Maybe one of us should stick our head in and check on him."

"Shouldn't we let him sleep, though? It's early." My fingertips drum over my knee at a rushed pace as I keep my eyes forward.

I feel the suspicious gleam in his gaze as he regards me. "Are you sure you're okay, Calla? You're acting twitchy."

"Am I?" I say nonchalantly. "Must be that coffee."

"No. This started last night." He hesitates. "Did something happen between you two?"

I can't take it anymore. "Besides me finding my luggage on Jonah's porch?" Which will be my official excuse when I'm questioned for my crime.

My dad's eyes widen. "*Jonah* had your luggage?"

"Hiding under a blanket."

My dad heaves a sigh of exasperation. "That son-of-a . . . I'll have a talk with— Oh, looks like he *is* up." He nods toward Jonah's door as it eases open.

My stomach clenches.

"I'll go over there later and make sure he . . ." His words drift as a stiff-bodied Jonah steps out onto the porch in the same sweatpants and T-shirt he fell asleep in. We're too far away to make out the stitched gash on his forehead.

I'm not, however, too far away to read the stony gaze in his eyes as he turns his attention to us, his muscular arms folded over his broad chest.

To glare at me.

Silence hangs inside the truck for several beats, my dad's eyebrows sitting halfway up his forehead.

Finally . . . "Calla, how long after Jonah fell asleep did you stay?"

"Not sure," I mutter, averting my gaze to the road. His tone is mild, but I can't for the life of me read it.

"And . . . what was it you said you did, again? Worked on the website, fed Bandit, and then . . . Oh, yeah, you looked at Jonah's book collection. That's all?"

"Yup," I lie with as much conviction in my voice as I can muster.

"There's nothing I'm forgetting."

"Definitely, nothing. But we should get going. Like, right *now*." I finally dare look over, to find my dad pursing his lips together tight, doing a poor job of smothering his grin.

"Yes, I think you're right." He throws his truck into gear. We lurch into motion and begin heading down the driveway, swerving to miss the deeper of the potholes.

Dead silence fills the truck.

And then, "Those muscle relaxers they gave him must be strong," he muses.

"*So* strong," I agree.

My dad's gaze burns into my profile, until I can't ignore it any longer. I turn to meet his eyes, to see the twinkle dancing in them.

We burst out with laughter. My own is mixed with an overwhelming wave of relief. My dad doesn't seem to be angry with me, at least.

By the time the truck reaches the main road, my dad is

struggling through a coughing fit, brought on by his mirth. "Oh, Calla . . . You've really asked for it now."

"He deserved it!"

"Yeah, I'd say so. But Jonah always has to have the last word. He's not gonna let you get away with this."

I fold my arms over my chest stubbornly. "He should be *thanking* me. Now people can see his face."

My dad's brow lifts curiously. "And seeing his face is a good thing?"

"He's less likely to be trapped in a cage and brought to the zoo." Do they even have a zoo in Alaska? I doubt it.

Dad bursts out in another round of gut-wrenching laughter. "For a while there, I was thinking something might have *happened* between you two. You know, with the tension from the accident and all. Maybe you two . . . *you know* . . ." He gives me a look.

My cheeks begin to burn. "*That's* what you were thinking happened last night?"

"I mean, it wouldn't be the worst thing in the world. He's smart, and hardworking. Seems pretty popular with the ladies." He chuckles nervously. "A father can hope, can't he?"

What did he just say? Is my father *actually* hoping that Jonah and I hook up?

Me and Jonah?

A flash of that face last night—a peaceful, handsome Jonah in slumber—hits me. I shove it aside. "I'm not falling for some sky cowboy," I say resolutely.

Dad chuckle-coughs. "God, Calla, you remind me so much of your mother sometimes."

"That's what she called the pilots up here," I admit sheepishly.

"Yeah, well . . . can't say she's wrong as far as Jonah's concerned. It's probably for the best, anyway. You don't need to be repeating our mistakes," he murmurs, turning into the road that leads to Alaska Wild.

Chapter 18

■ ■ ■

Agnes's eyes squint as she leans in and scrutinizes my computer screen. "I like the other one better."

I toggle back to the first picture-framing option.

"Yes. That one. It reminds me of a postcard." Agnes stands and slides her glasses off. "It's really coming along, Calla. And fast."

I lock the setting. "I should have it up in another day or two."

"You make it look so easy."

"It *is* easy, I swear. I'll show you how to do everything. And if there's anything you need help with, I'm always just an email away." How odd it is that only a week ago, we were emailing as complete strangers, yet to meet.

My phone rings then, and Diana's sardonic duck-lip selfie fills the screen. "I've got to take this," I murmur, climbing from my seat. I knew the call was coming. The text I sent her ten minutes ago would have her frothing at the mouth for details. "Do you want me to grab you a water?"

Agnes waves it off with a "no thanks," and returns to her desk.

Taking a deep breath, I answer my phone, thankful that the staff room is empty for the moment.

"You did *not*!" Diana gasps, in a shocked "I can't believe you did that!" way.

"The yeti is no longer a yeti."

"Oh my *God*, Calla! How angry is he?"

"I'm not exactly sure yet."

"Do you remember that time Keegan passed out drunk and his team shaved his—"

"Yes, and eww! Please don't bring that story up *ever* again." Diana's brother is like a brother to me, and the mental picture is still disturbing on so many levels, years later.

"Okay, I'm hiding in the mailroom and I have, like, thirty more seconds before Beef Stick comes looking for me," she whispers conspiratorially, and I'm picturing the tall blonde bombshell crouching behind the photocopier in her pencil skirt. "I don't have time for specifics right now. Just give me the final verdict."

"The final verdict is . . ." I open the fridge and begin testing the bottles of water to find the coldest one. "He's hot."

"Really? Like *how* hot?"

"You know that Viking fitness model guy's profile page I showed you a couple of weeks ago?" Pretty much the only guy with a full beard that I've ever found attractive.

She moans her confirmation.

"Yeah, like that. Only better."

"Tell me you got a picture."

"No!" I scoff. "I'm not going to take a picture of the guy while he's drugged unconscious!"

"*Really,* Calla? *That's* the line you drew?" she mocks.

I cringe at myself. "I know."

"So, he's hot but he's still a jerk, right?"

"Yeah, total jerk. I mean, not really. *Sometimes* he's totally a jerk and I want to punch him in the face," I amend. "And then other times . . . I don't mind him at all, actually." I'm not even as angry as I was last night anymore. Now I'm more focused on the growing tension that gnaws at my gut.

What if Jonah is genuinely pissed at me? What if he wants nothing to do with me anymore?

"So are you two gonna hook up?"

"*What?*" I squeal. "No!"

"He's hot and you have no emotional attachment to him. Perfect rebound material."

"I . . . No!" God, first my father, now my best friend? "Hookups aren't my thing—you know that." I'm either not able to detach my heart from the situation and end up hurt or I decide that I don't like the guy and end up full of regret. "Besides, he likes leggy blondes. *You* come up here and sleep with him."

"*Come on.* You *need* a rebound."

"Trust me, I don't. I haven't given Corey a second's thought since I've been here." Which only proves I didn't make a mistake in ending it when I did.

"Good! So then *do the Viking*!"

"I am *not doing* the Viking!" I burst out laughing, realizing how much I miss her. "I wouldn't even know where to start with him." How *does* a woman initiate something with a guy like Jonah, who's as likely to laugh at her for her attempts as throw her caveman-style onto the bed? She'd have to have a brass-coated spine just to try.

Diana groans. "Ugh. Beef Stick's calling my name. His voice is so annoying, I've started having nightmares. Gotta go now. Go and get this guy. And then call me tonight. We need to plan out the next week. Calla & Dee can't just be all Dee while you're off, flying around with your hot Viking."

"I know, I'm sorry. Things have been crazy around here." Calla & Dee has fallen by the wayside in my thoughts, right next to my ex-boyfriend. "And *no,* I'm *not* hooking up with Jonah." Satisfied that I've found the coldest water, I hip-check the fridge door. "That would be a *bad* idea— Ahhh!"

Jonah is standing a foot away.

"Call you later," I mumble, and hit End.

As handsome as he was last night, freshly groomed and peaceful in slumber, the sight of him towering over me now, the muscles in his cut jaw clenching as he pins me down with steely blue eyes, is as awe-inspiring as it is intimidating. His beard remains unruffled, and his hair, though somewhat disheveled, holds its volume like I intended.

He doesn't appear to be at all amused.

How long has he been listening to my conversation?

My face is burning. I attempt to regain my composure while I reach down to pick up the water bottle that slipped from my grasp in my shock. "You're supposed to be at home, resting," I say, trying to sound casual.

"I felt a compelling need to visit." His light voice is a stark contrast to his icy gaze.

My eyes flicker toward the stitches on his forehead. They should heal nicely, but even if they don't, something tells me Jonah can don an unsightly scar and still be attractive.

There's a tidily folded piece of paper in Jonah's giant paw, which he calmly unfolds. "'Dear Jonah. This is for the toy plane that wouldn't fit my luggage, for *stealing* my luggage, for not helping me get beer for my dad . . .'" He reads off his list of misdemeanors from the note I left, and I get caught up in watching his shapely lips move. How do they look soft, when so many of the words that come out of them are coarse? "'. . . for defacing my father's duck wallpaper, *if* that was you . . .'"

I keep forgetting to ask my dad about that, but something tells me it has Jonah's signature all over it.

Those lips finally curl into a smile. My eyes flit up to find his—crap, he caught me admiring his mouth—as he recites the last line from memory: "'Lastly, for crashing Betty and scaring me to death.'"

My heart pounds in my chest. I don't know why I added that last line. It certainly wasn't his fault that Betty went down.

Just as calmly and methodically, he folds the page up and tucks it into his back pocket, the move stretching his gray T-shirt across his chest, highlighting hard curves that I try—and fail miserably—not to stare at.

I struggle to twist off the cap on my water bottle, unable to find my strength for a grip.

Jonah wordlessly slips it from my hands. The sound of snapping plastic fills the room.

"So, how long did it take for you to work up the nerve to do it?"

I push aside my worries about what he might have overheard to level him with a flat, accusatory look. "No time at all, after I found my luggage hidden on your porch next to your raccoon."

"Yeah, thanks for feeding Bandit, by the way." He hands me back my water bottle, our fingers sliding over each other's in the exchange.

"How long have you had my things?"

"Since I flew back to Anchorage the next night to get them," he admits casually, without hesitation or a hint of remorse.

"But that's . . . You mean you've had my clothes sitting on your porch since *Monday*?" I punctuate the word with a smack against his arm.

He flinches and then reaches for his sore shoulder.

"Sorry," I wince, my anger dampened a touch. "And what, you got Billy to lie for you?"

"Nah. He had no idea I took 'em. He's been shitting himself and finding excuses, hoping they'd turn up."

I shake my head. "You're such an asshole."

Jonah's gaze skitters over my bare collarbone, stalling at the decorative lace strap of my bra. "You survived, didn't you?"

"So, what, you were trying to prove a point?"

"Didn't I?"

I sigh. "Just when I was starting to like you . . ."

A deep bellow of laughter sails from his lips and knowing eyes search my face. "Oh, I think you like me *just fine* today."

My cheeks flame again. Seriously, how much did he hear!

I move to get around him, to distance myself, but he smoothly steps forward, into my space, thwarting my escape. Making my pulse begin to race.

"You know it'll just grow back."

"Unfortunately, yes."

He smirks. "Unfortunate for whom?"

"For the people of Alaska. Thankfully I'll be long gone by then."

Jonah reaches up. I stiffen at the first sensation of his fingers fumbling with strands of my hair.

"What are you doing?" I ask warily, even as my body reacts to his subtle touch, shivers running down my arms and along my collarbone, skittering over my chest.

"I was just curious what your hair felt like. It's soft." He frowns thoughtfully. "And so long. It must have taken *years* to grow."

"Not really. I've never had it short."

"Never?"

Unease slips down my spine. "Never."

"Hmm . . . I think it would look good short." He coils his fist around it to form a ponytail at the back, his fingertips grazing the nape of my neck ever so gently. "Short like Aggie's."

"I don't have the right shape of face." I clear my throat against the wobble in my voice.

His intense gaze searches my forehead, my cheekbones, my jawline, as if evaluating my claim. "I'm sure you have enough makeup to fix that."

"I know what you're doing."

With a light tug, he releases his grip on my hair. "And what am I doing?"

"Trying to scare me into thinking you're going to get even by cutting off *my* hair."

He mock-frowns. "What? Like, sneak into your bedroom while you're asleep with a pair of scissors? I'd never do that. I'm not some sicko."

"I did not *sneak* into your bedroom," I snap. "And it's not like I disfigured you. I helped you."

"*Helped* me?" he repeats.

"Yes. Maybe now you have a shot at getting laid. As long as you don't speak."

The wicked smile he flashes makes my throat go dry. "Do you think I have problems in that department, Calla?"

"I mean with two-legged creatures." *You arrogant son of a bitch, you totally stood there and listened to my conversation.* My comeback might have been piercing and quick, but it's too late. He has a solid upper hand on me, because he knows as well as I do that, despite *everything,* last night's vengeful grooming session has caused a totally unpredicted side effect.

I'm now unmistakeably attracted to the yeti.

God, this feels like the ninth grade all over again. Billy Taylor, the captain of the hockey team, found out I had a maddening crush on him. The feelings weren't mutual—Keegan gently passed on the message—but my little-girl infatuation became a source for teasing from his friends, and I spent the entire school year ducking into classrooms and hiding behind taller students every time I spotted him in the halls.

That was the last time I ever let it slip that I might be interested in a guy before knowing that he was *definitely* interested in me.

And the major difference here is that Billy Taylor was a nice guy who never embarrassed me about it.

Jonah is *not* Billy Taylor.

"George said he saw you come in here." Agnes's sudden voice cuts into the tension. She rounds the table and wanders over to stand next to us. "You should have stayed home to rest." As usual, Agnes's scolding is weak, at best. I don't know how she's going to keep Mabel in line. Then again, how much trouble can a teenager get into around here, with no bars to frequent and alcohol difficult to find?

Still, her entrance feels like a timely rescue. "That's exactly what I just finished saying to him," I murmur, trying to regain some semblance of dignity.

"So . . . You're trying out a new look there?" she asks mildly, the corners of her mouth twitching. I didn't mention my transgression to her, but my father must have.

"Apparently," Jonah finally says. "Calla decided *she* needed a change."

"It suits you." Agnes's dark eyes flash to me and widen, the unspoken warning in them clear. *Do you realize what kind of hell you've invited into your life, you foolish girl?*

"It *does* suit him, doesn't it?" I make a point of cocking my head and letting my eyes drag along his jawline in an admiring way. "My neighbor's sheepdog always looks much better after getting clipped, too. And it helps with the fleas."

Agnes snorts.

I can't even begin to read the look that takes over Jonah's face as his eyes burn holes into mine, but it's made my stomach roll and my blood race all the same.

"Sharon wanted to see me about something," I lie, sidestepping around him. I stroll for the door, forcing my legs to move slowly, so as not to look like the sprinting chicken that I truly am.

Chapter 19

■ ■ ■

"Damn rain. Makes everything so damp," my dad mutters through another cough, his gray gaze on the living room window and the porch screen beyond, soaked by the steady rainfall. It started as a light sprinkle around two this afternoon—earlier than expected—and quickly evolved into a hard downpour that grounded the rest of the flights. Sharon's husband, Max, is stranded in Nome for the night, much to her dismay. "At least they're saying the worst of it should be moved out by tomorrow afternoon. Let's hope, anyway." *Cough, cough.*

"Can I ask you a serious question?"

It's a moment before my dad answers. "Sure, kiddo." The endearment is there, but the reluctance in his voice is unmistakeable.

"Do you have a thing for Julia Roberts?"

"Uh . . ." He lets out a shaky sigh of relief and then chuckles. "I don't know. Do I?"

I know what he was afraid of: that I was going to push for information about his diagnosis, his prognosis. That I wanted to know if these frequent coughing fits he's had the last couple of days are more than on account of damp air and running through a field. The truth is, though, I'm finding lately that I want to think about and talk about the coming battle as much as he does: not at all.

"You have every single movie she's ever been in, in both VHS *and* DVD. So, yeah, I'm pretty sure you have a *thing* for her."

A thoughtful smile stretches my dad's lips. "Her laugh. It reminds me of Susan's laugh."

I frown as the *Pretty Woman* movie credits roll along the TV screen, trying to recall the sound. "I never made the connection, but you're right, it does, kind of." Mom has one of those show-stopping laughs, an infectious melody that carries through rooms and cuts strangers' sentences short as they search for the source.

"You know, that's what made me introduce myself to her that night. I heard her before I saw her. And then I saw her and I thought, 'I've got to get up the nerve to meet that woman, if it's the last thing I ever do.'" He studies his hands in quiet thought for a moment. "She was probably living up here six months or so when I first noticed I hadn't heard that laugh in a while."

"Do you still love her?"

"Oh, kiddo. What your mom and me had . . ." His voice drifts as he shakes his head.

"I know. It was never going to work. It can't work. It will never work. *I get it.* But do you still love her?"

He pauses for a long moment. "I'll always love her. *Always.* I wish that was enough, but it's not. For a while there, I believed she'd have a change of heart and fly back. You know, spend a few months with her family and then come back to me, after the thaw."

"And she was hoping you'd have a change of heart and fly out to us."

"Yeah. Well . . . like I said, we were never gonna work. I'm glad she found someone who's good for her. And you."

"What about you?"

"Hmm?"

"Another woman."

"Oh." He hesitates. "I did try once, with someone else who means a lot to me. But we both figured out pretty quick that it's hard to make things work when another woman is already taking up center stage. It wouldn't be fair to anyone, to have to compete, and I don't seem in any rush to move on. I guess marriage just ain't for me."

"Are you talking about Agnes?"

"Jeez." He rubs his eyes and then chuckles. "You really are grilling me tonight, aren't you?"

"Sorry."

"No, don't be. It's good that we're talking about this. It's important to talk. I wish I had talked more, way back when." He sighs. "Mabel wasn't even two, so she doesn't remember. It wasn't ever anything official or *big*. Just some long talks, some ideas that *maybe* something could be evolving."

"And then it didn't?"

My dad's lips press together in thought. "Agnes is everything I *should* want in a wife. She's kind, and funny, and patient. She loves her family, and Alaska. She takes care of me even though I don't ask her to. I honestly don't know what I'd do without her. She'll make someone an incredible wife one day."

I wait for the "but" that I sense hanging in the air. Though I think I've already heard it before.

Yeah, well . . . I'm not Susan. That's what Agnes said my first night. She didn't sound bitter. More like resigned to the fact.

My dad sighs. "I keep telling her that she should find someone. There's been interest from other men. But she's never given them the time of day. I think she's getting as set in her ways as I am. So . . . we all just keep living like we do."

"I think it's nice, the way things work around here. The way you all look out for each other. I mean, Mabel brings you dinner . . . you leave a pot of coffee out for Jonah every morning . . . It's nice. It's like family."

"Yeah, well . . ." He scratches the gray stubble coating his chin. "They *are* my family."

"I'm glad to know you have people here who care about you." *Who will take care of you after I'm gone.* "And that I got to know them."

His mouth curves in a thoughtful frown. "Even Jonah?"

"Even *him,*" I admit reluctantly, adding an eye roll. Jonah, who thankfully seemed to be giving me a wide berth today as he helped my dad and Agnes rework flights after yesterday's delays, while I hid in a corner with my headphones on, finishing Wild's "history" page with a picture of my grandparents standing beside the first plane they ever bought.

Pretending I didn't notice every time he strolled by.

"Well, that's something." With a yawn, he shimmies out of his chair and reaches into his vest pocket. "Listen, I'm gonna step outside for a minute and then head to bed after. I'm beat."

I can't help but glare at the pack of cigarettes in his hand.

He notices, and sighs. "I've been a smoker for over *forty* years, Calla."

"And it's going to kill you if you don't stop." A reality that has been there since the moment we met face-to-face in the hallway for the first time, and yet it concerns me that much more now. Probably because I don't feel like I'm looking at a stranger anymore.

"Doc says it won't make much of a difference, so why put myself through that."

"I guess. If that's what your doctor said."

He opens his mouth, but then hesitates. "You're yawning. Go to bed, kiddo."

I *am* exhausted after last night's restless sleep. "Hey, do you think we could start locking the door at night?"

Dad frowns. "Why? Something got you spooked?"

"Besides the neighbor who wants to take hedge clippers to my hair?"

"Is that what Jonah said he'd do?" He chuckles. "He's not actually going to do that."

I level him with a knowing look.

"I would *never allow* him to do that to you," he corrects, a touch more sternly.

"You said so yourself . . . he's not going to let me get away with it, even if it's a *huge* improvement." Even if my blood raced every time I so much as heard his voice today, and my attention was only ever half on what I was doing, the other half wading through our past conversations, replaying words and looks, only now from the new version of Jonah, the one who'd stop me in my tracks if we were passing on the street.

I've somehow conveniently forgotten all the unpleasant exchanges and his games. *Those* were all the work of the angry yeti. My mind—or more likely my hormones—seems to be trying to compartmentalize Jonah in some sort of Jekyll and Hyde situation so I can freely lust over the hot Viking version.

"Don't forget, he hasn't been cleared to fly by the FAA yet. One call from me . . ." My dad winks.

I'm sure he's only kidding, but I appreciate it all the same. "Can we just lock the door anyway?"

He shrugs. "If that makes you sleep better, sure."

"Good, thanks." I collect our dinner dishes. "Oh, and I'm making overnight oats for breakfast. Do you want me to make you some?"

"I don't normally eat breakfast, but . . ." He seems to mull it over. "Sure. I'd love that."

"'Kay." I smile with satisfaction. "Night, Dad."

■ ■ ■

The heavy rain last night brought with it cooler weather this morning. Gooseflesh instantly sprouts along my bare skin as I step out of the steamy bathroom. I hug my towel tightly around my body as I dart to my bedroom, intent on dressing quickly.

I catch a familiar scent the second I step inside and pause to inhale deeply. That's Jonah's soap. But it's not possible. I locked the kitchen door before I jumped into the shower.

I scan my room warily. My phone and laptop are on the chair; the clothes I laid out for the day are on the bed, untouched. The rest of them hang neatly in the closet.

In a half-turn, I realize the problem.

The top of the dresser is bare.

Every can, every bottle, every brush. Every last cosmetic I own.

Gone.

I dive for my purse.

He's even taken my essentials from there—my compact powder, my mascara, my favorite blush lipstick.

"Jonah!" His name is a curse on my tongue. I rush out of my bedroom and down the hall.

He's in the kitchen, leaning casually against the counter with his back to the sink, his legs crossed at his ankles, eating a bowl of overnight oats.

My bowl of overnight oats.

A key dangles on a ring from his finger in a taunting way. A key to this house, I'm guessing.

"Where are my *things*?" I demand, my annoyance clouding all other thoughts for the moment.

His hand pauses halfway to his mouth, and his eyes drag over my body, stalling at my bare thighs for a few too many beats, reminding me exactly how short this towel is—about four inches away from me being mortified—before continuing his meal. "What things?" he says casually.

"Everything you took from my room."

"Oh. *Those* things." He takes his time licking the spoon. "They're in a safe place."

The white shirt beneath his flannel jacket has damp streaks over it. A dreary rain still falls outside, though it's lighter than yesterday. Light enough for Jonah to trek all the way home with my things and then back again just to taunt me?

"At my house," he confirms, as if reading my mind. "And you'll never find them."

"This isn't funny. There's over *a thousand dollars'* worth of makeup there." Eye shadow palettes that will crumble if handled roughly, and I'm guessing Jonah wasn't overly gentle.

"Shit. A thousand bucks? I think that's a felony in Alaska." Not that he sounds at all concerned.

"Maybe I should call the cops, then."

"Yeah. Good idea. Do me a favor, though, and make sure you ask for Roper. He's been complaining that he's bored." He points toward the bowl with his spoon. "This is good, by the way. What is this?"

My frustration with him swells. "It's *mine*." I storm forward and, with one hand still gripping my towel to keep it in place, I yank the bowl from his grasp. Taking a clean spoon from the dish rack, I spin on my heels and storm back to my room, slamming the door behind me.

A knock sounds a few minutes later.

"What!" I snap, yanking my leggings up over my hips.

"I'll give everything back."

"You'd better."

"Eventually."

A strangled sound escapes my throat. "You are *such* a dick!"

"What? I'm just helping you. Maybe now you have a shot at getting laid." His amusement rings clear as he echoes my words from yesterday.

"I don't have problems in that department, either," I throw back haughtily.

There's a pause. "Who's Corey?"

"My ex." I tug my socks on.

"Why'd you break up?"

Do I want to indulge his curiosity? Will he somehow use it against me? "We grew apart. Or got bored, I don't know. I ended it before I came here." I throw open the door to find Jonah leaning casually against the wall, his gaze on the ceiling above, giving me a clear view of a jutting Adam's apple. Even his neck is pleasant to look at.

Blue eyes settle on me, and I momentarily forget that I'm irritated.

"Why do you want to know about me and Corey?"

He shrugs. "Just curious." His gaze slides down the violet tunic shirt that clings to my frame and my black leggings below. The look on his face is unreadable, and yet it makes my pulse quicken all the same.

I sigh heavily and try a more civilized approach. "Jonah, can I *please* have my stuff—"

"No." There's no hesitation, no teasing inflection anymore.

"Fine," I say curtly. "I'll have fun trashing your house until I find it." Because he can't stay home all day.

I move to march past him, but he stops me with a swift hand on my side, and then his other hand on my other side, gripping me tightly as he herds me backward, until I feel the cool wall through the back of my shirt.

My hands fly up between us instinctively to press against his chest, unsure of exactly what's happening, my mind not registering much beyond how solid and warm his body is, how my palms curve around ridges.

Not until I dare look up, not until I see just how dark and intense his eyes have turned, do I begin to see it.

This newly found attraction might not be one-sided after all.

One . . . two . . . three beats hang as we seem to silently measure each other, as I struggle to grasp exactly *how* this has happened.

And then Jonah leans down and skates his mouth across mine, in a kiss softer than I could ever imagine him capable of. His lips taste like mint toothpaste and the brown sugar from my oatmeal, and the soft, freshly cut hair of his beard tickles my skin in an oddly intimate way.

I can't breathe.

He pauses, and then makes a second pass. He's testing me to see how I'll respond.

"I thought you didn't like my kind," I whisper, my fingers too timid to venture over this massive canvas of chest.

He loosens his death grip on my waist, letting one hand drop to curl around my hip while the other smooths upward, over my back and shoulder blades, to wrap around my nape. His fingers thread through my hair, pulling at it gently, forcing my head back. "I guess I was wrong," he admits, in a voice so deep and husky that I feel it in the depths of my belly.

And then he's kissing me without hesitation, his mouth coaxing mine open, his tongue sliding against mine, his breaths melding with mine. Blood rushes to my ears as my heart pounds with an intoxicating, addicting thrill I haven't felt coursing through my limbs in forever. Heat floods right to my core.

I'm vaguely aware of footfalls pounding up the steps outside, and then Mabel's loud, excited voice calls out, "Calla? Are you ready?"

Jonah peels away and takes a step back, letting out a soft, shaky breath as he goes. It's the first and only sign that I might be affecting him as much as he is affecting me.

"Hey!" Mabel stands in the hallway, dripping water from her canary-yellow rain slicker onto the floor, her wide-eyed gaze flickering back and forth between us. "What are you guys doing?"

"Umm . . . We're . . ." I stutter. Is she too young to sense the tension in the air? To figure out what she just interrupted?

"I'm just giving Calla something she needs," Jonah says, back to his normal, cool self, though with a hint of amusement in his voice.

I turn to stare at him, momentarily speechless. Well, if Mabel hasn't already picked up on it . . .

With a knowing smirk, he reaches into his back pocket and pulls something out. "Here." He tosses it in the air and I fumble to catch it. It's my antiperspirant stick. "See? I'm not a *complete* dick." He strolls away, playfully mussing Mabel's hair on his way past. Moments later, the door closes with a thud.

Mabel's face crinkles up. "Jonah bought you deodorant?"

I'm too overwhelmed to try and explain any of this. "What do I need to bring with me?" I ask, ignoring her question.

"Just yourself! I've got you covered." She grins and holds up her arms. A yellow slicker dangles from one hand and a stack of baskets sits in the other.

"Perfect." A morning of picking berries in the cold rain with a bunch of strangers is probably the best thing I can do right now, while I try to sort out what the hell just happened between Jonah and me.

And whether I want it to happen again.

Chapter 20

■ ■ ■

"Max has his heart set on 'Thornton,' after his grandfather." Sharon's lip curls in an unpleasant way.

I shrug. "It could be Thor, for short? That's a cool name. Unique."

"Except his mother would refuse to shorten it. Everything would be 'Thornton' this and 'Thornton' that." She rolls her eyes. "I've given up a lot, already, being here and all. I am *not* naming my son *Thornton*."

"I don't blame you," I mock-whisper. "Where are you moving to, anyway?"

"Back to Portland, Oregon. I can't believe I'll be home soon." Sharon's hand smooths over her belly in a slow, circular motion while the other reaches for another blueberry from the basket Mabel and I brought to the airport. After several hours of crouching in drizzle among an endless stretch of prickly bushes, my thigh muscles are still burning and I haven't been able to shake this cold-to-the-bone chill. "I still remember the day Max came home three years ago and said, 'Babe, guess what? I got the job! We're movin' to Alaska!' I didn't even know he'd applied." She chuckles, shaking her head. "Don't get me wrong, we're going to miss the people like crazy, but everything is *so* hard up here. And now we're going to have a baby to add to it."

I'm betting Sharon and my mom would get along well, commiserating. "And Max is okay with leaving?"

"For now. He's already talking about coming back in five years to work for Wren again. We'll cross that bridge when we get to it. Or should I say, *airstrip*."

In five years. I can't help but do the math. I'll be thirty-one in five years. Where will *I* be by then? Back in Toronto, obviously. How many trips back to Alaska will I have made? Will Dad come to see me? Will I still be living with Mom and Simon? Or will I be married and gone? Will I be rubbing my pregnant belly like Sharon is?

Will my dad be around for any of it?

I swallow against the lump in my throat.

A shrunken Alaska Native woman shuffles toward the desk, clutching a small weekend bag. Her gray hair is wrapped in a hot-pink floral handkerchief, but otherwise her clothes are drab shades of brown and green, meant for warmth and nothing more.

"Any news yet?" she asks politely, smiling. As if she hasn't been sitting in this lobby since seven this morning, which is how long most of these people have been lingering, according to Sharon. People who've been playing the waiting game all day, hoping that their flights will take off at some point. I count fourteen in total. Mostly fishermen, anxious to get out to their camps. It's easy to spot the ones who aren't from Alaska—they're pacing around the lounge like caged animals, peering out at the sky every time they pass the window, grumbling with impatience. Those familiar with how things work sit quietly in their chairs, their attention on their phone screens or their knitting needles, or those they're traveling with.

Planes were cleared for takeoff an hour ago. Half the flights have already left. Now it's just a matter of being called.

"The guys are loading it up, Dolores." Sharon smiles sympathetically at the woman. The supply plane that she's hitching a ride with was stuck in a village overnight and was just landing when I got here. "You must be excited to see your sister again after a year."

Dolores shrugs and mutters, "I wish she'd move down here."

To me, Sharon explains, "You should see the village where Dolores is from. It's near Barrow. I haven't been, but Max has. The sun hasn't set since when, Dolores?"

"Early May," the old woman confirms.

"Right. *Early May*. It'll finally go down in a few weeks. And then it doesn't come up for two months in winter. *At all.* We can't even fly there during the polar nights."

"They get their supplies in the fall, or not at all," Dolores confirms.

"And it's cold up there, all the time." Sharon shivers. "What's the high for there today?"

"Forty." Dolores tugs on her quilted coat as if to emphasize that.

I do the quick calculation in my head. That's three degrees Celsius at the beginning of August. I shudder at the thought.

Dolores's wise gaze zones in on me. "Who's this girl? Your replacement?"

Sharon laughs. "No. This is Wren's daughter. She's just visiting."

I get a curious once-over, much like the one I got from the woman at the grocery store. At least I don't feel as out of place today, with my bare face and my flannel jacket. And then her gaze shifts to something behind me. A genuine smile stretches across the old lady's face, showcasing misshapen yellowed teeth. "There you are."

"On your way to see Helen again?"

My heart skips a beat at the sound of Jonah's deep voice.

"Unfortunately. Are you taking me?" A hopeful sparkle dances in her black eyes. Does *everyone* in Alaska know and like Jonah?

"Not this time. But don't worry, you'll be in good hands with Jim." He moves in to lean against the end of the desk, a position that allows him to face both of us while he talks.

I can't seem to find the nerve to acknowledge him with a look or even a nod, and so I keep my focus on the old woman while watching him in my peripherals, all while my skin prickles with an electric current and my cheeks heat.

Three hours in the drizzle helped cool my hormones, both literally and figuratively. Letting that happen with Jonah this morning was a *bad* idea. I don't regret it—how can I regret anything that felt that good?—but it can't lead anywhere, so what's the point?

I'm going back to Toronto, where I belong, and he's staying here in Alaska, where he belongs.

It's a dead end.

It was a mistake.

Dolores's black eyes crawl over Jonah's face, pausing on his stitches. "I heard about the accident."

"Just a scratch—I'm fine. I'm ready to go."

Because you're insane.

She frowns. "There's something different about you, though."

"No, there isn't." His voice is gruff, but his tone is teasing.

"Yes, there is." She searches his face again. "I can't put my finger on it."

And I can't tell if she's joking or not.

"He finally got a haircut!" Maxine hollers from her seat a few feet over. She's a short, plump woman with a loud voice and an even louder laugh.

Dolores makes a grunting sound, then studies him another long moment. "I liked the old beard better," she finally states, as if he were waiting for her to pass judgment. "You're too pretty now."

He grins, a move that shows off those deep dimples. He's not in the least bit offended by her blunt and critical opinion. "Not as pretty as I'd look without it. Besides, some women like their men pretty." A pause, and then he turns to look at me dead center. "Right, Calla?"

I feel all their eyes on me as my face burns. I clear my throat. "*Some* might." *You ass.*

His knowing eyes crinkle with amusement. *An ass you want to kiss again,* he seems to be saying.

And he'd be right.

Bad idea, Calla. Bad. Horrible.

"Marie!" Sharon's excited shriek breaks up our intense deadlock. She waddles around the desk in time to greet the tall, willowy blonde woman who just came through the door.

Did she say Marie? As in *the* Marie? The veterinarian who flies in once a month to save everyone's animals? The crusader who vaccinated a raccoon for Jonah? The friend who Agnes is convinced wants to be much more than friends with him?

The stitched DR. MARIE LEHR across her jacket's breast pocket pretty much confirms it.

I try not to gape as I take in those mile-long legs clad in blue jeans and her long, golden-blonde tendrils of hair, damp from the rain and yet still falling around her shoulders in a natural sexy beach wave. She has lively teal-blue eyes surrounded by a fringe of lashes that are thick and long, but naturally so. Her nose is dainty, her lips are full, and while her cheekbones may not do much for her, the rounded shape of her face is flattering. I'd put her in her early thirties, with a fresh girl-next-door vibe. Not a stitch of makeup touches her face.

I remember wondering what kind of woman would interest Jonah. I feel like I just met her.

And friend or not, I'd bet money that he's slept with her.

Dolores is scuttling back to her seat as Sharon ropes her arms around Marie's neck. "Did you just land?"

"Uh . . . yeah. Rough flight." Marie returns the hug, but she seems discombobulated, her attention flickering from Jonah to Sharon and then Jonah again, as if not sure where to focus. "Okay, first of all, *wow,* look at that belly! And it's only been four weeks since I saw you last."

"*Only,* you say." Sharon groans, smoothing her hands over her midsection.

"And *you.*" Marie's eyebrows arch halfway up her forehead as she comes around the desk. "*What the hell,* Jonah?"

He folds his arms around her, pulling her against him. She's tall, but she looks petite pressed up against him like that. "What the hell, indeed," he murmurs. "Hey, Marie."

They break apart and she reaches up to smooth her long

fingers—with bare, neatly trimmed nails—over his beard, in a way that screams intimacy. The way a woman might reach up to lazily stroke a man's face in bed, after sex.

"I like it," she murmurs.

I'm sure you do.

How many times have they done it, anyway?

Does Jonah like to play childish games with her, too? Did he corner her in a narrow hallway to steal a kiss that first time? Did he realize she'd be coming in today when he was busy making moves on me this morning? Will he be MIA for the next however many days, while she's in town?

At least Jonah's hands aren't all over her. In fact he's moved back to his casual leaning-on-desk position. His gaze drifts to me. "I was the victim of a cruel and vicious prank."

I push aside my growing unease to roll my eyes dramatically for him.

He chuckles. "I probably deserved it."

"Probably," I echo, my voice laden with sarcasm.

Marie's teal eyes do a curious but quick down-and-up scan of me.

"This is Wren's daughter, Calla," Jonah says. "She's here, visiting."

"I didn't realize Wren had a daughter," Marie says slowly. She offers a hand and a smile, though it's not nearly as bright a smile as the one she flashed Jonah. "First time in Alaska?"

"Yeah."

"I picked her up from Anchorage last weekend. It's been . . . interesting, so far." Jonah smiles secretively and, dammit, I'm blushing again.

Marie's gaze darts back and forth between us, and there's no way she's as clueless as Mabel was. "So where are you in from?"

"Toronto."

"Oh, that's far." She says it in an "oh, that's too bad" way, emphasizing it with a pointed glance at Jonah. As if to make sure he realizes it. "And how long are you here for?"

"Another week."

"Okay . . ." If I'm not mistaken, a sigh of satisfaction passes her lips. *One more week and she's away from Jonah for good.*

"Unless I decide to stay longer," I blurt out without thinking.

Jonah's left eyebrow quirks.

I don't know why I said that.

That's a lie. I know *exactly* why I said it. An uncomfortable feeling pangs in my stomach.

I don't believe this. I'm jealous of Marie.

I caught my boyfriend of a year being handsy with Stephanie Dupont and I waved goodbye. Meanwhile, one moment of intimacy with Jonah and I'm ready to extend my stay so I can stake my claim against his attractive female friend.

This is what I get for kissing Jonah.

A coughing fit on the other side of the office door announces my dad a moment before he pops his head out from the office. "Hey, Marie. Has it been a month already?"

Marie's face splits into a wide grin. "It always feels too long for me, Wren. I thought you got rid of that chest cold already."

"Yeah . . . Guess it's hanging on there." No one not the wiser would notice the way he shifts on his feet, as if uncomfortable with the lie. To Jonah, he says, "The report says the fog has cleared for the time being, but there's heavy cloud cover. Possibility of light rain."

Jonah stands upright with a resigned sigh and I can't help but admire the shape of his chest, remembering what my hands felt like pressed against it just this morning. "I'll fly low. It's probably as good as it's gonna get."

"What's going on?" Marie asks, her eyes seemingly absorbed with Jonah's face.

"Going to pick up some hikers. They've been waiting at the checkpoint since Thursday."

"You want company?" she offers eagerly.

"I've already got it, thanks. Promised her a flight up that way. Might as well kill two birds with one stone."

It takes me a moment to realize Jonah's talking about me.

I struggle to wipe the shock from my face. He never promised me anything. Is this his way of avoiding time alone with Marie?

Or spending more time alone with me?

This is where I need to decline, to tell him to go ahead and take Marie. It'll send a clear message that this morning was a mistake, and that I'm not interested in repeating it.

"Are you ready?" He looks pointedly at me.

"Yeah, let's do it." *Oh . . . Calla.* An odd blend of excitement and fear churns inside me. *Am* I ready? Forget whatever's happening with Jonah for the moment. Am I ready to get back in a plane after watching him crash just two days ago?

Why does this feel like a test? Another "let's find out what you're made of" Jonah adventure.

Only this time, I care if he likes what he sees.

My dad eyes the two of us for a moment, as if weighing something in his head. Finally he turns to Jonah. They share a long look. "No risks," he warns him.

"In and out," Jonah promises solemnly.

■ ■ ■

"There's another one!" I exclaim, aiming my camera lens downward to try and capture the moose as it cuts through the river that snakes along the valley, the broad crown of antlers atop its head almost regal. "Those things are *huge*."

My eyes have been glued to the ground ever since we spotted a small herd of caribou grazing near the opening of the mountain range. It's an entirely different landscape on this end of the Kuskokwim River than the side that weaves through the tundra. Here, the valley is a mingling of tall, tapered evergreens, meadows with smatterings of pink and purple wildflowers, and wide, rocky river shorelines, the colors that much more vivid against the murky gray ceiling.

"You'll find pretty much everything up here. Wolves, caribou, reindeer, sheep . . ." Jonah's attention is on the flight path ahead, which I'm thankful for because we're flying low and on either side of us are mountains, their tops shrouded by mist. "Keep an eye out and you might catch a grizzly or three."

"Are there a lot?"

He chuckles. "You're in bear country. What do you think?"

I shudder, and yet find myself scouring the waters with new interest. "How long have these hikers been in here, anyway?"

"We dropped them off eight days ago."

"Eight days?" I try to imagine what that means. That's eight days of slugging camping gear up and down mountains. Eight days wandering around the wilderness—with bears, sleeping in a tent—with bears, searching for food—with bears. Eight days without a toilet or a warm shower. With bears. "That's crazy."

"That's pretty normal for up here. It's crazy if you don't know what you're doing. Hopefully these two did. They're a husband and wife from Arizona. I think they said it was their fifteenth anniversary, or something."

Pooping in a hole for eight days. "How romantic," I mutter wryly.

"Some people think so. Out here, in the middle of nowhere, you can do pretty much whatever you want," he counters, and I get the distinct impression that he's speaking from experience.

"Yeah, it's just them, a million mosquitoes, and the giant grizzlies roaming around their tent at night."

He chuckles. "They don't usually bug you unless you do something stupid. But that's why I bring a gun when I camp."

"And what, load it and tuck it under your pillow?" I shake my head. "Hell, no . . . You couldn't pay me to sleep out here and I don't care how experienced the person I'm with is."

"No?" A pause. "Even if you were with me?" He throws that out there so casually, and yet his words weigh heavily with meaning.

I swallow against the sudden flutter in my gut, unprepared for this quick turn of conversation, even though I've been rubbing my sweaty palms against my thighs in anticipation of it ever since we pushed through the doors of Wild. Jonah's been all business since takeoff, though, his fists gripping the yoke tightly to keep the plane steady against crosswinds that I was sure would sweep us off the runway.

He's been on the radio with other pilots almost constantly, heeding their warnings and navigating around patches of fog and heavier rain. Based on some of their reports, it doesn't sound like this weather system is in any rush to leave this side of the state.

Flying with Jonah today has been nothing short of tense, and an entirely different experience than the last time. I can't tell if it's because it feels riskier with the unstable conditions outside . . . or if it has more to do with the conditions brewing *inside* this cramped fuselage.

Even though I know it was a mistake, I can't stop thinking about that kiss. The rain, the turbulence . . . all competing with thoughts of Jonah's mouth on mine, and the way he was breathing when he pulled away.

And now we're in this misty valley and he's talking about us having sex. I mean, he didn't say that exactly, but that's what *I* heard, and I'm suddenly picturing the two of us stretched out naked on an air mattress with the door to our orange dome tent wide open to this great wilderness.

And it *does* sound insanely romantic.

"That might be okay." My eyes are locked on the river. I sound almost *shy*. When have I ever been shy with a guy who's so obviously flirting with me? Who I'm pretty sure has been flirting with me the last couple of days and I completely missed it. Who is making my nerve endings tingle and parts of me ache to be touched. Is he as turned on as I am?

Have his legs fallen apart that wide because he's got a—

"*Might* be?"

I push the illicit thought away with a throat-clear. "Yeah. You're a much bigger target for a bear, and I'm pretty sure I can run faster than you."

The deep chuckle that carries through the headset sends shivers down my spine and makes me smile dumbly. I'm becoming addicted to making him laugh.

Unfortunately, the playful conversation dies down as the drizzle grows harder and the wind begins to pick up. Jonah grips the yoke more tightly, his furrowed gaze on darker clouds ahead.

"Those don't look good."

"No. They don't," he agrees. "That's the thing about up here. The weather can turn on a dime. But we're not far off our checkpoint. We'll make it there."

"Okay." I realize that I trust him completely. It seems like a stupid time to ask, but, trust or not, I need a distraction from the constant jolting. "So . . . Marie. What's going on there?"

"What do you mean?"

I turn to watch his profile for clues. Maybe Dolores is right and he's too pretty now, because those full lips of his don't belong on a man like him. Neither do those lashes, which might be as long as my fake ones. "You know exactly what I mean."

Blue eyes flicker my way for a split second before returning to the sky. "Why do you want to know?"

"Just curious." I echo his words from earlier, when he asked about Corey.

He smirks. "Marie and I are friends."

"Even though she wants more?"

"Does she?"

I roll my eyes. "Stop playing dumb. You *know* she does."

He flips a switch on the cockpit panel. "Why do you care?"

"I don't."

He shakes his head. "You're such a Fletcher."

"What's that supposed to mean?"

"It means just come out and ask me what you really want to know, Calla." He sounds annoyed.

"Fine. Did you two ever date?"

"Nope."

I hesitate. "Did you two hook up?"

"Define 'hook up.'"

"I guess that answers that," I mutter, more to myself, letting my gaze drift to the mountain ridge.

"She kissed me once."

"And . . ."

"I can't give her what she wants. I'm not at that place in my life." He doesn't seem at all bothered to be telling me.

"She's really pretty," I hazard.

"And smart, and caring. But I just want to be friends with her. She knows it. I've been clear all along."

I can't suppress my sigh of relief fast enough.

"I take it that's the answer you wanted to hear?"

I turn away to hide my sheepish smile. He's too damn observant. And blunt. And inherently decent, if he hasn't taken advantage of the tall, blond, leggy veterinarian's attraction to him, at least once, in a moment of male weakness.

"What else do you want to ask me?" he murmurs.

I hesitate for only a second. What's the point of stopping now? "Why did you kiss me today?"

"Because I wanted to, and I knew you wanted me to." Such a simple, straightforward answer. Exactly what I've come to expect from Jonah. He pauses. "Am I wrong?"

"No." Unfortunately there are too many obstacles trailing it that I'm struggling to ignore. "Don't you think it's a bit risky? I mean, that it might complicate things, with everything else going on? Plus, I'm leaving in . . ." My voice drifts as realization dawns.

I'm leaving in a week. It'll be a nice, clean, uncomplicated end to whatever is happening between us.

A soft "Oh . . . right," slips from my lips. "Of course." That's *exactly* what he wants. And here I am, reading way too much into one kiss, especially from a guy I despised a week ago. This is why I don't do hookups.

"Of course, *what*?"

An orange bush plane suddenly appears in the sky, traveling toward us. It grabs Jonah's attention and splices our conversation. A moment later, the radio is crackling with a call-out from him, delivering an ominous warning about hellish headwinds and torrential rain around the ridge bend that he barely outran.

I feel my face fill with worry. "Are we turning around?"

"Can't. We're here, anyway." The right wing tips and we begin to descend.

Chapter 21

■ ■ ■

"This is definitely the right place?" I mutter, huddled within my slicker, my head bowed as I trail Jonah along a narrow footpath that cuts through the forest of spruce trees and leggy ground cover. It's a trek from where we left the plane. My jaw is sore from clenching my teeth so tight with that bumpy landing, and my leggings are soaked from rain that's coming down more sideways than straight.

"It's the *only* place around here."

A branch snaps somewhere to our right, loud enough to carry through the downpour. "Jonah . . ." I hold my breath as my head whips around, my eyes searching the trees.

"Relax. Our plane would have spooked most things. It's probably the Lannerds."

"Right." I speed up to close the distance between us all the same, shielding my eyes with my hand as I take in an archway. Someone constructed it out of tree trunks and rope. A hand-carved wooden sign dangles from the center; a set of antlers sits on top. It's fitting and oddly welcoming, out here in the middle of the middle of nowhere.

A small log cabin sits up ahead. It looks to be well cared for and supplied, the pile of cut logs and twiggy brush stacked by a simple wood door substantial. On the right is a rustic shelving unit that holds various boxes, tools, string, work gloves, and two black tanks with FLAMMABLE warning stickers plastered to them. Various tools hang on the exterior wall from pegs, protected from the inclement weather by a wide overhang.

"'Public Shelter Cabin,'" I read from the sign above the door, my eyes drifting to the enormous set of antlers mounted above it, and the snowshoes on either side. "Is this for anyone to use?"

"Pretty much. It's been here forever. Since, like, the 1930s, I think. It's mostly used during the Iditarod. That's one of the big dogsled races in Alaska," he adds, rapping his knuckles against the door. "Hello?" He waits three beats and then yanks the door open and walks in.

It smells exactly how I'd expect a ninety-year-old cabin in the mountains to smell—like musty wood and damp soot.

"They haven't made it here yet," Jonah declares, followed by a sharp, "Fuck."

There's certainly no evidence to suggest they're here now. The three tiny windows are all boarded up from the outside by plywood. The bunk beds in the far corners—simple frames of wood slapped together and bolted to hold—are absent of any sleeping bags.

The wooden picnic table beside the woodstove is bare of supplies. There *are* supplies here—lanterns hanging from hooks, rolls of toilet paper and tubs of baby wipes stacked on shelves, a jug of Crisco oil sitting on a long makeshift counter next to an array of pots and pans—but I suspect those were left by previous inhabitants, or by the caretakers.

"Maybe they left because we were late?"

He crouches down to open up and peer inside the woodstove. "No . . . with all this rain, they'd need a fire, and this hasn't been used in a while. Besides, they knew the pickup date would be pending weather."

"So, where are they, then?"

He stands and pushes a hand through his wet hair, slicking it back. "Good fucking question." His jaw clenches.

"Do you think they're lost?"

"They wouldn't be the first." He drums his fingertips against the table in thought. "They had a sat phone, but they didn't use it."

A darker, more sinister thought strikes me, after our earlier conversation. "What if something got them? You know, like a *bear*?"

"That doesn't happen *too* often," he murmurs, but he's wearing a troubled frown. "You didn't notice any tents or rain gear or anything when we were flying in, did you?"

"No. Nothing." The last sign of another human being—aside from the guy in the plane—was a fishing boat anchored on the river, a good ten minutes before we entered the mountain range.

He studies the dusty, worn wood floorboards intently. "They should have been here on Thursday night for a Friday pickup. That means they're almost two days behind."

"Did they say where they were going?"

"Through Rainy Pass. They gave me a map. They could be stuck up there because of the heavy rain, or they could have slipped along the muddy terrain. The river could have swelled on them . . . Who the fuck knows." Jonah wanders out the door to stand under the overhang, his gaze drifting to the mountain ridge that looms, in thought.

"You're not thinking of going back up to look for them, are you?" When he doesn't answer me, I know that's exactly what he's thinking. "You are *not* going up there in this to look for them."

He curses, his hands smoothing over his beard. "No, I'm not."

Relief overwhelms me.

He pulls out his satellite phone from his pocket. "I'm gonna call this in."

I huddle against the door frame, listening to rain beat against the roof and Jonah explain the situation to someone—my dad, I'm guessing. The connection must be poor, because Jonah is speaking loudly and repeats himself several times, emphasizing "no hikers," "heavy rain," and "staying here."

"What'd my dad say?" I ask when he ends the call, slipping the phone back into his pocket.

"He's gonna notify the state troopers. They'll have to start a search as soon as the weather cooperates. Nothing else I can do right now."

"Alright. So, *now* what?" I shiver against the damp cold. I still haven't warmed up from this morning's berry picking.

"Now . . . you and I are stuck here until we can fly out."

Something about the way he says "you and I" draws another shiver from me, this one not from the cold. "For how long?"

His chest lifts with a deep inhale. "Could be for the night."

"The night?" My eyes rove the cold, musty little cabin, stalling on the wooden base of the bunk beds. There's no mattress, no blankets, no pillows—not that I'd use anything left here.

No electricity, no plumbing.

"You think you can handle that, Barbie?" I turn back to find Jonah's piercing gaze settled on me.

Something tells me he's talking about more than just the rugged conditions.

My stomach does a flip. "Don't call me that."

"Prove me wrong, then," he challenges, taking a step forward, well into my personal space. I stand my ground, my heart beginning to race. Thoughts of missing hikers and bears and outhouses and bad ideas vanish, replaced by a simple one—that I desperately want him to kiss me again.

I tip my head back and gaze into intense blue eyes.

"You're Wren's *daughter*."

I frown. "Yeah . . ." What's he getting at?

"About what you said in the plane. I know where you were going with that." His brow furrows lightly. "You're *Wren's daughter*. I wouldn't use you like that."

"I'm not following." But my stomach is tightening with anxiety, that the next thing out of his mouth will be something along the lines of "You're right, it was a mistake and we should cool it."

Because, despite already seeing the end of the ride ahead, I'm ready to jump in the car and experience the thrill.

"I'm saying that I might take risks, but they're always worth it. Got it?"

"I think so?" Not really.

My gaze drifts to his mouth. *Ask me if I want you to kiss me again. Please.*

Abruptly, he pulls back. "We've got to set up camp. I'll start a fire when I get back."

"Back from where?"

"The plane. We need my gear!" he hollers into the wild.

I watch his retreating back, his shoulders hunched against the pelting rain as he marches down the path toward the plane.

Leaving me out here in the woods, all alone.

"Wait!" I run to catch up to him.

■ ■ ■

"You should have stayed put," Jonah mutters, crouching in front of the woodstove, shoving thin strips of wood into its mouth, the floor around him wet from the rain that drips off his body.

I probably should have, I admit, wringing water from my hair as I lean against the open door, taking in the tall weeds and wildflower blooms that bend under the rain's pummel. Jonah had just dragged out a nylon bag from the undercarriage when the skies seemed to open up with a deluge. We jogged all the way back, but it didn't matter. My rain boots, the slicker, none of it offered enough protection.

"Do you always fly with this stuff?" I eye the gear Jonah dumped on the floor, trying to ignore the beige case that holds a gun.

"Have to. A lot of it's law. Besides, you get stranded out here once and you learn to be more prepared next time around. We're lucky, though. We could be stuck in a cold plane for the night. Instead, we've got this cozy little paradise."

Our definitions of "paradise" are very different.

I hug myself tightly as Jonah strikes a match. Within moments, my nostrils fill with the comforting scent of burning wood. The flames begin to crackle.

"It'll take a bit to warm up in here." Jonah strolls past me, out the door, and around the corner. And I find myself holding my breath against the hope that he would have stalled there, would have looked down at me, smiled at me, grazed a hand against mine.

Anything.

There's an odd prying sound.

"Jonah? What are you doing out there?" I call out with a frown. I assumed he was going to relieve himself, something I'll have to do when I can't avoid that log outhouse any longer.

Suddenly daylight streams into the cabin through the tiny window on the left. Within minutes Jonah has the other two windows uncovered, too.

He reappears, his hair plastered to his forehead, raindrops dripping from his beard. "We need to close this door if we want to dry out." He pulls it shut behind him, herding me inside.

Despite the small portals in the walls, it's still dark in here, and it takes a few minutes for my eyes to adjust to the heavy shadows.

Jonah checks the fire, decides something, and then shoves a log into it. The fire grows.

"You're a regular Boy Scout, aren't you?"

"I know how to survive, if that's what you mean."

And thank God for that. I imagine being stranded out here with Corey. Last fall, the idiot threw wet logs onto a lit bonfire, and then nearly set himself on fire while pouring gasoline over them—and the flames—to try and get them to burn. Even I, a city girl, knew he was asking for trouble when he reached for that gas can.

I doubt any of my ex-boyfriends had particularly strong survival instincts. I can guarantee none of them have ever shot a gun.

But here's this rugged Alaskan pilot, his handsome face stony with focus, totally in control as he prepares our camp for the night, probably going through a mental checklist.

And I'm just standing here.

"What can I do to help?"

"There's a sleeping bag and mattress roll in there. Lay it on the floor over here."

"The floor?" I cringe at the worn boards.

"Trust me, it'll be more comfortable than those bunks. Plus it'll be warmer here, near the fire."

I follow instructions, quietly wondering if I'm getting this bed ready for him or myself.

Or for us.

My nerves flutter in my stomach at the thought.

Jonah starts peeling off his outer layers and hanging them on one of several wire clotheslines above the woodstove, until he's down to a clingy cream-colored crewneck that reminds me of long johns with its quilted material. The three buttons at the collar are undone, exposing the hard ridge of his collarbone and the top of the pad of muscle that stretches down over his chest.

"Give me your wet things."

"*All* my things are wet," I mutter, shrugging off the slicker and the flannel jacket. Even the hem of my tunic is soaked.

Jonah's gaze stalls on my chest a moment—given I can see his nipples pebbled beneath his shirt, I can only imagine what mine look like—before holding out his hand.

I frown at his palm, near the base of his wrist. "You're bleeding."

He turns his hand to inspect the gash. "Ah, shit. Yeah, I scraped it on one of the boards over the windows. It's nothing."

"It's *bleeding*. You must have a first-aid kit somewhere in here?" I dive down to begin rooting through the bag of basic survival gear—rope, a hunting knife, flashlight, iodine tablets for drinking water, ammunition—until I find a small white kit.

"I don't do Band-Aids," Jonah scoffs, tossing my raincoat over the line next to his things.

"Come here," I command softly, peeling the plastic wrapper away from the beige bandage as I wander over to him.

After a moment's pause, he holds his large, rough hand out.

With a painstakingly carefully touch, I wrap his injured palm, all the while feeling his intense gaze boring into my face. "There," I murmur, smoothing my fingers over his forearm, quietly marveling at the corded muscle and the soft tickle of ash-blond hair beneath my fingertips. "You've already ruined enough of my clothes with your blood." Words I never imagined saying to a guy.

"You asked why I kissed you."

I hazard a glance upward, to find his piercing blue eyes alight with heat. "And you said it's because you wanted to."

"That wasn't the right answer." He reaches up to smooth the wet strands of clingy hair off my forehead, his gaze wild as it skitters across my features. "You have been driving me fucking insane for days and I couldn't hold myself back for one more second."

"Really?" I say weakly, even as the tiny hairs on my nape prickle. This intimidating, sharp-tongued but soft-hearted, beautiful *man* is telling me he wants me. Badly.

And that's exactly what Jonah is: a man. All the other guys I've ever been with were just boys.

A swirl of nervous energy charges through my body, with a flooding warmth close on its heels.

It happens so fast.

One moment, I'm merely touching Jonah's arm and he's merely touching my cheek. The next, his hand is hooked around the back of my neck and he's pulled my mouth to his. There's nothing soft or tentative about this kiss. It's as if he's been counting down the minutes and hours since this morning, waiting for this moment, and now that it's finally here, he's not going to waste a single second.

I am stuck in the middle of an Alaska mountain range, making out with *Jonah*.

I can't believe this is happening, but whatever I convinced myself of earlier, this is a bad idea that I'm fully committing myself to for tonight.

His lips ply mine open and I taste his mouth for the second time today as his tongue slides in. Mint gum and traces of the cream soda he had in the plane. I don't even like cream soda, but on Jonah, I could drink an entire case.

My fingers begin to roam his body, crawling up his chest, reveling in its hard plains and his full, round shoulders, tracing the ridges of his collarbones and where they join his thick neck. Finally I let my arms loop around the back of his head so I can pull those full lips closer. If that's even possible.

My brain is still trying to process what's happening when he groans softly, "Calla."

I can only moan in response, as every square inch of my body below my mouth begins burning for his touch.

He adjusts his stance, setting his feet farther apart. His free hand splays across the small of my back and he pulls me flush to him, our bodies contouring against each other. I feel the hard press of his erection against my stomach.

His mouth leaves mine to find my neck and I let out a giggle-moan, the feel of his beard against my skin both intoxicating and tickling. It's followed by a straight-up deep moan as he drags his teeth over the same spot. "Your clothes are soaked," he murmurs, his hands sliding over my backside to test the hem of my tunic and my leggings, pausing to grip each side of me tightly, his fingertips digging into my flesh in a delicious way. He abruptly pulls away and takes two broad steps back. "Take them off," he demands softly, his voice low. "I'll hang them so they can dry."

He folds his arms over his broad chest and waits quietly, patiently, his fierce gaze locked on me, his lips parted.

"You, too." His pant legs are soaked.

"You first," he fires back, his eyes burning.

The cabin is dead silent, save for the drumbeat of rain. He's holding his breath, I realize.

With a deep swallow and a sudden case of nerves, I collect the hem of my long shirt and slide it up over my torso, over my chest, curling my arms to get it past my head.

Goose bumps erupt all over my skin as Jonah's eyes drift downward over my white lace bra, down over my flat stomach.

He holds out a hand and I toss my shirt to him. And still he waits without a word.

I kick off my rain boots and cast them aside, and then, curling my thumbs under the waistband of my leggings, I peel them away, shimmying the wet cotton down my legs and off my ankles, my socks going with them.

Jonah's eyes climb up my body and then drift again, stalling several times. "You're cold."

"Yeah." Even though every inch of my skin feels like it's on fire under his gaze.

"Better hurry up and finish, then," he murmurs with a crooked smile, my clothes dangling from his grip.

We both know that my undergarments are dry. Well, dry as far as the rain is concerned.

I feel light-headed as I reach back to unclasp my bra, letting it loosen and slide from my arms. "These *are* real, by the way," I murmur stupidly as cool air skates across my pebbled nipples.

His jaw clenches. "I see that."

I take a deep breath and then pluck away the elastic band at my hips, letting the skimpy lace fall to the floor.

"Fuck," he hisses. And then he's heading for the line, rushing to stretch and clip my things up with the available clothespins, while I stand in the cool, dark cabin, trying to fight the urge to curl my arms around myself. Something tells me Jonah prefers confidence.

"In the bed. Now," he mutters, and my heart begins to pound in my chest. I've never been with a guy who demands things like that. I never thought I'd find it a turn-on.

I drop to my knees on the foam pad—the width of a twin mattress—and pull the fully unzipped sleeping bag over my body, and then I quietly watch Jonah yank off his boots and socks.

He reaches over his head to peel his shirt off and I gasp as I get my first view of Jonah's broad back, his olive-toned skin stretched across muscle that fans out from his spine and toward his shoulder blades.

He turns and gives me an equally impressive view of his chest, coated in a fine dusting of ash-blond hair that continues downward, into a long, dark trail that disappears under his belt.

I stare unabashed as he unfastens his belt and buckle with confidence, pushing everything off with one move.

A light gasp slips from my lips as I take the sight of him in, feeling my eyes widen. Those unflattering baggy jeans hide the fact that his legs are thick and long and muscular, and coated with more of that ash-blond hair.

And that *all* of him is as well proportioned.

I feel my legs begin to part of their own volition.

I have to peel my eyes upward as Jonah strolls toward me, his smile wicked and cocky. God, I've come to love that smile. It vanishes just as quickly, though, the moment he's settling his massive body down onto the tiny pad next to me, lifting the cover off my naked body to make room for himself beneath it.

His bare skin is hot against mine and yet I shiver.

How have we gone from one surprise hallway kiss this morning to *this?* I am *not* this girl, I don't move this fast. And yet here I am, edging in closer to him, freely accepting his arm as he slides it beneath my head, welcoming his lips as they pry open my mouth, all while my heart pounds in my ears.

I drag my long fingernails over his beard for the first time, occupying myself with the delicious, scratchy feel of it while he seems eager to occupy himself with my body. Anticipation skitters along my spine, acutely aware of his hard length against my outer thigh as he toys with strands of my hair, before pressing his hand flat against my throat.

"Can't say I expected this turn of events," he murmurs, slowly smoothing his palm over my collarbone, over the contour of my left breast, stalling there a long moment before continuing down my stomach, my pelvis, farther . . . as far as he can reach, showing no hesitation as he seemingly memorizes my curves.

My breath hitches as that hand slides between my legs. He touches me far more gently than I thought him capable.

"You're nervous," he murmurs, his coarse fingers unexpectedly soft as they sink into me.

"No, I'm not," I lie behind a whisper and a kiss.

"Why are you nervous?"

I hesitate. "Because it's the first time?" It sounds like a question.

He seizes my bottom lip between his teeth playfully, before releasing it. "And that's the only reason?"

Do I admit the truth right now? That Jonah can be intimidating at times, that I've felt the strokes of his judgmental brush before and it wasn't pleasant, and now I'm in a *far* more vulnerable position to be judged.

He pulls away to peer down at me, his hand pausing its ministrations, his blue eyes shrewd as they study mine. "You know you're perfect, right?"

"Oh, *of course* I know that," I joke with faux confidence, trying to hide the fact that he's guessed at the real reason behind my nerves. "But I'm not your type. You know, blonde and leggy."

Good idea, Calla. Let's remind him of this right now.

His brow arches, but in his gaze I see confirmation of a guess. "That's not my type."

"But you said—"

"*You're* my type." His voice is gentle but he levels me with a steady gaze.

I pause, caught off guard by the seriousness in his eyes. "And what is that, exactly?"

With a deep sigh, he shifts, and then his mouth is following the same pathway of his palm. "Smart . . ." His tongue drags along my collarbone, back and forth several times, leaving a cool trail of wetness as it moves down to curl around my hardened nipple. "Fiery . . ."

I gasp as he sucks hard on it once before releasing it. His giant, muscular body shifts downward, pushing my legs apart as it moves, his lips pressing kisses down the center of my stomach, making my abdominal muscles tense. "Witty . . ."

I hold my breath as the coarse hairs of his beard tickle against my inner thighs.

He lingers there.

I shut my eyes and swallow hard, my mind screaming with anticipation.

"And, so damn beautiful . . ." He whispers, the words skating over me in a warm breeze.

I let out a soft moan the moment his mouth settles on me.

I can't believe this is actually happening. I can't believe Jonah is . . .

I stare up at the wooden ceiling of this shabby little cabin in wonder, my heartbeat racing as my hormones go into overdrive, flooding my body with heat.

He doesn't relent, doesn't pause, and the tiny, guttural sounds escaping his throat are heady with desire. Not before long, my nervousness has faded, and I find myself fumbling to weave my fingers through his hair, rolling my pelvis against his mouth, calling out his name with my desperate cries, the only sound for miles upon miles, save for the pounding rain.

By the time he climbs up to settle his hips between my thighs and push into me, I'm desperate for him.

My limbs curl around his body as I watch his broad chest heave with each thrust, and his hooded eyes alight with fire, our gazes locked, and I wonder how on earth I could ever possibly have *not* wanted this man.

■ ■ ■

"Am I going to wake up to find that gone in the morning, too?" Jonah murmurs, his voice scratchy and deep, but full of humor.

I trail the tips of my long nails through the soft, dark blond fuzz that coats Jonah's chest, deliciously damp from the sheen of sweat, circling first one nipple and then the other. "No. I think we'll keep this. But *this* . . ." My hand moves upward, sliding across his beard, tracing the hard lines of his jaw, the pad of my thumb smoothing over his soft lips. "I think I'll clean this up a bit more for you."

My head, settled against his chest, shakes with his deep chuckle. "What am I, your doll?"

I drag my fingers south, down the center of his chest ever so lightly, along the ridges of his stomach. I smile with delight when his muscles spasm. "More like my well-groomed action figure."

It's deathly silent in the cabin save for the constant drum of falling rain against the roof and his quickening breath as I follow the dark trail of hair below his belly button, itching to go farther, to tease his velvety-soft skin and watch him swell again.

"Don't start something you're not ready to finish," he warns.

I slide my thigh over his. "Who says I'm not ready to finish?" I can't seem to get enough of Jonah. I can't even look at his mouth without thinking of it on me; can't think of his hands without remembering where he's touched me. A nervous ripple courses through my body as the thought floods me now.

But I do hold back. I've found a blissful resting spot in the crook of his arm, my body pressed along his side, absorbing his warmth, and I don't want to ruin the peaceful moment.

"That fire needs another log."

I groan. "Don't make me move." The foam roll is narrow and thin, and it does little to disguise the fact that we're lying on a cold, hard wood floor that's seen countless boots, and yet it's easy to forget about that right now.

My stomach lets out a deep growl. "What are we going to do about food?"

"We're fine. There's a bunch of water, and we've got enough of this alone to feed us for days." He stretches an arm to reach into his duffel bag and pulls out two bags with leathery strips of meat in them.

"What is that? Beef jerky?"

"Basically." He holds up another with a deep rose color. "And this one's salmon."

I crinkle my nose at that.

"I take it that's a no to salmon?"

"I hate fish."

"Man, you are in the wrong part of the world."

"Where'd you get them, anyway?"

"Ethel. Remember her?"

"The woman who threatened to cut off her son's hand? Vaguely."

Jonah chuckles. "She gave them to me the last time I was at her village." He pulls a dark brown strip from the first bag and tears off a chunk with his teeth, his jaw tensing in a sexy way as he chews. "Here, try it." He holds it out for me.

I sniff. It has a smoky scent. "Is it any good?"

"Better than any store-bought stuff I've ever had. And it's all we have to eat, so come on." He taps my lips. "Take a bite."

I part my lips hesitantly, letting Jonah slide it in, his watchful gaze on my mouth as I tear off the tiniest piece between my front teeth. I let the intense flavor build on my tongue for a moment. "Not bad," I admit as I chew and swallow, and then burrow into his side with a shudder, the air cool against my bare back.

"Give me a minute." He presses a kiss against my forehead and then deftly maneuvers me off him.

I huddle under the covers and watch him grab another log from the small pile in the corner and carefully fit it into the woodstove, completely unabashed by his stark nudity. There's certainly nothing left of that skinny teenaged boy from the picture. He's all broad muscle and strength, perfectly proportioned, his thighs solid and thick. He makes Corey look like a gangly teen, and Corey's only two years younger than him.

"Do you go to a gym around here?"

"Not in a while."

"Then how—"

"Crazy good Norwegian genes. You should have seen the forearms on my grandfather. And I stay active." The flames begin to grow, adding light to the dim cabin and reflecting off his eyes, making the blue in them dance.

"Active like the past hour *active*?" Because the way Jonah was moving over me, his muscles corded and straining, his skin slick, he definitely got a workout. My thighs tighten reflexively at the thought. I can still feel him inside me.

Sharp eyes flicker to me before shifting back to the fire. As usual, he's figured out what I'm really asking and he's deciding if he'll make me drag it out of him or offer it up freely. "I was seeing a pilot from the coast guard for a while last year."

"What happened?"

"Nothing. She transferred back to the Lower Forty-eight."

"Do you miss her?" *What was she like? Did you spend a night on a dirty cabin floor by the fire with her, too? Would you still be with her if she hadn't left?*

He grabs the poker and jabs it into the stove. "I knew she wasn't sticking around, so I never let myself get attached."

I fidget with the slider on the sleeping bag's unfastened zipper, trying to push aside the dour thought that springs up.

Just like you won't get attached to me because I'm leaving. Another selfish thought quickly follows, that admits I *want* Jonah to grow attached to me. To pine and hurt for me after I'm gone. To care that I'm not there.

Because then I won't be alone in it.

But I'm guessing he's too smart to let that happen. "Are you always *so* honest about everything?" I ask mildly. Brutally so, sometimes. Though, I think I'm beginning to admire that quality. It's painfully refreshing.

I watch his face as it hardens with thought, his perfectly groomed jaw—the hairs mussed but still sexy—tensing. The mood in the cabin has suddenly shifted.

And then he sighs and, tossing the poker to the stone pad next to the stove, moves for the door, pushing it wide open. He simply stands there and watches the deluge of rain as it beats against the valley floor, his hands hooked on the wood above him, his naked silhouette framed by the doorway, cooler air flooding in.

I sense the need to stay quiet and let him work through whatever's on his mind, so I sit up and hug the sleeping bag tight to my body. And I selfishly admire his firm body. That ass I couldn't see in those styleless baggy jeans? It's there, alright. Round and rock hard, with two long red marks. From my nails, I realize. Several more marks span his back. I don't even remember getting that rough with him.

"My dad was like that. He'd come right out and tell you what he thought of you, and a lot of the time, it wasn't anything you'd want to hear. But he'd say it anyway. Couldn't help himself. It was like he'd explode if he didn't get it out." He chuckles. "When I met Wren, I didn't know what to think of him at first. He was this quiet man who kept his head down and seemed to just let things happen. Didn't yell about anything. He was about as opposite to my dad in every way as you could get. I don't think he knew what to think of me, either. I was pretty sure he was gonna can my ass within the first week. But George said I needed to come work for Wild, and I trusted George."

I smile, thinking back to my dad's words. "He said you were full of piss and vinegar when you started."

Another chuckle. "Definitely not sugar and spice, that's for sure."

"He knew you were a good pilot."

"It's funny, you know, my dad may have taught me how to fly a plane, but Wren was the first one to ever tell me I was any good at it. Maybe if he had, I wouldn't have bailed on the air force. Maybe I would have cared more to please him. I mean, I'd do anything for Wren." He pauses. "I know he doesn't have the best track record with you and God knows he has his faults, but he's up there with the best guys I know. I'm . . ." His voice drifts with a hard swallow.

"I'm really glad Agnes called me. And that I came to Alaska," I admit. That's the first time I've actually said those words. It's the first time I've truly felt them, deep down inside.

He turns his head, giving me his profile. "You mentioned staying in Alaska longer today."

"Uh . . ." *Yeah, in a moment of blind jealousy.* "I wasn't really thinking when I—"

"You should." His gaze drifts outward again. "For Wren. The next few weeks . . . months . . . are gonna be hard. It'd be better if you were in Alaska for them. With him."

"Is he even going to be around much, though? Sounds like he'll be in Anchorage most of the time."

Jonah's quiet for a long moment. "He won't ask you to put your life on hold for him, but he really likes having you around. I can tell."

That's basically what I'd be doing. Hitting "pause" on restarting my career at another bank, to wardrobe changes in Diana's Tahoe and fashion shots, to Simon's lattes and sage advice, to stilettos and clubs on Friday nights.

Back to a long-distance phone relationship with my dad.

And likely no relationship at all with Jonah.

My stomach tightens with the thought.

"Maybe you're right. I don't know what to do, though. I can't just keep rebooking every week. They charged me two hundred bucks—"

"See if you can cancel your return ticket and rebook it when you're ready."

I actually might be able to do that. Simon did say it was flexible. As usual, Jonah makes it sound so simple.

"Your life will be waiting for you when you go back, and it won't matter if it's next week, or next month, or next year—"

"Next *year!*"

"Maybe not that long," he mutters. "My point is, you won't lose anything by staying. That life will still be there to go back to."

My eyes drift over his perfect body again. I just spent two hours tangled up with this guy. "And what about this? If I did stay that long, don't you think we just complicated things?" Because I'm *definitely* feeling something for Jonah, and it's not just physical.

What will weeks, or months, of doing *this* do to us?

"Maybe, but I don't ever let that shit stop me from doing what I need to do. I live my life by the day. And today, you're here." He pulls the door shut and turns to face me. My eyes can't help but flicker downward. He certainly hasn't had an adverse reaction to the cold air. "But we can stop this right now, if you want, if that's going to be a deciding factor for you staying."

An unexpectedly strong wave of disappointment hits me at the suggestion, at the thought that I won't get to feel his mouth or his touch or his weight or his heat anymore. *No, I do not want that.* "Let's not get hasty."

He smirks. "I had a feeling you'd say that." He strolls forward to drop to his knees at the end of the foam mat and yanks the sleeping bag off me. Gooseflesh springs over my skin instantly. Jonah's eyes are like lasers drawing over my skin, taking everything in, deciding where to attack first.

I help him decide by stretching my body out for him, even as my stomach does a nervous flip.

His strong, rough-skinned hands seize my ankles and begin their slide upward, pushing my legs apart as they go, and all my worries about tomorrow are instantly forgotten.

Chapter 22

■ ■ ■

Thwack.

Thwack.

Thwack.

My eyes crack open to a dull, repetitive sound coming from outside. Dim daylight filters through the tiny portals, illuminating just enough so that I can make out the medley of frying pans dangling from nails against the wall.

I'm alone in our makeshift bed and the air is cold. I tug the sleeping bag tight under my chin and curl into a ball, instantly feeling the pull of sore muscles. I can't tell how much of that is from sleeping on this thin foam mattress, and how much is because of my night with Jonah.

The rain has stopped, at least, I note. That constant drum against the roof was a soothing white noise for me to finally drift off to in the wee hours, but now the ensuing silence is all the more deafening.

Thwack.

Thwack.

Thwack.

Curiosity finally wins me over. Throwing off the sleeping bag, I step into my rain boots and grab Jonah's flannel jacket from the clothesline, knowing it'll cover enough of me. Hugging it tightly, I step outside. A thick, gloomy fog has settled over the soaked forest, shrouding the tall spruce trees and the narrow pathway to the plane. Even the outhouse has disappeared. It's almost ghostly in mood, this morning.

Jonah is off to the left, his back to me, bent over a sizeable tree stump to position a log on its end. An axe sits nearby, next to a small pile of freshly split wood. He's wearing nothing but his baggy jeans and unlaced boots. I settle against the door frame and quietly admire the stretch and strain of the muscles in his naked back as he reaches for the axe.

"How'd you sleep?" Jonah calls out suddenly, his voice especially gravelly with the morning.

"Pretty good." I clear the scratch from my throat. "A bit thirsty."

"Well, that's a huge surprise," he mutters wryly. "That water we had should have lasted us a week."

"Yeah, if you're a camel." And you're not used to polishing off a two-liter bottle every day, like I do back home.

He glances over his shoulder, his gaze stalling on my bare thighs for a brief moment, before returning his focus to his task. He swings the axe, bringing it down on the chunk of wood. It splits in two.

If there's such a thing as beautiful form while chopping wood, Jonah has it. Or maybe it's just him that's beautiful, because I could watch that broad chest and tapered waist all day long. A flash of his powerful shoulders and arms tensing over me last night comes to mind and my lower belly instantly stirs with the memory.

On impulse, I duck back into the cabin to grab Simon's Canon. I manage to snap a few candid in-action pictures before he turns and catches me. "What are you doing?" he asks warily.

"Nothing. Just . . . I want to remember this." I smile, setting the camera aside. As if I could *ever* forget it.

He makes a grunting sound, and I can't tell if he's annoyed or just being Jonah. "I'll have the fire going again soon."

"What time is it, anyway?" The battery on my phone has long since died.

"Just after six."

I make the reluctant trek toward where I know the outhouse is, unable to ignore my bodily needs and just wanting to get it over with at this point. Jonah walked me out in the rain three times last night and howled with laughter every time I ran out of the dingy, dark little box. I've never peed so fast in my life, and I hated every second of it.

Shockingly enough, despite the lack of other basic comforts, it's the only thing I've hated about being stranded out here. Probably because Jonah has kept me well occupied.

"So, I'm guessing we can't take off yet?" I ask on my way back, slathering sanitizer over my hands. Tall, damp weeds lick my bare legs as I trudge through the grass, leaving wet trails against my skin.

"Not until this fog lifts. A few more hours, at least." Two halves of another log tumble to the ground with his powerful swing.

My stomach lets out a well-timed grumble. "Is there anything else besides that meat?"

"Protein bars."

"Right." Dried meat and protein bars. This can't be good for anyone's digestive system. "What would we do for food if we were actually stranded out here for a while, anyway?"

"We'd be fine. I've got my fishing rod and the gun." Jonah swings the axe.

Thwack.

"Of course." *We'd just go kill our meal. Naturally.*

The intimate, passionate Jonah from last night is absent this morning. He seems to be back to focused survivalist mode, much like he was when we arrived yesterday. I shouldn't complain—he's keeping me warm and fed—yet I ache for him to drop everything and kiss me again.

What if he's decided that last night was a one-time deal?

It probably *should* be, before I get in too deep with him. Who's kidding who, though? I'm already acutely aware of his moods and potential thoughts, and caring too much about them. Isn't that the first sign that you've waded in too deep?

Diana would swear it is.

But acknowledging that doesn't change the fact that I still want him. Badly.

I feel a pinch and slap my thigh with a hiss, squashing a mosquito against my skin. Another one lands beside the corpse, oblivious and ready to feed.

"You're about to get swarmed. They just came out," Jonah murmurs, grabbing an armload of wood and marching toward the cabin, his boot laces dragging through the grass.

He gets to work relighting the fire while I track down the few bugs that followed us in.

"Forget another bank job. I should just find someone to pay me to do this all day," I mutter with grim satisfaction.

"There's a small can of repellent somewhere in that bag. If you want to spray yourself."

"Why not? I'm already filthy," I mutter.

With another fire crackling, Jonah pulls his shirt off the line and slides it over his head. "Give it a few minutes and then stick one log in."

I frown. "Wait. Where are you going?"

He gives me a look. "You said you were thirsty, so I'm getting you water from the river."

"*Oh*. Thanks."

He grabs an old dented metal pot off the wall. "I want to check on the plane anyway."

I'm torn between a gush of warmth that Jonah's still catering to my basic needs and utter disappointment that he might have already had his fill of meeting my *other* need: him.

He heads for the door.

"Wait," I blurt out. "You forgot this."

He pauses to look over his shoulder.

I take a deep breath and then peel off his bulky flannel jacket. The cool air skates over my bare skin as I stand there in nothing but my military red rain boots, holding my breath, waiting for him to respond.

Hoping to God he doesn't deny me.

With a heavy sigh and a soft curse, he tosses the pot back onto the counter.

My stomach does a nervous but victorious flip as he reaches over his head to yank his shirt off. "Don't say I didn't take care of you out here," he warns, stalking toward me, his hands making quick work of his belt.

■ ■ ■

I pause to grab one last picture of the safety cabin, capturing the wooden archway in front and a partially cloudy mountain range in the background.

"Come on, we've gotta go!" Jonah hollers.

"And the angry yeti is officially back."

"What?"

"Nothing, I just wanted a shot of this," I mutter, stuffing my camera into its case. He's been in a rush ever since the fog dissipated not even a half hour ago, making quick work of camp cleanup so we could get moving. It's like he suddenly can't get out of here fast enough.

I'm trying to not take it personally.

He sighs heavily. "I'm being an ass, aren't I?"

While the actual apology doesn't come out, I sense it there. "At least you're learning when to admit it. That's progress." I trail him down the path, my annoyance fading almost instantly. His emergency gear hangs from his shoulder, the sleeping bag and foam pad once again rolled tidily and tightly, as if they didn't aid and abet in a night of private acts.

"How bad do you want to get home?"

"To be honest, I think I'm going to miss this place." I'm going to miss having Jonah all to myself. Despite the fact that my clothes and hair reek of smoke from the woodstove and I'm desperate for a shower and a toothbrush.

"I'm definitely gonna miss that table."

Heat explodes over my face as an image of that particularly intimate moment hits me.

But at least I'm not the only one who's still thinking about us.

What happens now, though?

We'll fly back to Bangor . . . and then what? I'm booked to leave next weekend, and yet here I am again, wondering if I should stay. Where exactly will that leave Jonah and me, though? Are we going to secretly screw in between hopping into planes and throwing around casual banter?

Or will I be waking up in Jonah's bed tomorrow morning?

As I quietly take in the powerful body I became so well acquainted with last night, I already know I'd much prefer the latter.

What would my dad make of that, though? He joked about Jonah and me hooking up, but would he *actually* be happy to find out that we did?

It's probably for the best, anyway. You don't need to be repeating our mistakes.

It's not like we're repeating my parents' mistakes, though. We didn't meet each other in some bar and fall madly in love. We didn't even like each other at first. And I'm not about to get caught up in some false romantic fantasy about moving to Alaska.

I like him now, true.

I think I like him a lot.

He's not like any other guy I've ever dated or crushed on. And while he's capable of making my blood boil like no one else, I feel a magnetic pull toward him that I can't explain.

But there's a very clear expiration date to whatever this is between us and I haven't lost sight of that.

Well, I *might* have for a few hours last night.

I will miss Jonah when I leave Alaska. And I *am* leaving Alaska at some point. That, I am sure of. The question is just a matter of when. And how many times I want a repeat of last night until then.

We step out into the clearing and for the first time since coming into this valley, I'm able to fully grasp the vast open wilderness before us, and how remote we truly are, two tiny figurines with looming walls of rock that reach to the sky on either side of us. The wide river ahead trickles and rolls over a bed of rocks and driftwood, the water shallow and sparse in places but continuously flowing.

Our plane sits where we left it, a small speck in a cavernous valley beyond, quietly waiting for Jonah to fly us home.

He pops the door for me and then goes about getting us ready while I take more pictures.

I can't help but watch his every methodical step, his hands—that were so attentive to me earlier—smoothing over the plane's body with near reverence; his gaze—that has been on every square inch of my body, many times over—now studying every square inch of metal critically.

By the time he climbs into his seat, my skin is flushed and I'm wondering what sex would be like in a plane.

"There's more room in here than I first thought," I murmur, eying the backseat.

He chuckles as he starts flipping switches. "We can't do this right now."

"Do what?" I ask innocently, even as my cheeks burn. *How the hell does he know what I'm thinking? And what is wrong with me?* I'm not normally needy like this.

He peers up at the daunting ridges and the wisps of cloud hovering around them. "We're going to go through the pass to look for the Lannerds."

Thoughts of climbing onto Jonah's lap fade as real life takes over. "We can't land up there, can we?"

"Not likely, but we should at least look."

I should have known Jonah would want to do that. He doesn't seem the type to be able to report a missing person and then simply move on with his day. I sigh with a hint of trepidation. "Okay. If you say it's fine."

"It is. Trust me." Jonah smooths his hand over my thigh, and my blood begins to race. "We can revisit that other conversation later. But for right now, I need your focus. And your eyes."

■ ■ ■

"And they definitely said they were going up into Rainy Pass?" I ask as we clear the last section of the mountain range, having found no signs of the hikers but plenty of tense moments where the cloud cover shifted to mask entire peaks. Dense trees and a vast system of lakes stretch before us, as far as my eyes can see. I sink back into my seat, taking what feels like the first deep breath since we took off, wishing for a stiff drink.

Jonah holds up a creased piece of paper with a map and a hand-drawn line with several x marks. "This was the planned route they gave me just in case."

Which we basically just flew over, as much as we could, anyway.

"So, now what?" I wince, the bumping and jostling from the turbulence having done little good for the blossoming caffeine headache behind my eyes.

Jonah's shrewd gaze studies the fuel gauge as he bites his bottom lip in thought. "Man, Wren and Aggie are gonna be pissed."

"Why?" I ask warily.

"Because they hate it when I change plans." Jonah's hands are tight on the yoke as he dips our plane to the right and brings us around. "And I'm changing plans."

■ ■ ■

"There!" I shriek, my adrenaline surging as I stab the air. A sagging yellow dome tent sits on the ridge to our right. One person—likely a female, given the long ponytail—is jumping up and down, frantically waving her arms in the air. The person beside her remains seated on the ground, propped up by a pile of rocks and covered by a neon-orange blanket. "Is that them?"

"They're *way* off course, but yeah, pretty sure that's them. And he's hurt." Jonah eyes the flat patch of ridge behind them with a calculating look that makes my stomach drop.

"You can't land here."

"I've landed on worse." After another moment of consideration, he shakes his head. "I could, but I wouldn't get back up with the added weight." He curses under his breath, and then with a sigh, he tips the wing toward them before leveling off. A signal that we've noticed them.

The woman falls to her knees and throws her arms around the man's neck, and I'm hit with a wave of chest-warming relief. God only knows what their story is, and what the situation is, but her joy is unmistakeable, even from the air.

Jonah gets on the radio. Within minutes, a search-and-rescue team have the couple's coordinates and a helicopter is en route.

"How'd you know to look here?" Jonah veered off in another direction on the way back.

"Just a hunch. Sometimes people get these two rivers mixed up." He drags a finger along the photocopied map. "They were smart enough to camp out where they did, though. If they'd stayed down *here,* there's no way we would have seen them and who knows how long it would have taken the rescue guys to fly out this way. They could have been out here for another week, easily." His chest heaves with a sigh and I catch the faintest "thank God," under his breath.

"That would have really bothered you, huh."

"It would have bugged the shit out of me," he admits. "I would have dropped you off, fueled up, and come right back."

"Is that why you were in such a rush to get back in the air?"

He wasn't being an ass. Well, maybe he was, but it's more that he wanted to find them.

Jonah pauses. "Nah. I was just afraid you'd take off your clothes again." His lips twitch as he tries to hide his smile.

I give his arm a playful smack and the corners of his eyes crinkle with his smile.

He reaches down to squeeze my hand before putting it back on the yoke. "Come on. Let's go home."

■ ■ ■

"This is gonna be a treat," Jonah mutters, steering the plane in with an air marshal's guidance, his blue gaze on Agnes as she marches toward us.

"She doesn't look angry," I say doubtfully. Agnes's face is typically serene. Sure, there's no wide smile to greet us. If anything, she seems hesitant to approach.

"She never does. That's part of her superpower."

"Well, at least we found the hikers. They'll be happy about that."

"Yeah. They will be." Jonah sets his headset down with a sigh, smoothing a hand over his beard. "But Wren hates it when I fly in on fumes, and this time I did it with you."

I frown. "Wait, what do you mean 'fly in on fumes'?" I look down at the gauge with new alarm as it registers. "Did we almost run out of gas? *In the air?*"

"Nah. She probably had another five miles or so in her." He pats the plane's door affectionately.

Five miles? Probably? "Are you *insane*?" Thank God I didn't know about that!

"Relax. I was watching the line and doing the math. If I didn't think we could make it, I'd have found somewhere to put her down."

"You mean like on a pile of rocks in a field?" Has he *already* forgotten that he crashed a plane a few days ago?

I get a sharp glare in return, a warning that throwing that in his face was not a good idea. "No. On one of the sandbars that we passed."

"Fine. So we would have been stranded in the middle of nowhere, without heat, eating beef jerky and protein bars?" I don't bother hiding my irritation.

"Hey, you're the one who was sizing up the backseat of the plane for us." He slides out before I can get a proper retort in.

Not that I necessarily have one handy.

My flare of anger fades to annoyance as I watch him round the nose. He pulls my door open for me and holds a hand out.

On impulse, I swat it away and hop down. My rubber boots hit the gravel with a soft thud. Just a week ago, showing up here in my wedge heels, I would have needed him.

God, what was I even thinking, wearing those here?

"So *now* you don't need me. Funny, I don't remember you pushing my hand away last night when I was—" He grunts with the impact of my fist against his hard gut.

"Shut *up!*" I hiss, giving him a warning as I glance around, hoping the air marshal didn't catch that.

He chuckles and squeezes the back of my neck in a way that could look platonic, except his fingers find their way past my hair to linger against my skin. "Hey, Aggie. Did rescue call with an update on the Lannerds?"

"They're taking them to Anchorage now," Agnes confirms. "Apparently, they got disoriented in the fog, and then Mr. Lannerd slid down a washed-out slope and broke his leg. Lost his sat phone in the tumble."

Jonah snorts. "That's an anniversary trip they'll never forget."

"Oh my God." Another wave of relief swarms over me. "What if we hadn't done that second pass?" What if Jonah hadn't thought to look where we did? He could have been out there with a broken leg for *days*.

"Feels pretty good helping people in trouble, huh?" Jonah's gaze searches the plane lot. "Where's Wren? Might as well get his licks in on me now."

Agnes's brow tightens. "Yeah, I . . ." Not until she turns those steady eyes on me do I finally see the pain and sadness that overwhelms them.

■ ■ ■

I hold my breath as I push through the door.

"Look who made it back," my dad murmurs, his voice groggy and weak. I've only ever seen him in his jeans and layers of flannel. He looks so different, lying there in his hospital gown.

So frail and vulnerable.

Mabel's in a chair next to him, her legs pulled to her chest, her arms wrapped tightly around her knees. Her eyes are red and puffy, with the stunned glaze of someone who sat down to watch a comedy, only to have the curtain pulled back and discover she's about to witness a horror.

They've finally told her about the cancer. I find no relief in that, though it was time anyway. She'd wonder why he wasn't home in the evening for their checkers games.

"Time to go now, Mabel," Agnes calls from the door.

She doesn't move.

My dad gives her an encouraging smile. "I'll be out of here soon."

"Promise?" she asks, her voice so feeble and childlike, and unlike her.

"Promise, kiddo."

Unfolding slowly, reluctantly, she climbs out of her seat, her dusty sneakers leaving bits of dirt. She leans in to give him a hug.

"Careful, Mabel," Agnes warns.

With a quiet nod, she moves to dart past Jonah and me, flashing me a look that is full of sorrow and youthful resentment. She's figured out why I really came to Alaska and she's not one bit happy that I kept her in the dark.

"Hey," Jonah calls out, as she tries weaseling past him. He reaches out and grabs hold of her before she has the chance to get away, effortlessly pulling her against his chest in a hug. She doesn't struggle, instead bowing her head and burying her face in his jacket. A single sob ratchets up from her lungs and it makes the already painful ball in my throat swell instantly.

Jonah quietly strokes the back of her long, dark hair with his hand for a few moments, and then with a deep exhale murmurs softly, "'Kay, go with your mom, kiddo."

They leave, and now it's just the three of us.

My dad's gray eyes skitter back and forth between us, before settling on me. "So, Calla? First night stranded in the mountains. How was it?"

"It could have been a lot worse, I guess," I admit.

"You two stayed at the safety cabin? I'll bet you've never stayed anywhere like that before."

"No, I haven't." And it's the absolute last thing I want to talk about right now, but I can tell my dad's trying to avoid dealing with the current situation for just a little while longer.

"Barbie had it pretty damn good, I'd say." Jonah chuckles.

I shoot him a glare, even as my cheeks flush. "Aside from the mediocre company. I'm looking forward to a hot shower and real food. I'm maxed out on beef jerky." Who am I kidding? My appetite has vanished.

"Beef jerky?" My dad glances at Jonah, his eyes narrowing curiously.

"From Ethel," Jonah explains. "Her homemade stuff. Calla liked it."

"Well . . . that's good." My dad lets out a soft cough and then winces.

"Does it hurt?" I look down at his chest, wondering where exactly the doctors stuck that long needle in. The one that drained the fluid that's been building up in his lungs, that had him wheezing last night.

"It's actually a lot better than it has been the last couple of days. They've got me on some good drugs."

Despair hits me in a wave. He's been suffering for days? "Why didn't you say something—"

"Nah." He gives me a resigned smile, waving it off. The hospital bracelet slides down his forearm.

"I'm sorry. We should have been there. But the rain and then the fog . . . Jonah said we couldn't fly." My eyes begin to burn with tears. It's all true, and yet I can't help but ache with guilt for how we spent the night and morning while this was going on.

"If Jonah said you couldn't, then I know you couldn't. Besides, I told Agnes not to say anything if he called in. I didn't want him taking any unnecessary risks to get here sooner. Don't worry, it's nothing. Just a complication. Wasn't even that serious. I'll be out in a day or two."

I let out a shaky sigh of relief. "I'm coming with you when you go to Anchorage for treatment." And I'm canceling my ticket as soon as I get back to my dad's. I don't know why I ever wondered if I should be here. Seeing my dad lying there, in that hospital bed now . . . there's nowhere else I could be.

My dad's gaze averts to his hands.

"Wren . . ." Jonah's jaw tenses. "This ain't right anymore. You need to tell her *now*, or I will."

A sinking feeling settles into my body. "What are you talking about? Tell me what?" I turn to my dad. "What's he talking about?"

"You're supposed to fly Dempsey and his crew up to their spot today. They're probably waiting for you."

"Wren—"

"Okay, Jonah. *Okay*." He sighs with resignation, pats the air.

"Why don't you get those guys where they need to go. Give me some time to talk to my daughter."

Jonah bows his head a long moment, and then he grips the side of my face and pulls my temple toward his lips, pressing a kiss against it, lingering there for one . . . two . . . three beats. "I'm sorry," he whispers, and then he's gone out the door.

"Well, it's good to see you're finally getting along," my dad murmurs, smiling.

"Yeah. Um . . ." Despite everything, I feel my cheeks flush.

"Pull up a chair. Stay a while." He gestures to the seat Mabel just left. It's still warm when I settle into it.

"What's going on, Dad?" I ask, my voice shaky with wariness.

He simply studies my face, long and hard.

"Dad—"

"Your grandfather had lung cancer, too. You knew that, right?"

"Yeah. Mom told me."

My dad nods slowly. "Same kind that I have. Small cell. It's more rare than the other kind and yet we both got it. And it grows fast. By the time they found it in him, his odds weren't great, but he figured he should listen to everyone else and do the chemo." He shakes his head. "Those last six months of his life were hell. He was in Anchorage a lot and when he wasn't, he barely got out of bed. My mom took good care of him, as good as she could, anyway. But it wasn't easy on either of them. By the time he called it quits on treatment, he was just a shell of a man." My dad chews his bottom lip a moment. "One of the last things he ever said to me was that he wished he'd just made peace with it from the beginning. He would have had less time, but at least he might have enjoyed it more. He would have spent his last days on his terms. That always stuck in my head."

Realization dawns on me, as I begin to understand where my father's going with this.

And the horrible, sinking feeling that settled earlier gives way to a numbing calm.

"But that was, like, thirty years ago. Everything's more advanced. The chances of surviving—"

"There's no surviving this, Calla," he says with grim finality. "Not this type. Not this far in."

"But you're fine." He's *nothing* like Mrs. Hagler was, with her decrepit body and her sallow skin, her oxygen tank rolling behind her. "I mean, obviously you're not fine *right now* because you're in the hospital, but a week ago you were *fine*." I don't sound like myself.

"Nah, I wasn't. I've just been good at hiding it. I don't have as much energy as I used to. And I've been having chest pains for some time," he admits.

"Because of the tumor?"

"Yeah. Partly."

"So they can shrink it. That's what radiation is for. And the chemo will kill the cells—"

"It's already spreading, Calla." Soft, gray eyes finally lift to meet mine. "It's in my lymph nodes. In my bones. All that stuff just buys me a tiny bit more time, and it won't be good time."

"How *much* time, exactly?" The question comes out in a croaky whisper.

"It's hard to say, but they gave me two, maybe three months, with it."

I suck in a sharp, shaky breath. "And how much without?"

He hesitates. "Four to six weeks at most, they're thinking."

A cold feeling spreads through my chest as his words hit me like a punch to the stomach. How is that possible? He looks *fine*. "I just . . . The doctors are wrong, obviously. They're always wrong, Dad! *Always*," I stammer as the words tumble out. "I hear stories all the time about how people beat the odds and survive for years."

He sighs. "Not always, Calla. Those are the stories that people remember because they need to. People need hope. But, not *always*. Not this time."

My initial shock ebbs as frustration and anger with his refusal to listen rushes forward. "So, that's just it? There's no talking about it anymore? There's no convincing you to at least try to live? For me? For Mom?" My voice cracks. I'm getting desperate now.

"If I let them pump me with all that shit, I'll be spending my last bit of time sleeping and puking, and in some hospital room for eight hours a day, five days a week, until I stop or I die. That's not how I want to go. I want to do it on my own terms." He reaches for my hand, but I find myself unable to take it and after a moment, his fingers fall lazily next to his side. "I thought about you, when the doctor gave me the news. You were the very first thing I thought about. I didn't know if I should call you right away, or if I shouldn't call at all. Wasn't sure if I had any right to. Figured you might not want to know, after all these years." His eyes grow glossy and he blinks the sheen away. "I'm glad Agnes didn't listen to me and did what I didn't know how to do. What I didn't have the guts to do. I'm so glad you came."

Another wave of realization dawns on me. "They knew how bad it was? Agnes and Jonah, they knew?" Have they been leading me on this entire time?

"I never told Agnes. I was planning to. And then the next thing I knew, you were on your way. I didn't know how you'd take my decision not to—"

"Bullshit," I snap. "You knew damn well that I wouldn't be okay with you just giving up. That *no one* would be. That's why you've been hiding it."

His lips press together. And then he nods. He's not denying it, at least. "I know you probably spent a lot of years angry with me. I figured, if I could just have one week to get to know you again, without this hanging over our heads. One week where maybe I wasn't disappointing you."

The week *had* been good, I'll admit. But now it's all gone to hell.

"So Jonah knew." I feel a sharp sense of betrayal as I say those words out loud, as the pieces click together. *That*'s why he's been pushing me to stay. Because when I get on that plane for home, I'll be saying goodbye to my dad forever.

The next few weeks . . . months . . . are going to be hard.

They'll be hard not because my dad will be fighting cancer. There is no fight.

He's already given up.

Without another word, I get up and duck out of the hospital room.

By the time I've reached the exterior doors, I'm running.

Chapter 23

■ ■ ■

Twenty minutes standing under a stream of hot water in a daze and I still can't seem to find any warmth or comfort in it. All I feel is the biting sting from the numerous blisters on my heels and toes. The distance between Bangor's local hospital and my dad's house must be at least six miles, and I ran all of it in my rain boots.

My arms feel sluggish as I lift them to my hair to scrub my scalp, working the shampoo into a heavy lather, releasing the scent of wood-burning smoke that my hair absorbed while in the cabin.

I begin to laugh. It's a soft, humorless sound—not really a laugh at all—as I remember my conversation with Diana, in the club that night. It feels like forever ago that I voiced a seemingly unbelievable thought at the time: What if I came to Alaska and somehow found the dad I'd always wanted, despite his many flaws, despite the fact that he all but abandoned me so many years ago, only to lose him again?

It's happening.

I found him, and now I'm going to lose him all over again. This time, for good.

He's breaking my heart all over again, whether he intended to or not.

I'm not sure exactly when the water pressure started going, but suddenly I'm standing under a sad trickle, my head covered in soapy suds, my body shivering from the loss of heat. "No, no, no . . . Don't tell me . . ." I fumble with the showerhead, adjusting it this way and that. Nothing.

I turn the tap all the way to the right. Nothing.

We've run out of water. Jonah warned me that this could happen.

I let out a heavy sigh of frustration and drop my forehead to the shower wall with a thud. "God dammit," slips from my lips.

And I finally stop fighting the tears.

■ ■ ■

A soft knock sounds on the bathroom door. "Calla?"

I press my lips to my knee to keep from answering. I can't deal with Jonah right now.

A moment later, he calls out more sternly, "Calla?" The doorknob rattles. "Let me in."

"Leave me alone," I mutter.

"Look, either you let me in or I'm coming in."

I don't answer. Don't make a move.

The floor creaks as he moves down the hall, away from the bathroom. But then he's back again and there's an odd metal-against-metal crunch. With a pop, the bathroom door eases open. I can see Jonah's distorted reflection in the shiny chrome tap, hovering in the doorway, but I don't turn around.

"What are you doing?"

"I ran out of water." How long ago was that, that I sank to the tub floor and curled my arms around my knees? It must have been a while. I've stopped shivering, stopped crying. My hair's still covered in soap, though the suds have flattened out.

He sighs. "Come on, you can use mine." He steps into the bathroom and stretches out a hand.

I ignore it, shifting away from him.

"Calla . . ."

"When did you find out?" I ask, my voice oddly hollow.

He settles his big frame on the edge of the tub, keeping his gaze ahead of him, on the vanity doors. He's still wearing the same clothes, the smell of smoke permeated into them. Last night feels so long ago now. "The same day Aggie told me what was going on, the day you came. I had a bad feeling when I pressed him for details. He was all wishy-washy about the treatment plan, about how many days a week he'd have to be in Anchorage, where he'd be staying. Then he took off and I flew out to get you." He studies his ragged fingernails intently for a moment. "I got it out of him later that night."

That's the difference between Jonah and me, right there. I just accepted my dad's reluctance to talk about it, because deep down I wasn't ready to talk about it, either. I was just as happy to avoid the truth that I should have seen coming from a mile away.

"So you already knew, that morning I came to ask for a ride to Meyer's." He's known *all along*.

His head falls into his hands, his fingers combing through his hair, making it stand on end. "He made me promise not to say a word to you or Aggie. Believe me, I wanted to so many times. I came close last night. But Wren wanted to be the one to try and explain his decision. I couldn't take that away from him." He pauses. "You can be mad at me all you want, you can hate my guts and not want to talk to me, but it won't change the fact that Wren's going to die, and we've all got to figure out a way to come to terms with that."

"Did you at least *try* to talk him into the treatment?"

"What do you think, Calla?" Irritation flares in his voice. "Don't you dare think for one second that you want this to happen any less, or that this is going to hurt you *more* than it does me, or Agnes, or Mabel. You're gonna go back to your life in Toronto with a memory of him. Meanwhile, we'll be here, feeling him gone every single damn day—" He cuts off abruptly, his voice turning hoarse.

"How are you not angry with him?"

"Not angry? I'm fucking pissed! Pissed that he waited so long to get checked out. Pissed that he didn't quit that shit years ago." His booming voice fills the small space. It's a moment before he speaks again, more calmly. "But Wren doesn't make rash decisions. He thinks long and hard about them. If even the doctors are saying they can only buy him a few extra weeks, then I can't blame him for not wanting to waste what he's got."

"What about the rest of us, who have to sit by and watch?" I ask hollowly. Hasn't he considered what this is going to do to the people who love him?

"He's convinced himself that he's making the best decision for everyone's sake and the thing with him is, once he's made up his mind, there's no turning him around. He's more stubborn than I am."

Like the decision he made to let my mom and me go all those years ago.

What *is* life going to be like around here with him gone, I wonder, as my eyes crawl up the molded shower wall. This little modular house with the tacky ducks felt so empty when I first stepped into it and, while it's still the same empty little house, I now have memories attached to it, to help fill it up. Of my dad's soft chuckle carrying through the perpetual silence, of the smell of his fresh-brewed coffee in the morning, of the sound of the floors creaking as he pads down the hallway after saying good night to me. Such little things—tiny, trivial slivers of his life that shouldn't count as memories—and yet I know they'll be the first things that come to mind when I think of him here, years from now.

And that's just within these walls. What about out there, beyond them? "What's going to happen to Wild?" I ask numbly. Jonah's not running things until my dad gets better.

He's running things until my dad dies.

And then what?

Jonah shakes his head. "I don't know. That's a conversation for another day. Not today."

"Why did you even let me waste my time building that website? It was totally pointless. And stupid."

"No, it wasn't. You wanted to try and help your dad. You were making an effort to know what he's been doing around here, all these years." I feel Jonah's heavy gaze finally venture over, to linger on my bare skin. He pauses. "What the hell did you do to your feet?"

"I ran home from the hospital in my rain boots," I admit sheepishly, curling my body tighter, suddenly feeling self-conscious about my nudity, even if Jonah saw every part of me many times over last night. Nothing about this moment feels remotely sexual.

"Jesus. They're all chewed up. I've got a first-aid kit at my place. You need to cover those blisters." He reaches for my towel, holding it out for me. "Come on. Water truck doesn't come until tomorrow. If you want plumbing, you better grab your things and stay with me." After a moment, he adds a soft, "Please."

Finally, I accept the towel from him.

Knowing that I need to be near him tonight, running water or not.

■ ■ ■

The bathroom door opens as I'm rinsing face wash from my cheeks and nose. "Almost done, I swear."

The curtain draws open behind me and Jonah steps in. Despite my dour mood, the sight of him naked stirs my blood instantly.

"Okay, *fine.*" I make to climb out.

He grabs hold of my shoulders, keeping me in place, his thumbs sliding over my slick skin, back and forth a few times, soothingly. And then his long, muscular arms are roping around my body and he's pulling me backward against him.

"I'm sorry," he murmurs, bowing down to nestle his face in the crook of my neck, his beard tickling my skin. "I wanted to tell you, but I also didn't. Don't hate me."

I let my head tilt into his. "I don't hate you." Far from it. I don't even think I'm angry at Jonah. I'm angry with my father, for the path he's chosen. With life, for how unfair it can be.

But Jonah . . .

Reaching up, I let my nails skate over his biceps a few times before gripping his arms tightly, returning the embrace. "I'm glad you're here," I whisper. I can't imagine facing this without him.

He folds in closer, tighter, until I'm cocooned within him, the hard press of his collarbone all the way to his thighs conforming to my body. I can feel him growing hard against my back, and yet he doesn't make a move to try to satisfy that need.

I think he's too busy satisfying another.

We simply stand there, holding each other until the water turns cold.

■ ■ ■

"This is *so* much easier when you're conscious and sitting upright," I murmur, slowly drawing the comb through Jonah's beard, feeling his blue eyes intently studying my mouth.

"And I've actually consented to it."

And I'm straddling your lap.

"Shhh. Don't move," I scold, frowning as my gaze shifts from side to side examining his jaw, making sure I've trimmed it evenly.

"How bad were your hands shaking that night?"

"I was fine *while* I was doing it. I was totally calm and in control."

"And after?"

"Petrified. My dad said I was twitchy."

Jonah's head falls back into the couch as he laughs. It's such a deep, beautiful sound and I'm momentarily lulled by it, admiring his thick throat, imagining my mouth pressed against it.

"You weren't, seriously, were you?"

"I was scared that I'd gone too far, and you were going to hate me again," I admit.

"What? I never *hated* you, Calla."

I give him a high-browed knowing look.

"No. Even when I was annoyed as hell and chewing you out at Meyer's that day, half of me wanted to see what you'd do if I just went ahead and kissed you."

"Really?" I smooth my palm along his jawline, appreciating the perfection. What *would* I have done? Probably freaked out. He was just the angry yeti back then. He made *me* angry. And yet now that I'm getting to know Jonah, I don't know how I ever *wasn't* attracted to him, horrendous bushy beard and all.

His eyes twinkle as if he can read my thoughts.

I toss the scissors and comb to the coffee table, satisfied. "There. I've fixed you up, as *requested*. I knew you were secretly vain."

"Did being your plaything for a bit make you happy?"

"Maybe," I admit wryly.

"Good. Figured we could both use a distraction."

"Yeah, I guess so." I sigh heavily as reality drifts back in. Smoothing my hand over Jonah's wrist, I turn it to check his watch. "I guess you have to go back to Wild now?" It's been a couple of hours since he found me curled up in the shower. I was sure he'd have left by now, but I'm so thankful that he hasn't.

"I don't want to," he admits somberly. "Ten years working there and this is the first day I want nothing to do with planes and people. But I should check in with all the guys. They're probably wondering why Wren hasn't called yet."

"Are you gonna tell them?"

"We all know Wren's not gonna jump on the phone and do it. Some of them have already heard, I'm sure. But, yeah, it's better they hear it from me than Maxine or one of their passengers. Plus I can't leave everything to Agnes to handle, not when she has Mabel to deal with, too." He sighs. "That poor kid. Wren's like a father to her. This is gonna absolutely destroy her."

I've been so focused on my own pain, I haven't given much thought to her. Now that I do, I note that there's no flare of jealousy behind his words, no spark of envy. Only sympathy. "I'll come with you. Just let me grab my phone from the house." I plugged it in when I got home from the hospital and left it there, having no desire to talk to anyone from back home.

I make to slide off, but warm, strong hands settle onto either side of my backside, trapping me in place. Jonah's gaze drifts downward over the fitted "But first, Coffee" T-shirt that Diana had made for me, to where my thighs meet his. He opens his mouth, but then seems to change his mind about whatever he was going to say. Steely blue eyes lift to meet mine.

"What?" I ask softly, smoothing my palms over either side of his jaw again. I can't get enough of the feel of his beard against my palms. That comment Diana made about how having me shave Aaron's face was too intimate for her liking? I think I get it now.

Jonah pulls my body flush to his, until his hands are gripping my back tightly in an embrace and he's buried his face in the crook of my neck, his hot breath skating over my skin, sending my blood racing.

I can feel the hard press of him between my thighs.

He wants me, but he doesn't feel right asking.

Reaching up to cocoon his head within my arms, I roll my hips, letting him know that it's more than okay.

■ ■ ■

The moment Jonah strolls into Wild's lobby, he seems to shed the coat of reluctance he wore in the car ride over, my hand cradled in his.

"Working hard, Sonny?" he calls out in that booming, deep voice, startling the Alaska Native couple huddled in a far corner—the only passengers waiting in the lobby.

Sonny, who was leaning over the front desk chatting up Sharon, stiffens immediately. "I was just finishing up my break. I'm gonna get back out there. We're almost done loading up for the last few runs," Sonny babbles, already taking backward steps toward the exit.

Jonah drops a hand on his shoulder. "Sounds good. Tell Clark to come see me when he's got a minute."

"Will do." Sonny bolts out the door.

"You are a horrible human being," Sharon hisses with an accusatory tone.

Jonah throws his hands in the air. "What did I do?"

"Oh, come *on*. You know you're intimidating."

"I am not." He turns to me. "Am I?"

"Sometimes," I admit. "And obnoxious. And annoying . . ." *And gentle and affectionate . . .*

"Alright, alright." He waves me off with a smirk.

Mabel is curled up in a chair next to Sharon, her head bowed as she plays a game on her phone.

Jonah pauses a moment to look down at her and his jaw tenses. "Hey, kiddo." He ruffles her hair.

She looks up long enough to give him a sad, shy smile, before ducking down again. Clearly not in the mood to talk, which is shocking for her. He leaves her be, disappearing into the office.

"I love your hair all up like that," Sharon says, gesturing toward my messy topknot. Her green eyes are full of sympathy, even as she tries to play it off casually.

"Yeah, that's called 'Jonah hid my hair detangler and my volumizer and every other beauty product I own in the name of revenge.'" I'll have to search his house later, when I care enough to. In the grand scheme of things, I've almost forgotten that I've been bare-faced for days. It's been oddly liberating.

"That sounds like something he'd do," she says with a soft chuckle, and then swallows. A pained expression fills her face. "We heard the news. I'm so sorry, Calla."

Word does travel fast. I wonder how exactly it came out. Not that it matters, really. I steal a glance at Mabel, and Jonah's words from earlier linger in my mind. The reality is that while he may be *my* dad, I have an entire life built back home that doesn't include Wren Fletcher, that hasn't for many years. Meanwhile, he's *everything* to people around here. Standing in Wild, accepting Sharon's condolences . . . It doesn't feel right. *I* should be the one offering it.

All I can manage is a nod, and then I duck into the back office. Agnes and Jonah are going over some scheduling and weather reports with George. Agnes flashes a sad, hesitant smile my way and I offer her one back. She's as innocent in all this as I am, after all.

I hold my phone in the air. "Do you mind if I use my dad's office for a minute?"

Jonah waves me in. "Nah, go ahead."

I push the door shut behind me, quickly scanning through all the "Did you see all your likes?", "Are you getting these?", "Where are you?", "Nordstrom's having a sale on your studded boots! Did you bring them with you? You need to get a picture in a plane with them stat!" texts from Diana that I don't have the energy or interest in responding to right now. There's also a "How are things?" text from my mom.

My chest tightens with dread. How is *she* going to deal with this news?

I need to call and tell her, and soon. But I find myself hesitating. Maybe because it'll seem more real, more final then. That voice is still there in my head, prattling away in a rushed, desperate tone, trying to convince me that the doctors are wrong about how serious it is, that my father has made a terrible decision, that he needs to fight, that *maybe* I can still get through to him.

And then Jonah's voice mixes in, his sobering words about coming to terms with the grim reality. It's on steady repeat.

Who knows when reality is going to sink in. But I do know one thing—I don't want to be thousands of miles away when it does.

With a deep inhale, I call the airline.

■ ■ ■

"She finally fell asleep about two hours ago," Simon says through a yawn. It's not quite five a.m. in Toronto. I left Jonah's house and trekked across the lawn to my dad's to check my messages—he really needs to join this century and get internet—and found several from Simon, telling me to call his cell, no matter what time.

Of course I panicked and dialed, not even checking the clock.

I should have known Simon would want to check in on me.

I've never listened to so much dead air over a phone as I did this afternoon, when I sat down in my dad's worn old office chair and called my mom to share the bad news. She barely spoke as I spelled out the reality of it all—that we were wrong, that they hadn't caught it early.

That they caught it *far* too late.

I talked with a wavering voice, shedding quiet tears, and I listened to the silence on the other end, knowing that what I was actually hearing was her heart breaking.

"She didn't take it well."

"No, she didn't." Simon's charming British lilt is a welcome voice. I realize how much I miss seeing him in the morning as I collect my latte with a grumbled thanks. I miss his dry-humored quips as I stroll through the house, always coming or going from something. I miss the fact that he somehow always knows when I could use an ear. I miss that he's always there for me, in a way that my father never was.

In a way that I had started picturing Wren Fletcher to be in the coming years, without realizing that I was actually doing it.

"How are *you* taking this, Calla?"

I peer up at the strings of Christmas lights dangling from the ceiling that I just plugged in. The bulbs are too big, the colors too dull, the light cast too weak, and yet the canopy they provide is somehow mesmerizing. I can't peel my eyes from them. "I don't know. I'm angry."

"About what?"

Simon knows exactly what. He just wants me to verbalize it. "That he didn't tell me sooner. That he's refusing treatment. Take your pick. It's all shitty."

"You're right."

"But . . ." There's always a but with Simon.

"No buts this time. You have every right to feel this way. I would be angry and frustrated, too, if someone I loved wasn't doing everything they could to stay with me for as long as possible."

"I just don't get how he could be so selfish! He has people who love him and he's hurting all of them."

"Do you love him?"

"Of course I do."

Simon sighs into my ear. "Well, that's something you wouldn't have confessed to so easily, sitting on the porch steps that night with me, now is it?"

"I guess not. I wouldn't have felt it then." And yet just a week later, there's no doubt in my mind that I love my father, and I don't want him to die. Which makes this all so much more painful. "But he doesn't seem to care about anyone but himself. He *never* has!" Even as I say the words, I know they're not true. "He doesn't care enough," I amend.

"Do you think he hasn't thought his decision through?"

"How *could* he have? I mean, who doesn't fight cancer?"

"It *does* happen, for various reasons." And Simon, for one, would know. He's had his share of terminal patients who come to him for help with dealing with their grim reality. "Did he explain his decision to you?"

"Yeah," I mutter, and I repeat everything my father told me earlier.

"Sounds like maybe he hasn't made the decision lightly."

"Maybe. But it's still not okay." It'll never be okay. "What would *you* do?"

"I'd like to think I'd go through with the treatment, at least to start, but I'm not in his shoes. Besides, your mother would have me hog-tied and dragged to the hospital if I even suggested skipping it."

"She should come here and do that to him, too," I say half-heartedly. "Or at least call him. I'm sure she still remembers his number. She sure dialed it enough times twelve years ago."

Silence meets my words.

"I mean—"

"There isn't *anything* about what happened with your parents that I'm not aware of, Calla," Simon says carefully.

I sigh. Of course Simon would know.

God, what a mess my parents are.

"I imagine Wren is quite scared," Simon finally offers as a way out of the awkwardness.

"He said he wants to die on his own terms."

"That doesn't mean he can't be downright terrified while doing it."

"I guess." And I ran right out of there today, leaving him alone. A sting of guilt pricks me.

We sit in loaded silence, my pajama-clad body wrapped in my flannel jacket and a layer of blankets, my gaze drifting out over the night sky, still much brighter than what I'm used to for almost one a.m.

"So I guess you don't have any wise words to make this all better."

"Sorry. No wise words," Simon says with a sigh.

"That's okay. Just talking to you helps."

"Good. And remember, you can be angry and frustrated with him for his decision but still love and support him through it."

"I'm not sure how to do that."

"You'll figure it out. You're a well-adjusted and self-aware young woman, and you make smart decisions."

"Calla! You coming back to bed?" Jonah hollers from somewhere unseen but nearby. When I threw on my clothes and left him to make my phone call, he was reaching for a leather-bound book on his nightstand, the sheet draped loosely over his bottom half. It was an oddly erotic sight.

Speaking of making smart decisions . . .

Jesus. Half of Bangor probably heard him.

"Let me guess . . . That must be that *horrid* pilot from next door that I've been hearing about from your mother," Simon says dryly. "Pray tell me, how is your vicious feud with him going?"

"I used up all my dad's water, so I have to stay over there tonight if I want plumbing." I could also stay at Agnes's house, a point I'm not about to bring up.

"Right. Well, that was kind of him to welcome you, despite your being mortal enemies."

"It *really* was." And Simon isn't buying my lame excuse for a second.

Jonah's heavy boots stomp up the porch stairs. He pushes open the door and I catch a flash of movement next to his feet. It's Bandit, scurrying in ahead of him, his beady eyes shimmering against the glow of the Christmas lights. He lets out one of those high-pitched chattering sounds.

I cringe. "Hey, Simon, what's your professional opinion about someone who has a pet raccoon?" I ask loudly, to make it clear to Jonah that I'm on the phone with my stepdad.

"Considering we seem to have two, who am I to pass judgment? Good night, Calla. Call me whenever you need to."

"'Night. Love you." It just rolls off my tongue for Simon. And I have yet to say it to my real father even once.

Jonah's gaze drifts over the ceiling of the porch. "You and Mabel did a good job."

"Yeah. It's kind of cozy out here now."

"Sorry, I didn't realize you were on the phone. You feel better after talking to him?"

"I don't know," I answer honestly. "Maybe. It doesn't make it okay, though."

"Nothing's gonna make this okay. Not for a long time. Come on." Jonah holds a hand out for me.

I take it and let him pull me to my feet.

And I can't help but think that it's Jonah who makes me feel better.

Or, at least, he makes me hurt a little bit less.

Chapter 24

■ ■ ■

My dad's dressed and sitting beside his bed when Mabel and I knock.

"Hey . . . How are my girls?" he murmurs, his gray eyes flickering to mine.

"Ready to whoop your butt tonight. And don't think I'm gonna let you win," Mabel says with a smile that isn't nearly as bright as usual, but is there nonetheless. She wanders in ahead of me, dragging her sneakers along the dull linoleum floor.

"I'd expect nothing less from a shark like you." My dad's lips twitch. "Did your mom drive you guys here?"

"No, Jonah did. He had to get his stitches out anyway."

My dad thumbs the collar of his jacket. "Well, that was good timing, then."

"What's this?" Mabel picks up the white folder sitting on the bed.

"Oh. That's just some paperwork I've got to go through. Nothing interesting," he says, smoothly plucking it from her grasp in a way that makes me think he doesn't want her seeing it at all. "Hey, kiddo, why don't you go and grab yourself something at the cafeteria." He pulls a bill out of his wallet. "We've got another few minutes before the nurse comes back."

Mabel snatches it up eagerly. "You guys want anything?"

He waves her away. "I'm good."

I shake my head and smile, watching her skip out the door.

Awkward silence lingers for a long moment, as I lean against the wall and my father fumbles with the folder in his hands, then casts it aside. What's it like to be him right now? To know your clock is almost up?

"Kinda thought you might be on a plane, heading back to Toronto."

"No." As angry and shocked as I was—as I *still* am—oddly enough, that thought never crossed my mind. "How are you feeling today?"

He takes a deep breath, as if to test his lungs. "Better."

More awkward silence.

"I called Mom."

He nods slowly, as if he knew I would. He doesn't ask what she said, though, or how she took it. He probably can already guess.

"And I canceled my flight."

He sighs and starts shaking his head. "You didn't have to do that, Calla. I'd rather you go back home with only good memories. Not with what's coming."

"Well, I'd rather you go to Anchorage and try to slow this down, but neither of us is going to get what we want, are we?" I step closer, to take a seat on the bed. "Are you scared?"

He looks down at his hands. "Scared. Angry. Sad. Full of regret. A little bit of everything, I guess."

I hesitate, but then reach over to place a tentative hand on top of his, absorbing its warmth.

What do you know? My mom was right. We *do* have the same knuckles, the same finger lengths, and, beneath my gel tips, the same short nail beds.

It's a moment before he reacts, placing his other hand over mine. He squeezes. "I'm sorry, kiddo. I really wish it wasn't going to end this way."

"But it is what it is," I say, echoing his words from that first night. My eyes stray to that folder again, to the HOSPICE label and the tagline, *Providing End of Care Support to You and Your Loved Ones.*

A painful ball in my throat swells. "So, what needs to be done?"

"Ah, don't worry about—"

"No, Dad. There's no avoiding this anymore. Besides, maybe talking about it will help me to start wrapping my head around it." How the hell do I do that? I'm twenty-six years old. Two weeks ago I was drinking martinis and struggling to find the perfect captions to go with pictures of my favorite shoes. I didn't even know this man outside of my imagination.

Now I'm about to help him prepare for his death.

He purses his lips. "I don't want to die in a hospital, if I can help it. There was a lady here earlier who gave me that pamphlet. She's going to come out to the house next week and talk about options at home. Pain relief, that sort of thing."

"Okay." He's going to be in pain. Of course he is. How much pain, though? What's that going to be like to watch? Will I be able to handle watching it? I swallow the rising fear, push it aside. "What else?"

"The funeral arrangements, I guess," he says with reluctance. "If it were up to me, I wouldn't bother, but I know Agnes will need it. I don't want anything fancy, though."

"So . . . no to a gilded casket and string quartet?"

He makes a soft sound that might be a laugh. "Definitely a pass on those."

"Okay. What else?"

"I've already started the ball rolling with the lawyer so, that's taken care of. I'll be leaving most of my money—"

"I don't need to know about any of *that*. You do whatever you want with it. It's yours." The last thing I want him thinking is that I'm sticking around for an inheritance. "But what do you think you want to do about Wild?" That's an entire company to deal with once he's gone.

"I talked to Howard from Aro Airlines about an hour ago. That's that regional airline that wanted to buy Wild. I mentioned them before. They've made me a good offer. I think I'm gonna take it."

"You said they'd swallow Wild up, though." My family company that's been around since the 1960s, that my dad wouldn't leave, will no longer exist.

It's odd; I hated it for so long, and yet the idea of that makes me sad.

"Eventually, probably. But to tell you the truth, it could be good for the villages and this whole part of Alaska in the long run, even if it is called something different. Anyway, they're willing to keep everyone on staff, and that's my only real concern. They want Jonah to run it, too. Give him a COO title or something like that. I'll have to talk to him about it. Not sure that's what he has in mind."

"He already said he'd do it."

"I know, but it's a whole different ball game, being tied up with a big company like that. He'd have board members to answer to and all kinds of new processes and policies." He smiles. "Don't know if you've noticed yet, but Jonah doesn't do too well with rules and authority, and people telling him what to do."

"Nope. Haven't noticed," I mutter wryly, earning his soft chuckle. "Either way, he'd do it for as long as they need him to." There's no doubt in my mind about that.

"Even if it means sitting in a chair all day, every day, instead of being in the air. Oh, I know. If there's one thing about Jonah, he's loyal to a fault. He'll do it long after I'm in the ground." My dad sighs heavily. "I don't want that kinda life for him. He doesn't suit it, anyway."

"Is there anything else?"

"Just keep livin', I guess." He gives me a resigned smile. "Try to have as many good days as I can, until I use them up."

"We can do that," I say with determination, giving his hand another squeeze. I don't have to be okay with it, but I *can* be here for it.

"Well, alright then." A slow, resigned smile curls his lips. "How about we start by finding Jonah and getting the hell out of this joint."

■ ■ ■

THE MOMENT THE attendant pauses at the end of the ramp outside the hospital's main doors, my dad is pushing himself out of the wheelchair. "Thanks. I've got it from here, Doug."

The attendant gives him a scolding look.

My dad holds his hands in the air, in surrender. "If I fall on my butt, I won't sue anyone but myself, I swear."

With a lingering pause, he finally nods. "You take care of yourself, Wren."

"Will do."

Doug spins the chair around and disappears through the doors, leaving us to cross the parking lot ourselves.

Jonah smooths a hand over the fresh pink scar on his forehead. "Don't know why I needed to see the doctor for that. I could have just pulled them out myself."

"But then you couldn't shamelessly flirt with her," I mutter. We found him perched on a patient table in the office of a forty-something-year-old blonde doctor, complimenting her on her husky dogsled team pictured on the wall and telling her he'll definitely come back to her the next time he crashes a plane and needs stitches.

"Do you think it worked?"

"Absolutely. She's on the phone with her best friend right now, saying she's fallen for a jackass with a death wish."

"Isn't that basically what *you* did?" he retorts.

My cheeks burn as I spear Jonah with a warning glare, feeling Mabel's curious eyes flicker back and forth between us. Whatever thoughts are going on in that innocent mind are thankfully held back by a mouthful of chocolate muffin.

"Well, isn't this a surprise . . ." my dad murmurs quietly, then starts to chuckle. The sound dies as he turns away to try to hide his grimace of pain.

But we all notice, and it throws a dark, sobering cloud over the moment of brevity the rest of the way to Jonah's SUV.

"Here," Jonah calls out, tossing his keys in the air for me to catch.

I frown. "Why do I need these?"

"Because you're driving."

"Funny." I make to toss them back, but he heads for the passenger side. "Jonah!"

"You think I'm gonna chauffeur your ass around for the next however long? Think again." He climbs in.

"I'll just call a cab," I holler through the driver's-side window, left open from the ride in.

"You're learning how to drive, *right now*. Get in."

"You don't know how to drive?" Mabel exclaims with a shocked frown.

With a sigh of irritation, I hold the keys out to my father.

"Don't you dare, Wren," Jonah warns sternly.

"Sorry, kiddo, my hands are full." He waves the small paper bag with his prescription in the air as he steps around me to duck into the backseat.

"I'll drive if no one else wants to!" Mabel chirps, her eyes lighting up. "I know how."

"You hear that, Calla? Even Mabel knows how. She's *twelve*."

"Of course she does." I climb into the SUV with reluctance. "I don't want to do this right now, Jonah." It wouldn't be so bad if we were on the empty road by my dad's house and we didn't have my dad and Mabel with us.

"Hey. Just trust me, would you?" He peers over at me, and I see a raw pleading in those blue eyes.

As if I can say no to that.

"Fine," I grumble, jamming the key into the ignition. "But for the record, this is a *bad* idea."

"That's what you usually go for, isn't it? Bad ideas?" he murmurs.

"Oh, you're *so* clever." And relentless, with the quips that keep corralling my mind right back to me and him.

"Do you guys ever stop arguing? God!" Mabel bursts, clicking her seat belt in place.

"Sometimes we do. Right, Barbie?"

We definitely weren't arguing last night. Or this morning, before getting up to come here.

Twice.

My dad clears his throat from the seat directly behind me. "Just stay to the right and stop when the sign says stop. You'll do fine."

"And don't hit the people walking on the side of the road," Mabel adds.

"I can't believe I'm getting driving tips from a twelve-year-old." With a sigh, I crank the engine. "I can't even reach the pedals!"

"Here." Jonah leans forward, gripping the back of my seat with one hand while he slides his arm down between my knees to the floor in front. With a click and a tug, my seat moves forward. "Better?"

I stretch my legs out. "Yeah."

"All right." His warm, strong hand lands on my knee, giving it a tight squeeze. "Just do what I say and we *might* make it home alive."

I grip the steering wheel, my nerves churning in my stomach. Suddenly, the streets of this dusty little frontier town seem too busy. But at least it gives us all something to focus on besides my dad.

I shake my head and start to laugh.

Damn yeti. That's exactly why he's doing this to me.

■ ■ ■

"Oh my God, no, Calla. Seriously. Forget about the stupid studded shoes." Diana sighs heavily in my ear.

"Whatever. I've already got it mostly done, anyway, with what you sent me." I toggle over the screen, testing the links to the pictures of Diana posing downtown with the city bustle in the background—the blur of people whizzing by on bikes and in cars, hordes of pedestrians milling at a street corner waiting for the light to change, rows of white tents that signal one festival or another. I can almost hear the buzz of life and I ache for it. "Aaron took some decent shots."

"And he complained through every minute of it. You wouldn't believe the things I had to promise to get him to agree in the first place."

"You're right, and I'm positive that I *do not* want to know." But I'm glad she's found a replacement for me.

She sighs. "So . . . when do you think you'll be back?"

I drop my voice. Even though the living room window is closed, I can hear Mabel's bursts of laughter and goading exclamations as she and my dad hover over the checkerboard. "I have no idea. A month? Maybe two?" Or will it be longer? Will I be here to see the first snow fall? Because, aside from some woolen socks, I am not prepared for that.

"God. That's . . . a long time."

"Yeah. But, I'm sure I'll keep busy."

"How's the Hot Viking?"

Oh man. "Still hot," I murmur, as an odd tingling sense courses through my entire body, like it does every time I think of him now. There's so much I have to tell her, but now is not the time to even hint at it. "I'll talk to you later." We end the call just as Agnes pokes her head out onto the porch.

"There's still some chicken left, if you're hungry. I already set aside plenty for Jonah." Agnes and Mabel walked into my dad's kitchen around three, while he was napping, Mabel's arms hugging her latest plucked catch from the farm, Agnes's laden with potatoes and carrots, and lettuce for a green salad. We hadn't made plans for dinner, but I was thankful to see them show up all the same.

By the time my dad staggered out of his bedroom, the house was smelling of roasted meat and we'd settled into solitary tasks—

Agnes with a book, Mabel with a game on her phone, and me with my computer—as if we all lived here.

He didn't say anything, didn't question it. Just smiled at us and sank into his La-Z-Boy.

"I'm full, but thanks." I offer Agnes a smile before turning back to my screen.

But she lingers, pushing the sliding door shut behind her. "Still working on Wild website stuff?"

"No." Is there any point? "Just keeping my mind busy." I toggle over to another screen, one of about thirty I have open, to pictures of my time here so far.

"That looks like Kwigillingok," Agnes murmurs, edging closer. "That's a nice one."

"No."

"No?" She frowns in thought. "I think it is."

The more I stare at it, the more I disagree. "It doesn't do it justice. At all. None of them do."

She tips her head as she ponders it. "Maybe it has a story to it that I can't see?"

"Maybe." On the screen, it *is* a pretty enough view, I'll admit. Not the barren wasteland my mother insisted was waiting for me. But it's just another picture from a plane, high up in the sky. You wouldn't know *why* we went—that it's where the little girl with asthma who needed the ventilator lives with her family and two hundred other villagers, on what feels like the very edge of the earth when you're landing.

You wouldn't know that Jonah pounded on my door and practically forced me out that day. Jonah, the broody bush pilot who started off as my enemy and has somehow evolved into something far more important to me than a friend.

Agnes settles down onto the edge of the wicker love seat where there's room. I sense that she wants to talk, as her gaze roams the porch, stalling on the lights dangling above. "Christmas in summer."

"Welcome to my life. My mom has lights up in our backyard all year round." Tiny, white lights that weave around the lilac bushes and Japanese maples and the trunk of the massive century-old oak tree that Simon has had to pay arborists tens of thousands to maintain over the years. This is kitschy by comparison, but it's still cozy.

"All this old stuff you dragged out . . ." She looks around us at the transformation. "I'll bet it's nice out here at night."

"It is, actually. We were out here last night after the sunset."

"You and Jonah?"

"Yeah."

"Hmm."

I ignore her curious murmur and keep scrolling. The pictures of Jonah cutting firewood appear and my finger stalls, my eyes caught momentarily on his hard flesh and his statuesque form, his olive-skinned complexion all the more so next to the misty fog.

"Now *there's* a fashionable look for your website." Agnes chuckles.

I keep flipping, pretending that my cheeks aren't red. I'll admire the rest of those later, in private.

"Marie was by the house on Saturday night, looking for Jonah. Forgot to mention that to him," she says casually.

"Big surprise." My tone is more clipped than I intend, a reaction to the way my stomach tightens instantly, despite what Jonah told me about their platonic relationship. Marie's not going anywhere. She's in Alaska for the long haul. Will he change his mind down the road and decide he *can* give her what she wants?

The very idea of Jonah with her—or anyone else—makes my chest burn. "Did you tell her we were stuck at the checkpoint for the night?"

"I did."

Good. I can't help the jealous little voice inside my head.

I feel Agnes's watchful gaze on me as I scroll through the rest of the cabin trip pictures, and I'm pretty sure the shrewd little woman somehow heard that. But, as always, she keeps those thoughts—and all thoughts about Jonah and me and whatever is going on between us—to herself.

"Listen, I was hoping you could help me and Mabel. Sharon and Max are leaving next week and we've been talking about throwing a little party for them at Wild."

"A party?"

"Yeah. Sort of a combo baby shower and farewell."

I hesitate. "I just . . . Do you think it's right to throw a party now?" I drop my voice. "With everything that's going on?" I mean, my dad's got a meeting with the guys from Aro later this week, to start the sale process. And he just got out of the hospital. It's going to take time for him to recover from that complication.

Plus, I'm sure I'm not the only one who's in shock over his news.

"If not now, then when?" Her black gaze drifts out to the wide expanse, to a regional airline descending from the sky. "They'll be long gone by the time Wren . . ." Her voice fades. She swallows. "Life will keep moving and changing, whether we want it to or not, Calla. There will be days to mourn, when it's time. But Sharon and Max are leaving us, and their baby will be born, and we need to celebrate the time we have with them while we have them here. That's all we can do with anyone." Her face slowly splits into a wide smile, even as her eyes shimmer. "Besides, it'll make Wren happy, to see everyone come together like that. He's always liked a good party."

I sigh. She's right. "Of course I'll help."

"Good. I ordered a bunch of cake mixes and some decorations and things a while back. They should be here any day now."

"I guess there's no such thing as Amazon Prime around here?" I say, wryly.

She gives me a look. "That *is* Amazon Prime."

We share a soft laugh.

But then her brow pulls tight. "I don't think I ever thanked you for coming." She reaches forward to clasp my forearm. "It feels right, having you here with us. I can't imagine doing it any other way."

My throat begins to prickle for the tiny woman, whose own heart has, however unintentionally, also been broken by my father in the past. And still she stands stoically beside him, offering her friendship and unrequited love.

How many hearts have been pained or broken because my dad decided to sit down next to my mom at the bar that night? I wonder. Would knowing what the future held have made either of them stand and walk out?

Something tells me no.

"I don't think *I* ever thanked you for calling me," I respond softly, thinking back to that night on the porch steps, wearing one shoe with Simon sitting next to me. It feels like a lifetime ago.

She inhales sharply. "You know, next to phoning Derek's parents to tell them about the crash, that was the hardest call I've ever had to make."

And all *I* heard was a stranger's voice. Some woman who was in my dad's life while I was not. Funny enough, she feels like the farthest thing from a stranger to me now. "Are you angry with him?"

Her lips wobble a little before she presses them firmly together, cutting off the rare show of emotion. "I love him and I'm here for him. That's all that matters."

The ever-patient Agnes. She would have been perfect for my dad. She *is* perfect for him.

The sliding door creaks open then, and Jonah steps out with a heaping plate of food. My heart instantly leaps.

"This looks good, Aggie."

With a gentle pat on my forearm, she collects my dinner plate and moves from the seat. "You're later than I expected."

"Lost a rudder coming home." He squeezes her slender shoulder on his way past, and then settles into the spot she just left, filling the space, his big, warm body pressing against me. He cuts into his chicken with a soft, "Hey."

I haven't kissed him since this morning. I feel an overwhelming urge to lean in and do it now, but I hold myself back. That's something you do when you're dating, and that's not what we are.

What the hell are we, though, besides two people finding comfort in each other while we watch a man we both love die?

Maybe that in itself is enough.

"So you lost a rudder?" I finally ask.

"Yup. Must have busted on the gravel bar I had to land on to drop off supplies," he mumbles.

"Is it dangerous?"

"Need my rudders to steer the plane. So . . . not ideal."

"Are you okay, though?"

He smirks through a mouthful. "I'm here, aren't I?"

The memory of Betty's crumpled body and a bloodied Jonah hits me then. That was just last week. *Days* ago. It seems like there's something new every day. Is this what life with Jonah would be like? Him coming home to dinner, telling me about the latest danger he's encountered as if it's just another day at work? Because that's exactly what it is for him.

I think I'm beginning to understand what my mother meant about living in daily fear. Here I am, only days in to this, and my stomach is already in knots over the thought of him crashing. Maybe that's because I already witnessed it once.

Or maybe it's because I'm not made for this bush life, just like my mother wasn't.

"What's that look for?" he asks.

"Nothing. Just . . . nothing." What am I supposed to say? This is Jonah's world, not mine. I'm just living in it for now.

He glances over his shoulder, as if making sure no one's hovering at the window, listening. "I moved around a bunch of things on the schedule for tomorrow, and the rest of the week. Figured you, me, and Wren could take Veronica and head out somewhere in the mornings. That way you can spend some time with him and he gets to fly. I'll co-pilot for him."

"That sounds amazing." And so thoughtful of Jonah. A small thrill sparks inside me. "Where will we go?"

He shrugs. "Wherever. There's all kinds of things to see. You haven't even scratched the surface of Alaska yet."

That Jonah would go to all the trouble to do this, for both my dad and me, makes my heart swell. "Do you think he'll go for it, though? I heard him talking to Agnes about going back to work tomorrow."

"You think we're gonna give him a choice?" He stabs at a piece of carrot. "If I have to throw him over my shoulder, he'll be there."

An overwhelming wave of gratitude hits me. I throw my arms around his thick neck, hugging him tightly. "Thank you," I whisper, my mouth catching his earlobe.

He lets out a soft groan that reminds me of the sound I woke to this morning, with his hard body molded to my back.

I close my eyes, longing to be that close to him again.

"Hey!" Mabel pokes her head out and I peel away abruptly. Her wide-eyed look tells me she's finally starting to clue in about what's going on between the two of us. "We're gonna watch *Notting Hill.* Mom's making popcorn. You guys are coming in, right?" Thankfully, given her crush on him, she doesn't seem resentful with me about it.

"We'll see," Jonah grumbles between mouthfuls, in a way that could translate into "not a chance in hell."

"We'll be there in a few minutes," I assure her, erasing the disappointment from her face. As soon as she's gone, I give his shoulder a smack. "Don't be an ass."

He sighs with exaggeration. "Fine. I'll make you a deal." I wait as he takes his time chewing. "I'll go in there and watch whatever the hell you want," he locks gazes with me, "but then you have to come over after Wren's gone to sleep."

A nervous flutter stirs inside me. "What, like sneak out of my dad's house as if I'm some teenager?"

His eyebrow arches. "Why sneak? You don't want anyone to know about this?"

"No, it's not that. I just . . . maybe it's easier if we keep this on the down-low? There's no having to explain or rationalize anything to anyone."

He shrugs. "Fine. I don't care how you do it, so long as you're in my bed tonight, and every other night that you're in Alaska." He sounds so resolute.

"What if I'm here for the next six months?"

His eyes drift to my mouth. "That's kind of what I'm hoping for."

I have to tell myself to breathe. "Deal." Because suddenly I can't imagine myself anywhere else.

Jonah frowns curiously. "Now, what is *that* look for?"

"Nothing. I was just remembering something my dad said." About how he knew it would never work out with my mom in the long run but he wasn't about to fight what was happening.

I think I'm starting to get it now, Dad.

Chapter 25

■ ■ ■

"So, people actually *choose* to do this for an entire vacation." I curl my arms around my body, readjusting my position for the hundredth time in the uncomfortable folding seat. We're on hour three of sitting in this rented tin can of a fishing boat. My hand is cramping over the fishing rod Jonah shoved into it, I reek of bug repellent, and I'm getting twitchy.

"They don't just choose to do it; they pay big bucks to get out here." My dad reels his line in a touch. "We make tens of thousands every summer, flying people in."

"Oh, wait! I think I've got—" Mabel pauses, then leans forward. "Nothing." She turns and gives us a toothy, sheepish grin, the same one she's given the last eleven times she's mistaken the current for a fish.

I swat at a fly buzzing around my head. "How long before we catch something and can leave?"

"Never, if you guys keep talking. You're scaring all the fish away." Jonah is stretched out in the chair beside me, his boots resting on the edge of the boat, his rod off the opposite side. He looks like a damn model in that pose, with his USAF hat pulled low and his sunglasses masking his eyes. Hour two was all about me stealing frequent glances at him and fantasizing about what we'd do tonight, until Mabel asked me why my skin was so flushed and I had to shut those thoughts down.

"I'm good with never," I mutter. "When are we leaving? I have to pee."

My dad chuckles.

Jonah sighs heavily, as if annoyed, but when he tips his head back to see me, he's wearing a smirk that's equally obnoxious and sexy.

This sucks, I mouth.

Say that again, he responds, his devilish eyes shifting to my lips, and I can read the dirty thoughts percolating there.

My cheeks heat. *Stop it.*

"Are you complaining about your tour guide's choice for today, Barbie?" he says out loud, grinning.

Any more protests I may have had melt instantly. "No. Today is perfect," I say with full sincerity and a warm smile. Because even if it's an overcast day and I want to toss this fishing rod into the lake and fly home, I know that I'm going to think back to this tin-can boat and Mabel's false alarms and the eerie quiet of this remote lake in the middle of the middle of nowhere, Alaska, and I'm going to remember it fondly.

Just like the last three days have been perfect. Because my dad has gotten to do what he loves—fly—and I've been there, sitting right behind him the entire time, watching his deeply contented smile for every second of every moment of it.

We've cruised through the Alaskan skies for hours each morning, over wide plains and icy glaciers, into deep valleys, circling around to get glimpses of brown bears roaming the wild.

And every evening, the five of us have gathered at my dad's like some cobbled-together family for a meal and evening that no one asks for but everyone seems to need, gravitating to that lifeless living room, filling it with life.

And every night, when my dad goes to bed, I duck out to Jonah's, making sure to sneak back in before my dad rises for the next day.

With a small, knowing smile, Jonah reaches across and gives my thigh a squeeze before turning his attention back to his rod. A peaceful, comfortable silence settles over the four of us as we all get lost in our private thoughts.

It's interrupted again just moments later. "I'm hungry," Mabel announces.

"Oh for fuck's sake, I am *never* going fishing with you two children ever again," Jonah mutters as my dad bursts out laughing, not bothering to scold Jonah for his language around a twelve-year-old. There's no point trying to censor that guy.

"Did you pack any snacks?" I reach across to smooth a hand over his shoulder, an excuse to touch him. "Maybe some of that beef jerky from Ethel?"

"*Beef* jerky?" Mabel frowns with confusion. "Nobody dries beef in the villages. There aren't any cows!"

I catch my dad's cringe and my stomach clenches as it dawns on me.

"What the *hell* did you feed me, Jonah?"

■ ■ ■

"Your mother had them strung up around the outside, up there." My dad draws a line in the air, along the top of the screens, before letting his eyes drift to the porch ceiling. "But I think I like this better."

"It's nice after dark."

"I'll have to stay up and see it, one of these nights." He butts his cigarette out in a can and pulls the outside porch door shut. "Who knew a morning of fishing would wipe me out like that?"

A lump forms in my throat as I study him quietly. It's been five days since he got out of the hospital. His complexion is still sallow. He's been ducking away for naps in the afternoons and wincing with his coughing fits, which are becoming more frequent, not less. And the past two nights, I noticed that his dinner plate has had less on it than Mabel's.

"Maybe we stay home tomorrow. All this flying can't help with you recovering from last weekend."

He waves my caution off. "Nah. I'm good. A night's sleep and I'll be ready to go."

I *want* to believe him. "Jonah said something about going to a bear park tomorrow."

"He must be thinking about Katmai. I haven't been there in years." Dad scratches his chin with interest. "Hope he called Frank."

"Is that the tour guide that you've done a lot of business with?"

"Yeah. Okay, good." He nods with satisfaction. "I haven't seen him in person in years. It'll be good to catch up."

Once last time, I add in my head, the feeling in my chest heavy.

He begins shuffling toward the house.

"'Night, Dad." I curl my arms around myself for comfort as much as warmth.

"'Night, kiddo." He pauses at the door. "So, I take it you've forgiven Jonah?"

I sigh. "I haven't decided yet."

"At least you didn't go hungry, up at that cabin."

"Muskrat, Dad. He let me eat *muskrat.*" A revelation that had me gagging over the side of the boat when I found out and gritting my teeth for the rest of the way home. Even now, I feel the sudden urge to scrub my tongue.

"That's Ethel's specialty. She's known for it. You liked it well enough, didn't you?"

I glare at him. *"Muskrat."*

He chuckles. "Fair enough. Well, Katmai is a good three hundred miles away, so we'll have to get an early start. Do me a favor and, if you forgive him enough to go to his place tonight, can you wake me up when you sneak back in in the morning?"

My jaw drops.

"I may be sick, but I'm not blind, Calla." He smiles. "It's okay. I'm . . . happy you two have each other."

"You're not going to warn me that we're making a huge mistake?" I ask warily.

"Do *you* think you are?"

Yes.

No.

"I know it's not forever. I know he's going to stay here and I'm going to go home." I feel like I have to say that out loud, to prove that I'm not some lovesick idiot, that I haven't deluded myself into thinking this is something it's not. And yet, I can't imagine being anything else with Jonah than what we are while I'm here.

Jonah *is* Alaska to me.

My dad smiles softly. "I've got a lot of regrets, kiddo. But falling for your mother has never been one of them." With that, he disappears inside.

■ ■ ■

"This is good, Calla. *Really* good." Agnes beams at me, and then turns back to Wild's lobby, which we spent the last two hours transforming into a blue-and-green party room with balloons and streamers for Sharon and Max's send-off this afternoon. "And we have a lot of food coming."

"I had legitimate cupcake nightmares," I admit, eying the trays that sit on the folding tables to the far right, near the receptionist counter. It took Mabel and me all day yesterday to bake and decorate the twelve *dozen* of them. Exhausted, I fell asleep in Jonah's bed last night while he was brushing his teeth. "How many people are coming, anyway?"

"More than I invited, I think." She laughs nervously. "Some of the villagers caught wind of it and are trying to make it down."

"It'll be a nice send-off for them, at least." I didn't realize Max and Sharon were so popular. "Do you know where my dad is?"

"In town, with the lawyers. He's trying to get the bulk of the paperwork finalized with Aro." Agnes sighs as she looks around. "Things are going to change around here pretty soon."

"But not today."

She smiles and reaches out to pat my bicep. "Not today."

"Okay, well, if there's nothing else, I'm going to run home and get cleaned up. I still have pastel green frosting in my hair, thanks to Jonah." And a sticky coating of it all over my body, where he decided to smear it before licking it off, but I don't think Agnes needs or wants to know those extra details.

Her dark eyes roam my face and then take in the messy pile of hair atop my head. But in typical Agnes fashion, she merely smiles.

■ ■ ■

"Moose meat . . . reindeer dogs . . . king salmon . . . herring eggs . . . bannock. That's a flat bread. You might like that." I trail closely behind Jonah as he identifies the various trays of food along the tables, courtesy of the eighty-odd people milling around Wild's lobby, most from Bangor, but plenty who took the river down from the villages. The place is alive with a buzz of laughter and friendly conversation.

Agnes was right, after all. A party is what we all needed.

Jonah points to a dish of glistening yellow cubes, a thick, dark skin lining one side. "You won't like that."

"What's that?" I point to a bowl of what appears to be white cream and blueberries.

"That's called Eskimo ice cream."

"Dairy?"

"Nope. And you *definitely* won't like it."

"She won't know unless you let her try it, Tulukaruq," a familiar voice behind us calls out.

Jonah peers over his shoulder at the old woman with the pink headscarf, his surprise clear on his face. "Ethel! Down the river twice in two weeks."

"Not just me. Josephine, too." She nods to a young woman of

maybe twenty standing over by the water cooler, with a thick jet-black braid that reaches her butt. A plump baby of maybe eight months with a full head of dark hair sits in a sling across her chest, his wide eyes alert and curious as they take in the many faces.

"Damn, he's gotten big, hasn't he?"

As if Josephine heard Jonah, she turns and then gives a small, shy wave.

"Give me a sec, would ya, Ethel?" Jonah says with a gentle pat on her shoulder, and I watch him wander over to them, his smile wide and genuine as they begin talking.

"Tulukaruq has a lot of soft spots, but I think his biggest is for the young ones," Ethel murmurs. She's wearing the same New York Knicks sweatshirt that she had on the last time I met her. I wonder if she's an avid basketball fan or if it's just something warm for her to wear.

"Why do you call him that?" It's the same name she gave him that day in Meyer's.

"Because he's a helper of our people, but he's also a trickster. It means 'raven.'"

I chuckle. "Yeah, that's . . . *so* perfect. 'Tulukaruq.' I might have to start calling him that."

Josephine slips her son from the sling and hands him into Jonah's waiting arms.

My heart unexpectedly swells at the sight of the exchange, of Jonah's enormous hands gripping the baby's entire torso as he holds him up in the air above him, bringing him down to let the boy paw at his beard. Jonah laughs and the boy laughs, and suddenly I'm able to picture Jonah as a father.

Jonah will make a good father.

And his family will live in Alaska with him. A truth that squashes my swelling heart back to reality.

"The raven and his goose-wife."

I turn to meet Ethel's sharp, wise eyes. "Sorry?"

"The story. Jonah is the raven and you are his goose-wife." She studies me for a long moment with a sad smile, and I get the distinct impression she has discerned everything there is to know about us.

Is she saying Jonah and I should get married?

"Excuse me, everyone! Can I just grab your attention for a minute."

My skin tingles as I turn toward the front desk, where Max balances on a chair, his hands in the air in a sign of surrender, waiting to collect the attention of the people in the room. "Sharon and I just wanted to take a moment to say thank you for coming out today to make this send-off extra special. But also, for making our time in Alaska something we'll remember for the rest of our lives." He's smiling wide as he talks to the crowd, his voice mid-timbre. "I'll admit, it was a bit of a shock when we first moved here. Can't say I'm gonna miss the long, cold winters, though something good did come out of that." He gestures to Sharon's belly with a red-faced chuckle, and someone lets out a whistle. "And I'm *definitely* not gonna miss the whole honey bucket thing in some of the villages." A round of chuckles erupts, and I make a mental note to find out what a honey bucket is. Something tells me it has nothing to do with honey. "But what we *will* no doubt miss are the people. How caring you are. How close you all are, how hard you work to keep your way of life. No matter where we go, we'll never find the same thing. I'm sure of it."

My gaze drifts over the crowd, to see plenty of proud smiles and nods, and a few tears.

"So, again, thank you, from the bottoms of our hearts." Max's hands press against his chest, over his heart, the sincerity pouring from him palpable. "And I promise, we'll be sure to bring Thor back for a visit as soon as we can."

Sharon clears her voice and shoots Max a glare.

"Okay, okay, so we haven't agreed on the name yet." He grins. "But if you guys all wanna do me a favor and start calling him that, I figure it'll be harder for her to deny me when the time comes."

A round of laughter goes up and Sharon shakes her head, but she's giggling now, too.

"Just a couple more things. I want to say an extra special thanks." He seeks out Jonah, who still has Josephine's boy in his arms. "Damn, man, a baby sure looks good on you."

Another round of laughter erupts, along with Jonah's holler of, "Don't rush me!"

"But seriously, Jonah, I've learned more about flying from you in these past three years than I'll learn the rest of my life. I still think you're one crazy son-of-a-bitch, landing on that mountain ridge not once, not twice, but *three times* just to get those climbers off there, but man, do you know how to fly, and I hope I get the chance to work with you again one day."

"Just come back to Alaska and you've got it, buddy," Jonah throws with a grin. "'Cuz you know I ain't ever leaving."

Everyone laughs.

Meanwhile my lungs constrict.

Jonah is not *ever* leaving Alaska.

I've been acutely aware of it since our first kiss, and trying to ignore it every time he rolls his body off mine, curls his arms around me, and we drift off into the quiet night. I've known and still I've gone to him, day after day, night after night, happy to take everything I can have while I can.

Never expecting to feel *this* much for him.

I haven't even left yet and already it hurts.

"Damn straight we'll be back. Five years. Tops." Max chuckles softly and then turns to search out my dad, who's milling in a back corner, his hands clasped casually in front of him, smiling quietly. Max takes a deep breath. "Wren, I want to thank you for believing in me enough to hire me—"

"Best thank Agnes, then. She's the one who pulled your résumé out of the pile and called you up for the interview."

"I just liked his smile," Agnes says with a shrug.

Another round of laughter.

"Well, you didn't just give me a job, but you gave one to Sharon, too. Lord knows she would have gone crazy here if you didn't, and I think you knew that. I mean, happy wife, happy life, right?"

A chorus of agreement sounds from the married men in the room.

"Whatever the reason, I owe you big-time for that, and for all the memories we've gained over these past three years with the Wild family. Sharon and I, we've been layin' in bed at night, reminiscing. Like, just this past January, when we got slammed with that massive storm and then it was, like, minus twenty for five days straight? Everyone was going stir crazy, so what do these guys do but throw a freaking luau, with Hawaiian music and food, and everything. Wren showed up wearing a grass skirt and coconuts. I swear, I've got the pictures!" Chuckles roll through the room. "And then there was that time last winter when we built that gigantic snow cave out back and lit it all up with candles. Wren hauled out the old grill and started grillin' burgers. It was like a summer barbecue, except with your nose hairs stuck together." Max sighs. "Man, we've had so many good times with you and everyone at Wild." He holds a hand up. "I *am* still sorry about the wallpaper. I didn't know how much those ducks meant to you, but if it helps at all, it was all Jonah's idea and I was drunk as a skunk."

And thus, the mystery of the duck nipples, solved.

My dad shakes his head, but he's smiling.

"I guess what I'm trying to say is . . . thank you, for giving me a chance to fly up here for you, for letting us be a part of the Wild family, and all the laughs. And . . . uh . . ." He bows his head a minute, clears his throat, and when he looks up again, I see the sheen in his eyes. "I sure am gonna miss you," he manages to say through a hoarse voice.

Sharon's hand goes to her mouth as she dips her head, trying to hide the tears that now roll down her cheeks. Other sniffles sound then. I dare to let my gaze wander, to see the awareness and sadness in everyone's eyes, the tense jaws, the resigned smiles. We all know what Max *really* means.

And suddenly this doesn't feel so much like a farewell party for the happy couple leaving Alaska as much as a final goodbye for the quiet man who stands in the corner.

His shoulders hunched inward.

His face sallow and drawn.

His tired eyes and stoic smile telling me what I've noticed but refused to accept.

Suddenly the air in this lobby is too thick, the buzz too loud, the gazes too many.

Slipping around the food tables, I wordlessly duck into the office and keep going, through the staff room, down a long, narrow hall. I push through the door and out into the warehouse. The garage-type doors are open, allowing in a cool breeze, damp from the mist. A few grounds crew look on curiously as they haul pallets of cargo across the floor, but no one says anything about me being in there.

I rush all the way through and beyond to the hangar, my arms curled around my chest for comfort and finding none.

Veronica sits alone in the corner. She must be inside for maintenance work. I dash for her now, climbing up with ease to curl into the pilot's seat—my dad's seat. I smooth my hands over the yoke for a moment.

And then I pull my legs to my chest, bury my face in my lap, and let myself cry as reality sinks in.

■ ■ ■

The door opens with a creak. Somehow I know it's Jonah without having to look.

"He's not going to last much longer, is he?" I ask through my sniffles.

After a long moment, a warm, comforting hand smooths over my shoulders. "He's going downhill fast."

Finally, I dare tip my head up to rest my chin on my knees. I can only imagine how red and blotchy my face is. For once, I'm glad to be makeup-free. "I should have called. All those years that I didn't call, I wish I had. And now there's no time left. You and Max and *everyone* else have all these great memories with him and the luaus and the winter barbecues and the stupid *ducks,* and I am never going to have that! I don't have enough time!" I thought I was all cried out, but a fresh set of tears begins to trickle.

I've spent the last twelve years dwelling on all the things Wren Fletcher isn't.

I should have had the guts to come and find out all the things he is.

Loaded silence lingers in the plane.

Jonah sighs. "You should have called him. He should have called you. Your mom should never have left. Wren should have left Alaska for you. Who the hell knows what's right, and what it would have led to, but it doesn't matter because you can't change any of that." His thumb draws a soothing circle over my spine, just below my neck. "My dad and I didn't have a great relationship; I think you've probably figured that out. It always seemed to be a power struggle with him. He didn't take too well to not having control over my life. Said a lot of shitty things and never once followed them up with an apology.

"Cutting him off and moving up here was the right thing to do; I knew that in my gut. Still, in those last few days, watching him go, listening to him tell me how much he regretted trying to force what he wanted on me, I kept playin' conversations in my head, over and over again, finding things I should have said or done, times I should have reached out. You can spend an entire lifetime doing that and still get nowhere." He lifts his baseball cap off his head and lets it settle onto his knee. "I found this a few days after the funeral, in his closet. There was a whole box of USAF stuff. Hat, sweatshirt, jacket . . . all still with tags on them, along with a card he wrote to me, telling me how much he loved me and how excited he was that I'd get to experience that life. I guess he had it all ready to give me after I was officially enlisted, and then he shoved it in the closet and tried to forget about it when it didn't happen." Jonah's lips press together. "He's been gone five years and I still feel guilty every time I look at this damn thing."

I rub away my tears.

"You're not alone. You've got me. And I've got you, and we'll get through this together." He slides a gentle hand up and down my arm.

"Even if I'm in Toronto?"

His chest swells with a deep breath. "There's this thing called a phone."

"*You* are actually mocking *me* about a phone."

"Oh wait, that's right. You don't like calling your friends," he mutters wryly.

I know he means to lighten the mood, and yet my stomach clenches. "Is that what we are? Friends?"

He curses under his breath, and then sighs again. "We're complicated. That's what we are."

There's that goddamn word again.

"Have you heard of a goose-wife?"

There's a pause and then Jonah chuckles, sliding his hat back on. "Ethel and her tales."

"She said you were the raven and I was your goose-wife. What did she mean?"

"It's just a silly story, about a raven that falls in love with a goose."

"And what happens?"

He chews his lip, as if deciding if he should continue.

"Fine. I'll just Google it." I slip my phone from my pocket.

He reaches over to seize my hand within his and sighs in resignation. "They stay together for the summer, and when she leaves just before the first snowfall, he decides to follow her south. But there's no way he can survive the flight across the ocean. Finally, he has no choice but to say goodbye and go home."

"Why doesn't she go back with him?"

"Because she's a goose. She can't survive the winter," he admits reluctantly.

My chest tightens. "That story doesn't sound so silly after all."

In fact, it sounds a hell of a lot like us. Maybe not the falling-in-love part, but certainly the rest of it. Though, whatever I feel for Jonah, I'd be fooling myself if I didn't recognize it as much more than a frivolous crush on an attractive guy.

"No, I guess it doesn't." The look on Jonah's face tells me he sees the truth of it, too.

■ ■ ■

Jonah and my father are waiting next to Veronica when I pull into Wild's parking lot in Jonah's truck.

"Did you sort out all the accounting stuff?" I ask, my spirits oddly high today, thanks to the clear blue skies and warm sun. In the three weeks that I've been here, this is by far the nicest day we've had.

"Yup," Jonah mutters, his arms folded across his chest and a severe look painted across his face.

"What's going on?" I ask warily.

"Nothin'," my dad murmurs, smiling, and I try to ignore the heavy feeling weighing down my chest as I take in his thin frame and his tired eyes. He went to bed last night right after barely eating dinner and was still asleep when I came home from Jonah's.

"So . . . where are we going today?"

"You and I are gonna go for a little spin around the block, kiddo," he says.

"Just us?" I glance at Jonah, to see his jaw clench. That's what's pissed him off so much.

"It's fine." My dad smiles with assurance. "Just this once."

I hold my breath.

After a moment, Jonah finally nods.

■ ■ ■

"You good?" My dad's voice fills my headset as he grips the yoke, his contented smile focused on the wide-open sky.

"Yeah."

"You sure?"

"It just feels strange," I finally admit. "This is my first time flying without Jonah in one of these planes."

He chuckles. "He's like George's hula girl, Jillian. He makes you feel safe."

"Jonah, the hula boy," I joke. "Ironic, isn't it?" I think back to the flight in that Super Cub. He didn't start out that way.

"You two sure have come a long way. I'm glad to see it." The headset carries his heavy sigh. "I'm giving him this plane, along with Archie and Jughead. Those weren't included in my deal with Aro."

"That's good. He'll take care of them."

"And his house. I'm leaving him that. It's not worth a lot, but at least he'll have a roof over his head."

"Dad, I don't want to talk about—"

"I know you don't. But just humor me, will ya?" he says softly.

I listen numbly as he goes through the division of his assets—of the houses, of the truck, of the checkerboard. That's going to Mabel. And the money from the sale of Wild is going to me. I don't know what to say about it, and I don't feel that I deserve it, but if there's one thing I've learned about my father, it's that there's no point trying to change his mind once it's made up.

"Dad, why did you really want to come out with me alone today?" I finally ask. It can't just be for this. We could do that on the ground.

It's a moment before he answers. "Talked to your mother last night."

"Really? She called you?"

"No. I called her. Thought it was time we caught up. I told her how sorry I was for hurting her. How much I wish I could have been what she needed. How much I still love her."

I turn my gaze out, toward the green tundra below, so he can't see me blink away the tears. I'm not stupid. He called her to say goodbye.

"I also had to tell her how proud I am of the woman you've become. Your mom and Simon, they did so good by you, Calla. Better than I ever could."

"That's not true," I manage to choke out.

"I wish . . ." His brow pulls as his voice trails. "I wish I'd called. I wish I'd got in that plane and seen your graduation. I wish I'd stolen your mom away from that doctor of hers and convinced her to come back with me. I wish I'd made sure you knew how much I thought about you. How much I've always loved you." His voice grows thick. "I wish I'd been someone different than who I am."

"I love you, too," I rush to say. "And I like who you are." It turns out he is the man on the other side of the phone, listening to me prattle in childish wonder. He's exactly who I wanted him to be, despite all his flaws, and all the pain he caused.

Pain that, oddly enough, has faded. Maybe with time.

Or maybe with forgiveness that I've managed to find in all this.

"This is my last flight, kiddo," he announces with grim certainty. He reaches over and takes my hand, and the smile on his face is oddly at peace. "And I can't think of a better person to have spent it with."

■ ■ ■

"YOU JUST CHEATED."

"I did not."

My dad gives me a knowing look.

"It's not cheating if I don't know the rules."

He smirks. "Even though I've explained them to you a dozen times now?"

"I wasn't listening." I push another piece across three squares and over five. "That's okay, right?"

"Sure, why not." He lets out a weak chuckle and his head lolls to the side. It's too much effort to keep it up these days. "I think I've had enough for today."

"Oh, darn." I smile teasingly as I slide off the hospital bed that the kind and soft-spoken Jane from hospice arranged to have set up in my father's living room. Collecting the checkerboard, I move it to the bookshelf in the corner.

And then I check the time on my phone.

"Expecting to hear from someone?" he asks, wincing as he struggles to adjust his gaunt body to no avail. "That's the eighth time you've looked at that thing in the last five minutes."

"Yeah. I'm just . . . Jonah was supposed to message me."

"He's finally learned how to use a phone?"

"Apparently not," I murmur, fluffing my dad's pillow for him.

"Don't worry. He'll get here when he gets here." He pauses. "Where are Agnes and Mabel, by the way?"

"They had a knitting thing in town."

"Knitting?" He frowns. "Since when do they knit?"

I shrug. "Since now?" I avoid his gaze as I adjust his bedsheets.

If he's suspicious, he doesn't press. He's too tired to question much these days. "Jonah gonna stay here again tonight?"

"Yeah, I think so. If that's okay with you?" I stopped going over there at night two weeks ago, when it became clear that my dad shouldn't be left alone. So Jonah took it upon himself to strip my dad's double bed and clean his room, and insist that he would be coming over here instead. We've been staying in there ever since.

"Yeah, that's a good idea. I want him here in case . . ." His voice drifts.

In case he dies at night. That's what my dad's saying.

"It's not happening tonight, Dad." Jane spent a lot of time walking us through what to expect. The shortness of breath, the organ shutdown, the mental deterioration.

All of us, including my dad, know it's coming and soon.

But not tonight.

I turn the TV on to the sports highlights for him. "I'll be back in a sec with your pills," I say, adjusting his covers and planting a kiss on his forehead.

I'm in the kitchen getting my dad's nighttime medications ready when Jonah's Escape pulls up into the driveway. Throwing my shoes on, I dart outside into the chilly evening, not bothering to get my jacket.

I breathe a shaky sigh of relief. "You made it."

Mom takes one look at me and, with a hand over her mouth, begins to cry.

■ ■ ■

"Hey Calla, would you mind grabbing me some water?" my dad calls in a croaky voice.

"Yeah, sure." I reach for the glass I've already filled, along with the pills.

My mom, as stylish as ever in a simple black turtleneck, fitted jeans, and collection of jewelry, wordlessly slips them from my grasp. With a deep, shaky breath, and one last thoughtful glance at the mallard ducks, she makes her way into the living room, her socked footfalls soundless against the normally creaky floor.

In fact, she's said very little since climbing out of Jonah's SUV.

This must be utterly surreal for her, to be back in Alaska after twenty-four years.

To see my father again, after so long.

Jonah wraps his arms around my torso from behind as we watch the reunion, one my father knows nothing of, that Agnes and Mabel intentionally stayed away for, to give them space. "Your mom is smokin' hot," he whispers into my ear, too quiet for it to carry over the sportscaster's droning voice.

"That's because Simon didn't hide all her makeup like some psycho," I whisper back.

Jonah pulls me tighter against him as we watch her quietly round the hospital bed. I'm trembling, I realize.

Probably because this is the first time I've ever seen my parents in the same room, that I can remember, and it's on my father's deathbed.

"Hello, Wren." Mom's eyes glisten as she holds the glass out in front of her with two perfectly manicured shaky hands, gazing down at the man who stole her heart so many years ago. Who she has spent almost as many years trying not to love.

Jonah's body stiffens, and I realize he's holding his breath along with me, as we wait three . . . four . . . five seconds for my dad to say something.

Anything.

My dad begins to sob.

And just like that, I sense a circle closing. Back to the beginning, and near to the end.

A calm washes over me, even as I turn and cry into Jonah's shirt.

Chapter 26

■ ■ ■

"I think I saw a black one roll under the woodstove," I call out from the wicker seat on the porch, a warm coffee mug in my grasp. "They bumped the bookcase when they were moving out the hospital bed."

A moment later, I hear Mabel's holler of, "Found it!" through the open window, followed by the click of the checkerboard latching in place.

"Good," I murmur, adding too softly for her to hear, "You can't play if you lose pieces."

And yet we're all going to have to play on with a big missing piece, I accept, as a painful ball swells in my throat.

Dad passed away five nights ago, surrounded by his loved ones, just like all those newspaper obituaries read.

He died as he lived. Quietly, with a resigned sigh and a smile of acceptance.

Leaving a giant hole in my chest that I can't see how time will ever close. And yet I wouldn't trade this emptiness for anything.

A waft of subtle floral perfume announces my mother's presence before she steps out onto the porch. "It's still so surreal, being out here," she murmurs, edging into the wicker loveseat next to me. "I can't believe he kept all this."

She's an anomaly here—in her silk blush blouse and pressed dress pants, her hair smooth, her makeup impeccable, her wrists sparkling with jeweled bracelets.

It's hard to believe these once were all her things, a long time ago.

"He kept *everything* that had to do with you, Mom." Including his love.

She takes a deep, shaky breath, and for a moment I think she's going to start breaking down again, as she has done countless times—the evening he passed, and the long, emotional days that have followed. But she holds it in as I reach to take her hand and squeeze, trying to silently convey my gratitude to her. I'm so glad she came. So glad I didn't have to argue or negotiate or beg. All it took was one text, one line of *I think you need to be here,* and she was on a plane three days later.

My father would never have asked her to come, but I sensed the utter peace around him as she sat in that chair next to him those last few days, holding his feeble hand.

I caught the smile that curled his lips as she laughed out loud over something on the TV.

And I saw the tear that rolled out from the corner of his eye, as she leaned forward and kissed him one last time.

"Jonah's at work?" she asks softly.

"Yeah. He said he'd be late tonight." He's been late every night. I can't tell if it's because he's avoiding dealing with my dad's death or because of the fact that I'm leaving soon. Probably both. I sense him slowly detaching himself from this—us—in probably the only way he knows how. I can't blame him, because I'm having a hard time coming to terms with our looming end myself.

She opens her mouth.

"Don't, Mom. I just can't hear it right now." He's the raven, I'm his goose-wife. He's rural Alaska, thriving on quiet nights and wild, crazy rides in the sky to save lives. I'm the girl who, now that my dad is gone and this house is eerily quiet once again—even more so—is feeling the pull of the city bustle. Of her old life.

One that Jonah does not fit into, no matter how much I wish he could. I wouldn't ever force him to try. In truth, I can't imagine it.

I see my mom's nod in my peripherals, as her gaze wanders over me. "You seem so different, Calla."

I snort. "I haven't worn makeup in weeks." My detangler magically showed up on my dresser a few weeks ago, after I threw a teary fit about my matted hair, but there's still no sign of my cosmetics bags.

"I can't believe you haven't murdered him for that."

"I know." I think of how angry and annoyed I was at him in that moment. It makes me chuckle now. God, Jonah can be such a stubborn bastard.

"But, no," she murmurs softly, still studying me. "I don't think it's even that. I don't know . . ." She lets her thoughts drift into the stretch of tundra beyond. "Are you sure you don't want to fly home with me? Simon checked and there are still some seats available."

"Yeah. I'm going to help Agnes clear out the rest of the house. See what other help she may need." That's a lie. I mean, I do want to help Agnes, but that's not why I'm lingering.

And the look Mom gives me says she damn well knows it.

With a heavy sigh, she reaches out to smooth a consoling hand over my leg. "I did warn you about falling in love with one of those sky cowboys, didn't I?"

"Yeah, you did." I try to laugh it off.

Until finally I relent to the onslaught of tears.

Because I'm not going home with one giant hole in my heart.

I'm going home with two.

■ ■ ■

"You can take that one with you." Jonah nods to the tattered paperback I was thumbing through when he stepped into the bedroom. "You know, for when you learn how to stay awake while reading a book."

My nostrils catch a waft of his minty toothbrush all the way from my spot on his bed. The guy spends an unnatural amount of time in the bathroom brushing his teeth every day, which is I guess in part why he has such a perfect smile.

I roll my eyes at him while brazenly gawking at his powerful body as he peels off his cotton shirt and tosses it into his hamper. Next off are his baggy, unflattering jeans, revealing muscular thighs and calves. "I'm going to teach you how to buy pants that fit you," I murmur mildly.

I expect a quip about treating him like a doll or something along those lines, but he merely chuckles.

Because it's an empty promise and we both know it.

This is the last night I'll be curled up beneath the blankets in his bed, watching him undress after a long day of flying, feeling my body warm to the promise of his hot skin and his hard torso and his enveloping arms.

I'm leaving tomorrow.

And this crushing weight on my chest tells me I'm nowhere near ready to say goodbye.

The mattress sinks under Jonah's heft as he sits on the edge, his broad, muscular back to me. He pauses a moment there, his gaze on the bedside lamp, but his thoughts seemingly far beyond it.

He hasn't said a word about my departure, besides confirming basic logistical details. He hasn't said much about my dad being gone, either, and I know that it's hit him hard; his jaw has been permanently taut since my father took his last breath.

For a guy who has always dealt with sensitive issues like a bull charging at a waving red cloth, I think my "Fletcherism" of avoidance has finally rubbed off on him.

In this moment, I'm thankful for it, because I'd rather spend our last night together making a memory than dreading our separate futures.

I push aside my sorrowful thoughts and crawl over to rope my arms around his chest from behind. I press my body in a tight hug against him, reveling in the feel of him this one last time.

■ ■ ■

I huddle in my layers of fleece and cotton as Jonah sets my two silver suitcases next to me. It's turned frigid these last few days. If I stayed any longer, I'd need to buy a winter wardrobe. Forecasters are calling for snow early next week. Villagers have been loading their boats with necessities ahead of the coming freeze, knowing they could be waiting weeks before their icy highway is safe to handle their ATVs and snow machines.

Meanwhile back in Toronto, my mom arrived to an unexpected autumn heat wave.

Jonah lifts his hat and smooths his thick ash-blond hair back. "That's everything?"

"I think— No, shit. I forgot my purse."

"Give me a sec." His shoulders are curled inward as he trudges back to Veronica.

And I wonder, for the thousandth time, if I'm making a mistake by leaving him.

"Here." He hands my purse to me, his glacier blue eyes meeting mine for a second before shifting away.

I hesitate. "Jonah—"

"You don't have to leave."

I guess we're finally going to have this gut-stabbing conversation after all, then.

"I do. My dad is gone. It's time for me to go home."

"You've got a home here, for as long as you want it."

"It's not the same. I . . . Your life is here, and my life is back there. This was only temporary." A lump forms in my throat.

"And you don't even want to try." His tone is thick with accusation.

"That's not fair."

"None of this is fair," he mutters, sliding his hands into his pockets, his gaze wandering to the nearby planes.

"Are you willing to give all this up and move to Toronto to be with me?"

His jaw tenses, and he curses under his breath.

"You know I'm right."

"Yeah. I know. Doesn't mean I have to like it." He looks at me with those light, piercing eyes, and I nearly lose my resolve. "Doesn't mean I don't want you to stay."

I take a deep, calming breath. "Maybe you could come visit me, sometime?"

He sighs with resignation, his eyes dropping to the gravel in front of us. "Yeah, I don't know when that'll be. Someone's got to keep Wild going until this deal closes. That's not for another two months." He kicks a stone with his boot. "And I told Aro I'd help them run things. Make the transition go smoother."

"How long will that take?"

He shrugs noncommittally. "Who knows. It'll take as long as it takes."

I nod. "So then maybe after."

"Maybe." He finally meets my eyes.

And I have the distinct impression that it will never happen. That time and distance will wear away at our feelings for each other, leaving nothing but stark reality and fond memories.

And that's probably all we were ever meant to have.

"Hey, Jonah! Calla!"

We both turn to find Billy standing there, with a wide, oblivious smile.

I swallow again. "Hey."

He reaches for my suitcases. "I'll throw these into the cab for you."

"Thanks." I check my phone. "I should get going. My flight is in less than two hours." And if I stay here any longer, I'm afraid I won't get on that plane.

Jonah pulls me into a fierce, warm hug that I let myself sink into one last time, cataloging the delicious feel of his strong arms around me and the intoxicating scent of his soap and *him,* though I've long since memorized it.

"We both knew this was never going to be easy," I hear him whisper.

"Yeah, I guess. I just didn't think it'd be *this* hard."

The sound of Billy's boots dragging along the gravel nearby steals the private moment away. "You know where I am if you need me," he murmurs, his voice hoarse, as he pulls away, peering down at me. His thumb brushes against my cheek, and I realize that I'm crying.

"Sorry." I try to wipe the streaks of black mascara off his shirt, but only rub them in more. He quietly handed me my cosmetics bags this morning when I was packing. They'd been hidden in his attic, all this time.

With a sharp inhale, he seizes my hand in his and holds it still for a few beats against his chest—against his heart—and then he breaks free and marches away, hollering, "Safe flight, Barbie!"

"You, too, you big angry yeti!" I manage to get out, my words cracking with sorrow.

I linger another moment, to watch him climb into his plane. To remind myself that in the long run this is the right choice.

I linger just long enough that my heart shatters fully.

And then I head home.

Chapter 27

■ ■ ■

Two months later . . .

"You know they have more cabs per capita in Bangor, Alaska, than anywhere else in North America?"

I catch the Uber driver's eyes flash to me in the rearview mirror before returning their focus to my street.

"There's this one driver named Michael. He's only twenty-eight and he has eight kids. No, wait—six kids." I frown in thought. "Seven kids in December; that's right. His wife should be having it next month."

"You said this house on the corner, right?" The driver eases in front of our big brown brick house.

"Yeah. Thanks," I mutter. He clearly has no interest in knowing about Bangor, Alaska's staggering cab population. I sensed that the second I climbed in, and yet I couldn't help but prattle on, as I've found myself doing more and more lately, as the acute pain of my losses morphs into a hollow throb with the passing days.

Still, each morning and each night and almost every hour in between, my thoughts wander to memories of fresh crisp air against my skin and the smell of coffee filling the tiny moss-green house, to the pound of my feet against the dirty, quiet tundra road, to the vibrating hum of Veronica's engine as she carried us through the vast, open Alaskan skies. To my father's soft, easy chuckle. To the way my heart would skip beats under Jonah's knowing, blue-eyed gaze.

I think about it all and my heart aches because that time in my life is over. My father is gone for good.

And so is Jonah.

I haven't heard from him in almost a month. We texted back and forth a bit, those first few weeks. But the messages were awkward—as I'd expect, coming from a guy who hates technology—and they quickly dwindled in frequency. That last text from him, the "Aro's keeping me too busy for anything else" felt like a brush-off. At least that's what I convinced myself it was. It was easier that way. It gave me an excuse to cut the cord that was already barely hanging on by a thread. But I still haven't found a way to stop thinking about him—wishing for him.

With my house keys in hand, I slide out of the Acura and begin slowly making my way up our driveway. The temperature is hovering just below freezing, enough to keep the asphalt coated with the light dusting of snow that fell earlier tonight.

I ease past Simon's car, and then my mom's, past the array of garbage and recycling and . . .

"Ah, crap," I mutter. It's garbage day tomorrow. Well, today, technically, as it's now one a.m.

I toss my purse on the stone pathway and then backtrack, to start hauling the bins down the driveway, one at a time. On my third trip back to fetch the recycling, I give the handle a sharp yank to pop the bin on its wheels. The lid lifts and a furry black face pops up in front of me.

I let out a shriek as I stumble back in my heels, barely catching my balance.

"God dammit, Sid. You get me *every single time!*" I yell through gritted teeth, my heart racing. "Why won't you hibernate!"

He chatters back and then leaps out of the bin to run under Simon's car, scattering a few cans on his way. Tim scampers behind.

A deep, warm chuckle from our front porch fills the silence.

My lungs stop working.

There's only one man who laughs like that.

I dart up the stone path, ignoring my heels in the cracks, to find

Jonah settled into one of the chairs, his legs splayed, his arms lying casually on the rests. As if it's not cold out.

"How do you know which one's which?" he asks casually.

"The white patch above Tim's eyes is wider," I mumble, still trying to process this.

Jonah's here.

Jonah's in Toronto.

Jonah has no beard.

"What'd you do to your face?" I blurt.

He runs his hand over his chiseled jaw. He looks so different without it. More like that picture of him with my dad from a decade ago. "I lost my groomer a while back and I couldn't find another one as good." His icy blue eyes rake over my black dress and heels as I climb the steps, my legs feeling wobbly.

"How long have you been here?"

"Since about nine. You were already out."

"Diana and I went out to dinner. And then out to a club." I frown. "You should have called. Someone should have told me—"

"You kidding?" He chuckles, nodding toward the driveway. "That was totally worth waiting out here for."

I stand there for another long moment, dumbly. I'm still in shock. "You stopped answering my texts."

The amusement vanishes from his face. "It was too hard."

"It was," I agree, offering him a sad smile. I knew I shouldn't be writing him, shouldn't be saying good morning and good night. I knew that keeping that connection wouldn't help either of us move on in the long run. Still, it took everything in me to stop myself.

And now Jonah's sitting in front of me.

"What are you doing here?"

"What do you *think* I'm doing here, Calla?" He sighs, shaking his head. "It's not the same."

"What's not?"

"Alaska. You've ruined Alaska for me." His tone is playful, and yet there's a hint of accusation buried within.

"I'm sorry," I mumble.

"Are you really, though?"

"No. Not totally," I admit with a sheepish smile and a tiny spark of hope, because maybe I'm not the only one who has been unhappy. Maybe I'm not the only one who might have accidentally, unintentionally found themselves in love.

He holds out a hand. I take it without pause, allowing him to pull me into his lap. I fall against his hard body and can't help the tiny sound I make. It feels even better than I remember it feeling.

Is this really happening?

Did Jonah fly all the way here, just to see me?

He hooks a hand around the backs of my thighs to pull my legs up, tucking my body closer to him, and then takes my hand in his, tracing the tips of my freshly filed and lacquered nails with his thumb. "Have you been—"

"Miserable." I push his baseball cap off, letting it fall to the porch floor, and press my forehead against his. "Nothing's the same here anymore." Or at least, *I'm* not the same. Sure, I still go out with Diana and our friends, but I ghost the second I can, preferring to linger on the couch next to my mom and Simon, listening to them bicker in their funny ways. Diana's drive to make something of Calla & Dee is still there, but I've been spending my time focused on my memories of Alaska, and my father, and Jonah—posting pictures that make me smile or laugh, and sharing the stories behind them, even if no one but me is going to read them. Simon says it's therapeutic for me. Maybe it is, but I just want to keep those days fresh and alive in my mind for as long as possible, because I know I'll never get them back.

I never wear makeup for my runs anymore and even when I do put it on, it's with a lighter hand. And the jacket Jonah bought me hangs in the front closet. I reach for it every time I find myself needing comfort.

It's ironic that no sooner had I gotten back to the city bustle that I was craving than I missed the simple calm and peaceful quiet that I'd just left.

Jonah smirks with satisfaction. "Good."

I can't stop myself from grazing the light stubble of his jaw with my palm and dipping down to press my lips against his, knowing that letting ourselves fall back into this routine will only make our parting that much more agonizing.

But I'll take whatever I can get, for as long as I can get it.

His tongue darts out to taste his bottom lip. "What have you been into tonight?"

"Just a martini."

His eyebrow lifts.

"Three martinis," I admit with a cringe. I was feeling the alcohol in the car, but oddly enough, I'm suddenly dead sober.

He groans, and smooths my hair off my forehead, his eyes roaming my face. "What the hell are we gonna do, Calla?"

"I don't know." I toy with the collar of his jacket, itching to slide my hand beneath it. "What about Wild? How's that going?"

"It's not gonna be Wild much longer. They're already talking about a new Aro logo for the planes. I told them I'll stick around for another two months, and then I'm out. I just . . . I can't." His jaw clenches. "Wren's gone. And, soon Wild will be gone, too."

The ball in my throat flares. "I miss him."

"Yeah. Me, too," he admits hoarsely, blinking several times. Against glossy eyes, I realize, and it makes me curl myself tighter into him.

"So what are you thinking of doing then, if you're not going to be at Wild?"

"I'm going to start up my own little charter company, for off-airport landings. Wren left me three planes."

"Yeah, he told me he was going to. That's good. People trust you to fly them in."

"Figured I'd sell Jughead and get something smaller. And then I could set up closer to Anchorage. You could help me with all the business marketing stuff, seeing as you're good at that. Figured being closer to a big city might work for you." He swallows. "Is that something you'd be interested in doing?"

"What? I . . ." I stammer, caught off guard. *Set up closer to Anchorage?* "What do you mean? Are you asking me to move there?" Is Jonah asking me to *move* to *Alaska*?

He fixes his eyes on mine. "That's exactly what I'm asking."

"I . . ." My heart starts beating wildly in my chest. "I don't know." That would mean going to Alaska for Jonah. Leaving my life for Jonah. Doing the exact same thing my mother did. "But what if I don't like it?" I blurt out.

"Then we figure out something that we both can handle."

"What if that means not being in Alaska?" I ask warily, because as much as I miss Jonah, I'm not about to sign up for that kind of life sentence.

"As long as I'm flying my planes and you're with me, I'll be happy. But this going-our-separate-ways bullshit? This isn't working for me, Calla." He gives me a stern look. That look he gets when he's lecturing someone about the way it is or the way it should be. "And I'm not just gonna give up without a fight and spend the rest of my life pining over you. That's where Wren and I are not alike."

Holy shit. He's serious. He's talking about living together and pining over me, something my dad did because he was *in love* with my mother. "I need to think about this," I blurt, my head spinning. A part of me wants to say yes right now. A big part. "I'm not saying no. But I need time to think."

"It's okay." He smiles softly. "You're a Fletcher. I expected as much."

I smooth my trembling hand over his jaw, still trying to process the sudden turn of events. This is the second time my life has been turned upside down on this front porch. Only this time, I think I already know what my answer will be.

Because I'd do anything to try and make it work with him.

Holy shit.

"Like it?" he murmurs, covering my idle hand with his.

"Yes, but you need to grow the beard back."

His lips stretch into a wide grin "Well, what do you know?"

"*Not* the yeti beard. The hot Viking one."

He makes a sound. "That reminds me . . ." I watch with interest and mild shock as he slips a new iPhone from his pocket. He hits the screen and pulls up my Instagram post from last week, the one that I captioned "The Good, the Bad, and the Yeti"; that tripled my following within days and has garnered thousands of likes, mostly from thirsty women.

I press my lips together to hide my smile as I admire the shirtless picture of Jonah, axe gripped in his hand, his jeans hanging so low and without any briefs, showing off that delicious vee and a trail of hair. It's the last one I grabbed, just as he turned to catch me in the act, and the best one in my opinion, his beautiful face—with a stern expression—and muscular upper body all the more prominent against the misty background.

"What's wrong with that?" I ask innocently.

"Do you know how much Aggie has been teasing me about this? She blew this picture up and plastered photocopies on the walls."

"I know. I sent her the jpeg." Agnes and I have exchanged emails about once a week since I came home. Mainly just check-ins to see how the other is doing, how Mabel is doing.

Jonah's eyebrow arches, and I note how well the scar across his forehead has healed. "There have been a dozen calls from people specifically asking to book me as their pilot."

"So what? That's nothing new. People know you."

"They've been asking for 'the yeti.'"

"That *was* a rather clever caption, though, don't you think?"

A slow, vindictive smile curls his plump lips.

Shit. "What are you going to do to me?"

His eyes sparkle with mischief as he pulls me into a kiss, but not before whispering, "I guess you'll just have to wait and see."

ACKNOWLEDGMENTS

■ ■ ■

Thank you for giving Calla, Jonah, Wren, Simon, Susan, Agnes, and Mabel a few hours of your life. When I set out to write *The Simple Wild*, I had a feeling it would be an emotional book, but I don't think I anticipated exactly *how* emotional it would be for me. There were times I found myself teary while writing and that *never* happens. But I tried to balance that sadness with humor and hope, just as life can be balanced with humor and hope, even during its hardest days.

The Simple Wild is my first book partially set in Canada and I promise, it won't be the last. I thoroughly enjoyed throwing in little Easter eggs that my fellow Canadians—especially GTA'ers—might appreciate.

Sometimes a setting becomes a character of its own, and I think that is definitely the case with this book. I spent weeks watching the Discovery Channel (*Flying Wild Alaska* is a fascinating documentary; if you're interested in learning more about Western Alaska and the life of bush pilots, I highly recommend it), reading countless blogs and travel posts, trying to thoroughly educate myself on this unique part of the world so I could depict it properly. For those of you checking your maps, no, there is no Bangor, Alaska, in real life (though there is a Bangor, Maine). I modeled my fictional town after Bethel, Alaska, but wanted to give myself some flexibility and creative freedom without feeling like I was "getting it wrong." Hence Bangor, Alaska.

A special thanks to the following people, and I hope I don't forget to mention anyone below (if I have, I am truly sorry). Thank you to Christine Borgford and Angel Gallentine Lee, who helped me collect general information about Western Alaska.

Jennifer Armentrout, Mara White, Andria King, Ola Pennington, Betty C. Cason, Kerri Elizabeth, and Kristen Reads, for sharing your own personal, painful experiences with losing a loved one to lung cancer. Please know that that day of speaking to you all was a somber one for me.

James "Wild Boy" Huggins, for your invaluable insights into flying bush planes.

KL Grayson, for educating me about hospice and helping me brainstorm through the challenges I faced surrounding Wren's declining health and how best to portray it. I had been spinning for weeks, trying to figure out the best way to tackle that. Our chats helped immensely.

Amélie, Sarah, and Tami, for running my Facebook group (especially when I'm on deadline and hiding from social media), making sure my readers know about my latest releases, and for *always* being excited to read my books.

Sandra Cortez, I can always count on you for honest feedback when I need it.

Stacey Donaghy of Donaghy Literary Group, for somehow hearing me hyperventilate over a text message and dropping everything to read this manuscript in a night.

Sarah Cantin, you are far more patient and wise than Simon. Thank you for bearing with me to the end and for always lending your ear.

The team at Atria Books: Suzanne Donahue, Albert Tang, Jonathan Bush, Will Rhino, Lisa Wolff, Alysha Bullock, Ariele Fredman, Rachel Brenner, Lisa Keim, and Haley Weaver, for all the work you have done behind this book, and on such a tight timeline (insert sheepish grin and profuse apologies here).

My husband and my girls, for leaving me be in my bat cave, with my bag of Cadbury mini eggs and my frazzled nerves.